IDIOT SAVANT

IDIOT SAVANT

ANTHONY M. ALIOTO
Illustrator: Luciano A. Alioto

RESOURCE *Publications* • Eugene, Oregon

IDIOT SAVANT

Resource Publications
An Imprint of Wipf and Stock Publishers
199 W. 8th Ave., Suite 3
Eugene, OR 97401

www.wipfandstock.com

PAPERBACK ISBN: 978-1-5326-6904-0
HARDCOVER ISBN: 978-1-5326-9171-3
EBOOK ISBN: 978-1-5326-9172-0

Manufactured in the U.S.A.   12/23/19

To Armine Ann

Contents

BOOK I

Fall Semester, 1969

 **BRUNSWICK STATE**
UNIVERSITY

MEMORANDUM – THREE DIRECTIVES FOR THE NEW SCHOOL YEAR

TO: REVEREND RICHARD BENTLEY,
            DEAN OF STUDENTS

FROM: H. RICHARD CRAVEN, PRESIDENT,
            BRUNSWICK STATE UNIVERSITY
            (FORMELY UNIVERSITY OF THE FAR NORTH)

DATE: AUGUST 30TH, 1969

DICK,

1. LET THEM TALK

2. KEEP THEM TALKING

3. ENCOURAGE THEM TO KEEP TALKING

FREE AND OPEN TO THE PUBLIC

Experience the Absolute,
Avatar, Guru,
The Divine Woo-Woo

THURSDAY,
SEPTEMBER 4

Sri GOODJOHN SACCIDANADA

Sponsored by
THE GREAT TRUTH CLOUD
8 LILAC STREET, HINNOM VALLEY

Ayamatma brahma

ONE

The Great Truth Cloud

SYLVIAN MATREYA DIDN'T FIT into our world and this is no exaggeration. His clothes always seemed too large for his body. His hair was limp and black where it should have been thick and gold. Using his distinctive method of speaking, he would have described each strand as a perfect example of Euclid's definition of a straight line. He didn't fit into his skin either, which was nut-brown, hardly that of fair Catholic Poland, the homeland of his Eastern European aristocratic ancestors.

Sylvian became quickly lost in the smallest of crowds. Even his draft board somehow missed him. He carried a 2-S college deferment that never seemed to expire. It should have been 4-F, unfit for military service.

Meeting him for the first time, people thought him an idiot. Most people ignored him and went their way. He went his way, happy to be ignored. It seems odd, then, that he would become one of those absurd university revolutionaries produced by that momentary lapse into infantilism labeled "the sixties," if what follows here can be believed.

The idiot for his part didn't mind being invisible if he gave it a thought, which would have been rare since Sylvian thought about little else except theoretical physics. Had he considered his condition, he might have realized in an "imprecise" way (his word) that he preferred invisibility since he found people bothersome.

Sylvian found it tiring to think and speak in words and concepts. Thoughts flowed through his brain in the form of abstract equations, sometimes analytical geometry, along with the accompanying graphical solutions.

Who can tell what the poor boy *really* thought or how his confused mind perceived the world?

Human contact counted for nothing, the empty spaces in a Cartesian graph he might have said, had he chosen to express the thought. Some, like hippies, fell into the category of negative numbers. Had he possessed the prerequisite self-awareness, he might have concluded that such dislikes were acquired characteristics, the inherited habits of Church and family, as our secular experts might say. But he lacked the very concepts for such insights. His internal reference was weak to quote from his medical file.

Sadly, the self-professed experts have never been able to explain his disappearance.

Oddly, then, Sylvian found himself engaged in a very uncharacteristic adventure that Thursday night in September 1969. He was on his way to a meeting—no, a Divine Woo-Woo Discourse—sponsored by the Great Truth Cloud.

Said Divine Woo-Woo, a god-like being whose title was derived from some long-extinct heathen language, was none other than Sri Goodjohn Saccidanada: Avatar, Groovy-Guru, an incarnation of the Absolute Intergalactic Brain, Supreme Yogi, a divine being, of whom Sylvian had never heard.

Physics students never attended such gatherings, Sylvian once told me. In physics one was either a genius or an idiot, he'd added. Idiots went into the humanities—and went to such things as anti-war rallies and Woo-Woo Discourses.

Sylvian may have been a rock-hard idiot in the eyes of the sublunar world, but in the upper spheres of physics, amid aether so subtle it might have been a vacuum, he was a transcendent being whose abilities verged on the mystical as one of his foolish professors explained to the authorities.

So what, in God's name, was he thinking—that Thursday evening so long ago?

He was thinking about a pretty elfin girl-child named Pearl, and thinking rather imprecisely.

Pearl—he never learned her last name—had noticed him. It went like this (paraphrasing his words from Confession):

Suddenly materializing out of smoke-filled air illuminated by bright autumn sunlight filtered through northern glass, which was the atmosphere of the Student Union, Pearl emerged like a garden fairy from a cold evening mist. She sat down at his table. Instantly she began talking about "this far-out, totally enlightened, fully awakened, incarnation of universal bliss, her Groovy Guru, the Divine Woo-Woo, Sri Goodjohn Saccidanada," and so forth and so on, of whom she was thinking of becoming an official devotee—but not a gopi—as soon as he acknowledged her divine status—

"I saw you—" her voice broke into little squeaks "—it's just so far out that I saw you here. You need to come. It's your. . . karma. I see people's karma, you know. Yes, I do. It's my nature. Are you listening? I had a vision. It was of this old saint that could float and live off the rays of the sun and drink Soma all day long and talk to devas and spoke all kinda far-out wise things. . . It's you, Sylvian, right? You are Sylvian Matreya? It's so far out—"

She giggled and played with her long blonde hair, twirling strands around her fingers. She gazed at an invisible presence somewhere over his head. It hardly mattered that he had not uttered a single word and could only steal glances at her before lowering his eyes in embarrassment.

"Will you come? Thursday night with me? Please?"

She smiled and displayed crooked teeth. She smelled like. . . a garden of herbs and spices. . .and fish.

"I know your name. . . Looked it up to make sure. It is. . . my vision, you know." She paused and took a deep breath as if she'd revealed the ultimate mystery of the universe.

"Christianity is finished," she abruptly declared, mesmerized by the invisible presence that apparently hovered directly above him. "Ain't much of a sacrifice when you know you're gonna come out perfect. What's the downer for that? God's a real son-of-a-bitch anyway. Ain't nothin' wrong but our own ignorance which is God's doin', if you buy the garden shit. Divine Woo-Woo says so. Gonna need a replacement. It's 'cuz of the Kali Yuga, you know. Kali seduced Christ. Was his wife, I think—"

Sylvian was a child of the Catholic Church even though—and I can attest to this—he barely grasped the rudiments of the faith. The Church was the bride of Christ he seemed to recall. Or was it the Pope? Mary perhaps? But which one? He couldn't remember. Surely not this Kali person, whoever she was. An actress maybe? Christ was eternal from the start, omniscient, all-powerful. . . He tried to remember dear Father Loeb's long list of attributes. He knew from mathematics that infinity was never finished even though it might be bounded, and yet some sets were uncountable, they couldn't be put in correspondence with the natural numbers. But Catechism was different. He always ended in an unbounded muddle. Theology gave him indigestion.

"It's a date then?"

He nodded something between a yes and a no.

"It's a date then."

He hadn't uttered a single word. He couldn't find a single word to utter. In three years at Brunswick State University, little elfin-hippie Pearl was the first girl to pay him the slightest attention. She even knew his name.

Only later, after he'd returned to the safety of his dorm room, did he consider the terrifying possibility that he was being lured into Hell like St. Anthony, the great desert father who'd been tempted by demonic legions of naked dancing girls. Unlike the desert father, he appeared unable to resist merely one of Satan's temptresses.

He met Pearl on the front lawn of the house at 8 Lilac Street. She stood near a sprawling porch jammed with people. The wood had been freshly painted in psychedelic swirls of yellow, purple, red and dark blue, clumsily suggesting clouds at sunset, puffed and stolen by the wind.

The porch railings and pillars were painted to look like gnarled old trees. The rest of the two-storied house was painted dark blue. Its original surface was blistered and peeled, bare wood poking through what remained of the old flaking paint.

The mass of people frightened him. His legs suddenly refused to obey his brain and his steps slowed to a shuffle.

Despite his fear of the devilish mob, Sylvian automatically sought equations that described the cloud-painted porch. He tried analyzing the dynamic patterns, silently computing the probable functions, giving the psychedelic mess a surrealistic mathematical life. The strange and threatening gradually became familiar.

Pearl proceeded up the walkway to the porch. She appeared stoned, but to most people she always seemed to be stoned. He lost her in the crowd.

"Peeaarl. . ." Anxiety added the extra vowels, yet another of Sylvian's problems: When he became agitated, he lost control of the language and mispronounced words. He violated grammatical laws as he called them, and he often made a noise that sounded like fingernails scraping across a chalkboard.

"Pleeaase. . . pleeaase, wait!"

With a toss of long silvery hair, she suddenly materialized. Her blue-gray eyes were wide and unfocused. Her mouth hung open.

People often remarked on how Pearl's responses could be weirdly unpredictable. She stared at the person who'd asked her something, never giving an answer or any indication that she'd heard the question. Sometimes she would babble in a whiny, childish voice, watching air spirits cavorting above a person's head. She said the oddest things, filled with profundity and wit had you asked her. No one took her seriously, not even her Groovy-guru as it turned out, although he pretended to (here we must not get too far ahead).

At that time she majored in art. Art, she said in one of her divine moments of inspiration, would save the world, but only after the establishment had crucified it.

The great Divine Woo-Woo told her that truly enlightened speech contained sediments of meaning. An enlightened being, he declared (or someone tripping on acid), might be able to tune in the thoughts of the Intergalactic Brain (or Brahman). The uptight ordinary world failed to recognize the profound wisdom and creative genius of those great seers like herself, which illustrated society's depth of ignorance, and arrogance when "normal" people were confronted by true spirituality, which was why benighted fools laughed at her. At least this is how she understood the Groovy-guru's Discourse.

She babbled it all to Sylvian. "Depths. . . and greater depths. . . and profound depths, very deep. . . Did I say profound?" He found it impossible to understand the surface.

Sylvian also learned that, besides art, her favorite subject was religion, and she was thinking of switching her major to philosophy although she'd yet to take a course. But then she hadn't made an art course either; she feared it might ruin her creativity.

She addressed the space somewhere over his left shoulder: "Oh wow, Sil, it's so freaky! Can't you just feel his presence?"

She'd stopped walking to utter these words of genius and so Sylvian was able to catch up despite the resistance he was experiencing from the mass of people. Newton's law of attraction broke down when it came to Sylvian and crowds. Attraction became the law of repulsion. Sylvian called it his version of the Cosmological Constant.

"Fre—eels what?"

"Him," she said, gazing up into the night sky. "The Divine One, the great seer, guru. . . You can feel his presence. The air just vibrates. The walls tremble when he speaks. You get high! It's his *tapas*."

He inhaled and caught the sweet odor of marijuana. The word *tapas* sounded vaguely familiar. Perhaps it was Latin, a word he'd heard in one of dear Father Loeb's little homilies.

"Hiss. . . what?"

She smiled her Parvati smile. When she smiled like this, she explained in one of her moments of Divine Inspiration; it meant that she'd assumed her goddess-Parvati-Daughter-of-the-Himalayas form and was poised on the cusp of divine ecstasy which was just like dying—and like sex.

The Divine Woo-Woo had yet to certify her goddess status, but she was confident he would do so when he got around to it.

Unfortunately for sacred ecstasy, but maybe not death, her crooked teeth slightly distorted her goddess-Parvati-Daughter-of-the- Himalayas form and transformed her from elfin-fairy into witch-girl.

She mounted the porch steps in a trance.

Shouldn't he be holding her hand like in the movies or on TV? Didn't he wanna hold her hand, like the Beatles song?

He heard a voice in his head. The voice was shrill and high-pitched and sounded like his mother. Then he realized that it belonged to his parish priest, dear Father Loeb. The voice was saying something about pagans, whatever they were. He couldn't understand. Was the priest urging him to flee? Or was it to feel?

Mixed with pot, he also caught the scent of incense. He felt sick. And then, against his will, he found that he'd stumbled forward and was suddenly on the porch.

The crowd smelled of unwashed bodies and slept-in clothes. Long-haired and oily, bearded and beaded, they were real hippies, not fad-following rich kids from Chicago suburbs. Authentic west coast hippies. How in God's name did they find their way to Brunswick State University stuck in this gray Midwest mill town?

He spied Pearl's hair shimmering in the doorway. Squeezing through the crowd, he followed her into the den of her groovy-guru as if attracted by some terrible force, maybe those *tapas* whatever they were.

The room was cavernous, like a vast underground cave. Interior walls had been knocked out. Blacklight made Pearl's hair glow like a beacon. Purple, red, orange and yellow paint splashed the floors and walls. Music blared. People laughed and talked and shouted and sang.

He recalled Father Loeb's descriptions of Hell. The floor and walls did seem to be made from molten metal just as the Dominican priest had taught him. Oh Blessed Virgin!

He'd lost Pearl again. The crowd jostled him, drawing him into this dark and dangerous cave of unnatural light. He stumbled and nearly fell.

Suddenly, across the cave at the far wall, a gleaming figure magically appeared and spread its arms as if to embrace the entire demonic horde.

The chief devil was a large man with long black hair and a wonderously thick beard. He wore a t-shirt dyed with crudely designed clouds and rainbows that blazed in the black light. The shirt seemed too small, for it covered roughly half of his massive belly.

Instantly Hell became silent.

The man produced what appeared to be a poorly rolled cigarette, lit it, took a deep draw, and surveyed the crowd. A devotee handed him an open can of beer. From somewhere in the spacious room, soft music began to play replacing the blaring rock.

Sylvian loved sound waves, heat waves, waves in general. Fourier analysis was one of his favorite subjects. Music enthralled him. He loved its mathematical purity, the fact that music was a thing in itself, a copy of nothing in physical nature other than itself, the closest sensate experience one could have of immaculate numerical relationships that existed in pure thought.

Music brought back memories of St. Barlaam, his invisible companion who'd mysteriously disappeared about the time he turned fourteen.

He heard an exotic combination of cello, drum, harpsichord, flute, and an instrument he especially loved (and he had no idea why he loved it or where he'd first heard it): the sharp twang of the Hindu sitar.

Unfortunately, there were also lyrics:

"A... UMM,
The rain is on the roof,
Hurry high, butterfly.
As clouds roll past my head,
I know why the skies all cry,
A... UMM, A... UMM, HEA... EA... VEN,
A... A... UMM..."

The fat man with the black beard took a long drink from his can of beer. He closed his eyes and began to sway back and forth with the music. His belly vibrated with the drums.

"The earth turns slowly round,
Far away the distant sound,
Is with us every day,
Can you hear what it says?
A... UMM, A... UMM, HEA... EA... VEN,
A... A... UMM..."

The sitar began to assert itself. Sylvian's head throbbed, he felt dizzy. Instinctively he calculated the relative volume of marijuana smoke to healthy room air. But the pulsation of the music seemed to shake the equations, jiggling terms, warping space, causing his mind to revolt against its mathematical habit. The smoky black light made him sleepy. Something seemed profoundly hilarious about the curious scene, but he was too scared to laugh.

Someone was speaking to him. The words seemed to flow into his ears as if riding the vibrations of the sitar. Perhaps the sitar itself had suddenly learned to speak English rather than the abstract language of waves.

Here stood a boy looking very young, like Sylvian himself, pushing the advanced age of twelve.

"Blue. . . Blues. . ."
"Huh?"
"Mood. . ."
"Whaa. . .?"
". . .Moody Blues. . .AUM. . ."

Blue, that was it, at last something precise.

The boy grew hair longer than Pearl's. He wore the weirdest clothes Sylvian had ever seen. The boy might have been a girl because he—she—seemed to be wearing a bright orange dress. But no, these were billowy pantaloons belted at "his" waist. It was a "he" Sylvian guessed, though it might have been a "she." Sylvian was too timid to ask. Long beaded necklaces of various colors, more beads than Sylvian had ever seen on anyone, even the most severe hippie, covered his torso. He carried so much jewelry that his slightest motion must have simulated lifting weights.

If this appeared strange, it was nothing compared to his soft baby-like skin. . . that glowed bright blue!

Body paint? The light? The smoke? It seemed natural as if the soft texture of the skin and its blue color were as integrated as the blue of a summer sky washed clean by a shower. The sitar gave sound to color.

"The Moody Blues," blue boy repeated. He smiled at Sylvian, flashing white baby teeth. "You're Sylvian Matreya, right?"

Sylvian gave him a startled look and nodded dumbly.

"Don't talk much, 'ay?"

Sylvian stared back open-mouthed. "You know. . . my name?"

"Oh, we know," laughed blue boy. He inclined his head towards the place where Pearl had vanished into the crowd. He stepped forward to redistribute his weight and prevent himself from toppling over.

"She's been talking about you ever since she had her far-out spiritual experience. The Intergalactic Brain—her *sensus Divinitatis*, as they say—confirmed it. It told her that the vision predicted Its manifestation. She wouldn't listen to anybody. I think *he's* finally given up on her. He's absolutely certain he knows."

"Whose nose?"

"Him, the Divine Woo-Woo, the Guru—Goodjohn Saccidanada. She says it's 'bout your karma. Between us, I think maybe she's right, and he doesn't know."

"What's. . . karma?" Here was yet another word, probably Latin, he thought Father Loeb might have used during Catechism.

"Like a bank account."

Economics was too imprecise for Sylvian and he turned away.

The Guru Woo-Woo opened his eyes and gazed at the crowd. His eyes were like his beard, light-drinking black. They swept the crowd until like the arrow of a magnetic compass they fastened upon this person, and then another, and then another. Naturally, his divine gaze passed over the submerged form of Sylvian Matreya who was as visible in a crowd as a shadow in the dark.

Woo-Woo began to chant: "*sarvabhutastham atmanam sarvabhutani catmaniksate.*"

Blue boy translated: "He sees the Atman in all beings and all beings in the Self."

The crowd chanted along, repeating Goodjohn's exact words. A few began to cry, whether in ecstasy or pain Sylvian could not say.

Goodjohn paused and gulped down more beer. Then, in a low, gurgling voice, sounding very much like a drunken Hinnom Valley mill worker muttering to himself in some dark tavern near the river, he said: "It ain't 'bout you. You're ignorant. You got your pinched little thoughts. You got your silly little needs. Your stupid little wants. What'd ya doin' here? What ya lookin' for?"

He seemed to get viciously angry. He ranted for a few minutes, slurring the words so badly that no one, least of all Sylvian, could understand him.

Then, as if the season instantly changed from autumn to spring, he threw back his massive head and roared with maniacal laughter.

"Ain't 'bout you. Ain't 'bout religion. About ME. Your minds are stuck on needless things, on display, on empty pleasures, on their world, their nightmares, what they call good—"

The crowd emitted a collective sigh. Sylvian heard more weeping. He also heard gasps of "yes," and exclamations of "far-out" and "right-on" and "you, you, love you—"

His eyes radiated the Divine Presence, as Pearl had said and many in the crowd experienced, except Sylvian. His Divine-Presence-stare seized them and transported them into glorious states of rapture, as Pearl had said, except Sylvian remained un-transported. And all of these miraculous communications were the result of the Guru's most significant (and well-practiced) pause.

His divine laughter broke the spell.

"The Divine Woo-Woo don't know you-yoo and regards you-yoo with divine indifference."

This piece of unanticipated bad news brought forth not a few moans and more weeping, which was most likely not due to divine ecstasy—especially from the female devotees.

"I'm God. *Aham brahmasmi.* Beyond good and evil. *Ayam atma brahma.*"

More Latin words Sylvian should've known.

"So bring your wandering minds to me. Worship me. Revere me. Be Me-minded. Then will you be dear to me. Then will the Divine Woo-Woo not regard you with indifference—

"Abandon your small desires,

"Come to me,

"And I will liberate you."

"Oh yes!" the chorus sang.

He fixed his Divine gaze on a dark-haired girl in the front row.

"So, baby, are you really happy? Yes? No? Maybe? Don't know?

"Well, are you?"

The girl shook her head.

"What's that?"

Another shake, very nervous.

"Ah, a no? Not here? Where? The ignorant world of products and parties? Grades and degrees? The assembly line of school, college, career, family, funeral, see-ya-later? Society, religion, education just bring you down—"

The girl bowed her head as if praying.

"Actions spring from beliefs. Beliefs spring from mind. If mind is deluded, action is deluded. Get it? You got to be Me-minded. Devoted to the Divine Woo-Woo. Show me your devotion."

The girl nodded and emitted a soft moan. The crowd nodded and moaned. Sylvian felt a sharp pain behind his eyes.

Foam flecked the Guru's beard. His skin appeared rosy, flushed, even in the black light.

"Action arises from mind which is Spirit. I am the Spirit, the Absolute. Do you wish to be spiritual?"

YES. A few people said the word aloud; many more mouthed it silently. YES. OH YES.

Sylvian felt as if he were watching a weird movie, or in the Cathedral listening to Father Loeb recite the liturgy as he administered the Eucharist.

"Then come forward, my *gopis*."

The girl got up and did as the holy Guru ordered. She knelt at his feet. Other young women joined her and formed a kneeling semi-circle around Goodjohn. They held hands and swayed back and forth, gazing up at their Groovy-guru, some faces aglow, others weeping, others nodding vigorously. Though her head was bowed and her hands clasped in prayer, Pearl appeared to hang back.

"Give up the self and its little thoughts. Give yourself to the Spiritual. Give yourself to ME!"

Swaying back and forth, as if in a trance, the dark-haired girl unbuttoned her blouse. The other young women did the same, very slowly and deliberately as if performing a sacred ritual.

Goodjohn said: "Ahhh. . . Give up your small relationships. Unhealthy desires, insecurities, cravings drive them. Transcend them. Reject them. The only relationship that matters is your relationship to your Guru."

Sylvian forgot about Pearl, forgot physics and math—he forgot his name.

He turned and noticed that Blue Boy had vanished. Sylvian saw a crease in the crowd where the blue hippie had left a trail. He darted towards the door as if pursued by all the fiends of Hell, reaching for his innocent soul with grotesque claws.

The fat devil bellowed. Sylvian felt the demonic voice in the middle of his chest. Making the mistake of Lot's wife, he turned around for a peek at Sodom.

Goodjohn was blazing. Flames sprang from his head. His fingers spewed bolts of blue fire like gas jets from a stove. His eyes, hair, beard, belly were ablaze. Surely he'd burn the house down. But how could Hell burn down?

No one seemed to notice the fire.

"Sil!" A shrill voice cried from the blaze. It was Pearl. And then he realized that she was a. . .*suckyoubus*. Yes, that was the word Father Loeb had used when he taught the boys about witches during their lesson on sex education. Amazing that he would remember a word. Terror was good for vocabulary.

A witch-suckyoubus. Sylvian broke her invisible hold and bolted through the door, fleeing the inferno.

He made the porch, tripped and fell, skinning his elbows and knees. Although it bore the pungent stench of the paper mill across the river, the night air awakened him like a hard slap on the face.

He managed to pick himself up and run—actually stumble—down Lilac Street.

He knew as surely as a proof in Euclid that she was a female demon, one of those "suck-you-buses." Woo-Woo must be Satan himself, or undoubtedly high in the chain of infernal command.

Dear Father Loeb taught the parish children that Christ commanded them to be holy as God the Father is holy. Sylvian wanted to be "holy," although he wasn't sure what being holy exactly meant. "Imprecisely," he sensed a strange thing in himself, as odd as his dark skin and straight black hair. He felt—oh, horror —a resistance to the divine command. There was some weird thing inside that resisted the Church and Christ's teachings. And now it seemed the seed had brought forth noxious fruit.

But then, miraculously (he might have said that it was God's gift he remembered the words), he heard Father Loeb's sermon on St. Paul's *Letter to the Romans*, which he'd never read—but why did he need to read any ancient texts after listening to Father Loeb?

Paul, according to his beloved parish priest, taught that demons lived in the flesh, especially of little boys. Usually when they slept the demons came out. But they could be easily aroused, by rock-music, for example, and especially hippie girls. And now, Sylvian realized, by Divine Woo-Woos and their gopis, and blonde-haired fairy-suck-you-buses named Pearl.

Hell had spewed forth Pearl and sent her to drag poor Sylvian Matreya into sin.

Of this he was certain. Father Loeb had said it. Scripture confirmed it. QED.

TWO

In the Library

CLASSES BEGAN ON MONDAY. Sylvian had the weekend free. After his experience the previous night, he was in no mood to take one step out of his dorm room.

No matter how hard he tried—even to the point of cracking his new physics textbooks and working a few of the easier problems—he couldn't subtract Pearl from the jumble of variables that threatened to overwhelm his sanity.

Friday evening he ventured out to the Commons for dinner. The lines were short. The majority of the students living in his dorm had not yet returned to school, among them his new roommate whose name he didn't even know.

Waiting in line, a flash of blonde hair suddenly brushed his shoulder. He turned. Some clean-cut boys dressed in jeans and old football jerseys were pushing each other, laughing, making faces, and arguing. Many were stocky, a few fat. They'd been eating commons' food for quite a while. Most were business majors. They cursed with gusto. They were loud and pushy. SHS was back early for specialized training.

SHS was a corps of students recruited by the Dean of Students, Dr. Richard Bentley. SHS stood for Students Helping Students. They monitored extra-curricular activities—some people added curricular activities. They spied on radical professors and reported back to the administration. They made certain there'd be no anti-war rallies, teach-ins or protests against the war. Dean Bentley created a select branch of SHS for "the special needs of Negro Students." "Negro SHS" encouraged hard work and spiritually, and preferred Martin over Malcolm, Jesus over Mohammed, Mary over Joan, and cultivated disdain for the likes of Bobby, Huey, Eldridge, and especially Ali.

Dr. Bentley was very disappointed when he found that not one "Negro student" had joined the organization. This year, he planned to petition the faculty to make it mandatory.

But eyes other than SHS were watching Sylvian. He turned and caught a flash of light. . . a white-clad server, a student.

Sitting alone at his table, walking back to his dorm, even in the stairwell, he felt *her* watching. Just at the edge of his vision, teasing and laughing, but when he tried to catch her, she vanished into thin air.

Pearl was following him! The air was thick with the perfume of an herb garden, or maybe it was fairy-dust, which Sylvian thought of as LSD, but which Father Loeb labeled the devil's drug, not to be confused with the devil's weed, although the distinction, other than the method of ingestion, was lost on Sylvian.

In the early morning hours he was awakened by the sweet odor of said weed mixed with the sour smell of stale beer, probably beer processed through human organs. A shadow glided into the room. The bed on the other side of the room creaked. He heard the twang of springs giving beneath weight. His new roommate. Was he "a head"? A drunk? Smelled like both.

Sylvian sprang out of bed at the first hint of daylight. He was afraid to glance at the other bed. Dressing quickly, he made it to the Commons just as they'd begun to serve breakfast. He was the only customer.

While the rest of the Brunswick State University slumbered peacefully on this cloudy Saturday morning—the air over Hinnom Valley was thick with the combined odor of paper mill and brewery—Sylvian drifted across campus to the library.

Deserted campus greens, empty college buildings, lonely paths, the hushed feel of impending rain in the damp air, Sylvian spun around several times sensing movement. Furtive shadows haunted the windows of abandoned classrooms. Wraith-like creatures lurked behind trees and buildings. He heard soft laughter, Pearl's whining soprano tingled with songs of mirth. Smell of herbs, and spices, and now, curiously, fish.

Pearl was laughing at him.

When he turned around, she vanished. When he stopped and listened, the laughter faded away. He risked a bleating: "Pear. . .lll. . .?"

No answer. No Pearl. Then, as he resumed his walk, he heard the fairy voice and glimpsed a flash of blonde hair. . . Nothing. It was maddening.

He ran the rest of the way. He made the stairs of Crowley Library. He sensed that she was close behind, laughing, gasping, breathing so heavily that he felt the heated moisture of exhaled air on his neck.

He sped up the stairs between the colossal library pillars and bent over sputtering like a deflating balloon. He'd never run so far and so fast in his life.

The library courtyard was deserted. A slight drizzle made the dull reddish brick surface glisten.

Shaken and terrified beyond anything he'd ever known (even his father's beatings), Sylvian dove through the doors, thankfully unlocked, into the sanctuary of Crowley Library.

The library was his temple, a refuge from people and society. He loved the quiet. Here silence was normal. Here the spoken word brought rebuke. Here he could choose his companions from among the long-dead authors preserved in pages filled with abstract symbols. He could forget messy, imprecise, embarrassingly personal flesh, and blood human beings.

Books always said the same things. They never argued. You never had to look into their faces and perceive the hypocrisy glinting in their eyes (not that he could). He read what he liked, discarded what he didn't, especially if they threatened his beliefs or made him uncomfortable. Their voices were his to command, turn them off if he desired and they could do nothing about it—they could not even raise their voices in protest. They were at his mercy. He possessed power, they security. The very dullness of the place was comforting.

Suddenly he had an inspiration. Crowley held a reasonably decent collection in the areas of philosophy and religion. He would look for something about Sri Goodjohn Saccidananda and the Great Truth Cloud. Who were they? Why had they suddenly appeared in quiet Hinnom Valley and what in the name of Christ did they want with him?

Or maybe they wanted nothing. Perhaps it was just Pearl?

He didn't want to think about Pearl.

He searched everything: periodicals, newspapers, registries, lists of religious organizations, names, telephone and street directories—everything. He even sought the Intergalactic Brain.

And discovered nothing. He went through the entire reference library looking for religious or exotic Eastern sects that referred to clouds. He found plenty of clouds but no Great Truth.

The search took the whole morning and part of the afternoon. According to the omniscient library, the house on Lilac Street didn't exist. There

was no such person named Goodjohn Saccidananda, or the Guru Divine
Woo-Woo, or Intergalactic Brian for that matter. Last year's student directory listed no Pearl. He had to admit that since he'd never learned her last
name, such lacunae were hardly conclusive.

He finally sat down at a table and thought about it. Over the years,
he'd observed any number of strange individuals lurking about the university like so many young vagabonds and academic gypsies. Sometimes these
strangers might audit a course. But most of this wandering-scholar subclass
hardly ever endured an entire semester.

Sylvian recalled the time when one such ethereal spirit spent a day
in his optics course, which in the catalog bore the suggestive title: *Waves
and Light*. This longhaired individual told him that: "man, waves are groovy,
especially good waves, you know, good vibrations. It's all about feeling good
vibrations, man." The feeling-good student wasn't aware that *Waves and
Light* was a physics course until the professor began to cover the blackboard
with differential equations, which Sylvian loved and could solve as easily as
he breathed.

That was enough. The phantom student of good-vibes vanished, obviously disappointed. Mathematical analysis didn't make it as good waves.
Neither was it groovy. He never came to class again.

Later in the student union where many such specters gathered, Sylvian
heard the would-be physics student complaining loudly about the professors at this "maybe-versity." How narrow, stupid, irrelevant, and unenlight-
ened they all are. . .

He was sitting with a group of similarly clad rebels, sharing a pitcher
of the local brew, Butcher Beer, the only brand allowed in the union. He
seemed to be giving a political speech that carried to Sylvian's table near the
windows.

". . .and the whole fuckin' bureaucratic, anal-retentive, Hitlerite, concentration camp mentality of credits and degrees!" he bellowed, thoroughly
enraged.

"Man, but they gotta teach somethin'," said a boy at his elbow. "You
gotta read somethin' and get tested on it—"

"I read voraciously!" yelled the orator, waving his arms and nearly
knocking the pitcher over. "I read significant works! Not the repressive—
and-repressed—heroes of the decadent educational establishment. Such
scribblings are rolls of toilet paper written for neurotic bourgeoisie house-
wives, the stupid cunts. It's all bullshit moronic garbage that gets printed
only 'cuz it's fuckin' money-making, inauthentic candy for mindless capitalism, 'cuz of repressed cunts that reads that shit—"

He paused long enough to gulp down more Butcher beer. Sylvian thought that he strangely relished the unfairness of the system and that he was oddly obsessed with "repressed bourgeoisie cunts," just as many people saw communist subversives behind everything and everyone they despised. Then Sylvian was an idiot when it came to reading human motivations and grasping the slippery hidden messages in people's talk. Human speech was so imprecise. He was probably mistaken.

". . .no, not that shit, but good books. Books you won't get any fuckin' credits for 'cuz they're dangerous to the fuckin' Pig Empire. . . 'cuz they tell the truth 'bout fuckin' pig values, fuckin' pig repression, fuckin'. . ."

One thing he knew from experience and with some precision was that there existed a connection between beer and language. He wasn't sure if the relationship was causal, but it was there. He thought of it as the "geometric exponential increase of the word fuck as a direct function of the volume of alcohol consumed."

The information on Goodjohn Saccidananda approached absolute zero. Goodjohn was probably a kind of full professor of that invisible university inhabited by intellectual rebels who read important books. They came and went, sampling universities like restaurants. Goodjohn would surely vanish in no time given the ambiance of conservative Brunswick State University, a school that had been founded by the local brewer old Frederick Butcher von Brunswick and was practically owned by the Butcher family (and Boots Lumber) who were the majority on the Board of Trustees.

Reaching this proof, Sylvian decided to climb the wide stairs to the second floor and escape into the science stacks.

Although the library seemed deserted, he had that eerie feeling that someone (or something) was watching him from among the stacks. Worse, no matter how hard he tried, he couldn't stop thinking about Pearl. He desperately wanted to stop thinking about Pearl because it hurt to think about Pearl, and, well, mathematics (sometimes the Church) usually rescued him from all his problems, and when it failed this meant that the problem was beyond reason and not worth his effort and so he no longer bothered to think about it.

He scurried up the stairs praying that he'd find something interesting. Perhaps he'd discover some offbeat physics treatise that had been forgotten or rejected. He harbored a special love for the crackpots and was inexplicably drawn to crazy theories. He admired scientists who'd become objects of contempt and ridicule. This admiration was the only irrationality he allowed into his life (he might have said had he been able to put his thoughts into the proper words).

He found himself in the east wing amid the dusty rows in the six and seven hundreds. He gently touched an old crackling volume, a comprehensive text on thermodynamics from the last century.

Someone was standing behind him.

The sense of human presence came from body odor.

He'd stepped into a sickly sweet cloud of smoke. Somewhere, within the dense fog stood a living human chimney. His eyes began to sting. The smell seemed identical to the scent of his unseen roommate.

"It ain't natural, Bilbo," said a raspy voice within the pungent cloud, "like, One Ring to bring them all and in the darkness bind them, in the land of Mordor—"

"Huh?"

"Science, man, the One Ring of Power, belongs to the Dark Lord hisself—"

"Wha. . .at?"

"Ain't you never read Tolkien, man? It's all there. Middle Earth is reality."

Sylvian's eyes burned, but he knew with immense relief, and yet some disappointment, that this could not be Pearl.

"Reads. . . what?"

"Tolkien, idiot! He's the only one worth readin'. He wrote stoned, you know. Gotta get high to understand him. Tolkien was high forever. Everybody's read Tolkien. At least freaks. Don't you know that hobbits smoke pipes full of the best grass there is?"

"Who're you?"

"Jerry Wolfe. Call me Frodo."

"Gerry Volfe?"

"Jerry Wolfe. And you're Samwise Gamgee from the Shire. Ain'nit far out?"

"No. Sylvian Matreya from Chicago."

"Yeah, sure. But fuck, Sam, that's all illusion. We really live in Middle Earth."

"You're. . . my roommate?"

"Jerry Wolfe according to the Dark Lord-fuckin'-establishment."

"What're you talkin' about?"

His eyes no longer stung, although they were still wet, and he gazed at Jerry Wolfe through tiny prism drops of water. Jerry was short and stocky and dressed in black: black tee shirt, black jeans, black army boots. He had thick and wild red hair, shooting out in all directions like a forest of corkscrews. He seemed desperate to grow a beard, but it was so sparse and scraggly that it caused his skin to appear more pimpled than it was, although Jerry Wolfe's particular brand of pimples was the deep blotchy kind. The red beard made his face appear raw. He had blue eyes and a large nose, broken in the middle. His lips curled when he spoke, making every word a sneer and every sentence sound sarcastic.

Nonetheless, Jerry Wolfe was painfully earnest even when high.

"Well, shit, man," Jerry appeared to be looking for a book as he muttered: "Jus' like they toll'd old Bilbo, such wealth ain't natural and nothin' good'll come of it."

Suddenly he turned and studied Sylvian. His red eyebrows seemed to glow as his brow furrowed, heated by mental concentration. Jerry required a great deal of effort and not a little time to express a thought.

"Hey man. Are you my new roomie? You're into the Ring too?"

"Huh?"

"Yeah. Saw your books. So what's a good book on. . ." Jerry thought hard, so hard that any moment his head might burst into flame. They were in the thermodynamics section after all.

"On. . . on. . . nuclear fission?"

"On what?"

"The One Ring, man. One Ring of the evil Dark Lord, Sauron the Great, to bind us all. Fuck, Sam, nuclear fission. . . how they make the fuckin' bomb."

"Any book on atomic theory. Chemistry. Not before the '40s."

"No, man. Not theory. That's Mordor shit. I mean how the fuckin' thing works. How the fuckin' Orcs made it. You know. Materials and shit. . . and, uh, how ta put it all ta-gether. I'm into revolutionary action—"

"Engineering. South Wing."

Jerry sighed and muttered a forlorn: "Shit." He looked pensively at Sylvian and scratched his beard, irritating the already irritated skin beneath. Slowly and painfully, he squeezed ideas out of his brain like thick glue from a tube.

Finally he asked: "So, my loyal Sam, what'd 'er doin' in the berry?"

Sylvian suddenly had an inspiration. Jerry Wolfe of all people might know something about Goodjohn Saccidananda and the Great Truth Cloud.

"Lookin' for information. . . about this, uh, master, Divine Woo-Woo, Sri Goodjohn Saccidananda, and his Great Truth Cloud."

"Lemme think," Jerry said.

Time slowed to a stop as they approached a black hole.

Jerry's eyes widened, and he grimaced in pain.

"Saruman!" he cried, "Saruman of Orthanic, a wizard like Gandalf but turned traitor and sold out to the Dark Lord. Did too much acid. A real downer, man. Saruman's got this real cool voice that'll just blow your mind, but it's a mindfuck in the end—"

"Whoosse Saruman?"

"The wizard that betrayed Gandalf. . ." Jerry concentrated.

"Goodjohn. . . Ah, this head named John somebody that came up from some straight place out west but turned out to be a freak and crashed here in the Val. Turned on a bunch of chicks who think he's just groovy. It blows my mind that he ain't been busted yet. I mean, ain't been offed by the Riders of Rohan."

"John whose?"

"Or is it Jonathan?" Jerry was thinking again. "Hey, man, I wouldn't fuck with them. Heard some real bad shit 'bout 'em."

Sylvian waited anxiously. Jerry's extended lapses of conversation meant that he was making the journey from Middle Earth to Hinnom Valley.

"Oh yeah. I know now. Talk is he's been charged with some kind of sick crime in California, offing some chicks and carving 'em up into pieces the size of Elvish Runes. Real heavy perversions, man, like that Sharon Tate babe. A real bummer, Sam. He split that scene and crashed here in no-where's-ville till the pigs out west give up."

Jerry focused his eyes on Sylvian as if truly studying him for the first time.

"Hey man, stay away from him. Might be a quack, might be a pervert. He fucks with people's minds. Blasts 'em with real strong acid and then lays it on 'em that he's God or Jesus Christ, or some Eastern freak, divine-somethin', some groove—"

"Guru?"

"Yeah, far out. A Grooveru. . ."

Jerry concentrated so hard that he broke out into a sweat. This effort took a very long time. It appeared that a very significant thought was forming in his brain.

"Oh, hell, man. Religion is a mindfuck, like some invisible cop that peeps into your brain even when you're stoned, and then you get busted. Religion is the opium of Amerika."

At that his shoulders sagged, and his next breath came with difficulty. Then Jerry came to a decision.

"Hey, Sam, forget 'bout the Clouds, Isengard and that slimy Saruman. Who needs 'em. They're a bad trip. You gotta come with me to the Council of Elrond."

"What?"

Jerry had slipped back into Middle Earth where the hobbits smoked pot, as did their creator. Reading books was useless, Jerry often said, unless the author was trippin'. Otherwise, all one got was bourgeoisie drivel, dismal capitalist landscapes populated by hollow characters, bullshit plots driven by greed and display, where nobody ever expanded their consciousness and nothin' was real. Apparently, he'd picked up this credo from the invisible college in the union.

"To a meeting. I know these far-out people. You just gotta deal with reality: the war, Amerika, the Pig Empire in Czechago—fucking Mordor. You gotta deal with reality! There's these far out people who are hip to what's happin' in Amerika, and they're into revolution, man."

Now he seemed to concentrate on a row of books behind Sylvian, where the titles read: *Entropy and Statistical Analysis: An Introduction; or Thermodynamic Equilibrium in Nonlinear Systems: A Dynamic Approach.*

Sylvian followed his glassy-eyed gaze and wondered if he were reading the titles. On the other hand, this was Crowley's east wing, and that meant there were much older and stranger books interspersed with serious physics texts, books written by Sylvian's beloved crackpots, bearing titles like *Heat-Death and the Goddess Isis,* or *Botlzmann's Equation Discovered in the Great Pyramid of Cheops.*

"You're a scientist? A physicist?" Jerry stated the questions as if reading the titles. "So, man, you dig reality too, and you could get into revolutionary action. Shit man, these people dig reality and they read radical stuff by authors who raise consciousness—"

His voice thickened with awe.

"They read far-out shit 'bout politics and Amerika, and economics, how it's all about profit and bread and offing anyone that don't dig that bag, and that's what the war's really about, man, blowing away blacks and freaks and poets that don't believe in the Pig Empire of Amerika."

Jerry gasped for air. "They're the Elves, man. High Elves. Higher than hobbits 'cuz they got the most excellent shit. You gotta come to their meetings 'cuz you understand the One Ring of Power and you can build the thing—the Ring. But you can't tell anybody where you're goin' or who you are, 'cuz there's the Nazgul that is searching for the One and if they find you—"

He gave Sylvian a strange look.

"You dig the bomb, right?"

Sylvian shrugged. He wasn't sure what "digging the bomb" meant. It probably made sense in this Middle Earth place, but how could he know never having been there.

"Like, you want to do something for the people that's suffering? Liberation not escalation. Fuck the Establishment. You know, 'up against the wall, motherfucker this is a stickup!' Be a revolutionary hero of the oppressed people."

Sylvian felt his heart beating loudly in his ears. Every muscle in his soft body began to quiver. He dropped his eyes in embarrassment. He wondered how Jerry could have ever seen so deeply into his dreams, his silly vision of himself as a great Polish revolutionary from family legends. The stupidity of it: people repelled him and yet he had always yearned to bring them freedom and happiness, like his Polish ancestors, like Christ. He loved the people but couldn't stand being around them.

He stammered, "yes. . ."

"Far-out, man. You gotta come and meet the High Elves. Especially Anita. Maybe she'll let you join the movement."

"Movement?"

"Yeah." Jerry dug into his chin, scratching hard. His voice fell to a whisper, dark, and conspiratorial. "The People's Will. It's a worldwide movement, underground, bigger than fucking SDS, real revolutionaries. And you just gotta hear Anita, man. Ain't nobody like her. She's the Lady Galadriel of our time."

Jerry appeared unable to continue. He wandered for a moment through the strawberry fields of Middle Earth. But not forever. He gazed at Sylvian and came to an important decision.

"I'll take you, Sam. She just blows your mind. Anita Anarcharsis. She's a trip, man. A real revolutionary. Still, gots a bullet in her head from 68 in Czechago."

"Don't have much time. Physics is pretty demanding—"

"Hey man, don't get uptight 'bout it."

"Ain't—"

"Shit, man you are. Uptight and wired. Just forget I said anything 'bout Anita."

"Okay."

"But stay away from them Clouds, Sam. They're a bad trip."

"Yes, stay away," Sylvian said softly, really meaning it.

"And don't breathe a goddamn word 'bout what I toll you 'bout Anita and the People's Will. Mordor's got ears and eyes all over."

"Won't," Sylvian promised.

Jerry turned and began to make his way through the stacks slowly.

"Looks like fucking Gollum," he muttered.

THREE

Introduction to Philosophy

A GIRL RESEMBLING PEARL floated into Sylvian's philosophy class.

Lots of girls grew long hair; lots of girls had blonde hair. The "set" of long-haired blonde girls was quite large. The "set" of girls who wore bells and beads and went braless was considerably smaller, at least here at conservative BSU. The set of long-haired hippie blonde girls named Pearl who'd encountered him in a vision and was a devotee of the One Absolute Divine Woo-Woo Guru was smaller yet. Single-membered "sets" were rare.

He sat well hidden in the back row. He didn't smell spices (or fish)—and certainly not sage, rosemary, and thyme.

The "set's" eyes were half-closed. She glanced neither right nor left. Finding her way to an empty seat two rows in front of him, she settled in like some flimsy apparition of shadows and luminous smoke. He wondered why she didn't keep sinking clear through the chair, through the floor, and into the earth.

Then he heard a whining sigh.

Pearl.

Sylvian sank deeper into his seat and prayed to all the saints that she wouldn't notice him. Her being in the same class could not be coincidence. What did she want? What did her groovy-Guru freak want?

Feelings were so imprecise and changeable. A sudden desire arose in him: that she would turn and see him; that she'd come and sit next to him. Why did he crave what he so desperately wanted to avoid?

Pearl stared at the blank surface of her desk as if reading something carved into its wooden surface. She'd brought neither notebook nor paper, and no one ever defaced the surface of desks in BSU classrooms. The other male students in the class stared at her. Many nodded knowingly. The women, mostly well dressed, hiding beneath layers of make-up, reeking of perfume, hair in tall beehives mortared in place by cans of hairspray, blessed her with contemptuous glances. Some emitted scornful little exhales of breath, an exercise to which they had devoted a great deal of practice, like a musical instrument. They were quite talented.

Sylvian dreaded the class and had put off taking it as long as possible. Damned general education requirements. Would he be forced to speak? They did that in humanities classes. Unlike the mathematical precision of physics, humanities depended merely on words. Some people, he'd once heard it said, attempted to reduce words to symbols that could be manipulated by the established laws of logic.

But this avoided the issue, as far as Sylvian understood it. No matter how perfectly symbolized, words could not account for themselves. They floated free from things, like insubstantial clouds, changing shape, changing phase, transforming from mist to rain, to soil, to grass and trees and grain, maybe even people. Spoken or written, logical or not, it didn't matter, slippery words were the curse of his life.

People kept coming in. The class continued to grow. Forty? Philosophy 100 was a top-rated course. It was easy and fun, Sylvian had heard from the "heads" in the dorm. The professor was a freak. He sat on the desk in "half-lotus"— thus spoke the heads—and rapped far-out shit for an hour. Then people went home and did philosophy. The projects they did when they did philosophy could be anything from a term paper to a painting or piece of sculpture, a play, a speech, a musical demonstration—one student constructed a necklace from roach clips and labeled it the "the higher mind's circle of fire." He received an "A."

Jerry Wolfe did much of the advertising. The professor's name was Doctor Hallerman. Jerry had taken the class last year. It was the "most excellent" class he'd ever had at BSU. "It was relevant, man."

Jerry had written this "really brilliant" political philosophy paper comparing the Joint Chiefs of Staff to the Nine Ringwraiths of Sauron the Dark Lord. Professor Hallerman called it "significant," and "a real contribution to contemporary political theory," and had given it an "A."

Professor Paul S. Hallerman continually invited students into his office for philosophical discussions. He often could be found drinking coffee with students at the Union or a student bar. The extremely fortunate, those with an exceptional talent for philosophy, attended evening book discussions by invitation at Hallerman's home. Some discussions went on deep into the night.

Such "selfless devotion to his students," as he called these tutoring sessions, sprang from his fond memories of the continental European education system in which professors served as mentors to the young. The bond between teacher and student became closer than the family bond between child and parent, he would say in tones of wistful longing. Professor Hallerman wanted to be more than a hired brain. He ached to become a "spiritual parent," he said.

To this end, Professor Hallerman would begin his introductory courses with an explanation of the family relationship—the parent-child fetish; he called it—of twentieth-century capitalist America.

Jerry had instantly grasped the truth of Hallerman's revelation. The family, the professor-prophet lectured, is an economic entity. The father as proprietor of the "means of production," by which Hallerman meant the necessities of life, actually owned the family. Viewed in such a way, the wife and children are his possessions because their very biological existence and maintenance depended upon the father.

The wife, who performed the actual physical work of that maintenance, comprises no more than the protoplasmic vacuum cleaner. As such, she counted as a single item in the long list of the father's possessions. She was an essential, often pleasurable item to be sure, but after all the pious rhetoric, all the fancy bourgeoisie talk about "love" and "partnership," the wife in economic terms of use and labor value ultimately comprised a comfortable, serviceable, animated piece of machinery.

For the benefit of religious students, Hallerman noted that the Bible, with its view of the family, was a "pre-capitalist capitalist" document. The Tenth Commandment, for instance, forbade a man from coveting the possessions of his neighbor, and those possessions included his neighbor's wife. She was, therefore, a product, but at the same time, a means of production. God, Hallerman quipped, was a bourgeoisie father long before there was such a class. God was omniscient, at least economically. He foresaw the coming of capitalism.

And now you children, the Great Man would say, giving them his benevolent but slightly cynical smile, are even less than that in the context of the bourgeoisie capitalist family structure. Beware lest the gypsies happen along and the price is right.

The brighter students would laugh uproariously, knowing Professor Hallerman's penchant for irony and indirect speech. Most of the other students, being typical Brunswick State University scholars, frowned worriedly

and squirmed and felt mildly outraged especially when the talented professor made references to "the Jewish lad" as he liked to call Jesus and "his
bourgeoisie dad" as he liked to call God. Admire him or not, everyone
agreed that Doctor Hallerman was indeed a brilliant lecturer, and even the
most conservative students sometimes admitted that he saw through a great
deal of deception. Such jokes usually set up dangerous truths.

"Naturally dees things hurt unt are very shocking to you," Professor
Hallerman would continue in soft, sympathetic tones. "But, you see, such
is point: mawkish reverence for family is another example of fetish of commodities that poisons capitalist culture. Like all fetishes unt neurotic obsessions, it ist irrational. You are a possession. . . You vill do as I say. Mine. . .
belong to me. . . to the family (which is mine). Under my roof, eating my
food. . . mine, mine, mine."

Inevitably, this last string of "mines" would bring forth nervous laughter from the entire class.

"Zsoo. . ." Professor Hallerman would bless them with his most benevolent grin and give his words a stronger German accent. . .

"Zsooo. . . dis bonds of yours to family ist ultimately ones of economic
necessity on your part und irrational fetishisimus on your father's part.
Needs become wants. I prove it to you. Ask for money. Say, for tuition, without any strings."

Abruptly he dropped his accent and became hip.

"Oh man, freak out! Bread with no attachments? The ole man shouts:
Are you zonked? You respond: Hey man, how 'bout parental love? Love?
Yeah, free love? Oh man, double freak out. Love without commitment? Love
without responsibility? What he really means is love without ownership,
without attachments, without capitalism. Love without commitment means
love without capitalism. It's still really my wife, my kids, my girl."

The offhand reference to the Temptations generally brought forth more
laughter and new respect for his wit and cleverness. Hallerman knew that
his students, conservative or not, were today-people. They loathed history;
history was about the dead. History was all about delusion, oppression, and
war. Nothing significant happened before the hip people turned on. They
were into the "now." He made sure that he was a "now" guy.

Such opening lectures served as warmups for his "real serious" critique
of the system. Oh sure they paid their tuition, and yes of course he accepted
a salary for teaching—man, he worked in the system. That's just the point;
he cried with real passion and fire. By being more than mere teacher, by
caring enough to spend endless hours with them, caring for them without
any economic reward, without "moneytheist" attachments, loving them
for themselves—"all you need is love, man"—Professor Hallerman actually

tossed a bomb into the capitalist, bourgeoisie, neurotic, alienating, inauthentic, subhuman, criminal "fetishisimus" for possessions that reduced people to commodities.

Zsoo. . . Professor Hallerman taught philosophy to liberate his students from false bourgeoisie values. He alone truly loved them as human beings. He'd become a greater threat to the system than Che or Mao.

The administration felt the same way. BSU President H. Richard Craven especially despised Hallerman. Unfortunately, Hallerman achieved tenure before Craven had assumed the Presidency. Some said Craven had actually been hired to weed out such radicals and that he'd been relatively successful in this enterprise, especially in the History Department where he managed to sweep out such firebrands as the infamous Doctor Jonathan Burke, who was a real subversive and would hold teach-ins along with his equally radical wife, a veteran of Czechago. (Craven probably owed his position to the fact that he'd married a Butcher girl, Charlotte Butcher, who died in an unfortunate auto accident a few years later.)

Hallerman stood at the top of the President's list. He seemed to enjoy the attention and acted quite recklessly as if to provoke the President.

Sylvian sat in the back of the classroom half-heartedly trying not to stare at Pearl.

Hallerman wore a denim shirt and an old pair of washed-out jeans. He resembled one of the mill workers except for the beads and the silver peace medallion he wore around his neck. Unlike any mill or brewery worker in Hinnom Valley, he grew hair past his shoulders and wore a neatly trimmed beard, gone partially silver. Stuck permanently in his late middle years, Hallerman reminded Sylvian of Michelangelo's Moses, horns and all.

Hallerman claimed that he'd been educated in Europe, although the official faculty profile listed University of Chicago. His student-disciples said that he was a political exile, an anarchist philosopher who'd escaped from some iron curtain country. No one knew if he had a wife or children, although rumor said that in said unnamed country his family had been imprisoned and ultimately murdered by the secret police.

He assumed his cross-legged position astride the front table and began in a bored tone to rattle off the course requirements. These "requirements" actually reduced to one "requirement": a rather vague "philosophical project" on some rather ambiguous "philosophical issue" that was "relevant to what was happening now," or something to do with "happening," which was also rather vague, given that his voice had fallen into a muttering drone.

The professor's eyes appeared to be focused somewhere over their heads. They were sitting in the basement of Dumbley Hall so he couldn't be staring out of a window.

Resting her head on top of her folded arms, Pearl had gone to sleep.

With all the "bureaucratic refuse of a neurotically repressed system" out of the way, Hallerman let out a long sigh and began his lecture, addressing the white brick wall at the back of the room.

Sylvian tried very hard to follow the "lecture" and to write down the salient points. But he couldn't locate any "points." The lecture was a map without coordinates. He was instantly lost in a raging sea of words illogically strung together, or at least organized with a logic he failed to grasp. Everyone else nodded and wrote, and understood everything correctly, except for Pearl, who slumbered through the revelation.

As far as Sylvian could see, the Great Man was talking about something he called *Sein*. The fact that he called it—this, whatever it was—*Sein* seemed very profound and deeply significant.

"Therefore, you must see into *Sein*," he intoned significantly, "how it is with *Sein*, not *seiende*, or even *Dasein*, for such are objects of our grasping bourgeoisie perception, and grasping them distorts them, and rapes them, and forces them into naïve objectivity, which they are not, and so traditional philosophy is another form of repression, as is Amerika itself. Dig it?"

He paused and sipped from a coffee cup, allowing these mighty thoughts to sink in. Most of the students wrote furiously, some covering a page or two in their notebooks. Sylvian, utterly lost, wrote: "*Sein* is not bourgeoisie."

"Bourgeoisie capitalist culture is mired in *Dasein* and has thus forgotten about *Sein*," the prophet-professor continued. "The essence of reason thrown rootless into the world of *Dasein* is calculative thought—"

Relieved that he'd understood something, Sylvian quickly wrote: "*Dasein* is calculus."

"—and the inhuman result: Not only is *Sein* forgotten by *seiende*, but calculative thinking becomes the highest order of reason, delimiting *Sein* by *Dasein*, and henceforth you have the absurd neurotic obsessions with course credits, grade points, class percentage which in adult life become bank accounts, net worth, religion, patriotism, the work ethic, and the fetish of commodities. Just think of how your parents live. They've completely forgotten *Sein*."

The students wrote furiously. Many nodded. How could his parents, good Catholics, have forgotten their *Sein*? Sylvian would have to ask Father Loeb.

Abruptly a male student sitting in the front row shouted: "What about Vietnam?"

Professor Hallerman smiled benevolently at the back wall. "Vietnam is another of the consequences of forgetting about *Sein*. It is a realized reality of the principle that flows from that forgetting, which is 'the Nothing nothings.'"

Now here, undoubtedly, was a significant principle of philosophy. Sylvian wrote it down quickly. "The Nothing nothings."

"Vietnam is the result of a male-dominated warrior caste society addicted to violence as the sole solution to every problem," declared a girl sitting in the far right seat in the first row. "All that stuff 'bout how Amerika is so good and generous, and virtuous. . .always been bullshit. . .napalming poor villages, defoliating, indiscriminate bombing, mass killing is. . .sickening, Amerika's sick. . ."

"Vietnam is capitalist imperialism and the military-industrial complex conveniently feeding off of cold war paranoia," declared the student who first posed the question.

"Which arises from an obsessive violent male culture that's the result of frustrated sexuality and monstrous penis insecurity," the young woman declared, anger creeping into her voice.

The young man shook his head. "No, sister, you got it upside down. The violent militarist society comes from the private ownership of the means of production and the exploiters' need to dominate the working class that produces labor-value commodities, as well as the need to create new markets, stealing natural resources, and stock-pile cheap labor from formerly colonial peoples."

The young man—Sylvian saw that he had short hair and seemed well groomed—glanced at Professor Hallerman for approval, which Hallerman bestowed by smiling benevolently at the back wall.

"—cold war lies and propaganda serve the system. Any sort of colonial liberation might give the imperialist country's own working class certain ideas that would be dangerous to the capitalist oppressors and their government stooges—"

"Cool it with the lecture, Eugene," the girl groaned, interrupting him.

Sylvian thought that she looked like a cherub from the stained-glass biblical scenes in St. Stanislas Cathedral. Round face with wide eyes and a down-turned mouth set in a perpetual pouting frown, she seemed sad and severe at the same time, chewing her bottom lip. She worked very hard to control her emotions, which seemed obvious to everyone but Sylvian.

"The male fetish for control and power born of penis insecurity," she said again, tension in her voice. "Capitalism is the result of male aggression not the cause."

Eugene shook his head. "Nope," he said in a superior tone, "you got it backwards, sister. Capitalism breeds aggression, and aggression becomes oppression. We need to assimilate a new consciousness."

The other members of the class were furiously writing. Sylvian tried very hard to think of something to write in his notebook and became very anxious when nothing came to mind. He was quickly falling behind in what was supposed to be the most accessible course at BSU. Hurriedly, he wrote down all he could think of, "nothing is male."

"And what'd ya all know 'bout oppression?" shouted a black student with a huge afro sitting next to Sylvian in the back row. He was the only black student in the class.

"We the ones been lynched and whipped and shot and we is done talkin' 'bout 'ssimilatin' into middle-class America 'cuz white honky middle-class America ain't got no conscience. Capitalism, communism, ain't no difference to us. We the internal colony of white America. We the oppressed!"

Black people generally frightened Sylvian. Their excessive anger, their aggressive tones, the simmering violence that seemed about to erupt in the next moment, the rapidity of speech, the sheer volume as if every word were a shout of anger (and pain), or, conversely, a hoot of laughter—all this scared him. Such behavior, his father and mother said, proved that blacks were closer to the animal kingdom than whites, a million years behind in terms of evolution—"just out of the trees," to quote President Nixon.

His parents accepted evolution only when applied to blacks. "Normal" people, of course, were created by God as described in Genesis about six thousand years ago. Adam and Eve were white; black people evolved from a son of Noah, Sylvian forgot which one. Liberal Catholics—communists, his father said—held that all humans derived from Africa. This was obviously wrong, Father Loeb said (and Sylvian's father agreed), since the Garden of Eden was in the Mideast. Modern archaeology confirmed its location, but here Father Loeb wasn't too clear on the details.

Professor Hallerman smiled and raised an eyebrow. He sipped his coffee but remained silent. He seemed to be enjoying the discussion. The students were doing philosophy.

Another male student, one sitting next to Pearl (who still appeared to be asleep), spun about and glared at the black student, who glared back in turn.

Sylvian shuddered—not for the first time or the last. He recalled the description of Satan he'd heard from the nuns at St. Stanislas when he was six; the portrait had given him nightmares.

The young man looked frightfully satanic. His hair and eyes were wickedly black. Although he did seem to have a haircut, hair grew from his head in a wild tangle, thick and black, as if it'd never been combed. He possessed an immense forehead and sharp cheekbones that gave his eyes a slight slant and thus an evil glinting look. His lips were full and sensual. Worse, he wore a sharply cut goatee that gave his face a goat-like aspect exactly like the nuns' devil. He wore thick rimless glasses that seemed to magnify his piercing dark and evil eyes.

The devil of Sylvian's nightmares had come to life. Sylvian couldn't take his eyes off him. Satan frightened him, no doubt, but also proved compelling.

"What's Black Power against the armed might of Amerika, James," the Satan snarled at the black student. "Riots and ghetto wars gonna play right into the hands of the fascists. Give 'em the excuse they're lookin' for to wage genocide on black people. We fight for real emancipation! We have real power. We—"

He stopped suddenly as if an alarm had gone off.

"Jus' words," James shot back. "White devils is always preachin' liberation, emancipation, integration, freedom. But what'd we got in all these years? Nothin'! Ain't got nothing 'cept white man's religion without Black Power."

"You of all people know we are more than words," the Satan growled back.

"Oh yeah," James laughed sarcastically, "we knows. You and your big radical girlfriend. You sooo crazy. Gonna shake lots of folks real good. Randal the revolutionary."

"You know who we are and what we are capable of," Randal the devil answered. "It'll happen. Soon."

"Oh yeah and then daddy'll come and bail you out, hey Boots?"

Sylvian identified the devil. This identity was the first clear definition he'd encountered in philosophy class: Randal Boots, Boots Lumber and Paper, a child of the mill owners, the mighty family Boots of Hinnom Valley.

The student named Eugene interrupted. "Without party discipline, no revolution has a chance. History proves it."

"Oh yeah," James said again. "Disciplined by our own Eugene Vico."

"Revolution without an ideology is mere rebellion and doomed to failure, like your ghetto riots, James."

"Gonna be a war of colonial liberation. Right, Randal?"

Randal decided upon a strategy of stubborn silence.

"The class war will come only after the consciousness of the proletariat has been awakened and raised by the Party," Eugene recited.

As if reading his lines from a script, Professor Hallerman chose this moment to grace the class with his wisdom. The brilliant professor's wisdom was a question addressed to the cherub.

"Well, Miss Butcher, anything to add?"

Butcher! Sylvian experienced yet another profound shock. She had to be Cathy Butcher of the brewery family. Jesus, Mary, Joseph, and all the Holy Saints, what a class. Children from the two most prominent families in Hinnom Valley attending the same class with student revolutionaries, black power militants, and the most radical professor on campus.

"No, nothing," she said frowning.

"Cathy, you know it's more than words," Randal muttered.

"Anyone else?" Professor Hallerman asked, raising his arms and spreading them wide as if still following a script.

Suddenly Pearl lifted her head. "It's because of Puritanism and Christianity," she declared in her most plaintive monotone.

Professor Hallerman put down his cup, put away his smile, and looked at the class for the first time. He focused on Pearl and gave her a most severe and thoughtful frown.

Pearl stared at a point just above Hallerman's head. Her mouth hung open, and she exhaled a whining sigh.

"Well, Miss?"

"Pearl."

"Well, Miss Pearl, please continue."

"Repressed," she sighed as if it were obvious. "Religion. Christianity is a bummer. Like, no one's had a healthy orgasm 'cuz of it. Capitalism is Puritanism without God. So everything's 'bout desires, but capitalist desires, and they ain't natural, so. . ." she paused as though she'd lost the thread of her argument, or perhaps realized that there'd never been a thread, which didn't seem to matter to her, since she concluded ". . . sex lost its holiness 'cuz of Christianity, which is capitalism and repression, and no free love, and so no healthy organism—"

Professor Hallerman nodded gravely and said: "Repression."

"Like wow, repression starts a big ego trip too," Pearl declared, sounding amazed at her inspired discovery, "and, like, this ego trip is, like, Death, and. . ."

"Ahhh," said Professor Hallerman, "and have we repressed that too?"

"Yeah! We got all these hang-ups 'cuz of Christianity and its repressions, and so we screw other countries. . . which is why we're in Vietnam!"

Professor Hallerman studied her, waiting for more. But she put her head back on the desk.

"Well, Miss Pearl, that was truly profound," Professor Hallerman announced. Especially your penetrating analysis of capitalism and sex. I certainly hope the rest of you got that down."

The class wrote furiously.

Sylvian again experienced the terrible anxiety of being lost. He felt as miserable as the day he'd hidden a candy bar in his coat pocket during confession. In total agony, Sylvian wrote: "Christianity nothings—and this is why we're in Vietnam."

The class was concluded. Professor Hallerman had done his job liberating young minds. Their assignment was to read Heidegger's *What is Philosophy?* By Thursday.

Later that evening, Sylvian paged through the philosophy anthology, frantically searching for this Higher-digger. He stumbled over strange sounding names, read a few sentences from some, and understood nothing. The Nothing did nothing indeed. He feared he'd never graduate.

But here we've forged too far ahead, for the nothing problem was nothing compared to what befell him that afternoon and changed him forever. Let's observe how revolutionaries are made.

FOUR

Class Consciousness

PERHAPS PEARL HAD ABANDONED her effort to recruit Sylvian Matreya for the Great Truth Cloud. Perhaps she'd appeared in his philosophy class by mere coincidence. As soon as the class ended, taking no notice of him, Pearl melted into a crowd of students. Sylvian felt immense relief—and yet a stinging disappointment. He'd become invisible again, even to a sweet garden-fairy of the unseen realm.

Dear Virgin Mother, he ought to be relieved at his escape. What if Goodjohn Saccidanada turned out to be what Jerry Wolfe claimed? What if Pearl was the killer's baited hook? Thank you, Holy Mother of God—

The powers of Hell are legion and come in many guises; Father Loeb taught his young charges in Cathedral School. Every ancient religion worshipped demonic offspring, Father said; even the simple fairies of the Celtic peoples were demons spawned in Hell. Fraudulent eastern gurus were the most depraved of the infernal lot. Sly devils, they adopted Jesus himself into their temples of barbarous idolatry.

Assigned the task of seducing him (Satan loved to corrupt innocence—and the simple-minded), Pearl was a member of that swarming devilish host. They blended into wild nature. Changelings and shape-shifters, they appeared to human beings only when they chose, usually to work mischief through beautiful sounding but noxious doctrines. Adam's sin had fatally corrupted nature too. Father Loeb drummed this fact into the heads of his impressionable charges—and thus had been given over to the rule of the dark powers. Only the strength of the Church stood between frail human beings and the demon-inhabited world.

He'd experienced a very narrow escape indeed. But he was not an innocent. Oh no. Alluring desires sprouted like weeds from the sinful soil of his soul. He'd almost betrayed his beloved parish priest. . .and Jesus himself who'd suffered for him on the cross, come to think of it. Jesus and Father Loeb—in Sylvian's mind they merged into one. The guilt made him physically ill. Tears rolled down his ashen cheeks.

"Hey, boy, you sick?" James was staring down at him.

"No—"

"Don't look so good."

Fright pushed aside the terrible weight of guilt. It was impossible to speak.

James shrugged. He studied Sylvian.

"Say, boy, you Indian or somethin'?"

"Uh, no—"

"I mean Hindoo?"

"NO."

James shrugged again, gathered his books and headed out of the classroom, one of the last students to leave save for Sylvian the great sinner.

"No," Sylvian called after him, knowing that James couldn't hear him and thankful for the fact. "Not Hindoo (whatever that was). Polish!"

Polish, he repeated to himself, ancestor of the heroic revolutionary Count Kalka Janski Matreya. Sylvian Matreya, descendent of nobility. Oh, the Holy Virgin. Tears burned his eyes. His mental image of the warrior Count fit his older brother Karl. He, the runt of the family, was a little boy with strange dusky skin and a language problem, more comfortable with the abstractions of mathematics than the "imprecise" society of people, a disgrace.

Tears still burned in his eyes as he emerged from the basement of Dumbly Hall into bright September sunshine. He squinted and blinked like a mole. The tears played with the light—he knew the geometry of it—splitting and refracting the rays. This brief mathematical reverie made him happy. He forgot his fear, his dull ache for the succubus Pearl, and his stupid, infantile dreams of Polish heroes.

Through a maze of light-born sines and cosines, he automatically headed southwest, down Pine Avenue towards the residence halls. His dorm was one of three newly constructed high-rises and named for an early founder of Hinnom Valley, a certain Doctor Schleiermeir—Schleiermeir Hall. It sat on the very southwest edge of campus, part of a canyon of high-rises, about a half-mile from Oakwood Park, Sylvian's favorite place in Hinnom Valley.

Sylvian had no more classes. It would be a great day to gather his physics books and head to Oakwood Park. Besides the library, Oakwood Park was his refuge from the incomprehensible human world. The Park included a large, roughly triangular section of thick woods, an open field, a lagoon, and a steep hill upon which sat the oldest tree in Hinnom Valley christened (for reasons nobody seemed to know) the "von Jahn oak." The origins of this mysterious name—nor the sinister rumors that dangled from it—didn't concern Sylvian, mainly because he'd never heard them. He loved to sit against the ancient gnarled bark and vanish into the shadows of its soothing shade. There he would doze away the hours. Sometimes he dreamed his old dream of St. Barlaam, the strange saint no one knew, not even Father Loeb.

He made the right turn off Pine Avenue and headed through the main campus, through the complex of old administration buildings with wide-open greens, crisscrossed walkways and narrow paths. University Greens contained monuments and statues, some very large. They were usually the figures of individual university benefactors astride high stone pedestals that resembled miniature ziggurats.

This region of administration buildings, greens and statues, was roughly circular and referred to as the "Ring," or, to honor the country of many of the founders of Brunswick State, *das Kreis*. On fine days such as to-day students crowded the Kreis, lying in the grass, talking, reading, tossing footballs, some furtively drinking from cans of (Butcher) beer, which was strictly prohibited by university regulations although seldom enforced, except if the beer originated from some company out-of-town, say Milwaukee or St. Louis. Pot smoking, however, instantly produced the campus police.

Sylvian floated through das Kreis lost in the mathematics of the rainbow. Unexpectedly, his dreamy wandering brought him into the epicenter of a storm. Something incredible was happening in das Kreis.

He had wandered into the middle of a demonstration.

His absent-mindedness had to be an "unbalanced remainder" of his dream. . . or imaginary space created by complex numbers. The administration of H. Richard Craven forbade demonstrations on campus. Not once, even during the tumultuous year of 1968, had BSU endured the mildest disturbance.

Here was a demonstration during the first week of classes.

Sylvian had encountered a logical impossibility, anti-war "demonstration," at BSU. More precisely a public debate.

❖❖❖

About one hundred students milled about the statue of a certain General Klaus von Brunswick, one of the Butcher-Brunswicks from whom the school took its name. The great man's image cast in bronze stood nearly eight feet tall and rested upon a five-foot base. It had been erected in the 1850s and looked its age: the metal skin had become discolored; years of slow deterioration, coupled with fraternity pranks, had broken the pointed beard and snapped the sword. The spike had disappeared from the helm, and boot toes were missing. The stone base was worn smooth. Given his miserable condition, the exaggerated Napoleonic pose of the brave General appeared ridiculous.

Sylvian was overwhelmed by the terror of finding himself in the middle of so many people. No university police were about, nor any university officials, nor members of SHS. Hulking shadows, however, haunted the windows of the administration buildings.

An exponential increase in terror nearly brought him to his knees when he discovered that he'd wandered into the middle of a tight group of blacks. God took pity on him and gave him strength, and he kept his feet. Here was James from philosophy class. James, wearing that look of disdain and anger, was listening to a young man speaking from the base of the Brunswick statue.

The speaker was another philosophy student, Eugene Vico.

Eugene wore all denim and looked exactly like a mill worker, except for the fact that his clothes were spotless and obviously new. He was wearing wire-framed glasses and looked very scholarly.

He spoke beautifully in a rich baritone that somehow seemed too dense and sturdy for his skinny frame. Without mechanical aids, his voice carried effortlessly across das Kreise. And how eloquent his words. So precise, so brilliant. Every word was perfectly pronounced and annunciated. Every symbol, every metaphor, made perfect sense and communicated exact, unambiguous meaning.

Sylvian was entranced, unable to move as if that magical voice had somehow seized his free will. For the first time in his life he entertained the previously nonsensical possibility that the pure aesthetics of human speech might approach the precise beauty of mathematics. He was so mesmerized that he hardly understood what the young orator was saying. Something about classes, parties, discipline: perhaps Eugene was giving advice about on how to obtain good grades.

But then James' voice tore into silky speech, shattering the magical vocal spell, as a night siren often breaks deep sleep.

"Ain't no classes in America!" James shouted. "Ain't no such thin' as class consciousness, juss honkey bullshit. Everybody's out to get theirs. Ain't no workin' class gonna revolt."

Eugene appeared unruffled by this outburst. He fixed James with a thoughtful look, raising his eyebrows as if Hallerman had asked him an exam question that had a distinct and straightforward answer.

"Of course there are classes, Mr. Rutledge," he replied calmly. "The mill workers, brewery workers, the maintenance people here at BSU, even the professors—all share the same objective economic conditions of having to sell their labor. Therefore, they constitute a proletarian class. And we students comprise this class too. We are in job training. We're the raw material manufactured into products by our so-called education, to be purchased by the clients of the university, those businesses that contribute to BSU."

"Shit!" James spat. "Yeah, Eugene, you just go tells that to them whitey mill workers 'cross the river. Then you tells them that they gotta unite with their black brothers and sisters at this 'versity." He laughed sarcastically. "Go ahead, Eugene. Get the shit kicked outta you, boy."

The black students gathered in a tight knot around James, perhaps twenty, pretty much every black student attending BSU, erupted in derisive laughter, causing Sylvian to cringe.

Eugene's unruffled serenity began to show a few tiny cracks. He actually raised his voice.

"Black and white unite!" he shouted. "Raise the consciousness of the working class. The socialist revolution must begin with the realization of proletarian class unity."

"Raise some hell!" someone behind Sylvian shouted.

"Right-on!" Voices rose in a chorus.

Most of the white students had already begun to edge away from the small group, leaving only Sylvian among them. But he was so small and dark that no one, black or white, seemed to pay attention to him.

"Ain't no socialist revolution," shouted James Rutledge in the same angry tone. "Is gonna be a colonial revolution. We is a nation. We is an oppressed and conquered nation, victims of imperialism, juss like our brothers in Africa. We a nation thats been enslaved by whitey imperialism and aggression. Like this Hindoo kid here, like in India." He pointed at Sylvian. "We like Jesus and the Romans. Jesus was a black man and the Romans were white oppressors. Whitey done killed 'em 'cuz he taught black power. All that other pacifist shit in the Bible is whitey trying to lie 'bout what Jesus really taught. They gave us the Bible to pacify slaves. We got the Bible and they got us. Jesus was a black man who taught black power. He taught liberation. Black power! Black power!"

A thunderous shout greeted this declaration.

"BLACK POWER!"

For reasons he could have never put into words, Sylvian suddenly felt a powerful wave of sympathy for James and his companions. He felt their suffering and lived their alienation. He was one of them. Imprecise feelings could still be quite powerful.

"No, no—" Eugene cried, spreading his arms, appealing to what remained of the crowd.

"—we must have a disciplined party of white and black—to teach the proletariat, to raise class consciousness, to lead them. White and black unite!"

The black students laughed derisively.

"Hey, Eugene!" shouted James, "who leads? You? Who decides?"

"Decides what?"

"Decides what's best for us poor childrens."

"I. . . don't understand?"

"Boy, don't you feel guilty? cuz you really does think that we inferior. We jus' big childrens that's got to be lead by the likes of you. You jus' can't admit to yourself that you believes blacks really is inferior. All your raisin' consciousness is only for power over poor folks you secretly believes is inferior."

This declaration brought forth a mighty shout of BLACK POWER! A crushing wave of noise swamped Eugene's reply. He began to experience problems speaking. Red-faced, swollen with rage, he choked on words he sought to hurl back at his tormentor. White students in the crowd began to hiss and shout: "Why don't you coons go back to Africa. . . Go back to your fields, Sambo—"

Amid the escalating pandemonium, a huge woman wearing a flowing gold-trimmed cape, black boots, and jeans, mounted the base of the statue. She instantly dominated the scene. Her hair was wild, curly and black, flying out in all directions. Her face was heavy, her jaw almost brutal—her thick neck cushioned by rolls of flesh. Her eyes were strikingly blue, hypnotic, and overpowering. She was too old to be a student, but her age seemed indeterminate. She might have been thirty or sixty.

The huge woman quickly brushed aside a flustered Eugene. She seemed as large as the statue itself.

Her voice boomed as if she used a loudspeaker. "Marxism, socialism, New Left, Old Left, class consciousness—FUCK ALL THAT! It's all DEAD! Daddy's politics. White-man's power trip. All isms are wasms. Only Marxists here is the Groucho kind!"

She pointed a finger the size of a Polish sausage at James.

"Black power ain't the way either!" she thundered.

Sylvian noticed that several white students had taken up positions at the platform's base. They shouted their approval.

Sylvian recognized Jerry Wolfe and the satanic Randal Boots from philosophy class. Randal was gazing up at the wild creature with a combination of reverence and awe etched across his sharp features. Sylvian recalled the faces of many Cathedral parishioners as they gazed upon the statue of the Virgin Mary.

Surely this caped woman was no Virgin Mary, for she yelled: "FUCK IT! Power is the fucking Establishment. We're all oppressed proletarians. We gotta destroy the whole damned thing! DESTRUCTION IS THE FIRST ACT OF LIBERATION! All of us, black and white, are OPPRESSED, RE-PRESSED, SUPPRESSED AND IMPRESSED!"

Even the blacks had to laugh at this.

"The working class is a Victorian myth. What do you think this university is? Nothing but a tool-shed for future capitalists! You're all slaves, white and black, and you don't even know it. Students are the proletariats. Students are the revolutionaries."

She spun on Eugene who seemed to fade in her shadow.

"Organization is oppression. Jus' what the fucking Establishment wants. Party, state—" she lifted her eyes to the brick buildings behind— "education, administration, management, public relations, politics, FUCK IT ALL. WE REJECT IT ALL. REVOLUTION NOW!"

At that moment the university police arrived.

FIVE

The Making of a Revolutionary

UNIVERSITY POLICE DID NOT carry firearms but they did wield sticks filled with lead. Usually, they were retired military men or former mill workers, or dropouts from the Hinnom Valley police force.

University cops despised and resented students; at this age, males ought to be in the military defending America in Vietnam, not wasting time frolicking in college sandboxes. What the hell did young women need with a college education? Most smart co-eds were ugly girls who couldn't find a husband. Or lesbians.

"Auxiliaries" took up positions at the boundaries of the green like spectators at a sports event. Auxiliaries were members of SHS, mostly football players—some were frat brothers, and others belonged to Christian youth groups.

The police line parted. A phalanx of auxiliaries advanced on the dilapidated statue and the revolutionaries who held it prisoner. They carried baseball bats and wooden beams. They hooted and yelled obscenities at the protestors.

"Go home and take a bath! Fuckin' commies! Go live in fuckin` Russia! Go to China, sons-of-bitches. We don't want you in America stinkin' up the place. Commie bastards!"

One unusually large fellow with a crew cut and huge belly shook his bat and bellowed: "All right, assholes, fun's over. Be good little boys and girls and go home."

The white students, now probably less than fifty, scattered like fright-ened puppies. The police roared with laughter and smacked any student who got close enough, propelling them on their way.

"That's right," boomed crew-cut who acted as if he was the leader of the student army, "How 'bout you spades?"

The line advanced. James and his friends glared at them and retreated towards the statue. Sylvian was too terror-stricken to move. Then, once more, he experienced a great wave of compassion for the blacks. He'd never felt anything like it, as if he'd become someone else. It was all so vague, but he felt. . . black.

He felt hands on his shoulders firmly pulling him away from the on-coming stampede. James had not forgotten the little invisible "Hindoo." "Come on, kid, 'fore you get hurt."

The black students retreated to the statue's base dragging him along.

He looked up at the fearsome woman revolutionary. She was glaring at the police and their auxiliaries, snarling like a cornered she-bear. Surely she would fight.

The phalanx came on, swinging their bats, laughing and shouting obscenities.

"Go home and take a bath, monkeys!"

Sylvian would never be able to say what exactly happened next, except, perhaps, in the language of physics: Several simultaneous events occurred instantaneously in a single region of space-time.

Less precisely: The whole thing exploded into chaos.

SHS and the frat boys charged old General von Brunswick.

A crazy melee broke out around the heroic General. It seemed as if, for a mad instant, the ruined statue suddenly came alive and began to swat at people with its rusted sword. The giant woman let out an ear-piercing shriek and collided headlong with Eugene Vico. She knocked him off the pedestal as easily as if she'd swatted a fly. At the same instant, Randal Boots and Jerry Wolfe, standing below her perch, suffered a head-on collision of their own. Literally head-to-head. Running like two darting rabbits, they slammed heads together, reeled back senseless, and collapsed at the feet of the bronze General—his conquered foes, vanquished and prone at his feet. But the old warrior, obviously suffering from poor eyesight and advanced age, completely ignored this, his most significant victory.

The black-capped shrieking banshee, having disposed of poor Eugene, who'd fallen in the grass next to Boots and Wolfe, clambered off the stone platform like a huge spider. She displayed utterly fantastic agility for a person of her mass.

She hit the grass at full gallop. The cape streamed behind as if caught in a mighty gale. Her high-pitched screaming exploded painfully in Sylvian's ears. She seemed to be anticipating the blows that were about to descend upon her.

She charged directly at little Sylvian Matreya.

"Out of my way, RUNT!"

He couldn't move and James had left him to his fate. He stood directly in the path of this rolling avalanche of the revolution.

Crew-cut flung himself at her, baseball bat raised.

At that instant—perhaps in violation of Einstein's special relativity—a simultaneous event occurred in a different region of space-time, in this case, the fairy world. Unbelievably, Pearl appeared standing beside the victorious General. He smelled fish. She was laughing through her crooked teeth and calling to him, that he should follow her. . .

"OUT OF MY WAY, RUNT!"

"Pearl." He threw up his arms. "Blessed Virgin."

CRASH!

He thought that the blow came from crew-cut's bat. But he never knew who or what slammed into him. A terrible pain exploded behind his eyes, and his sight snapped off like a burned-out light bulb. Instantaneously (for the third time), he fell to the grass and dropped into darkness. His last thought was that he'd peed himself.

And he had.

Sylvian remained unconscious through the rest of what the university administration called "an unfortunate riot—the work of a tiny minority of glib and arrogant activists, and black radicals." Later, Jerry Wolfe informed him that he'd been ambushed by "one of the fuckin' pigs who'd crept up behind him—the cowardly bastard—and tried to off him with a loaded club."

"Jus' like an orc," Jerry concluded, failing to mention that he too had been unconscious throughout the battle.

The pig-assault changed Sylvian's life.

A single blow to the head awakened him to political reality in Amerika.

She mildly regretted running over the little Indian kid. But Anita Anarcharsis wanted to avoid any ill-considered confrontations with the pigs. The Masters had not spoken. Not yet.

Crew-cut and his teammates chased her through the Kreis, gaining on her, but only for a few seconds. Then she began to pull away. They were linemen, not sleek distance runners, and despite her size, Anita's endurance was that of Satan himself.

After about a hundred yards, they gave up. Many finished their unanticipated workout coughing, bent over, hands on knees. Three lost their lunch.

"Goddamn, she's fast!" Captain Crew-cut gurgled and spit; he was one of the unfortunate who'd vomited.

"Too bad she's a fuckin` commie," observed a teammate.

"Shit man, women ain't allowed to play football anyway."

Students fled the green like frightened rabbits. General Klaus von Brunswick still stood in his victorious pose, rusting away but undefeated. Bodies lay scattered at his feet, mostly black.

The university police wandered about, laughing and joking, searching for someone to arrest. They'd squelched a riot after all. There should be arrests. And there would be. The blacks.

A paunchy sergeant with a bull neck and bald, bullet-like head, along with two companions, who obviously patronized the same grocery and barber, began to cuff the bodies at the base of the statue.

"Hey Billy, ain't this here that Boots kid?"

Billy the fat sergeant squinted. "Yup, at's 'em. Help 'em up, Pete."

Pete grabbed a dazed Randal by the back of his pants and heaved him to his feet.

"Yeowww! My nuts!" Randal yelped. "Police brutality!"

"Hey, asshole. Better git the hell outta here, or your ole man'll cut those nuts clean off! Ain't that right, Pete?"

"Yup," Pete laughed, shaking Randal and causing him to shriek with pain. "Might cut off his allowance too. Then poor baby'll have to go to work."

"Or to Nam," Bill observed.

"Yea. Study gooks in their rice paddies."

The police roared with laughter. Pete released his prisoner. Holding his groin, Randal staggered away. They exploded in laughter when he collided with a red brick administration building and became a casualty of war a second time.

Entertained by The Randal Boots Show, they didn't see Eugene Vico drag himself to his feet, shake like a wet dog, and scamper off.

Now the battlefield was empty save for little Sylvian. And James.

They didn't see Sylvian flattened in the grass like a swatted insect. On this day, his odd curse of invisibility saved him from arrest.

Perhaps too, they didn't notice Sylvian because their attention was focused elsewhere. Everyone had fled the green or had become prisoners of war save for Sylvian and James Rutledge.

James stood defiantly beside the statue, facing the police.

"I thought all you children had gone home," growled sergeant Bill. The other university police crowded in beside him, clubs in hand. They'd stopped laughing.

"All the children's gone home," said James.

"No, they ain't. There's still one left."

"Like I says, the childrens is gone. You must be blind, pig."

Bill took a menacing step. "Better get your ass outta here right now, boy, or we'll see who's blind."

"Ain't no boy, motherfucker."

They swarmed on him like a cloud of flies. Hoarse wordless grunts and growls, obscenities, and then a rain of sickening thuds—they beat him to the ground and kept punching, beating and kicking. Their clubs became slick. The grass went from green to red. Their clean khakis were soiled. Blood splattered the statue's pedestal.

They kept beating until they were exhausted.

Bill, panting like a dog, shouted: "Did you see how this coon attacked me?

"I'm arresting this bastard for assault and battery, attacking an officer of the law—" He glanced at the red-dyed stone. "—destruction of public property, resisting arrest— What else?"

"Inciting a riot," someone suggested.

"Communist subversion," added another.

"Ought to be shot for treason."

Bill kicked James viciously. Two other police grabbed him under his arms and lifted him. He seemed limp and broken. His head lolled, mouth open, blood pouring from his nose and mouth.

"Boy, you a goin' ta jail."

A boy approached the still-unconscious body of Sylvian. An extraordinary boy to be sure, he wore stripped silk bellbottoms held up with a wide belt, no shirt but loads of brightly colored beads. Someone had dipped him in a vat of blue body paint. He was a musician, for he carried an instrument, slung over his shoulder that might have been a small trumpet but more or less resembled a conch-shell. His hair was long and black, which was the same color, or negation of color, of his eyes.

He gazed down at Sylvian and sighed. Then he laughed, and his laughter sounded like cymbals and bells.

His laughter seemed to signal a choir of young women, who abruptly joined in. Dressed in the most outlandish clothes—formless silken sack-like gowns of red, orange, and purple—they formed a circle and began to dance, singing like brightly feathered birds in some unknown, antique tongue. They chanted and called, and laughed, and executed extravagant contortions, waving their arms, gyrating and twirling.

The women appeared focused on Blue Boy who, a strange grin tuning his thick lips, regarded a trampled Sylvian.

"Now's not the time for faintheartedness," Blue Boy said. The blue-hippie bent down and whispered into Sylvian's ear: "Arise, into battle. Your time has come."

With these words, Blue Boy produced a porcelain flask and forced liquid, which might have been tea, down Sylvian's throat. The poor child coughed and gagged, yet swallowed the entire contents of the flask. He opened his eyes and shut them quickly. When he opened them again, Blue Boy and his female horde of dancers had vanished.

He awoke transformed. Whether it was due to his collision with the giantess of the revolution, or some drug administered by the blue apparition, no one, especially Sylvian, would ever know. In spite of the uncertainties surrounding his rebirth, one might say his spiritual birth, young Sylvian had taken his first step on the path of revolution. He was a victim of police brutality.

Ghostly shadows rustled behind the window blinds of the President's office high above the green.

Dean of Students Richard Bentley turned his back, sighed, and shuffled over to his chair near the President's substantial antique oak desk. President H. Richard Craven, who'd been standing on the other side of the window, peeking through the blinds, followed the Dean and took his exalted seat. He leaned back in his stuffed leather chair, swiveled about, and fixed his gaze for several minutes on the crossed medieval swords that hung on the wall behind his desk.

Bentley tugged thoughtfully at his trimmed beard, which was gray and distinguished. Craven, contemplating the imitation swords, angrily tossed his black-rimmed glasses onto the polished desk surface. His sharp nostrils flared and twitched, giving his face a weasel-like appearance.

Bentley knew from the familiar signs that the President fumed. His fleshy ears blazed bright red and his pale, blotchy skin seemed to glow like polished metal in the sun.

Bentley waited patiently for the outburst, fingering his wide white tie.

Ministers such as Bentley were accustomed to such things. They knew how to handle the extremes of emotion, how to calmly listen, nodding in sympathy and wincing in empathy—meanwhile recording it all, every tiny bit of information. Who knew what infinitesimal dust mote or what insignificant smudge might prove useful in some future situation? Bentley smiled ironically behind his serious dignified expression, thinking how similar a Protestant councilor could be to a Catholic priest in the Confessional. Similar but not identical. Counseling was not a sacrament, though many ill-informed people treated it as such.

The explosion finally came. Craven slammed his open palm on the desk and shouted: "Goddammit, Dick, the people of Hinnom Valley, especially my dear in-laws, generously support this fine institution of higher learning and they don't want it to become a dumping ground for outside agitators, radicals, and black revolutionaries!"

Bentley pulled at his beard and replied carefully: "Well, President Craven, I do not see it quite this way."

"Hell, Dick! How then? American boys are dying in Vietnam 'cuz of these bastards. Commies see such things and are inspired. Hell, did you hear that communist punk down there?"

"Eugene Vico?"

"Card-carrying commie bastard. Givin' aid and comfort to the enemy. Takes orders directly from Nikolai Lenin. Ought to be hanged for treason. I want him expelled immediately."

"Well, I think that would be a mistake."

Craven's ears turned a deeper shade of crimson, and his nose twitched. "Why?"

"Because he's harmless," said Bentley calmly, "and useful besides. We should let him talk all he wants, as you yourself advised. In fact, given your third point, we ought to encourage him."

"Inciting a riot is not what I had in mind."

"With all due respect, President Craven, he's not the kind to do anything. We should begin a so-called dialogue with him. Negotiate. Talk. Make him feel, well, important."

Craven squinted suspiciously at Bentley for a few minutes. At last, he murmured: "Yes, I see. You want to play a little game? Get someone to spy on him, infiltrate his group? Administer a slight push here and there, like Anita and the People's Will?"

"Something like that, but in the open. Not all the mystery and sneaking about. Not all the occult nonsense. Vico's too hardheaded for that. He'd suspect anything that smells of mysticism."

"Hummm. . ."

Bentley could see that Craven had begun to calm down.

"Marxists are the easiest to manage. It has to be scientific, though, nothing mysterious, religious. And by the way—" Bentley had to tread carefully here— "Vico doesn't need to take orders from anyone, not even Vladimir Ilich Lenin, who, uh, died in 1924. Too bad we can't lock the library. It all comes out of books."

"So we can use 'em?"

"Assuredly."

"What about the big witch? I saw her down there."

"We've been over the Anita thing before. She cracked when her husband ran off with that brainless nymph who fell for his Age of Aquarius rap. My informant feeds Anita similar nonsense, and she swallows it whole. Sailed off to the East on her swirling magic mystery ship. I've thought up a few rather interesting wrinkles for her and the People's Will. They're no problem."

"What about those black animals?"

Bentley put on his most concerned mask, one that combined regret with toughness, stern duty with clerical pity.

"Expel them. Every last one of them, I'm afraid."

"Now you're talking, Dicky. How 'bout arrest too? I'll call ole Chief Dick Butcher."

"Yes, that too. I confess I see no way to control Black Power."

"Shoot it out of existence?"

"May come to that. Those people are serious. Isolate them in their ghettos maybe. Let 'em kill each other. Bringing them here, into civilized society, was a mistake."

"Should have never let 'em in the university."

"Well, the grants—"

"We can expel them and still keep the money, can't we?"

"I think so. Yes. Let the good Christian black kids stay. Expel the radicals. They're the smartest, but they'll never graduate."

"Goddammit, Dicky, I'm feeling better about this now. Shit, you might even say that the riot was useful."

Bentley smiled at what was was precisely the conclusion he'd wanted the President to reach.

"Indeed, very useful."

But then he assumed his troubled and dejected expression.

"Still, I'm not altogether happy, President Craven."

"Oh?" Craven's eyebrows rose and his nostrils flared. Bentley imagined a wet ferret or a weasel about to steal an egg.

"Goodjohn has always been difficult to predict. And he gets nuttier every day."

"The stupid Woo-Woo hippie?"

Bentley had trouble believing that Craven had not made the connection. Summoning his clerical powers, he thought it best to play along and not ruin the President's mood. Unless Craven knew quite well the identity of the Divine Woo-Woo and was playing Bentley himself? No, he wasn't that devious—

"Him."

"Hell, Dick Butcher says they're harmless. A bunch of acid heads."

"I don't know—"

"Shit, they ain't done nothin' 'cept drugs. I can have the Chief bust 'em."

"No, not yet, I still may find some use for them—"

Craven grinned, showing his fangs, now reminding Bentley of a slavering badger about to bite. "What you got in mind, Dick my boy?"

"Well, nothing yet. They still concern me. There's something odd about them. Something I've never seen before. They could turn out to be a real threat."

"Ah fuck 'em. Dopers and dropouts. Can't park a bicycle straight. Wouldn't know how to start a fire with a gallon of gasoline and a box of matches. I'll get Chief Dick to bust 'em."

"I don't know. . ."

Craven would not allow his sudden swing into this joyous mood to be denied. "Hell, Dicky, you're right. This riot turned out to be a good thing after all."

He leaned back in his chair and toyed with his glasses. "Goddamn but this is a great job. It's really an exciting time to be the President of a major university. You know they call me Pa College. Like I'm a father to them. Ever since dear Charlotte's been gone, this place has become my life. Maybe someday you'll be a college President yourself, hey Dicky?"

"I'm quite happy nurturing students," Bentley replied quickly and with some alarm.

Craven eyed him and his nose twitched like a hungry rat sniffing garbage. "Yeah, you ministers are still priests at heart. Father Dick. Especially with the young ladies."

"As Dean of Students I do feel a certain, shall we say parental responsibility for every student, male and female. Just as you do, President Craven."

"Not like me," Craven answered him with a scornful tone in his voice.
"Not like me—"

And thank God for that, Bentley thought. He smiled back, his most
concerned smile and silently prayed that Craven wasn't planning to go off
on one of his little "Presidential junkets," as he liked to call them. He was
already showing signs by cozying up to Cathy Butcher for God's sake.

And Bentley would have to deal with the frightfully messy cleanup.

SIX

A Special Child

BEFORE WE GO ANY further into our story, I think a short pause is in order. Please don't expect an edifying sermon. I feel the need for a little essay on context since all of this happened so long ago.

It occurs to me that I should have written an introduction. Saving, I honestly don't know what I could have said to prepare any normal person for—and here I think we need to be honest with ourselves—the depravity of those wild years. Church and State still suffer a temporal hangover. I mean to say that today's so-called progressives, religious and secular, are descendants of those deluded children.

Nowadays every straight-thinking person grasps the pure lunacy of that time, that it indeed was a series of childhood tantrums.

I seem to recall one of those radicals who, sad to say, came from the Catholic clergy. If you can imagine such a foolish little man; he certainly didn't deserve the title "Father." I once heard him say that our dear Lord Jesus was a hippie. Long-haired, bearded, dressed in rags, Jesus revolted against the Establishment of his day and organized the working class (the pious fishermen of the Galilee!) into a revolutionary party. He urged them to seize the means of production, by which he meant the land, the Temple, the wealth of the elites, and share everything in common, including their wives.

Can you imagine such nonsense? I mean, Jesus's teaching was purely spiritual— "blessed are the poor in spirit."

The silly little Priest claimed that Jesus practiced free-love too. He married Mary of Magdala, and the marriage was an open one, which was "right-on."

It was as if for a moment our country went collectively insane. Except, I need to make clear, it was never more than a tiny minority, who became the darlings of the mainstream press and Hollywood, who put on the show. All theatre. Intellectually bankrupt and never a revolution at all, the sixties deserve to be forgotten. So why write?

Let us say that I can't get poor Sylvian out of my head even after all these years. Nor can I forget those tragic events that shook our "non-versity" as the cynical Professor Jonathan Burke used to call BSU. Looking back, it all seems so incredible.

Kindly grant, then, dear reader, this short biography of our subject in place of a proper introduction:

The "Mattayya" (old spelling) family was among our most faithful parishioners. They were loyal to our Holy Mother Church and our beloved country, and they implanted these values in their children. The youngest, however, had already become a worry long before the opening of this tale.

Immigrating from the Grand Duchy of Warsaw, Karl Matreya, the future revolutionary's grandfather, came to Chicago and learned the printer's trade. He founded a small bookbindery and printing shop near Kosciuszko Park. The Company specialized in religious books: Bibles, catechisms, theological words and manuals, liturgical works, and some secular works, all with the *imprimatur*.

The business prospered. Karl became the exclusive printer for St. Stanislas Cathedral. Eventually, he married the youngest daughter of Baron Leon Janski, a distant relative (although nobody knew exactly how). While still in his teens, Baron Janski had fled from Warsaw to Chicago in the aftermath of the Polish tragedy of 1863. Some said that he had attempted to assassinate the Russian Tsar Alexander II, but he neither confirmed nor denied said accusation.

Grandfather Karl never uttered a word about the old country. He was American he unhesitatingly declared whenever someone asked about his ancestors.

Karl and his wife Maria Janski had two daughters and a son. The son was named Leo, after his maternal grandfather Leon, and was born in January of 1912 when Karl was in his fifties.

Leo eventually inherited the bookbindery, Matreya and Son Company. Like his father, Leo worked hard at the business and maintained (and improved) his connection to the Church. He became wealthy enough to purchase an estate in Highland Park. His first wife, a Polish girl from a humble background (nobility graced not her family) died quite suddenly in her late twenties. Leo did not remarry until his late forties.

His second wife was some twenty years younger. Lorraine Blank was the middle daughter of the prestigious Blank family from Milwaukee. Her grandfather, Arthur Blank, had been a prominent member of the liberal Frankfurt Parliament of 1848–49. Prussian soldiers arrested him after an especially vicious speech he gave in May of '49, in which he referred to Frederick William IV Hohenzollern as "a bloody-handed pig-traitor to Germany." They would have executed him had he not chosen exile in America. I sometimes wonder if Sylvian inherited the revolutionary disease from him.

Leo and Lorraine had two sons: The oldest named after his grandfather Karl, born in 1950, and the youngest, our tragic dark-skinned boy, born in 1952.

Karl looked like all the Matreyas, a wild blonde bear of the Polish woodlands. A tremendous athlete, he could become arrogant and occasionally rude, traits his father indulged, I'm sorry to say. You see, Karl was a throwback to the old Polish warrior-nobility, and such characteristics bespoke the aristocratic values of an earlier, heroic period. At best, an average student, he got bored after a year of college and joined the Marines.

Sylvian was a changeling. Leo often wondered if gypsies were roaming Chicago, stealing babies and replacing them with misfits and pygmies. Unlike the other Matreyas, he was short and dark. Perhaps Ukrainian blood flowed through his veins, perhaps Mongol from the time of Batu Khan's Polish invasion. Who can say? In him the German and Polish bloodlines seemed to have dried up like ancient riverbeds, exposing the dark soil of Asia.

Sylvian refused to grow. He refused to talk. When he did speak, he made silly mistakes in grammar and pronunciation. Such childish blunders were at first cute and endearing. Unfortunately, they lingered as he got older until by age ten the cuteness had become stale. He sounded mentally disabled and appeared stunted. Except for his straight hair, he might have passed, God forbid, for a Negro.

A steady stream of specialists, family doctors, assorted medical and psychological saviors, took charge of poor "developmentally impaired" Sylvian Matreya. The experts finally decided that the problem wasn't physiological, say a congenital abnormality—oh no. Yes, Sylvian did indeed appear to be mentally "slow," as they said in those days, and dwarfish to boot.

But he did not entirely fall into the statistical category of the mentally or physically impaired even if you adjusted the parameters and fudged the factors. Our most highly respected specialists pronounced him "normal." His parents found some solace in that.

What the good Lord takes away, however, He sometimes repays in strange ways. What we perceive to be natural evils, say arbitrary and needless suffering caused by natural phenomena—I often teach the parish children—are God's mysterious purposes at work in the world. In the end, a greater good will arise, although in Sylvian's particular case, as in a few others, this is often difficult to determine. To repeat, it is all for the greater good, I say.

One morning, in Sylvian's twelfth year, he surprised his parents by babbling about a strange dream. He'd dreamed a dance of odd- looking symbols, letters burning like church candles, spinning about his bed in a mad chaotic whirl. Suddenly, as Sylvian rubbed his eyes and pinched himself awake, the fiery symbols snapped into line as if some drill sergeant had barked out an order. Then he heard beautiful music. The symbols themselves were singing to him, but not in any language. Pure sound bubbled up from various shapes and positions in the sequence. He possessed no words to describe it. The music made him weep with a deep longing.

Naturally, his baffled parents had difficulty understanding what he was saying. He usually lost control of the language when he became excited. The dream made him ecstatic, maybe for the first time in his life.

Leo was tempted to slap him as he often did when he lost his patience with Sylvian's "special problems." A strange note in the piping child's voice stopped him. He felt an odd tingling in his fingers as if the sound of the boy's voice awakened memories, not in his brain but his skin. For a moment, he felt pity and compassion for the unfortunate child, contempt, and guilt for the many "corrections" he'd administered, especially in public places when the kid became embarrassing.

The guilt feeling passed. Leo remembered his parental duties and drew back his hand to strike the runt—

Lorraine stopped him. "Wait, Leo, let 'em talk. He ain't never talked so much in his life."

"He's babblin' nonsense!"

"Not all of it. Listen."

Leo heard it too. Sylvian kept repeating a word, a name. It was Saint. . . Saint somebody. . .

"What?" Leo was still itching to hit him. "A Saint? A Saint done talked at you?"

A Saint! A saint was inside the music. The music gave birth to a saint, immaculate like. . . The boy surprisingly pronounced the word "immaculate."

His parents had never heard of this music-saint. The Dominican Fathers at St. Stanislas had never spoken the name, nor had they heard it. (Indeed, we had not).

"Says it slowly," Lorraine prompted.

"Saint. . . Bar. . . la. . . am. . . Saint Barlaam."

"Sounds like a clown's name," Leo said. "Ain't never heard of no Saint Barlaam."

Lorraine agreed.

Sylvian started to cry. He became completely incomprehensible.

There was too such a Saint (they thought he said something to this effect). St. Barlaam had appeared to Sylvian. The Saint didn't speak. Instead he arranged the floating symbols just like a child playing with blocks, not forming words but—Lorraine followed this better than Leo—happiness?

There was meaning in the arrangement of the symbols. Sylvian didn't know what exactly they meant only that he felt thrilled and joyful, happier than he'd ever been in his whole life.

The Saint did not utter a word. He juggled the burning symbols. And finally, the symbols spoke meaningfully to Sylvian through that sweet music.

The music spoke of how the heavenly chorus of angels sings at the foot of God's throne in the Empyrean sphere, as Father Loeb described it and the children of St Stanislas believed it. The angels sing the praises of God's mighty creation in the deep purple-black of space amid the rumble of infinite speeding galaxies. . .oh yes, they sing of numbers beyond infinity, so far beyond that only God's mind can comprehend it all. The symbols sang the angel songs. Sylvian repeated the whole thing perfectly, as Father had taught.

Lorraine believed she followed most of this fairly accurately. She feared that the experts were wrong.

". . .dose symbols is the mind of God!" the boy declared in a powerful voice that even Leo could understand. "Immaculate."

At that, Leo slapped him, slapped him quite hard, enough to split his lip, and knock him down.

"There'll be no blasphemy in this house, goddammit!"

Lorraine pulled a weeping Sylvian to his feet, scolding him about disrespect for his father, about his stupidity, his lies, and his hundred other failings.

Then she pinched him hard and shoved him out the door, screaming that he'd be late for school. Additionally, he needed to shut up about his stupid dreams.

Sylvian's only attempt to tell his parents about his dream and the silent Saint Barlaam ended with a slap, a pinch, and a shove out the door. He, of course, confessed the whole thing to Father Loeb, begging the learned Dominican to tell all he knew about this Saint, who he was, his story. Father Loeb said to him that he'd never heard of a Saint Barlaam, except for a certain Barlaam of Calabria, a medieval theologian who was more Orthodox than Catholic and therefore suspect. Sylvian had better not talk any more about this Barlaam, for if such a person had visited him in a dream, it must be the Devil, or a devil.

He never mentioned St. Barlaam again.

The unknown Saint invaded his sleep one more time and then never returned. His last dream of Barlaam followed the same sequence of events, only this time Sylvian cursed him and turned his head away just as Father Loeb had ordered him to do.

St. Barlaam had appeared dressed in gaudy colored rags like some hippie with beads and long flowing hair. He seemed to give off. . . well, a kind of bluish glow.

Apropos to my responsibilities, and without violating the sanctity of the Confessional, I advised his dear parents to search his room for drugs. Naturally, they found none. Leo gave him a beating for causing a priest undue concern.

Soon after the Barlaam affair, Lorraine picked up the phone one evening and heard the lisping voice of Father Schmidt, one of the St. Stanislas teachers. Father Schmidt was calling to inquire about Sylvian's "special talent."

Thoroughly jaded by such phone calls, Lorraine replied with dignified fury that yes, she was quite aware of Sylvian's problems and had been so for twelve years, and a teacher of Father Schmidt's outstanding academic achievements need not trouble himself over such things, for neither she nor the good Father possessed either the training or the knowledge of the countless distinguished experts who had examined the poor child and pronounced him developmentally slow—

"No, no," Father Schmidt somewhat rudely interrupted her, "I ain't talkin' 'bout his silly little speech confusions."

"I dare say them's hardly silly to his parents," Lorraine answered dryly. "I'm wonderin' how much of dis problem is comin' from da lousy teachers thats he's had?"

"Ah, dear Mrs. Matreya, really. Whatever you think of St. Stanislas, I must tell you that we think very highly of young Sylvian. He's a genius if I'm not mistaken."

Lorraine's Teutonic jaw dropped in astonishment. Only for an instant. Father Schmidt, she guessed, was playing a cruel joke.

"Perhaps you knows Alderman Jackowski? He's a very good friend he is and a very large contributor of the Cathedral. I believes dat he sits on the school's board of directory too. Ain'nit so, Father?"

"You should know that today your son identified a six-digit prime," Father Schmidt said quickly.

"A what?"

"A six-digit prime. A number that can only be divided by itself and one. It's impossible to identify large prime numbers so quickly in your head. Sylvian did it. At least I think so. It's hard to say without a lot of checking, but he says that he sees the answers dancing before his eyes."

Father Schmidt could hear Lorraine's heavy breathing through the line.

"He's not an idiot savant," Father Schmidt hurried on. "I spent the afternoon testin' 'em. He sees geometry too. He developed Euclid's 463 proofs in the order of the *Elements*! He says he sees 'em in his mind falling into place. He hears 'em making music too. He says the symbols are alive."

The Priest's voice grew even softer. Lorraine could barely hear what he was saying.

"He knew 'bout stuff I ain't never taught. He said he could see the operations in his head. I mean tough stuff: differential equations, variations, matrices. He's a native speaker of mathematical languages."

"Well he's actually adopted," Lorraine blurted into the receiver.

"It's uncanny. I'm not able to follow all of it. I think that he's derived Bernoulli numbers, infinite series, set theory, stuff I've only heard about, and some I ain't."

"Jesusmaryandjoseph," Lorraine groaned, "more therapists. First his stupid dreams and now dis. Leo'll probably give 'em a good beltin.'"

"I think we can get him a university scholarship," Father Schmidt said.

Lorraine gave an incoherent grunt.

"I've taken the liberty of callin' a friend of mine up north. There's a cozy university up dere named Brunswick State of the North. It's perfect for Sylvian: small, conservative, nurturing—"

Abruptly Lorraine screeched: "Damn teachers don't know nothin' 'bout Sylvian!" She slammed the receiver down and flew upstairs to give Sylvian a good slap for causing a teacher to call his parents at home.

❖❖❖

It turned out to be true. Dopey little Sylvian did indeed possess an exceptional talent for mathematics. He also showed a taste for physics. And he did receive a full scholarship to Brunswick State University.

Leo forbade him to follow a course of study in pure mathematics. Theoretical or pure mathematics, Leo declared, was a complete waste of time. Physics was different. Engineers were well paid.

Sylvian said that he wanted to study theoretical physics. Maybe become a professor. Leo flew into a rage. He would have none of it. Professors of physics, like mathematicians, were mostly Christ-killing Jews. Einstein was a Jew. Lots of 'em was communists too. Marx was a Jew. Most professors were leftist subversive Jews. Queers besides, he added.

Sylvian received the required beating for thinking such a thing, and applied to the engineering school. He scored perfect on the mathematics section of the particular entrance exam administered to underage first–year students on scholarship.

Thus did little Sylvian Matreya come to Brunswick State University.

He passed his first two years quietly, working hard, spending most of his time in the library. But then he committed his first real act of rebellion. Without telling his parents, he switched his major to theoretical physics.

It is probable that his parents, had they found out, would not have cared. By this time they were so thankful to be rid of their "special child" that he became something of an afterthought: "Yes, we gots a younger boy dat's away at the 'versity. . ."

Karl, his older brother, was now a captain in the Marine Corps and had gone to Nam. He won a bronze star. Leo bragged about his Polish warrior-nobility ancestry, the aristocratic blood that flowed in Karl (from Leo himself).

Yeah, the other kid is gone to the 'versity. Leo hoped that he stayed away from the communists and the Jews, the drug freaks, sex maniacs, and especially Negroes. They's all ruining the country and making it tough on war heroes like Karl.

Yeah, Leo would just as soon forget about his other kid.

Lorraine was thankful to be rid of the experts and teachers. They didn't care what weird stuff he studied at BSU even if they could understand it.

So, Sylvian rebelled by studying theoretical physics. . .

Until Pearl, Goodjohn Saccidanada the Divine Woo-Woo, and the BSU riot.

❖❖❖

Thus concludes my little interruption. I promised no sermons. Allow me, however, a brief moral lesson.

In my humble opinion, Goodjohn Saccidanada was, at best, a fraud. It may even be said that the Great Truth Cloud was an ancestor of recent New Age cults. They were a mystical band of atheists and nihilists such as those our most saintly Holy Father, also from Poland, warned us against many years ago. Anita was a deluded feminist-communist who, in my expert opinion, was quickly seduced by satanic powers, which, despite the babblings of arrogant scientists, are very much active in the natural world.

It's all old age primitivism. Paganism. Goddess worship. A whole satanic world revealed—an abominable brew distilled back then, still flowing active today. It reminds me of those old frat parties when everyone brings something—wine, gin, whiskey, rum, vodka—and dumps it all into one massive vat of lemonade or Kool-Aid. The only prerequisite was alcohol content; your guru, Maharishi, Spiritual Master, Ascended One had to be some pagan wise man. They even made Jesus a freak. They fed weak and fearful egos. Theirs was a kind of intoxication, but of the oldest type, the ancient promise of the devil: "Ye shall be gods."

People adopted names and terms of which they knew absolutely nothing. Read anything from those times, and you'll see. Pure ignorance, abysmal superstition. But if it felt good, if it shocked the "Establishment," well then, do it.

There were always frauds and criminals, revolutionaries and anarchists, nihilists and atheists quite willing to take advantage of such naive and rebellious ignorance.

Goodjohn was one, Anita another.

SEVEN

Awakening

"Gonna join the People's Will," Sylvian declared. "Wanna fight pigs! Free peoples. How can a rational person live for the next second knowing such oppression exists?"

He stabbed the heart of his overcooked steak with a knife. His asault met with little success. The blade was dull, and the steak was already dead.

Jerry Wolfe glanced around nervously. "Keep your voice down, Sam. Got to be Ringwraiths listening. I know there are orcs. Mordor's reach is long."

Students crowded the cafeteria at the noon hour, but nobody seemed to pay any attention to Jerry and Sylvian.

"Stuff you Tolkien shit!" Sylvian howled. "This's reality!"

Jerry looked hurt. "Sam, man, you've become really. . . mean. You gotta cool it. Get stoned or somethin'. Take the edge off. Man, you ain't no fun. I mean, you're becomin' a real downer. Man, all of a sudden you're old."

"Is serious." Sylvian glared menacingly at Jerry. His lips curled. His skin appeared darker. Coals smoldered in his dark eyes, a cold fire that gave the baby-skinned face an odd and frightening hardness, like features of a Brunswick statue, as if he'd become a hollow rusted shell housing fire. His speech had mysteriously improved, if only slightly.

"Informers, man," Jerry whispered, looking sideways. "Fucking SHS is really FBI. Maybe even CIA. Been trying to crack the People's Will for years. That riot las' month got 'em real uptight. Anita says we can't trust nobody."

He cast a wary eye at four young women sitting nearby. They wore layers of make-up, puffed hair, their sweaters tight, and they giggled incessantly.

"School's crawling with FBI. Anita's got to be careful, calling meetings and planning revolutionary action. Gotta make sure of people. Gotta be totally committed to the movement."

"Am committed," Sylvian snarled. "Am awake."

"Yeah, well, we ain't no SDS. We ain't no New Left, or Old Left like fucking Vico. We're serious."

"Toll you, stupid head. Establishment's totally evil. Is simple mathematics: Total evil must be totally canceled. It all deserves to perish—"

The young women at the next table got up to go. Their giggling reached a crescendo. One of them brushed against Sylvian.

He leaped to his feet, fists raised. Jerry gasped in astonishment. The idiot was at least an inch shorter than the shortest coed, and his threatening pose looked comical. Jerry thought that the whole act was a joke. Sylvian then proceeded to demonstrate the error of this assumption.

"Stupid little cunt!" he howled, "touches again and. . . kill you!" He looked like a flustered two-year-old venting impotent rage upon some inanimate object, some toy that refused to yield to the child's omnipotent will.

The women stared at him for a second and then exploded in laughter. "Oh, wow! Sorry. Far out. We're sorry little boy. Oh wow. . ."

Sylvian swept the dull butter knife off the table and waved it in their faces. "Will kill you, sluts!" he screamed. "Will!"

People around them had begun to stare. Many were laughing. Jerry reached over the table and tried to grab him. Sylvian stabbed at Jerry's outstretched hand. He missed, of course.

"Sylvian, man, cool it. SIT DOWN!"

Sylvian glared at him, shaking and trembling as if he were having a seizure. One of the coeds said, "Oh wow, is he ill?"

"Yes, he's ill," Jerry said loud enough for everyone to hear. "I'll take care of him. Sorry."

They returned to their giggling and whispering, gave a collective shrug and left. Sylvian slumped back into his seat, looking exhausted. He still clutched the knife. "Is serious," he muttered.

Jerry looked worried. "Man, you got to be careful. For your own good. Got to be secret. Invisible. Fucking FBI's all over. Thank the elves, the People's Will is a match for 'em, man. We're part of this huge network that Anita calls the White Order. It's worldwide. Gonna start the real revolution when the time is ripe, when the High Elves—the Masters, Anita calls 'em— give the signal. Until then, you gotta remain invisible so the People's Will can't be infiltrated by the Establishment. Gotta be quiet, man."

Sylvian laughed. "Why'd she speak at the demonstration if she wants to remain invisible?"

"She had to answer that asshole Eugene."

"Marxism makes sense. It's precise."

"Anita calls it a revolution in the library. A bunch of abstractions about commodities, production, surplus value, class-consciousness, objective conditions. . ." Jerry recited the words as if from a sermon he'd heard repeated many times. "Nothing but formulas. It's bullshit."

"It's scientific, stupid freak."

"Man, what's happened to you? People's Will is science. Anita says workers is just another gear in the System. Ain't revolutionary at all 'cuz they been bought out by the bourgeoisie. It's bread and circuses, man. They got their nice homes, their cars and TVs, their bourgeoisie vacations—they're as empty as those brainless chicks you wanted to off. Ain't no classes in Amerika. Just one lousy tune repeating itself like a scratched record."

"Then why didn't she debate Vico?"

"She don't give a shit about Vico. She spoke 'cuz of James. We need 'em. They're violent. They'll do the deeds that needs to be done."

"Is violent too!" Sylvian declared. "I'm black. Jus' look at me. Can't be Polish. Parents lied. Everybody's liars, even the goddamn priests. Delusion is infinite. Wanna join The People's Will!"

"I'll ask Anita. There's gonna be a secret Council of Elrond soon. We gotta be careful."

He wrote something on a napkin, folded it, and gave it to Sylvian.

"Memorize these directions and then burn them. I shouldn't be doing this before Anita says it's OK, but shit man, you're a physics major, right? You know all about the Rings of Power?"

"Theoretical physics," Sylvian said mockingly. "A real genius. Ask anybody."

"Far out."

"I'm committed to revolution. Everything is an illusion. All that exists deserves to perish."

"Wow, man, you're more like Gandalf than Sam," exclaimed Jerry Wolfe.

That evening, alone in his dorm room after physics class, Sylvian looked into the mirror and knew with certainty that it was true: He'd been adopted. He was not he; was not a Matreya descended from heroic Polish nobility. If not Polish, then was he a changeling? Negro? Indian?

Studying the dark skin, black hair and eyes, he recalled an old, insignificant even. Gazing into the dresser mirror with his new eyes and awakened mind, he sunk into a past memory.

Early Sunday morning before Mass at St. Stanislas, once again the devil, there in the very pages of his Catechism, Satan was causing confusion (as is the nature of the Devil). He couldn't grasp the meaning of the anagogical sense of scripture. In mathematics, a finite continuum, a line segment for example, potentially contained the infinite, as he understood it. Except he could not grasp how "eternal destiny" (which itself made no sense since eternal meant no passage of time while destiny assumed time flowed to a conclusion, and so one ever got there) existed in the finite events of scriptural history. He couldn't put the problem into words.

After Mass, dear Father Loeb remarked to his parents in an offhand manner that little Sylvian seemed a bit slow, unlike big brother Karl who'd instinctively grasped the Catechism, ingesting it whole and complete, and could repeat it by rote. Sylvian's *sensus divinatatus* seemed stunted, the priest said, as any atheist. He appeared religiously retarded.

His dear mother Lorraine had answered quickly: Oh yes, this was indeed so, but Father should know—here she'd lowered her voice—that we adopted little Sylvian, alas. Yes, yes, after Karl we wanted another child, only the Lord God hadn't answered our prayers—if Father cared to recall—so we adopted. "Who could've known that he was so. . .backwards?"

Suddenly his dear mother realized that little "who could have known" was standing right next to her holding her hand and had heard this revelation, which required no divine intuition to grasp. Embarrassed by the slip yet afraid to lie to a priest, she patted the oily black head and said so everyone could hear that despite his backwardness they loved him almost as much as Karl, "I mean," she quickly corrected herself, "as much as Karl."

Later, she explained to Sylvian that the whole thing had been a rather silly mistake on her part, the result of habit which like all practices had become thoughtless. She'd slipped into the habit of referring to Sylvian as a "special child" because of his, uh, idiosyncrasies, and well, this might result in "other things, and of course he was their natural child, even if he was so different and, well, there'd never been idiots in their illustrious family tree. . ." So, naturally, she sometimes slipped into "other things." And, she added contemptuously, "Do you honestly think we'd adopt a Negro?"

He also recalled Holy Week when they read to the children the gospel story about Peter's denial of Christ. Peter had denied Christ three times. At least his mother had only denied him once. And yet Simon had become the first Pope because he was named Rocky, which is how Sylvian understood the Aramaic name, Cephas.

Gazing into the mirror, feeling deep pain, he knew that his mother had lied. He bunched his fists and felt a burning hatred. He hated them all. It had all been delusion. He was finally awake. He would not be fooled again.

He too was capable of lying. After all, he'd had good teachers, especially the priests who piously lied in the name of God.

Now a terrible plan began to take shape in his mind, piece by piece, like a mathematical proof. He saw in the mirror a terrifying design for revenge. He winced as if stung from the inside. Excitement and disgust overwhelmed him. How in God's name could he consider such a fearful thing?

But they'd all lied to him. They'd abused him, laughed at him, and beaten him. They—the Establishment, the System, the Church, his parents—deserved terrible retribution.

He would be patient. He would be sneaky, deceitful, convincing. At last the hideous thing formed whole and sharp in the mirror like a fully developed film; he could see it leering behind his eyes, slavering and waiting, a misshapen shadow from the darkest pit of his bruised mind.

He'd feel no pity for any of them. They'd created the monster. They were responsible. All that exists deserves to perish. He was merely the instrument. He had awakened.

For two weeks, Pearl slept through philosophy class. For two weeks, he smelled herbs and spices, and fish, and knew that once again she was following him. He knew she was an informer.

One night Jerry came up with the theory that the Clouds were the FBI infiltrating radical BSU just as they'd done at Berkeley. He told it to Anita, he said, but he would not reveal her response; that was party business. Sylvian believed him. He was an innocent, Christ-like, stoned, and stupid at the same time. He was Frodo.

Sylvian had tried to read Tolkien but couldn't. The whole thing seemed childish, like one of Father Loeb's little parables. There didn't seem to be any women in Middle Earth, and certainly no sex.

Then, after two weeks, he decided to act.

He caught her in the hall after class.

He actually touched her—more than touched—grabbed her by the arm and spun her around. She gasped and looked startled, mouth open, grinning foolishly, stupid and stoned at once, that is, Christ-like.

Then, something passed through her, and she giggled, twirling her long hair with her fingers.

"So you're gonna come," she said in her nasal whine.

"Come where?"

"To the Clouds. With me. You got to tune in, turn on, and— (she couldn't remember the rest of it) with the Divine Guru. He'll confirm you."

"I've been confirmed. Why do you want a zero, Pearly?"

She sighed as she always did before she spoke. "I know about your rebirths, Sylvian Maitreya."

"What exactly do you know?"

"Everything."

"Oh yeah? Then you know 'bout a brilliant physics student that's descended from Polish nobility? How big brother's a marine captain in Nam? How dear loving parents are so disappointed width the other kid? Who's special?"

Pearl looked directly at him. "I know that you were incarnated on February 3, 1952," she said in a voice he'd never heard before. "And this is your final rebirth."

He stared at her. Rebirth was bullshit, like the resurrection. She knew his birthday. Jerry Wolfe was right. The place was crawling with FBI. They had to have a file on everybody. A middle-aged devil that Goodjohn Fraud, an idiotic little misfit. He had to be careful.

"Zsooo. . .?" He imitated Hallerman's accent.

"So you might be him."

"Am nothing, nobody, zero, a vacuum, emptiness. Ain't heard of no damn *him*."

She shook her head and sighed. Her voice slipped back into its whine: "You don't understand. If you're really him—Goodjohn needs to know. He doesn't believe me. Says he's the Divine Avatar. I need you to show him—"

"Have you heard about that Charles Manson creep?" he interrupted.

She looked away. "Everyone has. . . poor Sharon Tate, a sacrifice like Jesus."

Sylvian shrugged. "Jesus is a lie. You be careful, Pearly. How much do you actually know about this Goodjohn? Might not be too healthy."

For the first time, Pearl looked hurt. Her elfin face twisted unnaturally into a frown.

"Maybe not you," she said slowly.

"Yup, babe, maybe I ain't nothin'. Don't forget, the nothin' nothings."

"Not you?"

"Better tell your Creepjohn this bit of news. Save him any more trouble. Go after real radicals like Vico. Me, I'm from Middle Earth."

She gave him a long look and then floated away.

After that, she never came to philosophy class again, and he no longer smelled gardens and fish all over campus. She vanished, just like Father Loeb's Celtic faire-folk. Of course, Father Loeb was a lying bastard, as were they all. What revenge he had planned.

Physics, he began to suspect, might also be a pack of lies. With his awakened vision, his new mind formed by the combustible chemicals of hatred and skepticism, he now saw the old magic as nothing more than human conceit and delusion. Physics changed like the weather.

His terrible plan, however, called for him to continue with the charade. Therefore, he closed his new eyes, temporarily disarmed his explosive mind, and played the idiot.

Physics itself, as if in response to Sylvian's monumental change, became unbelievable, even for God, he suspected, who must have confused himself when he created such a universe. Nonetheless, physics was the One Ring of Power as Jerry Wolfe (Frodo) would say. Revolutionaries needed to know it if only to build weapons to blow the mind (and everything else) of the Establishment.

So while the newly awakened revolutionary insisted that this too was a delusion, the old idiot perceived a deep, exquisite beauty within the confusion. The old idiot had the feeling that he'd touched something sacred, something so beautiful that even God, if such a monster existed, would catch His divine breath in surprise and awe, and worship in the Temple of science.

After two years of what now appeared to be a mere initiation, Sylvian was at last permitted to enter the inner holiest of holies and view the central mysteries. He was allowed at last to study Restricted and General Relativity. Next semester would be Quantum Theory.

Every Thursday night, Sylvian and two other neophytes met off campus near Oakwood Park at the home of Professor Gustav Adolph Olaffsoon who according to rumor had studied for a summer with Neils Bohr at the Copenhagen Institute. The university often referred to Professor Olaffsoon's "international reputation," especially on the occasion of fund-raising functions. Sylvian never heard him mention one thing about his exploits, his work, publications if indeed he had any. He resembled a lost hobbit like Jerry—and appeared consistently stoned.

Professor Olaffsoon taught Relativity like a tape-recorder. Never interacting with his students (all three of them), never acknowledging them or their questions, never indulging in personal asides like Hallerman, for two and a half hours he did nothing but explain the mysteries—speaking as if from the Absolute Elsewhere.

And what mysteries. The revolutionary Sylvian suspected the authorities—this time his physics teachers—plotted a vast conspiracy. They'd manufactured truths to serve the interests of the capitalist oppressor. Classical physics was only good for gross technological, corporate, conventional warfare, capitalism and its social system. Except it wasn't true. Or else, Olaffsoon was lying, or crazy, or joking. Most likely he was stoned.

They started with the Michelson-Morely experiment. Every other experiment he'd ever studied, from Galileo's inclined plane to Newton's prism, to Faraday's electromagnetic induction, confirmed or refuted theories. Michelson-Morely refuted physics, not merely theory but the foundations of everything Sylvian had spent so much effort learning. The friendly Newtonian term "S," space, absolute, and immobile like a universal blackboard upon which all material things moved and changed; the good old "t," time flowing across the universe like a single thread binding every event—the old terms became strangers to him, monstrous fantasies, mocking him for believing what seemed to be the foundations of rationality itself. They transmuted into. . .what?

Professor Olaffsoon's eerie serenity compounded the shock. Light and motion are reality. Do not trust common sense. Einstein called common sense acquired prejudices. Coming or going, moving into or away from light, at whatever velocity your coordinate system adopts, light travels at the same speed. On the moving earth, a spaceship, a star out in space; moving towards the star or away from it, the speed of light never varies. Plus or minus your velocity, in vacuum light goes past at the same rate.

Then Olaffsoon proceeded to demonstrate how Lorentz calculated a solution to the puzzle and how Einstein in 1905 calculated the same answer but how Einstein changed the meanings of "S" and "t"; how they made light the speed limit of the universe; how he abolished simultaneity across the universe.

That night Sylvian walked home under a new sky. Craning his neck, he gazed upward and into space; he experienced a vastly different world. Space, now, pulsated, moving fluidly, breathing; it was a living thing. He felt time speeding up and slowing down, even coming to a standstill. Only light proved absolute. Separate temporal events were no longer simultaneous, even in the mind of God. God couldn't know everything at once. There was no "at once." Therefore God had lied. By the laws of physics, it was impossible for him to be omniscient. What a shit.

Professor Olaffsoon proceeded from Special Relativity to General Relativity, from inertial motion to acceleration and gravity. Another

Establishment fable. Gravity was not a force. It was the very fabric of space-time. It was geometry. The new tensor calculus cut through everything he'd learned, for what was straight had now become curved. What was a plane became a sphere, and the sphere ballooned into four dimensions. What was clear had become dark and distorted. Two years of meek and obedient dedication to Newton now appeared to be the result of manipulation by perverse professors who themselves were slaves of a wickedly false system.

With an odd coldness, Professor Olaffsoon cremated reality every Thursday night. He never seemed to notice the three of them, never acknowledged them. He spoke to the dining room table. Like St. Barlaam, the professor was a dream only Sylvian could see.

What is truth?

Brutality and repression were mere surface blemishes on the vast body of delusion. It, the Establishment, was an insatiable beast fattening itself on the death of its cells. It drained the blood of its servants, stealing their lives, leaving them empty corpses of straight lines and standard time. Sylvian looked about and perceived a massive funeral parlor. IT created a world of inexhaustible suffering. Everything was meaningless. He felt a wave of sick anger that once again flowered into poisonous hatred.

One night he gazed for nearly an hour at a picture of Einstein in his textbook: the sad yet sparkling eyes, the mocking grin, the humor and sarcasm of a man who refused to listen to common sense.

Deep in some unacknowledged part of his mind, an imprisoned thought whispered that revolution was not the correct response to the Establishment. It had to be something more subtle. Nonetheless, he refused to give up hatred. All that exists deserves to perish.

The brilliant Professor Hallerman turned out to be a false prophet.

At first, Sylvian thought that truth might be found in his "Daseins" and "Way to Being" and "Existenz" and "transcendental subjectivity," and other mysteries. He thought about these marvels until his head hurt. In the end, a severe headache was all he had to show for the effort. In philosophy, space and time remained as always, delusions.

He mustered the courage to seek the great man's help. Alas, every time he attempted, he found the famous Professor occupied, usually with some beautiful if not too bright young lady.

The Professor could be heard saying things like: "You are really making it, really digging it. You are zsoo intelligent. Did you know that?"

"Oh, Professor Hallerman, I don' think so."

"Paul."

"What?"

"Call me Paul, we are no feudal aristocracy here. Und I do think zsoo. You've got a real mind for philosophy. Vhat ist your major?"

"Well—" an embarrassed giggle "—I don't know yet. Maybe English— I just adore romance novels."

"Ach, no! Vhat a waste of lovely mind. Let me be your advisor."

"Oh, I don't know—"

"Ah, have I made you nervous perhaps? You play with your hair. Have I gone too deep?"

"What do you mean?" A hasty lowering of eyes.

"Maybe you have questions und yearnings you find difficult to accept? Philosophy perhaps awakens them. Like: Does God exist? Is God dead?"

"Well, I've been brought up Catholic, and I go to Mass with my mother when I'm home. Sometimes with my boyfriend—"

"Yes?"

"Wow, Dr. Haller. . . Paul I mean, like no one ever asks such questions. You're so. . . wild!" She glanced at him, smiled and quickly looked away.

"Do you talk about such things as death of God with your boyfriend?"

"Oh no. Whenever I say anything about philosophy his face goes blank and his eyes glaze over."

"Too bad." Professor Hallerman shook his head sadly and clicked his tongue. "As your friend, because I so much respect your remarkable intelligence, I feel that it is my duty to warn you that intimate relationships cannot merely be based upon physical attraction."

Another glance, now quite nervous.

"A fine mind like yours, such a beautiful person as you, needs intellectual nourishment alzso."

"Yes." Reluctant agreement.

"Vell! I think you should really consider majoring in philosophy. I would be thrilled to give you all kinds of extra help. Perhaps, a weekly tutorial session in the evening, at my home. We could do that. I'm a very dedicated teacher you know, like an Eastern guru. It would be *frohlich*, uh, *voller Freude*—how you say?—joyous, uh, lots of fun, to nurture such a beautiful mind as your own."

A nervous laugh. "Not me—"

"Ja, ja! Why, we could take this afternoon and go to Oakwood Park and sit beneath the old oak, or walk off in the secluded little wood there and talk philosophy. About the death of God."

A few moments of silence and then: "Oh, Professor Hallerman, you've been so kind, and a real help. But my boyfriend is waiting for me, and I've got to go."

He gave her his most concerned look. "I'd just love to nurture your beautiful mind und be your guru—"

Close to the speed of light, the beautiful mind housed in an equally lovely body was out the door and walking briskly down the hall.

"Yesss?" Professor Hallerman directed the word at Sylvian who had been waiting patiently while listening to this "philosophic dialogue." He'd noted how the Professor's German accent tuned in and out like lousy television reception— "tune in, drop out—"

"Needs an explanation, like what'd you mean by—"

"Oh, dammit!" the Professor glanced at his watch. "I'm late for that damn meeting! Uh, Mr. . .?"

"Nothingness that nothings."

"Yeah, far out. I'm zsoo late. Does anybody really know what time it is?"

"Not according to Relativity."

Hallerman cocked his head. "Ja, vell, come back tomorrow unt ve'll speak about it."

He brushed past Sylvian, slamming his office door. Nothingness was left standing alone in the hall now more determined than ever to join the People's Will and realize his terrible revenge.

EIGHT

Saturday in the Park

SATURDAY AFTERNOON IN EARLY October, the weather unusually warm and bright, Sylvian reasoned that Oakwood Park would be crowded. If he had any lingering doubts about the revolutionary path, revolutionary physics shattered them. He'd join the People's Will. Alone in the park, Sylvian would gird himself for the coming ordeal of his rebirth. He'd rescue people from their ignorance and oppression. But today he wished the "people" would just go home and leave him and the grass in peace.

Why not seek shelter in the library? He'd reached a new understanding of the library too: the library with its volumes upon volumes containing the scribbling of every genius who ever lived was, to his reformed mind, his new eyes, a hothouse of lies and delusions excreted by intellectual eunuchs who were castrati for the System. Now he hated libraries.

As luck would have it—in the past he'd have called the acausal conjunction between two disparate events a "sign"—he found the park deserted.

A torpid lagoon sat in the center of Oakwood Park like the nucleus of a dying cell. West of the pond grew a densely wooded area; east stretched a large field gently rising to a blunted edge like the rim of an old plate. At its crest, perhaps fifty yards from the lagoon stood a massive oak, which was the largest and oldest tree in the park. Local gossip said a pecular von Jahn individual had planted the oak over a hundred years ago.

The old Sylvian loved the von Jahn oak. He loved it for its soothing shade, its enduring age, its hoary corrugated bark. The body of the tree was like sinuous wooden cables worn smooth by the weather and the flow of time. The von Jahn Oak had endured everything from lightning filled tornadoes to the hard icy blasts that came down from Canada. Its ancient surface was defaced by generations of student graffiti, yet it had not lost its dignity.

Today he viewed the oak differently. It stood as a symbol of his awakening. Today in its shade he'd plot his new revolutionary career.

It never stormed when he sat beneath the great oak. In all probability, this had been mere coincidence, a foolish figment of his formerly ignorant imagination filled by lying priests with their blessings that robbed even chance of its innocence, just as they'd robbed him of his very sanity. Wasn't faith in what did not exist, what never existed, a form of insanity? The definition of madness itself?

In warm weather Hinnom Valley sweltered under a stagnant haze; its citizens would gag and gasp on the thick odor of paper pulp that oozed from the mill or the sour smells of hops that issued from the brewery. Yet Oakwood Park, especially in the vicinity of the von Jahn Oak, remained a world apart, pure, immune to the stench.

Sylvian gazed across the lagoon and briefly considered the strange phenomenon. It didn't matter. What does not serve the revolution is a useless waste of time.

Burn down the Park! Oak burns quite nicely. Burn, baby, burn.

He pictured the forest going up in flames. How densely packed its oaks. How dry its pine trees. There were a few cedars, old and hard, an island of birches, some maples, elms here and there. Rumor said that an ancient grove of northern pines formed a kind of inner ring, planted by the Indians for some sacred ritual. Burn baby, burn.

Seize the means of leisure. . .

The tiny forest comprised all that remained of the original growth before the coming of the Butchers, the Brunswicks and the Boots. Once a mighty wood, dark and impenetrable, sacred to the Indians, the grand forest had been slowly decimated by axe and saw until it shrunk to this tiny corner of the park. He'd finish the job. Everything that exists deserves to perish.

Well, now, I realize I should not interrupt the flow of our tale. Saving I do need to suspend the narrative for a moment—for the legitimate purposes of providing much-needed background information since our Sylvian is so unreliable. I promise that this interruption will be brief, but it is crucial. What follows is pure legend, so I've heard.

I'm afraid that it will be tricky separating fact from fancy since our poor little Sylvian, as should be clear by now, utterly failed to do so. Like you, I noticed that after the blow he supposedly suffered during the bloody insurrection instigated by black radicals and white atheists, his verbal abilities mysteriously improved. I would say that the problem merely transmuted. By this, I mean that his speech confusions became "interiorized." He used words correctly, it is true.

Nevertheless, the match of thoughts with words became faulty. That is, he used the oddest words to express even stranger thoughts, and thus it often seemed that he jumbled imagination with perception and seriously skewed reality. He pronounced the words correctly enough—and that was an improvement—except they were the wrong words.

I'm confident that drugs had something to do with it. Or that crazy Park affected him like a drug long before his monumentus change. Primitivism is as powerful a hallucinogenic as LSD, our Church has always taught. Needless to say, his friendship with Jerry Wolfe (who, I ought to mention, came from a rather wealthy if troubled Jewish family) didn't help matters.

So, very little of what follows can be trusted.

Before I return to our Sylvian, however, I need to relate one other bit of information, which I'd once heard: No one ever set foot in the Park's wooded area.

Rumors claimed that young people, mostly female, had disappeared in those dark woods. Names were never reported to the police, nor did anyone ever personally know someone who'd vanished on such and such a day. No bodies had ever been discovered, and no one was officially reported missing. You might say that people who went missing never existed in the first place, but this is obviously nonsense, which proves the fictitious nature of the stories.

Naturally, a college town with its large transient population always seems to be missing people. And naturally, everyone had heard about the old Indians and their sacred grove of evergreens. Still, there were rumors. By the fall of 1969, the stories had multiplied, becoming detailed and more grisly than ever.

It's a strange process, you know. No one person really starts a rumor. Such reports do not enter the world fully developed. They seem to develop spontaneously over time, like the weather.

For whatever reason and from a multitude of invisible sources, gossip whispered lurid tales of children and young coeds who'd been murdered deep within the wood in some sort of satanic ritual.

Descriptions of terrible, inhuman mutilations found eager ears. Strange figures haunted the fringes of the wood-—people said that the Hinnom Valley police knew everything but hushed it all up so as not to create a panic. Charles Manson had escaped jail and taken up residence in Oakwood Park.

Well, here I must not get too far ahead of our poor naive hero. We shall see about these rumors shortly.

As I've said before, those years marked the beginning of the cults that today poison our Christian civilization. Many claim some fake Eastern pedigree. In reality, these so-called Eastern "ways" were crass materialistic, atheistic, amoral con-jobs masquerading in a pseudo-mystical cloak of nonsense taught by some megalomaniac, sex-crazed sadist who knew a smattering of Sanskrit, Chinese, Japanese or Tibetan. Hence, they were capable of any crime, which they rationalized by calling it "liberation." Every rational person knows that it all comes from Satan.

Once you see beneath the colorful, exotic silken words and gestures, you become aware that all of these so-called "awakenings of the west" are nothing less than the old tricks of the Evil One.

Believe yourself equal to God. Think yourself divine. You can do anything; cure any disease (how many fail at this one, but there's always some reason!). Everything is permitted. Complete self-gratification. Total hedonistic license and an excuse for any crime.

Yes, I know, I've said all this before. But it needs repeating. "Enlightenment" is nothing but the old temptations the dark spirit whispered into the ears of our first parents.

Alas for Sylvian.

He leaned back against the old tree. He noticed a large root exposed like an old bone breaking the skin of the soil. He saw faded carvings on its weathered bark as if the ancient tree bore scars from whippings suffered over years of slavery.

Even the von Jahn Oak was an oppressed class. Maybe he'd spare it the coming destruction.

He closed his eyes and tried to imagine the tree's pain and suffering. He thought of James Rutledge. He felt the blows. His hatred burned.

Suddenly somebody was standing next to him.

For an instant, he thought he'd fallen asleep and this was some kind of nightmare. Fear shot through his body. He attempted to spring to his feet. But he got tangled in the root and pitched headlong into the grass.

An irritating falsetto voice commenced laughing: "Ha, ha, ha. . . No need to get up. . . ha, ha, ha,"

Sylvian sat back on his heels and peered up. Anger elbowed fright aside.

He had to be dreaming. Standing there was the weirdest looking person he'd ever seen. No, not "ever seen. . ."

Blue Boy. This time the skin was dark, darker than Sylvian's, and nearly black. Blue Boy was not a child, nor a man, nor a woman, not even a boy. He—whatever you'd call him—had long, wavy hair black as a starless sky, dark eyes, full lips that glowed red as if he wore lipstick, a thin, delicate nose, and a round face without edges. He wore a large number of beaded necklaces, covering a hairless chest. Shirtless, he wore a vest embroidered with designs resembling peacock eyes in blue and green. His wide, stripped elephant bell-bottoms were blue and green.

An eerie glow appeared whenever Sylvian turned his head. The effect, Sylvian would later say, was a function of vision displacement. From the side, at an angle, the strange being glowed bright blue like a cloudless sky.

When his glance slid askew, he perceived, as out of the corner of his eye, a bluish jet of flame.

Blue Boy from the night at Goodjohn's, but Blue Boy altered. In the full sunlight, he appeared black. The effect could not be real, Sylvian reasoned, merely the fault of his perception.

"May I sit?" Blue Boy inquired. He spoke with an accent Sylvian could not place.

"It's a free country," Sylvian muttered.

Blue Boy—actually black-brown when Sylvian stared directly at him— sat in a painful-looking way, twisting his legs like a knot, heels to thighs, back straight and head held high. He showed no sign of discomfort. In fact, he appeared extremely relaxed, certainly more at ease than Sylvian.

"You like this tree?"

"Maybe."

"Old tree. The oldest. This place was once called Deer Park."

Sylvian glared at him. "Don't like hippies following me around. Hippie."

"I'm Kris."

"Don't give a shit what you're called. Said it before, don't like hippies that sneak around like cats at night. Ain't gonna join the Clouds. So, fuck off."

"Oh my, Pearl was right. You have changed," said Blue Boy, his voice cracking a little as if he repressed a sob. He seemed about to say something else but stopped himself.

"You bastards been spying on revolutionaries. Maybe you ain't no hippie. Maybe you're the FBI."

"This is the oldest tree in the valley. It is—"

"So what? Are you the CIA?"

"—the von Jahn Oak." Blue Boy's falsetto became the sound of someone crushing fallen oak leaves underfoot. Although Blue Boy, apparently named Kris, was fuckin' FBI or CIA (he had to think like Jerry if he was to be a member of the People's Will), he found himself straining to listen. Something was absorbing, maybe even hypnotic (and therefore dangerous) in the hippie's tone. The sound itself captivated him. Like a physical force of attraction, like gravity, aside from the fact that old-style fuckin' physics was a lie. Gravity did not attract, spacetime warped. Like the rest of the degenerate Establishment, it was twisted.

Kris didn't stink like other hippies. He smelled of flowers, of apples, of jasmine, even wild onions. Like Pearl, a vast and varied herb garden spoke to Sylvian.

"Yes, yes, the von Jahn Oak, named after old Gottfried von Jahn. Because the old guy's buried right beneath it."

Sylvian gave a start and instinctively drew away from the exposed root.

"Right here. They didn't put a cross over him. Didn't mark the grave, 'cept by this tree. Wow, man, but these roots are growing right out of the corpse, I'm thinking. Out of the casket."

Son-of-a-bitch FBI pseudo-hippie was waging psychological warfare.

"Gottfried von Jahn right under our feet. The old heretic himself. Did you know that? Yes, yes. Devil worshiper, magician, alchemist, murderer. He was a strange one, I think. Maybe only the Church knows what he really was, perhaps only the Jesuits can tell the truth of it."

Kris paused and adjusted his strings of beads. "I'll tell the story," he said firmly.

"Don't wanna hear no goddamn story," Sylvian said hotly. But he knew that he really had no choice in the matter. FBI Kris had hypnotized him. The FBI loved to plant false stories—rumors, lies, innuendos, all meant to subvert the revolution. Delusion had become an art.

"Gottfried von Jahn came from a Catholic family that lived in Silesia during the last century. He attended Koinigsberg University, where he studied philosophy and theology. After taking his degree he became a priest, and after that, he joined the Dominican Order.

They say that Father Jahn was an expert on heathen religions, especially those that the Majesterium believed a challenge to the Church. He became quite good at winning back doubters, especially those who'd been corrupted by false religions. Father Jahn was also famous for his deep spirituality and compassion—rare for a scholar, don't you think? No inquisitor he, they say that he respected the dignity of the person no matter how lost that individual appeared, even the wicked. His very presence radiated beauty and serenity; a golden glow seemed to surround him. He felt sympathy for the very doctrines he refuted. Perhaps compassion was his undoing.

His fame brought him to Rome. The Magisterium asked him to lecture at the Collegio Romano on the subject of Christ and Krishna, even though a handful of conservative cardinals thought him a dangerous heretic exposing the false doctrine taught by fools. He claimed that Christ was simply another Avatar, an incarnation of Vishnu the Sustainer.

In Rome, however, his virtues outshone his faults, and his personal sanctity came to the ears of the Pope. He was brought into the Vatican to serve as the Pope's chief advisor on interfaith dialogue, which at the time did not exist, except it *sounded* liberal.

This was, you understand, the age of Italian Unification, the "Resorgimento." The Pope, Pius IX, believed that the secular state was an assault upon the Holy Church worse than any pagan faith. He issued the infamous *Syllabus of Errors* which condemned the modern world, everything from biblical studies to democracy.

Now the Pope was obsessed with prophecies and illuminations, and visions of the Blessed Virgin. He believed that Father Jahn was an enlightened spiritual councilor sent by God to fortify the Holy Father in this desperate hour.

Father Jahn surprised the Pope by advising compassion and humility in the face of secular power. The nation-state, he said, was like a ravenous tiger. We must demonstrate spirituality, poverty, selflessness, and the gift-giving virtue of Christ. If the state requires our body as sustenance, why, then we must slice off our limbs gladly with great compassion. We must offer ourselves as to a starving beast. If the Italian state requires Catholic Rome, we will give it Rome.

Such advice infuriated this Pope. I mean, why be Pope if one had to surrender Rome and Central Italy? Nonetheless, Father Jahn's spiritual power was uncanny. In his presence, the Pope's critical mind seemed to go to sleep. When Father Jahn spoke, he perceived the world differently, as one sees the lake-bottom when its waters are stilled.

But Cardinals close to the Pope fumed and plotted, and spoke openly of heresy inside the walls of the Vatican. The Jesuit Fathers provided them with clandestine aid, composing learned articles on Father Jahn's heathenism. Did not Father Jahn claim that the holy Gospels were filled with contradictions? Did he not scandalously argue that the Gospel Jesus is a false messiah, sounding just like the perfidious Jews? Did not the real Jesus teach "God-consciousness."

Naturally, all this is rank heresy. It is also deplorable history and a manipulated exegesis, as the Jesuits have said. It makes Jesus into some kind of swami or guru. And Jahn, having achieved "Christ-consciousness," became Jesus himself.

If we were to speculate, the Jesuits told the Pope: "Jahn is an agent of creeping secularism since his so-called sanctity actually renders the faith ridiculous. He almost certainly is a heretic who not only harbored sympathy for heathens but is secretly one himself."

What is compassion, they asked the Pope, except toleration for evil? What is humble open-mindedness but an open invitation to demonic possession? What is "Christ-consciousness" aside from the madness of a boundlessly inflated ego?

The Pope became suspicious and fearful. Father Jahn, Satan's agent, had become his advisor and was privy to the darkest secrets of the Vatican.

Father Jahn heard the whispers. One day he announced that he was leaving Rome. The Pope feigned surprise, yet he agreed.

As the priest withdrew from the Holy Father's presence, the Pope's little dog who had previously fawned over him gave a menacing growl. 'Perhaps,' the Pope noted, 'our beloved little Thomas heard you say something wicked.'

Kris paused as if he couldn't recall the rest of the story. Seemingly earching his memory, he said in a voice that sounded a little like Pearl's nasal whine: "Oooo, okay. So then, von Jahn fled Rome and completely disappeared from Europe for many years." He sat back.

"Some said he traveled east where he studied with strange occult sects and mysterious gurus. He discovered a magical talisman that gave him supernatural powers, and which he used to commit all sorts of crimes.

"The Jesuits later claimed that the talisman—some said it was a book, others a set of symbols he'd written down and memorized—was the work of a mad guru who murdered young women in bizarre rituals, and these rituals bestowed miraculous powers upon the wicked spiritualist. Nearly everyone agreed that the talisman, whatever it was, a book, a string of symbols (perhaps a simple sentence or an equation), had been created with the blood of innocents.

"After many years, he came back and haunted the German lands, students who are always susceptible to fraudulent swamis. He was a heathen hobgoblin haunting Europe."

"What bullshit!" Sylvian exclaimed. "Where'd you hear this?"

"From Goodjohn. Before he experienced his awakening, he was a professor of history right here at BSU. He taught a course on local history. One day he discovered an old book in the library, containing the story of von Jahn, I presume. He thought it fiction at first, and that's how he taught it. But something changed him. He experienced some kind of awakening. I don't know the details. I'm not a member of the inner circle of the Clouds. I only know he became the Divine Woo-Woo, Avatar of the Intergalactic Brain, Groovy-guru—"

"Hates the son-of-a-bitch Goodjohn!" Sylvian said, hoping that by insulting Goodjohn he'd get rid of Kris. "Don't like Pearl either." Even as he said the words, he knew he was lying, and very precisely.

Kris didn't seem to hear him. He closed his eyes along with his ears.

"Know what? Goodjohn says that the Jesuits harbor a secret order within their Society, an order of assassins dedicated to killing heretics and prominent leaders of pagan cults. They doubly hated von Jahn for being both a Dominican and heretic. They were sly and crafty, those Jesuits. They are assassins with clean hands. They use the innocent, the unsuspecting, to spill blood in the name of Jesus Christ. These days they are practically invisible, an invisible college.

"So it happened that von Jahn fled Europe and came eventually to America, to this very town. He settled in Hinnom Valley posing as a simple farmer. You could have seen him right here herding his cows. He was a cowherd. Yet he became rich."

Kris opened his eyes and lowered his voice. "Then one day in that very same grove across the lagoon they discovered a young girl's body. Oh man, it was sick, perverted stuff. Some satanic ritual, like they used to say—and still do—about the Jews stealing Christian children, drinking their innocent blood and eating their tender flesh in a diabolical mockery of the Eucharist."

Sylvian gazed into the wood and shuddered.

"Pretty soon, people began to notice strange things about farmer Jahn, like how he demonstrated an uncanny business sense as if he knew exactly what people were thinking. He seemed to know people's secret desires, cravings, hidden things such as the small points of pride, pettiness—their deepest falsehoods.

"Then it happened that the new parish priest preached a sermon one Sunday in which he claimed that Gottfried von Jahn was no simple farmer but an agent of the infernal realm. Aye, the priest swore, von Jahn made a pact with Satan sealed by human sacrifice. In return, the devil gave him forbidden knowledge, like old Faust. Dig that!

"I'm thinkin' that this simple parish priest was not so simple. I'm thinkin' he was a Jesuit in disguise.

"So, the priest tells 'em that von Jahn is some kind of evil sorcerer corrupted by cursed knowledge, which comes from dabbling in heathen religions, and how he'd fallen into the depths of perversity by practicing ritual murder.

"Freaked 'em out, he did. Whole town went crazy. A mob made up of the best citizens went looking for von Jahn at his farm, to lynch the devil-worshiper just like in a Frankenstein movie.

"But the sorcerer knew they were coming. He fled the farm.

"Goodjohn says that they burned his house anyway 'cuz they discovered all sorts of evil things. Disgusting, unspeakable things: beakers of blood, urine, preserved body parts from his victims, bones, hair. . . Place was crawling with live snakes, poisonous ones, not native to this area. Exotic Asian plants too. They burned it all."

"But where'd he gone? The priest told 'em that the evil one had fled into these very woods. Right here."

Kris gestured across the lagoon. Sylvian followed the pointing finger and thought he saw a robed figure lurking among the shadows of the old trees.

"At this point, the story gets real freaky. When they came here, von Jahn raised some kind of dense fog that acted like a powerful acid trip. With von Jahn's acid, every trip was bad. . . real bad."

"Just as the townspeople entered the wood, they were attacked by monsters. Weird shit sprang out of the vapor: flesh-eating Manticoras, sirens, basilisks, griffins, demons from strange lands, Christian devils. Of course, it was only an acid trip. But the good citizens went berserk and started shooting and stabbing one another. Lots of 'em got killed by mistake."

"By pure luck (the priest said it was the hand of God), a bullet hit von Jahn who'd been watching the insane melee from right here behind this very tree. At the moment von Jahn died, the fog lifted, and they all came to their senses. They found the body. The priest made 'em slice off the head, throw it into the lagoon, and bury the rest of the corpse right where you're sitting."

Sylvian leaped to his feet. "Bullshit!" he shouted without much conviction, "shit, shit, shit—"

"Goodjohn found the book manuscript in the university archives. Goodjohn was a historian like I said."

"Fuck Goodjohn and his mindfuck!"

Kris rose to his feet with a fluid motion that Sylvian would have thought impossible given his pretzel-like sitting pose. In fact, it seemed as if he floated to his feet. Towering over Sylvian, Kris appeared like a giant baby, smooth and squishy and very soft.

"Oh, you've become so—angry. Anger is poison, and she wants you without defilements."

"Why me?"

"Pearl had a vision, she says."

"Says what?"

Kris paused and stared at him. He seemed to be carefully considering his next words. Then he shrugged and said: "Of course she was probably high. Who knows?"

"Tuned in," Sylvian observed.

Blue Boy gave him a funny look. "You know, the Jesuit Father ordered the forest burned too. First, they searched the old Deer Park, and they found something all right. They discovered a deep pool, a natural well surrounded by granite boulders. And, man, the pool was bottomless. White, eyeless fish lived in those black waters, white eels, crayfish, and salamanders all eyeless.

"The priest ordered the townspeople tear up the rocks and seal the pool, which he called Satan's Well. The fog, he said, was actually mist from the devilish pond. That the pool of water was sacred to the heathen Indians proves it.

"One more thing. In class one day, Goodjohn remarked that his manuscript could be identified by a Latin inscription sown into its cover with golden thread: . . .*vir sui divinus revelationibus sublitissimus imaginalionibus, undefessis laboribus ad coelestia, atque humana mysteria. Ex Deo nascinur: secunda luna, MCMLII.*"

". . .a man initiated into mysteries and secrets of heaven and earth by divine revelation, subtle thought, and unrelenting labor. We are born of God: February 1952."

"Lying bastard, FBI! You made this all up to discredit the revolution."

"Why don't you ask Pearl?"

"Fuck off, pig."

Sylvian took a step back, turned and ran. He didn't look back to see if the blue hippie followed.

Jerry Wolfe shook his head. "It's Mordor, man. Black Riders after you 'cuz they know you got the Ring, Sam. Tryin' to trap you in dark webs of the wraith world."

Sylvian was too tired to mock Jerry for his pothead Tolkien obsession. He'd given up trying to grasp the references. Only potheads understood Middle Earth. Only potheads read that shit.

"Clouds are FBI, man, you know, Nazgul. FBI's probably trying to recruit a snitch to rat on Anita."

Staring out his dorm window, Sylvian, filled with rage, howled: "Won't be a snitch. Wanna be a revolutionary! Join the People's Will. Won't fall for fascist lies ever again."

"All right, man, I believe you." Jerry went to his desk and wrote on a scrap of paper. "Bilbo's map to Anita's."

"Ain't no snitch," Sylvian declared. "Everyone else is."

"Can't trust nobody." Jerry Wolfe agreed. "Amerika is a country of snitches."

NINE

Vanguard of the Revolution

THE SCRIBBLED DIRECTIONS—WHICH HE'D memorized and then burned—took Sylvian across the Casimir River into working-class neighborhoods. Jerry insisted they go separately.

Here the streets shrank into narrow alleys. Houses became two and three-story bungalows, ugly and dilapidated, many a century old. The streets tended to curve, dead-end or cut diagonals from the river. Haphazard old cow paths had evolved into a sophisticated urban hive. The reeking paper mill sat on the riverbank spewing waste into a sluggish current. It seemed that every street found its way to the mill like arteries and veins to a heart, in this case, a diseased organ, one that beat and infused refuse into the once-pure arteries of the river.

Fresh from the Olaffsoon Oracle, Sylvian visualized the streets as "world-lines," geodesics, bending and twisting in the presence of the mill's gravitational field. The energy tensor describing the changing field actually revealed the curvature tensor, which constructed the texture of space-time and hence determined the geometry of the field. The very fabric of existence is crooked, Sylvian decided. Matter was the gathering of the coordinate web—no sharp edges, no cut-offs, no separation of this and that. One big set of mathematical functions, all bent and crooked; yet the mathematics was beautiful. Professor Olaffsoon was like St. Barlaam.

He walked through the darkened streets following the map of memory, lost in a mathematical dream.

He passed children playing in the streets, old people sitting on porches, noisy taverns with blaring music, drunken arguments, and mad laughter.

TV's silver glow flickered in windows. Life in its individual manifestations was too variated, too disparately separate. It could not be condensed into a simple, beautiful mathematical symmetry. Therefore life was ugly, he concluded—everything that exists deserves to perish.

He came upon a gang of young townies occupying the porch of a, particularly run-down frame house. Street signs in the neighborhood had been vandalized, and he'd wondered if he'd missed a turn.

A snarling voice came from the porch: "What'd ya lookin' at, college punk?"

Sylvian peered into the shadows and identified vague shapes and the bright glow of cigarettes.

"Maybe the asshole's deaf," said a girl's voice.

"Thinks he's too good to answer."

"One of them goddamn hippies. Probably a fuckin' commie."

A thick shadow lumbered onto the sidewalk and planted itself in front of Sylvian, blocking his way.

The porch-dweller was big. He wore a dirty tee shirt stretched thin over broad shoulders and a powerful chest. His skin was pimply with open sores, even on his arms. He had a military haircut, like Karl.

"Where're ya going, hippie?" He peered down at Sylvian. "Boy, you're dirty. Need a bath."

"Hey Tom," called a voice, "see if he's got any money." A chorus of approval greeted this suggestion.

"Yeah, good idea," Tom said. "Hey, college asshole, got lots of money I'd bet."

"Sure he do!" called out a girl. "Lucky for him too. Daddy's money keeps 'em out of Nam."

"Not like Weasel."

"Who?"

"You know, the wrestler. Got drafted in '67 and got his head blown off during Tet."

"Shit."

"Hear what happened to Mac?"

"Mac?"

"Fat Macquitty. Stepped on a mine around someplace called Tam-key. Came home ball-less and without a leg."

"So, draft-dodger, how 'bout makin' a contribution to the war effort."

"Maybe he ain't patriotic."

Tom stared at Sylvian. "Hell, he ain't even American. You some kinda Indian?"

"Say something, asshole!" a voice shouted from the porch.

"You're all. . . oppressed by the. . . fu. . .fuck. . .in' Systematic. . . Nothing that nothings!" Sylvian blurted.

Tom burst out laughing. "Jesus Christ, Dave, listen to this. He's some kinda foreigner that ain't learned to speak right. Can't be in college."

"So what?" Dave sneered.

"Ah, leave 'em alone," said a girl.

"Yeah, leave 'em alone," agreed the chorus.

Dave, however, stepped down to the sidewalk, waddled over and shoved Tom aside.

"Hey, watch it, fat boy."

Dave was much heavier than Tom, even though he was a head shorter. His extra weight was like bread dough. His face had an oily shine, and his mouth hung open, resting on a double chin. He exhaled beer. Meanness glinted in his small eyes.

"What's this shit 'bout oppression? Gimme your money, punk. It's gonna be my possession."

"Oppression," Sylvian mumbled.

Fat Dave grabbed him by the arm. "Gimme your fuckin' oppressed money, asshole."

"Hey," called the girl, "leave 'em alone. Can you see he's a doffuss—"

"Yeah, pick on somebody you own size."

"Ain't nobody Dave's size," Tom said mockingly.

The chorus applauded with hoots of laughter. Sylvian laughed along in order to maintain his solidarity with the working class. Vico had that right.

"Fuck you!" Dave drew his fist to strike Sylvian. In a flash, Tom grabbed his wrist and twisted it, forcing him down on his knees.

"Yeeoow. . .!"

"Let the foreign kid alone," Tom said softly.

"Man, you're breakin' it! Let go. You don't know your own strength."

Dave twisted and pulled, but for all his bulk, he might as well tried to dance with one of the iron statues on the campus. Finally, with a forceful shove, Tom released him.

Dave went sprawling to the sidewalk. He scrambled to his feet and holding his wrist in obvious pain. Then he retreated down the street as fast as he could lumber.

As soon as he deemed himself safely down the block, he turned and started screaming: "Fuck you! Motherfucker! Son-of-a-bitch motherfucker—"

Tom took a step after him. Dave squealed another string of mother-somethings, turned a corner, and ran for his life.

Tom was laughing.

"You lost, kid?"

"Looking for. . . somebody's house. . ." Sylvian had to be careful. Even if these were proletarians and therefore members of the oppressed class, there might be informers among them, like the Clouds.

"Jesus Christ, Tom, how can he be in college? He's an idiot. Like I said, a doffuss."

"Hey kid, you're Indian, right?" Tom asked. "Probably studying science, huh?"

"Study physics."

"Who're yer looking for?" asked a girl.

Despite his terror, Sylvian felt a kind of sadness. How bleak these dwellings, how desolate these people—even Fat Dave's meanness seemed to spring from misery. He lacked the words to describe these vague feelings, yet he recognized that they were similar to what he'd felt for James. Sadness pushed his fear aside.

"I'm looking for the house of Anita Anarcharsis."

Abruptly Tom became furious. He grabbed Sylvian by the shirt and shook him. "What'd ya want with that lying bitch?"

"Hell, Tom, she's a hooker. That's what he wants."

Tom shook his head. "She's a whore, all right. Her and her playground revolutionaries."

"Wanna join 'em," Sylvian gasped. "Wanna become People's Will and off pigs and burn down banks and stores and churches and the mill. . . and book binderies."

Tom suddenly let him go and laughed: "Somebody's playing games with you, boy. Anita Anarcharsis? People's Will? More like Anita Burke and the People's Pimps. Only revolution is in her bed."

This brought forth a roar of laughter from the porch.

"Wanna join," Sylvian pleaded. "Really. . . man. You can be. . . uh. . . up front with me. Wouldn't betray the vanguard of the proletariat. Really."

Tom shook his head. "Little boy, why don't you go home? Back to India."

"I'm Polish."

Tom hesitated. He felt sorry for the foolish little boy; there was something strange about Sylvian, maybe his innocence. "All right, I know where the old whore lives. Got to see this for myself. I'll take you there. Ain't seen Anita Burke for ages."

"Anarcharsis," Sylvian corrected him with as much force as he could muster.

Tom howled. "Should be Anita Amazing— Hey kid, what's your name?"

"Sylvian Matreya."

"Far out, Silly Man. Let's go see this here revolutionary."

Sylvian was forced to trot to keep up with Tom's powerful, military-like strides. The effort winded him and turned his legs to rubber.

They were walking along Lyon Street, Tom said, although Sylvian couldn't see any street signs. They seemed to be climbing. On this side of the Casimir River, the city was packed into rows of cheap multi-family houses built among hills. Street lamps were burned out or smashed. Glass littered the pavement, garbage filled the gutters, the street smelled of vomit. Houses looked dark and forbidding.

They turned a corner, going west in the direction of the brewery.

Curtained windows glowed dully like evil eyes in the shadows of a dark forest. The streets reeked of strong smells as the odors of strange cooking mixed with the stench of clogged sewers. Urine and excrement sloshed through the gutters. Everything was permeated by the sharp stench of hops and malt from the brewery.

The street played music all its own, now a dull rumble, now a piercing cry, now a whistle, now a pain-filled sigh just beneath the threshold of conscious sound. The neighborhoods groaned in agony, in unrelenting pain, or rage. In a moment, as though the street took a breath, an eerie calm spread like a blanket; watchful eyes became aware of the intruders and marked their progress.

Tom strode like a lion on the savanna. The hulking shapes that passed them slunk away into the darkness like jackals.

An old drunk approached, muttering to himself; he seemed to be carrying on a single person argument. Suddenly, just as he came abreast, he screamed and threw away a sandwich he'd been eating. The shock of this sudden move scared Sylvian so bad that he wet his pants. Tom just laughed. The drunk wobbled past. At the corner, Sylvian bent over and vomited into the gutter.

"The people's will," Tom observed.

They walked for what seemed hours. Finally, Tom came to an abrupt halt in front of a peeling wooden house, dark and squat, fronted by a tiny yard of bare soil. Vines and weeds broke through the concrete walk. Sylvian hoped Tom wouldn't notice the wet spots running down from his crotch. Goddammit, revolutionaries don't pee in their pants.

"Is this it? Don't see no meeting."

"There's always a meeting. That's all they do. Talk—"

He gazed thoughtfully at Sylvian and shook his head.

"Little boy, take my word for it, this is just a big pile of bullshit. A couple of years ago, after I got back from Nam, I took the G. I. Bill and went to that university—" Tom gestured to campus "—and there was this professor named Jonathan Burke. He's gone now. The bastards fired 'em.

"I loved the guy, man. He explained everything 'bout the war, why I'd been drafted when the rich kids got to stay home and fuck around and go to college. Man, he explained why the country ain't really free, why some people got it easy and others ain't got it at all. He knew. He knew what was really happening. How they lie to us all the time—"

"Yes!" Sylvian agreed.

"I got to know him. I couldn't understand hardly any of the reading, but I knew that something was really bad with this country even though I couldn't explain it as good as him. I'd been a stooge. I killed people for the fucking rich bastards that lied to everybody so that they'd get more power. B'cuz, man, it ain't just greed for material shit—its greed for power. They wanna tell people what to do, how to live, what to believe—"

"He made me believe. You never doubted what he said.

"He said I was smart, that I could help the cause, I could help people like him actually change things. Man, I believed."

Tom became angry. "Something happened to him. He found some book or somethin' in the 'brary. . . started talking weird shit, 'bout God and stuff, and how nothin' is real, and he's a god-something or another. . . and, wham, he's back to the revolution. Back and forth, from God to revolution—

"He invited me to his house to discuss how I could help, how I could be a worker in the revolution. So, I goes to his house one night. Do you know where it was?"

Sylvian shook his head.

Tom jabbed the air with his middle finger.

"This very same fucking house. Right here. Professor Burke lived among the poor working class. And guess whoose his sweet wifey?"

Sylvian shook his head.

"Shit. What a doffuss you are. Anita! Anita Burke. I first met her here."

He gazed at the ugly house and spoke almost gently, wistfully: "It was so weird. There were all these people, mostly college kids, and in the middle was Jonathan Burke sitting on the floor and smoking a joint. All these stupid little girls. Like a rock star surrounded by groupies. In fact, he called 'em *gopis*, whatever that means. He was talking some crazy shit, 'bout blowing up the administration building, the chemistry labs, the science building, 'bout occupying Craven's office, assassinating people like the mayor, the mill owners, chief of police, killing off whole families like the Butchers and the

Boots. There was no end to it. They were goin' to stick it to the Establishment. Murder, arson, bombing—"

"Yes," Sylvian breathed.

"Shit, man, it was just like Nam. Nothing ever made any sense. We just went in and waxed what they said was Charlie, but I never understood anything 'bout it. I mean the strategy. Just waxing the place. Burke was saying the same thing. No more illusions, no more oppression, just destruction like in Nam.

"I saw what he was really about. The stupid little chickees loved it. They got off on it. They just ate up the violence and the thrills, man. Stupid rich bitches got off on revolution. All talk and fuck."

"And there was Anita. She was loud and big, always smoking, hair all over, a black cape. Man, she never walked; she blew about like a monsoon. She talked a storm, like those monsoons in Nam, just kept pasting you with an endless torrent of words, smoking and talking, pounding you with words.

"You're a vet, she booms and grabs me by the arm, hard, man, 'cuz she's big and strong. Says that they can use me.

"And then she starts talking crazy too, 'bout marriage and how it's really bourgeoisie bondage, a contract of female oppression. Suburbia is a gushy concentration camp, she says. The Amerikan housewife is nothing but a glorified prostitute. She gets her clothes, and fancy house and social status and even her identity by simply fucking like any common slut, but at least professional hookers is honest 'bout it. The bourgeoisie housewife lives in a delusion, and she goes to the PTA and the Church in order to suppress the truth that she's nothing but a fancy hooker who ain't really any good at it like the professionals—-"

Tom had to gasp for breath. "Man, she could talk a person to death.

"Next she starts in on the professor's line, 'cept that now all the murder and arson and bombing is gonna be the homes of bourgeoisie. Insane, man! We're gonna kill hookers that don't know they're hookers, and that's how we strike a blow for liberation. And then in the middle of it she asks me if I brought any weapons back from Nam and if I know how to manufacture explosives and home-made bombs, and if I could teach revolutionary fighters how to kill and stage assassinations, and carry out incursions into bourgeoisie strongholds—"

"Yes!" Sylvian cried.

"Hell no. I got the fuck outta there. Never went back. Never went back to old Burke's class either. Had enough of education. Same maniacs as in Nam. I went to work at the mill."

"Wha'at happened to Professor Burke?"

"I believed in him, the son-of-a-bitch. I loved the guy. He disappeared right after that. I heard he split out west with one of them stupid little babes, some little blonde fairy thing dumber than a fence-post but a hot little cunt. They went west. Some say Craven had something on Burke and Burke knew it, so he split before the shit hit the fan. Anita went crazy. Bastard Burke just lied to everybody."

"Lots of people lie."

"Still wanna go in?"

Sylvian visualized the huge woman at the riot. He recalled the power, the energy, and her fiery words. "Is she violent?" he asked.

Tom laughed. "Like a volcano."

"Let's do it," Sylvian said.

TEN

Old Left, New Left

Tom rapped on the door.

A sliver of light appeared, glowing dull red as if the interior of the house were on fire.

A head materialized, then a gray metallic barrel.

Tom leaped aside, pulling Sylvian with him. He grabbed the barrel and twisted it away. "Be cool, man," he shouted into the crack, "we ain't no pigs."

"Who is it?" snarled the head behind the door.

"Tom Sargent and a college kid named Silly Man."

"Hey, let go, asshole and I'll see about it."

Tom released the barrel. The door slammed shut. A few minutes later, the door opened, this time wide enough for a person to squeeze through. Tom went in without hesitation. Sylvian slunk in behind him.

"Shit, man, why didn't you say you were an old fighter?" said a shape standing behind the door.

"Cuz there ain't no old fighters. Ain't nobody here fought. All we did was talk—"

"Things have changed, man. Time for talk is over. Establishment would just love to keep us drugged on talk. We gonna act, man. Revolutionary action. We gonna talk with bombs and rifles." He shook an M-16 at Tom.

Sylvian's eyes stung in the crimson light. He squinted at the speaker and got nothing but dream-like impressions. The young man, bearded and dressed in army fatigues, wore a bandoleer of ammunition and a web belt. He was a white kid, although he grew a huge afro. He tried to look grim and

95

dangerous, yet he was unable to hide the child-like innocence in his wide eyes and the adolescent awkwardness of his gestures.

Tom laughed. "Oh yeah? Well, the moron that stole that weapon ought to get some clips for it."

"I got 'em. . ."

"Oh yeah? Wouldn't load it if I was you. Might shoot yourself."

Behind the fearsome revolutionary and his afro, knots of people stood about talking loudly, gesturing, drinking, and smoking. The room was vast; interior walls had been knocked out just as inside the Cloud house. Music reverberated; creating visible waves across the room, swirling through a vaporous atmosphere.

Sylvian tried to pick up the words: "I do be—lieve. . ." (or, "I don't be—lieve") ". . .that we're on the Eve of Destruc—tion. . ."

His father usually fumed when the radio station played that song. Father Loeb had called it satanic communist trash. Of course, all rock music was part of the communist master-plan to demoralize the young and produce artificial neurosis, which was designed to goad teenagers into riot and revolution. Rock-music was destroying the American-Christian way of life. It was communist brainwashing. His brother Karl had said that the guy, Barry. . . Barry Mac-something. . . ought to be hauled out and shot. No patriotic radio station should play such garbage.

"I gotta get back to my post," said the guard. "Anita wants to see you. She'll be out of the meeting pretty soon."

They wandered into the crimson gloom, lost in the vast spaces. No one seemed to notice them.

". . .I say we bomb Craven with one of them pressure-plate detonators. Some TNT, batteries hooked to metal plates, blasting caps. Firing pin can be a simple nail on a metal plate."

"What'll that prove?"

"What'd ya mean?"

"Don't you understand revolutionary tactics at all? The Vanguard occupies radio stations, TV, newspapers, banks, the post office. We call upon the masses to rise up. We divert the pigs with thousands of false calls—"

"Shit! Craven will just call in the National Guard."

"Let him. As long as the media is in with it. We'll appeal to the troops, to the enlisted men not the officers. Enlisted men are working class. We're fighting in the name of the working class. We'll plead with them: Brothers, don't fire on the sons and daughters of the working class! Don't fire on your people!"

Sylvian knew that voice. It was formidable and smooth, humorless, impatient, self-conscious—Eugene Vico.

"Ain't you been listening to anything Anita says? The whole fucking thing, workers and owners, troops and officers, students and teachers, is the goddamn Establishment. We gotta off 'em all."

Vico's adversary looked just like Che Guevara as if he'd stepped right out of the popular poster and come to life (for Sylvian, Che Guevara was a poster) . . .like Che, except for his large ears.

"The proletariat must be educated. It's a question of false consciousness. They want the workers to think of themselves as the bourgeoisie. That's what TV is all about." Vico sounded a bit exasperated and tired as if he'd been arguing all night with a poster that possessed oversized ears and yet couldn't hear.

"Why don't you try educating the mill workers yourself," said the Che. "They'll make you eat your Marx page by page. Man, they is totally corrupted."

"Corrupted? Paul, you make it sound like original sin. It's economics not religion. This is category confusion. They're ignorant, not evil."

"The whole Establishment is evil!" exclaimed Che-Paul.

"Evil must be totally erased," declared a girl standing next to him. She had long black hair, straight and silky as if she'd ironed it. Her oblong face resembled a frowning Cher. "Total evil, total annihilation," she said, singing the phrase in a light, airy voice, unlike Cher's deep-throated rasp. She, too, was painfully sincere.

Eugene shook his head. "People act evilly. Morality is an interpretation of acts, not a cause, not something indwelling as, say, the old idea of a metaphysical soul. Look at how morality changes over time. Economics dictates morality. If capitalism needed slavery, there'd still be slavery. And there is, under another name—"

"Evil is evil," the Cher declared. "Power to the people!"

"Don't you see your contradiction?" asked Vico wearily. "If it's all evil, why say power to the people?"

"Anita says that destruction is a creative act," Paul recited.

"Bakunin said that."

"What?"

"She's quoting the Russian anarchist Michael Bakunin."

"Anita said it! I was there when she thought it up. She's always coming up with far-out slogans."

Eugene sighed. "It's like this: the working class is alienated from what it is to be a true human being. Humans objectify themselves in some form of labor. You actually inject your subjective, individual talent into the objective material world. You become who you are through labor. The object contains your labor and creative labor is what shapes the world and gives it value. It's what makes us different from the animals."

Paul, the Che, shifted from foot to foot, muttering: "shit, shit, shit—"

The Cher's eyes glazed over, just like the real Cher.

Sylvian edged closer. Vico was reciting a formula. He was drawing a beautifully transparent calculus flowing through rigid Euclidean space, Sylvian's old familiar "S" and "t" in their proper forms, not the craziness of Professor Olaffsoon's seminar.

Vico cried: "Listen! This is scientific. The product of your labor is you. When you reflect upon it, when you freely give it to your fellow social beings and witness its use for the good of society, then you fully realize yourself as an actual human being.

"But if your labor becomes coerced, inauthentic, forced and necessary, in the service of another, then it is no longer human. It is slavery. You become someone else's *property*. You no longer work to enjoy your creative powers, you work for the benefit and the profit of another, and you are alienated. Even your leisure time is not yours. The market determines leisure. You work and play in the service of the Capitalist."

The Cher shook her head.

"What do you get in the place of your self-realization as a freely creative worker?"

"Money!" Sylvian cried out in glee, oblivious to everyone around him. It was so beautiful. He could almost see symbols in the thick air, the differential functions, the variables, the inverse relationships. "Money!" The obvious answer.

"Who the fuck is this?" asked an irritated Paul. "Your little brother?"

"I thought all the Negroes were in jail," said the Cher.

Eugene stared blankly at Sylvian. "You read Marx?"

"No. . . The answer is. . . obvious. It's. . . necessary."

Eugene muttered in a strained voice: "Money is an abstraction, a mere sign of value. All value in society is determined by the class that owns the means of production. Money has no intrinsic value. Can't you see what it does to people?"

"Ask the black kid," said Paul.

"They become Nothings," said Sylvian happily. At last Hallerman's class began to make some sense.

Eugene lost control. "Look, you little. . . whoever-you-are, why don't you shut up and let me finish! It's alienation! Not Nothings. Ignorance does not lead successful revolutions."

"Oh and our Eugene does, 'cuz he really knows Marx," said Paul the Che sarcastically.

Vico ignored him and said: "Alienation means that a person no longer works for self-fulfillment as a social being but solely for the accumulation of money. People become their money, abstractions—"

"Nothings," Sylvian repeated.

Vico tried to ignore him. "Money becomes more powerful than any god. It is. . . the Supreme Good.

"People become abstract. Marx said it. As an individual, I may be dishonest, rude, arrogant, without a shred of compassion, but if I have money, I am honored and respected. I may be lazy, but if I have money I can hire other people to work for me. In terms of money, the more I have, the less I am. Capitalism is the total contradiction of humanity."

"Nothings," Sylvian repeated, but with less certainty.

"Will you shut the fuck up! I'm giving the lesson here!"

Sylvian, however, was flying through the upper spheres of physics. "But. . . but it's all wrong. All this assumes Euclidean space. . . Cartesian coordinates." He felt suddenly depressed. There was no going back after Olaffsoon's seminar. S and t were illusions, and he had to let them go.

"The black kid says it's all wrong," the Cher remarked.

"Ignorant little shit!" Vico spat. "This is scientific. I have proof. Don't people shun work like the plague? Do you think the mill workers like that stench? Don't they work just to earn money? They live for recreation, for eating, dressing-up, sleeping, fucking. They live for animal functions. What is animal becomes human. It's a world turned upside-down—"

"No," said Sylvian, "it's old science—"

"So what are you going to do about it?" boomed a great voice.

Suddenly she was there, swooping down like a huge black bird. Her cape flapped as if she flew with dragon's wings. Wild black hair, long and curly and streaked with silver, formed a massive plume of congealed night. Despite the formless cape, one could see that her body was thick and muscular. Her nose was wide with flaring nostrils, her eyebrows dense, her jaw powerful, and her skin coarse. Her eyes, however, were startlingly blue, captivating, hypnotizing, alluring—and dangerous.

She was smoking a cheroot, blowing great puffs of smoke. She was a dragon flying through sulfurous air of her own making and breathing fire.

Anita Anarcharsis was revolution incarnate. An exploding terrorist bomb. The Eve of destruction.

A crowd gathered around her as smoke around a blazing fire.

With fantastic quickness and power, she slapped a huge claw on Sylvian's shoulder and held him like a captured worm.

"I know you!" Her words penetrated to the bone, causing his heart to flutter by the force of their vibrations.

Holding on to Sylvian, she turned and glared at Eugene.

"Black kid's right, Eugene, my boy. You got it all wrong. Old Left is ancient history."

Eugene sputtered: "We've got to awaken the workers. . . organize a vanguard of students who know the truth. We will lead—"

"Bullshit! Words. Nothing but words. Nobody's gonna listen. Nobody's got the patience, the endurance. Old Left is beautifully useless. New Left is infantile. People only hear acts."

"Acts will follow—"

"Double Bullshit!" She shook a massive fist at Vico.

"World's insane like the kid says. Still made some sense in Marx's day. But that's all gone now. It's totally depraved. Insanity is sanity. The world doesn't even know it's crazy. Thinks itself sane. Remember when you were a little kid, hiding under a desk in case of a nuclear attack? Duck and cover? Absurdity was your real education. World's gotta be fumigated. Gotta start from zero. Destruction is a creative act."

"Insanity," Eugene whispered.

"You got it, Eugene. Disruption, chaos, explosions, murder. . . No goals, no Utopias. No more library vomit. Crazy old books written by crazy old men. No ends at all. Just means. Blowing minds."

Her fingers dug into Sylvian's shoulder, giving him deep bruises.

"All that exists deserves to perish. Ain't that right, kid?"

"Yes," Sylvian whispered. Who could disagree with this female colossus?

"I don't trust the little punk. Hear he's been hanging around the Clouds. They're agent provocateurs. And now he knows our safe house, no thanks to fuckin' Jerry. We gotta waste 'em right now."

Randal Boots stood next to Sylvian. He acted like a prosecuting attorney. Dressed in a black turtleneck, black pants, leather jacket—glasses, hair, and goatee, all back—it seemed as though Satan himself had joined the revolution.

"Nothing personal, man. Revolutionary tactics."

"Yeah, nothing personal," added Che of the big ears. "It's democratic centrism."

Anita laughed, "Shit, Randal, that's ridiculous."

Cathy Butcher, looking gloomy and grim as always, said: "Randal's over-dramatic."

"This ain't no debutante ball," Randal shot back. "This is revolution, and we gotta use the rules of the *Catechism*."

Anita let out a great booming laugh. The walls shook. "*Catechism* says that even potential informers must immediately be killed."

"Ain't no informer!" Sylvian cried with as much force as he could inject into his weak voice. "Ask Jerry—"

Jerry Wolfe squeezed through the crowd. "Hey, he's hip. He's a hobbit, maybe even a wizard like Gandalf. He knows how the orcs make the One Ring."

Randal muttered a profanity. Eugene shook his head, and Cathy looked more morose than usual. Anita erupted into peals of laughter.

"He wants to join the elves. . . the White Order."

Anita stopped laughing. "What? You told this child about the White Order?"

The room became silent; someone turned off the music. No one dared speak.

"Uh. . . not everything. . ."

Cathy clicked her tongue against her front teeth, "I told you, Anita, not to recruit any more BSU students, especially pot-heads."

"We'll have to off 'em both," the Cher observed matter-of-factly.

"Why don't you do it, Vesta. Remember though, it ain't gonna be like on TV. Blood all over. Just spurts out like a hose. Ruin your nice clothes. And the smells. Nothin' like you can imagine." Tom materialized out of the smoky red light.

"Holy shit," cried Vesta the Cher, "Tom Sargent! I thought you'd gone and re-upped."

"Went to work at the mill. What about you? Still at the brewery?"

"Yeah. It's a bummer."

"How's your brother?"

"Ain't seen 'em for a year. Ever since I went to Czechago for the Convention."

"Where's Craig?" Tom glanced around.

"Broke up," Vesta sighed, "after Czechago. All he wanted to do was get stoned. Gave up the fight. Said it was useless. But, goddammit, it ain't. We got something here, Tom. We're the People's Will. We got connections to something really big and serious, a real—"

"Vesta!" Anita was staring at Tom, fixing him with those magnetic eyes.

"Things have changed," she said, "after fuckin' Jonathan skipped out to Colorado I made contact with—"

She broke her gaze away from Tom to Sylvian. Instantly, it seemed, she came to a decision.

"Downstairs," she ordered. "I'm calling a meeting of the Central Committee. The rest of you take off. In twos and threes, fifteen minutes apart. And watch out for those Clouds. FBI got files on everybody."

"What about this punk?" Randal asked.

Sylvian suddenly went berserk. He flailed his arms wildly, trying to punch Randal. He kicked, and spat, and screamed a string of incoherent threats. Tom was forced to grab him, lift him clear and pin his arms. Inbetween wrestling a hysterical Sylvian, Tom couldn't help but laugh, entertained by the scene playing out.

"Wanna join!" Sylvian gasped, struggling against Tom's powerful grip. "Just give me a gun. . . do pigs. . . bomb, burn. . . Is serious!"

"He knows the secrets of Mordor," said Jerry.

"What?"

"You know, the One Ring."

"Oh yeah? Well, ring or not he might be useful. Small and innocent like a twelve-year-old. Perfect for terrorism, hey? Yesss. . ." she blew cheroot smoke into his face. "You might be useful."

She drew herself to her impressive height, which was, in fact a shade over Tom's. "You are about to become a member of the most important progressive force in the world," she announced. "You'll be part of the greatest change in human history. It's gonna be incredible, absolutely revolutionary. A whole new world like nothing before. We are the People's Will."

"Yes. . ." Sylvian breathed. And everybody, except Tom, whispered with him: "Yes."

"You have your orders!" she barked, breaking the spell. "The Central Committee. Downstairs!"

"Not you, Eugene."

"But Anita. We're a coalition of parties. I belong with the Leadership too."

"Nope. Masters say no Marxists."

"But why?"

"Because the Masters ordered it."

"For what reasons?"

"Eugene, my boy, the Masters, don't give reasons. It's how they test a true revolutionary. They wish to know how far a person has evolved beyond corrupt bourgeoisie consciousness. They say no Marxists on the Central

Committee. I don't ask for reasons. I simply obey. It shows that I've evolved and become worthy of the Masters."

"Absurd!"

"To the uninitiated, yes."

"Who are these so-called Masters?"

Anita gave a great guffaw. "Really, Eugene."

"I don't believe a word of it."

"Oh come, let's not jettison that precious self-control."

"There's no secret revolutionary cell of invisible, all-powerful Masters living in the mountains out west."

"If you say so."

"I say so."

"Big things are coming, my boy. World's headed for a huge jolt. You'll see."

Eugene inhaled deeply. "You're all crazy. At least Marx is rational. You're just as crazy as. . . Fourier, or Saint-Simon. Crazy utopians. Did you know that Fourier thought there'd be a future Age of Harmony in which the seas would change to lemonade, the poles marshmallow, there'd be six moons for lovers and wild animals would become tame? Yeah, there'd be anti-lion, anti-whales to pull ships. Is this you?"

Anita chuckled: "Maybe, my boy, maybe."

"We'll see which revolution the masses join. Your mystical garbage or scientific socialism."

"No need for that."

Long rows of florescent lights made the basement seem more like a laboratory.

Workbenches covered by a litter of tools, boxes, batteries, wires, cans, ceramic jars, beakers, test-tubes, and even—Sylvian recognized them instantly— Bunsen burners lined the walls. The labels read ammonium nitrate, paraffin, potassium nitrate, sodium carbonate, sodium chloride, sulfur. There were even jars of Vaseline and resin. Interspersed amid the clutter was an array of firearms: handguns, rifles, military M-16s. Some were in pieces and others still packed in grease.

In the very center of the basement sat a high rectangular wooden table covered with green felt. Odd-looking, charred letters had been burned into the felt in the center of the table:

Ayamatma Brahma

Anita found her place in an antique chair at the head of the table. On her right sat Cathy Butcher, next to her Randal Boots. On her left was Vesta-Cher and Che Big-ears (Paul was actually a graduate student in the Psychology Department). These four, plus Anita, made the Central Committee.

Sylvian, Jerry, and Tom seated themselves at the far end of the table. Jerry, who'd never been "downstairs," looked nervous and a bit ill. He could be heard muttering: "the Mines of Moria. . ."

Tom was grinning. Sylvian had become invisible.

Anita opened an old notebook and began to read: "The true strength of the Order of the People's Will is dependent upon revolutionary solidarity. All friendships, feelings of devotion, family ties, social obligations, all attachments whatsoever, inside and outside the movement, are determined solely by the degree of usefulness to the cause of the all-destructive revolution."

She glanced at Jerry Wolfe. He trembled and let out a tiny moan.

"Have you, Jerry Wolfe, brought this person into our movement fully conscious of this our most important rule?"

"Oh, Lady Galadriel. Yes. He knows the secrets of Sauron."

"What the hell does that mean?"

"May I interrupt this, uh, formal initiation?" asked Randal.

"What is it?" Anita sounded and looked, profoundly irritated.

"We, uh. . ." Randal turned a page in a notebook similar to Anita's. He found his place and began to read: ". . .the revolution renounces all peaceful pursuits and seeks only the destruction of the whole ignoble existing fascist order. For this purpose only does the revolutionist study mechanics, chemistry, physics, medicine, science in general—"

"Oh, yes!" Sylvian waved his arms as if to answer a question in class.

"Yes, what?" asked Anita.

"Study physics. Physics can cause real damage. . . like. . . an atomic bomb placed in a bank or somethin'—"

"That's what Jerry was thinking, the One Ring," said Randal. "The kid knows everything. We could nuke the fucking capitalists out of existence. Nuke my ole man's mill that exploits the workers—"

"Jesus Christ!" Cathy Butcher exclaimed. "Are we criminals?"

Tom shook his head and gave a bitter laugh. "Little's changed," he said, addressing the table.

The others waited for Anita.

Anita closed her eyes for a few moments. Then she fixed Sylvian with her stare and said: "We don't act except by the will of the Masters. Nothing they've ever revealed would lead me to believe that such acts would be among their tactics."

She paused. "I do like this kid's audacity, though. It's an interesting idea—"

Randal shifted in his seat. He flipped a few pages, jabbed his finger on the place he'd been looking for and read:

"The revolutionist has broken with the Establishment not only in words but in deeds. The revolutionist breaks every connection: social, educational, all laws, appearances, generally accepted conventions, morality, sentiments, hopes, desires, personal interests, and attachments, for the purpose of total and complete destruction of the present evil system—"

"Fuckin' Jonathan wrote that shit!" Anita shouted, sending spittle flying across the table.

"You still read from it."

"Only useful parts. What's approved by the Masters."

"I'm getting sick of always waiting for these so-called Masters," said Randal, rising from his seat. "I like the kid's idea."

"Be respectful when you speak of the Masters," Cathy warned him.

"Fuck you, rich bitch."

"RANDAL, SIT DOWN!" Anita boomed.

He glared at her. Slowly, like a deflating tire, he sank back into his seat. There was no resisting Anita Anarcharsis.

Jerry Wolfe fumbled in his shirt pocket and produced a joint. He lit it, inhaled deeply, and then offered it to Sylvian. "Here, man, take a hit of Gandalf's tobacco. It'll calm your nerves."

Sylvian had never smoked pot in his life. Now he accepted the crudely rolled paper and inhaled in imitation of Jerry. His throat and chest began to burn. He tried to hold the smoke as he'd seen Jerry do, but he exhaled with an explosion of coughing and gagging.

The table erupted with laughter. "Pass it around," said Vesta.

The joint went quickly around the table. Everyone except Anita and Tom took hits. Randal smoked more than the others. Anita lit another cheroot.

"Is everyone cool?" asked Anita.

Randal glared at Cathy, but he nodded.

"Now listen," said Anita, "this ain't '64 or '65, and we ain't talking about Selma or Berkeley or Detroit or Watts. We ain't talking about free speech or disintegration or voting. This ain't about burning draft cards or campus protests. We ain't gonna try to levitate the Pentagon like those acid-heads in '67. Amerika ain't greening. It ain't no magic, swirling trip, and it ain't no love train. Haven't you learned anything from what happened to the Panthers? Ain't Czechago taught you nothin'?"

Vesta nodded grimly, her eyes half-closed and her mouth half-open, looking more like Cher than the real Cher. "Yeah, I saw it. Pigs got all the power. When they say no, man, it's over."

"Who's really fighting the war? There're all these race riots, then, wham, the war escalates. Now we got Nixon. You just watch. He ain't gonna end the war too soon. He's gonna use it to off radical blacks and radical students—anybody who can't afford a dodge."

"State has the monopoly on violence," Cathy added. "No revolution succeeds without military collapse—"

"What about Tet?" Randal asked. Sylvian saw something in Randal's eyes, something besides anger, but which Sylvian in his innocence could not identify. It didn't look healthy.

Anita waved her hand impatiently, brushing the words out of the smoky air. "Forget about Vietnam. It's surreal, like some TV show. That's all it is, 'cept for people like Tom here. It's a TV show that comes on at five-thirty. Yeah, it chews up the blacks and the poor, but that ain't enough. It just ain't real, even to the Establishment that's running it. You watch. When it becomes too inconvenient for the Establishment, they'll pull their dicks right out."

"They're settin' up this new lottery," said Cathy.

"So—?" Randal muttered.

Anita sounded exasperated: "Pigs got to manipulate protest and opposition. Something that my dear Jonathan Burke, Ph.D., didn't grasp. . ." She looked at Tom. ". . .protest, even violent so-called revolutionary protest, just plays into piggy hands. Don't need a war to manipulate people. Old Jonathan didn't get it 'cuz he was just a thinker, an ideologue like Vico."

"So escalating the war or ending the war, or changing the political structure, or voting, or even revolutionary class struggle isn't gonna change a thing," said Cathy, "it's the whole insane System, everything. . . reality itself. . . the rocks and trees and soil. . . it's all corrupt."

"Sounds like the bourgeoisie has already won," said Randal glumly. "Like my goddamn ole man keeps tellin' me. I gotta stop making waves and start making money."

"Ah, my boy, this is why we have the Masters. They've remained secret. . . waiting, planning. They know the truth. They're beginning to move. They have plans for the People's Will. Don't you worry. It's gonna happen soon. We're gonna blow Amerika away."

Sylvian clapped his hands in childish glee.

Randal looked doubtful. "So, give us a little clue how and when this is all gonna happen?"

Anita laughed: "Tell you the truth, Randal my boy, I don't know. But it's coming real soon. Masters gotta keep it all secret, even from the troops. cuz of infiltration. Believe me, though, Amerika's gonna have its senses stripped."

"If it's because of infiltration, then we should off this little punk," Randal declared. "Fuck physics. I change my opinion. Jerry says he's in with the Clouds. Clouds are FBI for sure. Whether he's aware of it or not, they're usin' him to get to us."

Sylvian looked as though he were about to speak, yet stopped himself.

"He went to only one meeting," said Jerry quickly, "with an elf maiden, who fucked him later."

Tom laughed at this. The others looked troubled.

"Shit, maybe we will have to kill the kid," Vesta muttered.

"Democratic centrism," said the Che.

Anita closed her eyes and appeared to go into a kind of trance. Minutes passed. No one dared speak. Randal stared intently at Cathy. Jerry lit another joint, which he proceeded to smoke by himself while gazing at Anita.

"Far out," he breathed, blowing smoke, "like, she's doin' telaphoneology with them Masters."

"Telepathy," Sylvian whispered into his ear.

"Yeah, that—"

Anita opened her eyes and studied Sylvian.

"Can you get inside the Clouds?" she asked him.

Sylvian failed to comprehend what she was asking. He was determined not to pee in his pants again this evening.

"Brilliant!" Paul exclaimed. "I love it. Infiltrate the fuckin' FBI. A double agent."

Sylvian finally got out a squeaky: "Yes."

Anita grunted: "Good." She looked at the notebook, flipped a page and recited: "Do you wish to see the very roots of the suffering of the people, the corporate state, be utterly and mercilessly destroyed, so that the last vestige of domination, alienation, falseness, repression, hypocrisy, and manipulation is burned to ashes, leaving the complete liberation of the masses?"

"Yes—"

She ignored his answer and continued: "Will you snuff out in yourself all tender, softening sentiments of kinship, friendship, love, and gratitude, except for the cold passion of revolution?"

"Yesss—"

"Congratulations. You're a member of the People's Will. Your first assignment is to infiltrate the suspected FBI front called the Great Truth

Cloud. Such are the orders of the hidden Masters of the White Order, given directly to me, of which the People's Will is a battle arm."

Randal shook his head: "I don't know, the kid seems goofy—"

"The movement needs such," said Cathy. "We struggle against an insane system run by madmen. We fight in the name of a people who have themselves been brainwashed by all sorts of goofy superstitions—"

"Like your ole man," Randal laughed.

"And yours, Boots."

"Enough," Anita ordered. "Meeting's adjourned. By the way, nobody says anything about this to Vico."

"What about him?" Paul gestured at Tom.

Anita grinned. "Well, Tom, what'd ya think now?"

"I think you still know how to rap real good, Anita Burke. . ." Tom paused. "And I guess I would like to stick around and see if any of it is true."

Anita gave him a wink. "You do that, Tom. There's a place for you in the People's Will. You'll see very soon. It's gonna be unbelievable."

ELEVEN

Pearl's Path

WEDNESDAY, OCTOBER 15, 1969: thousands took to the streets protesting the war in Vietnam. All around the country, on almost every college campus, students poured out of their classrooms into the crisp October air. Even members of Congress joined in the antiwar demonstrations, the largest to date.

Not, of course, on the campus of Brunswick State University—neither in the town of Hinnom Valley. The day passed with its usual mechanical routine, the mill, the brewery, the university, grinding out their particular products. Nonetheless, tension flowed through the stagnant air, as though one felt the faint rumblings of a storm just over the horizon, yet the rain never arrived. Nothing marred an otherwise perfect day except an uneasy sense of impending violence. No clouds rolled in, and no storm broke.

Professor Paul F. Hallerman canceled his philosophy classes to demonstrate solidarity with the nationwide antiwar movement. Announcing his decision, he was careful not to use these exact words. When questioned by the administration, he pointed out that it was standard procedure to allow students time off to complete their philosophy projects, and this was entirely in keeping with the principle of academic freedom, which, by the way, was the *raison d'etre* for tenure at all legitimate universities and colleges across the country.

Neither the People's Will nor Eugene Vico's Student Marxist Party, or whatever he called it that week, took to the streets, except to go to class and work.

That weekend, Sylvian went home to Chicago. In fact, his parents ordered him home. His brother had returned from Southeast Asia (again) with
yet another silver star and a second purple heart. The family had planned
a huge celebration, and, naturally, Sylvian needed to be there to greet the
hero. Father Loeb would be coming for dinner that Saturday evening, and,
of course, the whole family had to be present whenever a priest came; and
Father Loeb had mentioned to Lorraine at Mass how he would dearly like to
see her "special child" too.

The moment he stepped in the front door, Sylvian felt as if he had
stepped out of a dream into the real world. Would they detect his stupen-
dous revolutionary change, he wondered?

They barely noticed him. He was invisible as usual. After all, this was
the real world.

Sylvian went to Confession and unburdened himself in the presence of
Father Loeb. And as surely as time flows in one direction, so too, once in the
Confessional, did the full story of his radical change pour out.

Father Loeb listened patiently, grasping about half of it. At home, Sylvian's language problem mysteriously reappeared.

The good priest warned Sylvian to stay away from drugged nihilists
like Jerry Wolfe, who was a Jew besides, which the priest found highly significant. He wasn't sure if Anita or Kris, or even Pearl were even real people.
Like St. Barlaam, they might be symptoms of Sylvian's "special problem."
Goodjohn Saccidananda was almost certainly a fictitious character, perhaps
a drug-induced delusion.

The priest's authoritative certainty jolted Sylvian and forced him to
reconsider the past months.

Old habits reasserted themselves. The old Sylvian returned, and old
Sylvian returned to school.

He did his best to avoid Jerry Wolfe. He stopped going to philosophy
class, although he discovered later that Hallerman had canceled the entire
final month of classes. He tried to forget the demonstration, the police assault on his person, and his awakening. He made an effort to believe in God,
the Holy Mother Church, and the goodness of America.

"Where're ya goin' Sam?" asked Jerry Wolfe, peering up at him as through a
fog. It was noon, and he was still in bed.

"Oakwood."

Jerry moaned and swung his legs out of the tangled mess of soiled sheets and a dirty blanket. "Shit—" With a grunt and loud belch, followed by a fart, he fetched a can of beer from under the bed. Butcher Beer.

"Goin' to Mirkwood? How come you ain't been to Anita's? You're in the movement, man."

"Don't have the time. Got to studies. Got courses. Going to the park to study in peace."

"Fuck! Goddamn courses are irrelevant. Professors are stooges. University's nothing but toilet training. They're all bourgeoisie parasites—"

Jerry took a sip from the can.

"Man, students are oppressed. Kissin' ass for grades is class discussion. Shitin' out propaganda is exams. Repressed, guilt-ridden, filth-ridden corpses is culture, man, like some fruity lyrics from the fifties when everybody fit into the same clothes except a few losers and blacks, and everybody looked and acted like Ozzie and Harriet, and God was this old white guy with a long beard, and nobody ever fucked 'cuz we all got here on the wings of fucking storks, and the whole thing was big fucking lie 'cuz the only real God is money, and 'cuz—"

"Goin' to the park," Sylvian sighed. "Goin' to the park ain't no political act."

"Hey man, take a drink of this. It's water from the Ents."

"No, thanks."

"Ah, come on. You'll feel groovy. Its Ent-water, uh, called *Ayahuasca* in Elvish."

Sylvian grabbed the can and drained it in one gulp. The sudden violence of his act startled Jerry.

"There, you stupid head. Satisfied?"

"Wow, man—"

The beer tasted sour and was without carbonation. It brought back memories of Goodjohn. It might not have been beer at all. It was more like tea. Jerry liked to mix drugs.

"Man, you gotta come back to the revolution. You're Sam, man. Gotta infiltrate Mordor."

"That so?"

"Yup. Masters ain't revealed everything yet, but they toll'd Anita that Tom should be on the Central Committee. Randal don't like it. Says Tom ain't nothing but a big dumb ugly redneck. But the Masters done toll her, so he's in."

Sylvian shook his head. "Crazy—"

"Ain't crazy. I'll tell you what's crazy. Member them Clouds we thought was FBI? Lass night the local pigs shut 'em down! Raided the Cloud house for dope or something."

He dropped his voice to a conspiratorial whisper: "I heard from this chickee at Anita's that the cops went after Goodshit and he escaped into fucking Mirkwood and lost 'em, man."

"How could they be the FBI if the cops are after them?"

"Shit, man, stupid local cops don't know nothin'. Maybe it's just a ploy to throw us off the scent. You know, the dumb local cops make it look like they is a west coast cult."

"Where'd they go?"

"Mirkwood. And listen to this: the chickee says that the stupid pigs went into the park after him and got themselves lost. Took 'em an hour to get out. So they didn't get ole Goodshit. Everybody gets lost in that place."

"What did she look like? This chickee."

"Shit, man—" Jerry had to concentrate. "She looked maybe twelve, thirteen. Long blonde hair, real straight. Little tits, tight sweater. Spacey. One of them really weird chicks, witchy-like, kinda flaky, screwed up. You know, like that Mia Farrow—"

"Pearl," Sylvian whispered.

"Yeah, like that. Baby white—"

"Her name, idiot!"

"Didn't tell me—"

Sylvian gritted his teeth. "She came to Anita's house?"

"Yeah, came with Vico, I guess. Vico is always trying to get people to follow him, trying to convince people that he's gonna be famous some day. . . got a destiny. . . shit like that. He wants to organize a student strike to protest Craven's expulsion of the blacks."

"A. . . strike?"

"Says students ought to boycott their classes. Professors too. Go stand beneath Craven's window and scream shit at him."

"At least somebody's trying to do something."

"Fuck, man. Ancient history. Strikes and shit, like Berkeley. Didn't change a fuckin' thing. Establishment's stronger than ever. Nixon's president. Protest is like farting in the wind, stinks for awhile but just gets blown away."

"When's the strike?"

"Monday, I think. Vico just blabs everything. Administration's got to know. This is BSU. Snitch U. He'll be lucky if twenty students show up."

"What about Pearl?"

"Who?"

"The chickee, asshole!"

"Jeez, Sam. Cool it. She stayed awhile. Tried to argue with Vesta Higgens. Weird shit. I thought Vesta was going to punch her. But Vesta finally gave it up and toll her to get lost, which she did. Went back to Mirkwood and Goodcreep."

"She went to Oakwood?"

"Ohoo. . ." Jerry held his head and sank back into his pillows. "All this talk is givin' me a real bad headache—"

He let out a long pathetic groan. "Don't follow her, man. There's some bad shit that goes down in them woods."

But Sylvian had already made his decision.

The day turned bright and mild, more like late August than November two weeks before Thanksgiving. By noon, the temperature had climbed to sixty; an hour later, just as Sylvian entered Oakwood Park, it pushed to seventy. Surprisingly, the park was deserted.

He sat beneath the von Jahn oak and gazed across the field to the lagoon, trying to pierce the looming shadows of the wood. Bereft of leaves, the trees still seemed impenetrable like a dark temple supported by massive barked pillars. There were tall evergreens among the oaks, birch, hazels, and elms. Axe or saw had not touched the place. Hardly a breeze stirred those branches as if somehow the wind itself decided not to blow into the wood.

Sylvian's eyelids grew heavy. The book sitting on his lap remained closed. The warm sun beamed down on his back, massaging his skin with soft fingers. His eyes closed.

His stomach felt bloated. It was a curious thing that Jerry's stale *Ayahuasca-beer* (probably a foreign brand; Sylvian had never heard of the company) kept him from falling asleep. He shouldn't have downed so much in one gulp.

Serene, peaceful. . . Images marched behind his closed eyes: Pearl, Anita, Jerry. . . the Cher, Che of the Big Ears. He perceived quite clearly the figure of Kris, the blue hippie. Guru Woo-Woo failed to show up in the procession. Neither did the Intergalactic Brain.

Sylvian snapped up and opened his eyes.

Something had changed.

The wood appeared brighter; the lagoon seemed a deeper green. The oak's shadow had grown. Angles, lines, their ratios—the trigonometry of shadows— had all been altered as if he'd blinked and the world had changed. The alteration was multivariable; he'd have to use partial differential equations.

Sunlight bathed a broken nest of cityscape on the western horizon. It was a city like none he'd ever seen. Towers of spiked glass and metal mimicked palaces showcasing exterior staircases and inclined planes that crisscrossed and intersected. The geometry of lines created an impossible composition. The city looked somehow Mid-eastern, though he'd never seen a Mid-eastern town in his life. He felt an alien presence, dangerous, threatening, Jerry's elves perhaps but more insect-like, and not of flesh and blood. And yet the fantastic city felt more real than Chicago.

Hours passed in a moment, and the short autumn day began its rush into the dusk. The alien city seemed to fade with the fading light, dematerialize, leaving behind this unearthly reality that seemed to play tricks on his senses.

How did the entire afternoon pass so quickly? Time really was relative, he thought.

Movements from the trees were just at the fringe of his perception. Once more, he experienced the odd sensation of reality shifting as if something new were unfolding out of multi-dimensional space.

He studied the wood. A flight of birds? The light seemed steady. No wind.

It now seemed to him that wood itself had moved, expanded as if it took a breath. Inhale, then exhale, it expanded and contracted. The very fabric of space was breathing.

Goddamn Jerry. Goddamn hippie and his foreign beer.

He closed his eyes tightly. It'll wear off. "Just wait and be patient," he said aloud.

A voice answered: "I've waited."

Not again. Had to be a dream—a bad trip. The voice sounded like it belonged to Kris the blue-hippie.

He rubbed his eyes vigorously and dissolved the world in a wash of tears. Then he staggered to his feet, fists clenched.

He peered into a brilliant fog. Lines and angles wavered and merged in a flood of refracted light. Liquid droplets were bending the rays, rebounding, reinforcing, canceling—oh; he knew the physics of it. He saw the world through a stack of rainbows, like a pack of transparent rainbows with cards shuffled at random.

He heard someone speaking about "kalpas" and revolutions and saviors, and suddenly he realized the voice didn't belong to Kris.

Pearl.

Pearl was gazing at him and laughing gently: "I've been looking all over for you, Sylvian. I even checked out that wild woman's pad. This guy from class said you'd been there. But you weren't."

"Pearl—" he moaned, shaking his head. "What'd you want?"

"You," she said.

He tried desperately to focus his vision. The girl did seem like Pearl: long blonde hair, pale skin, crooked teeth. But the being was Pearl without her garden, Pearl minus her fish-smell. Drugs, of course, affected the olfactory sense as well as sight. She, this faerie-like being, wore an ankle-length hooded cloak of heavy green material with a blue scarf around her neck. She looked like a greeting card faerie or a pagan woodlands nymph.

"Stay away! You FBI. . . agent."

"Take a walk with me, huh. Please." Smiling, she offered her hand.

"Where?"

"There." She inclined her head. "There's a path that goes into the forest."

A sudden breeze rippled the surface of the lagoon as if her slight motion had initiated a cascading series of waves in the stagnant air.

"Heard bad things 'bout this place."

"Oh, no. It's a good place. A good place to be alone." She winked.

"It'll be dark soon—will get lost."

She laughed merrily. "We might get lost, yes."

"Not even the pigs go there."

"Oh, Silly. Come with me. Please?"

Language is so imprecise, he silently groaned. Nonetheless, he wasn't a complete idiot. He had to hear what she was really saying, as Jerry later told him, shaking his head. "Man, Samwise, in our age Gollum's become a little girl."

He felt dizzy. He thought that he heard music coming from the wood. It was faint yet the vibrations spread through his body. She was irresistible. He had to follow.

"Are you coming?"

He felt her hand on his arm. Her fingers burned.

She led him across the field, around the lagoon, and into the forbidden wood.

"Can't see," he protested weakly.

They reached the edge. The trees magically changed into black pillars. Of the devil's temple, he imagined. The music stopped. Everything was still and silent, brooding, and waiting.

"Path's right here," she laughed.

The wood swallowed them. To Sylvian, it appeared much more significant than a few acres of trees left over from the days when it was a real forest.

Forms dissolved into a cold mist, which was like a wintry breath arising from the earth itself, as if the wood exhaled. The vapor became luminous, transformed into tiny droplets of light.

It seemed as if they were going downhill. Except. . .Oakwood Park was flat. Hinnom Valley was, after all, just that, a flatbed river valley. A country of vast spaces and wide vistas, the crazy park had expanded into something more extensive than the town that contained it.

"Do you see the path? Bright and clear like a holy river. It's the path you must take."

He didn't see the path; he could barely see her. He did feel her burning fingers on his arm.

"Where're we going?"

She stopped, and he crashed into her. He felt her entire body press him. He felt her warmth, the brush of her hair on his face, sweet and fresh.

"We're going to a. . . happening. Lots of mellow people will be there."

The luminous mist evaporated. Ahead something glowed like a fire burning at the bottom of a deep well. The trees became leafy as if the season changed back to summer.

The light ahead became brighter. He hesitated.

Pearl glanced over her shoulder. "What's wrong? Don't you like me?"

A new note in her voice frightened him.

"Don't you want to kiss me?"

He flinched. She was mocking him like all the others, telling lies. Must not forget. Pearl was another FBI-stooge, planted to seduce honest revolutionaries, destroy the moral strength of the revolution. Vicious anger washed over him like a cold shower. The new, dangerous Sylvian came back.

His small body shook, his fists clenched. "Hate you!"

She laughed, and her laughter sounded like the bells of St. Stanislas, eerily deep and resonant, far too deep for elfin Pearl.

He spun around, began to run. . . and slammed right into a massive oak. He ran in a straight line. The tree had not been there a moment ago. He stumbled and fell and sank into oblivion.

Music brought him back to the world. Somewhere, faintly, guitars played, electric organs, drums. . .the sitar. Voices mixed in, people, a crowd. He heard them singing and laughing (at him, he guessed), all of it somewhere in the impossibly expanding wood.

He rubbed his eyes and experienced a world that appeared disjointed and fluid. His senses refused to work together. Each sense registered its particular impression without coordinating its data with the others.

Pearl was still laughing like a cathedral full of bells. A plump figure loomed behind her, one he could not make out except as a vague, shadowy form.

"Hey Silly, open your eyes. Huh, please?"

The crowd behind her took shape and split up into a mass of dancing devils, just as Father Loeb had always described Hell. Red, yellow, blue, green—grotesque, distorted bodies—humans, animals, many he could not identify—they leaped about in a mad frenzy.

They danced and laughed, and wailed. They howled in unbearable pleasure (or agony), screamed in hysteria, roared in mad laughter.

Pearl stood in the center of the dance and grinned at him.

He scrambled to his feet. All lies. All delusion. Everything was a lie. Everything that exists deserves to perish.

Then the demonic horde and the hounds of Hell abruptly faded back into the darkness of the trees.

A shadow stepped forward, a large-bellied middle-aged man, nearly bald, bearded, and dressed in ordinary jeans with an embroidered vest like those he'd seen on the most ardent hippies of Lilac Street. The jacket contained strange symbols, an alien script that reminded him of St. Barlaam.

Sri Goodjohn Saccidananda. The Absolute, Groovy Guru, the Divine Woo-Woo, Master, Savior—

The FBI agent. Murderer. The Charles Manson of Hinnom Valley.

The Groovy Guru wore a smirking grin and carried his customary can of Butcher Beer. Peering owlishly at Sylvian, he winked and took a swig.

"Ahhh. . ." Goodjohn belched. "Want some?"

Sylvian shook his head.

Goodjohn raised his left hand and bellowed. "Hey, COOL IT!"

"Go away, you fat son-of—" Sylvian shut his mouth. He was supposed to infiltrate the Clouds.

"—what'd ya hippies want? Always sneakin'. What'd ya want?"

"Come over here!" Goodjohn waddled off to a spot in the tangled brush. He seemed to be looking for something. Pearl's gaze followed him; she heaved a worshipful sigh with every move he made; yet she was also frowning.

"Stupid little twit," Goodjohn snarled. He turned and slapped Pearl hard on the face, knocking her to the ground. Blood dripped from her mouth.

Sylvian was suddenly enraged. He raised his fists and stepped between them.

Goodjohn gave him a knowing look. "Want her, don't you?"

Sylvian glared back. The fat bastard could read minds.

"No, I can't," said Goodjohn, reading his mind. "Don't concern yourself with her. I've just imparted divine energy, *Shaktipat*, enlightenment by touch. Might cure her of her fantasies. She thinks she's Parvati, Daughter of Himalayas. Only one Divine Being here."

"What'd you want?"

"She thinks you're the Savior." He pointed at Pearl still on the ground, head down, softly weeping. "She won't listen. So, the Divine Woo-Woo must enlighten her."

"Don't know what you're talkin' about."

"Come over here."

Not knowing what pushed him, trying to look fierce and determined, Sylvian obeyed him. Goodjohn stared at him.

"Here," said Goodjohn. "This belongs to you."

"It's nothing but someone's old cloak, maybe a priest's robes. . ." Sylvian said. Looks like it's been patched. Made from pieces of rag. Goodwill."

"See the embroidered inscription. Do you recognize it?"

"Don't know." Sylvian thought it might be the robe worn by St. Barlaam from his old dream. Strange symbols, possibly a script, were sewn into the old fabric.

"Try it on."

Infiltrate the Clouds. He heard Anita's words in his head.

He shook the dirt from the old robe and wiggled into it. As small as he was, the gown fit tightly. Too tightly. Clearly made for a child; Sylvian took a deep breath, nearly splitting the seams.

"Rags don't fit."

"*Ayamatma brahma*," said Goodjohn, reciting the inscription. "What's it say?"

"Don't know. Maybe it's an equation."

Goodjohn laughed. "Pearly dear, I toll you. After I gave up the stupid teachin' racket, I went to India. My guru delivered me from repressive reason. I found *the I* behind I, the truth behind the dream. It's all about ME, not him. Pearly dear, you need to be me-minded."

Pearl staggered to her feet, wiped the blood from her mouth, and said: "But the old one? What he wrote—"

Goodjohn shook his head and drank his beer. "Nobody wants that. I'm the Avatar of the Intergalactic Brain, Divine Woo-Woo."

He finished the can. "People want God. That's what moves 'em. Anything that doesn't waver, doesn't break apart, disintegrate, fly away. Stable as worms buried in the earth, not birds carried by unpredictable winds."

"Birds eat the worms," she answered. The awe had gone out of her eyes, the worshipfulness from her voice.

"Rocks then! Mountains. Ever seen a mountain walk away?"

He was getting irritated. As he raised his hand, Pearl cringed.

"Look, I'm Jesus too—Moses, Mohammad, Krishna—and I say that people want mountains and laws that descend from their peaks. Forget this foolishness, Pearly. It never worked. Now go join your sister gopis like a good little girl. We're cuttin' outta this non-versity. Goin' out west, to the mountains."

"I've seen mountains walk," she whispered. "I've seen them run over the wide ocean."

He frowned. "You better stay outta intellectual matters. Your talents are for other things, more down to earth—"

Pearl looked at Sylvian. "Why did your ancestors come here from the Old Country?"

Sylvian stared at her dumbfounded. His head ached, and his eyes watered.

Goodjohn gave a mocking laugh. "Why do I waste my time trying to educate such as these?" He turned and waddled off, followed by his horde of demons.

Sylvian's head throbbed, and throbbed some more, as though he'd been struck again by that police club, the one that had awakened him to the reality of oppression in Amerika.

And as he'd previously done, he fainted.

Cold air brought him to consciousness. Wearing his usual white cotton shirt, Sylvian fumbled in the dark. He accidently grabbed at the old robe, pulling it over his head. His fingers frozen stiff, he fastened the buttons in the wrong holes. The mistake hardly mattered. The thing actually fit better when its buttons were askew. The world was crazy.

How stupid to fall asleep in Oakwood Park in the middle of November. What awful nightmares. Goddamn Jerry and his. . . *Ayahauser beer.*

"Hey man, is that you?"

"Who's there?"

"Oh, wow, man. Sorry, I scared you. It's me, Kris. Remember?"

"Kris. What the hell you want?"

"Wow, check out the duds. Did you join the priesthood? Hey man, did you have a bad trip? I was on my way to party with the Clouds. You know, dance with the gopis. Do you want to come along?"

"No."

"Just thought—"

"NO."

"OK, man—"

Kris turned to go, but then he stopped and said: "You know, pigs shut down the Cloud house on drug charges. But it's really political. Everybody's living in the park. It just blows the pigs' minds. Can't find 'em. I mean, every time the pigs search the park, it's like hide and seek. We got them chasing their piggy tails. So, man, if you change your mind just come on in and we'll find you."

He turned and broke into a loping run, beads and hair bouncing, trailing streamers of blue light. He sped around the lagoon and disappeared into the dark where the wood began. Sylvian thought that he heard music coming from that quarter, flutes and pipes.

Lying bastards. Jerry was right about 'em. Got to stay out of this place. But his task was to infiltrate the Clouds. Shit.

On his way back to the dorm, he took a detour. His mind was clear, his eyes steady, his hearing reasonably healthy. The park was as he remembered it, not some otherworldly zoo. He found his way around the lagoon, to the deep end, where there was no bottom, and the fish were eyeless. Unbuttoning the old robe, he wrapped it around a rock and threw it into the dark waters. Returned to Satan himself, he thought.

Walking the dark November streets, he suddenly wondered: *Why did* his noble Polish ancestors come to Amerika from the Old Country?

TWELVE

Strike!

H. RICHARD CRAVEN CLOSED his office door and poured himself a brandy. He exhaled a long sigh and settled into his rich leather chair. Its partially inflated cushions embraced his weighty body with a soothing caress.

On this particular dismal Monday, Craven's mood was as overcast as the weather.

He'd been pursuing *her* for most of the fall semester. But she was wise to his subtle hints and treated him like a little boy.

Merely twenty, the age of an undergraduate at BSU, and yet she mocked him, laughed at him, and treated him with disdain. Him! Christ, the majority of students thought of him as their father, a father-god beneficently overseeing the campus from the lofty heights of Eckhardt Hall, guarded by General Klaus von Brunswick standing his eternal watch at the gates of the President's palace.

Although there were times when Father's actions seemed inscrutable, most students believed that whatever the President did, his mysterious decrees and actions had to be in the best interests of the University and its students. Years might pass, decades, but they'd eventually discover it was all for the best.

This morning, however, anger burned deep in his guts like acid. It made him physically ill. Frightening thoughts rose to the surface, visions so terrible that he thought someone else had momentarily taken over his mind and body. Dismembered human bodies on plates as in a grocery store, choice slices, intestines like sausages, brains, tongues, eyes, all human, all for sale, and he was the butcher. He was so hungry, impossibly hungry, that he wanted to eat them all.

He shook his head and slapped his forehead—

He'd easily overwhelmed the others, but subtle hints had left her unmoved. There was no response to his most blatant behavior even to the point where he was brushing up against her. She was untouchable, like one of those idiotic statues in Kreis. She was stone.

The others sometimes demonstrated dismay, guilt, sorrow, even loathing—of him, of themselves, of BSU. They might tell someone: parents, boyfriends, ministers. Sometimes the whole thing threatened to explode. An outraged but fumbling threat, trying to intimidate him with some ridiculous blackmail scheme.

Christ, he owned the miserable school. The stupid Regents: businessmen, bankers, wealthy and mostly senile widows, the ministers (no priests or rabbis, of course), all of them owed him an enormous debt. He'd saved the pitiful place. He'd started the "market research program," as he liked to call it, which, when he dared to be honest with himself, really constituted a devious set of schemes designed to milk the alumni, the state, and whatever foolish foundations bought into his slick marketing of a new program, which he labeled "entrepreneurial education," but was little more than high school shop class— more or less, a capitalist pre-school.

He'd established new methods of "personnel management"—in reality, an absurd rulebook of incomprehensible procedures to keep the BSU faculty and staff underpaid, overworked, and obsessed with the trivial. BSU was one big family, he would often say, and he liked to think of himself as god-the-father.

The Board of Regents loved it. He protected their money and spared them responsibility. And so he'd earned absolute trust. He could do as he pleased.

With a few irritating exceptions.

Alas, now to the miserable business at hand. Reading the folder, his dreary mood became worse. Female revolutionaries, indeed, he thought. Goddamn, college education just ruined good girls. It was much easier to manipulate draft boards: A favor is done, a name dropped, a contract and every long-haired radical found himself protesting jungle-rot and cow snakes. Naturally, the new lottery would pose problems, but H. Richard Craven understood the first principle of power: With enough imagination and foresight, everything could be manipulated.

As he anticipated, Bentley's little schemes seemed to be working. He turned a page. He suspected that the People's Will was all talk and that in the end none of this foolishness would prove necessary. Intellectual radicals—revolutionaries who read books—were very similar to most academics. They loved to talk.

On the other hand, they shunned physical labor like the plague. Ha, physical work frightened them—they might find themselves out-of-breath and sweating, for Christ's sake. They might suffer sleepless nights, even drop a few pounds. *Beware, Caesar, yon professor has lean and hungry look.*

He came to the final page of Bentley's recommendations. He shrugged and put his initials on the document.

Next, he turned to the flier calling for the strike. Eugene Vico and his Student Marxist Revolutionary Vanguard—

He read the pamphlet. Yeah, a little repression would trigger something like this. Maybe now he'd be able to get that slippery bastard Hallerman.

He made a few notes in the margins, scribbled a directive for campus security and the Hinnom Valley Police Chief. He was reasonably sure he wouldn't have to call in the National Guard. He knew what the Governor would think of that.

He turned to Vico's personnel file. Bright enough kid in a rather mechanical way. Does well in the sciences, has decent writing skills and an aptitude for mathematics. Until this year, he had not joined a single student organization.

Craven turned a page. Wealthy, north shore family; they'd even contributed to the endowment. Family business in Racine, a restaurant, but real wealth came from other sources, not listed. Eugene was an only child. All private schools, now BSU.

Christ, what made the little punk turn Marxist? Probably that son-of-a-bitch Hallerman pumping his German philosophy into empty heads. Philosophy was about as useful as weighing empty space. It was all pompous foolishness, but with precision. And now a strike. He'd get Hallerman yet.

Craven leaned back and took off his glasses. He'd heard it once long ago, in some long-winded lecture during his student days. Marxism was a mirror image of capitalism in that both assumed materialist, fully determined reality. God forbid that he'd ever have to manipulate the mystical Clouds. Marxists presuppose that all sane questions had technical answers, that all needs were material only. Their shrill babble about alienation and human spiritual needs was a kind of infantile economic temper tantrum, like a room full of two-year -olds squabbling over candy. Bentley might say something like this.

Take a child, raise it on a ton of sweets until its very blood turns to sugar, dump a million toys in its lap, keep its environment filled with loud noises and bright lights—a never-ending deluge of TV, sports, radio, music (preferably loud), and be sure to give it enough of an education to manipulate the gadgets. Then, when this quivering mass of protoplasm grows up, you explain to it how these terrific experiences are called "leisure." Best of all, this thing leisure (or pleasure), can be extended into adulthood, expanded in quantity and quality until new, exciting things once impossible for a child, like sex—that is, the sex promoted by Playboy and Hollywood in which the wealthy, successful guy gets to bang an endless stream of bunnies as the reward for his financial success—become possible. (No "free-love" garbage) As long as the protoplasm works hard in the System, makes money and doesn't make waves, the possible becomes attainable. On the other hand, things such as protests could be made part of the System, such as new fads, mod styles, hip cool, and all for a profit.

The System never failed. So how the hell could the little shit turn Marxist? Had to be Hallerman.

The strike would be a kind of warm-up for Thanksgiving. Maybe he should give a TV interview. He could make some big announcement, perhaps a fake concession, promise a breakthrough. Must be sincere, though. No use being cynical.

The ultimate solution, Carven knew, would be to slow down the economy and turn the energy of protest into job seeking. Never give the children time to really think about things, which meant changing the curriculum, so they never encountered those lean and hungry minds.

Despite its usefulness, it would probably help to stop drafting the little bastards, at least the middle-class kids. There were undoubtedly enough hee-haws in the United States who'd swallow the horse-pill of pious patriotism. The media could easily be manipulated to shower praise on the stupid shits. Right or Left-wing, it was ideally compliant, since it was, after all, another section of the corporate leviathan.

No more anti-militarism. The media would transform soldiers into heroes rather than instruments of oppression; murderous goons for what Eisenhower called, "the military-industrial complex." To be fair, Eisenhower must have been going senile at that point. They would become selfless heroes, the fair-haired warriors who kept the dark forces of evil at bay. Best for everyone they did not know the truth. Child-like innocence was as pliable as heated wax.

It is still the greatest country in the world, goddammit. Competition releases the most potent creative forces, despite what some leftist parasite bleated about alienation.

He wrote a little more, yawned, and leaned back in his chair. His eyes came to rest on the framed public relations brochure that hung on the wall; one Craven himself had written the year he'd become President. He felt immense pride and loved to re-read it, savoring every word like some juicy morsel from a rare steak. The brochure said:

> Brunswick State University is built upon the solid, hard-working character of the original settlers of beautiful Hinnom Valley. Proud of its heritage, its strict, unyielding adherence to those firm and lasting truths instead of the shifting sands of current fashion, BSU is dedicated to molding the whole person: intellectually, morally, and spiritually. Taking the noblest human endowments: friendship, trust, the capacity for love, curiosity, BSU molds your young person into a competent citizen, a professional, a good person, through the stern yet rewarding process of socialization and training.
>
> Education at BSU provides the tools for life. It is a kind of machine tooling of the young to fit them snugly into the world of today and of tomorrow. Given this solid foundation, they will live their lives happy, free, and productive. They will comprehend the value of work without becoming servile; they will mesh with society without becoming a non-entity, and they will surely not suffer the misery of having "to find themselves" as so many of today's sadly misguided youth lost in some drug-induced fantasy.
>
> Our students know what they are: graduates and proud alumni of Brunswick State University.

Let them strike. H. Richard Craven was no Clark Kerr.

At noon on Tuesday, the twenty-fifth of November, Eugene Vico climbed the Klaus von Brunswick monument and in a chill sleety rain declared a strike against "Dick Craven," and his "fascist gang of administrative stooges."

Surprisingly, the Kreis was fairly crowded despite the foul weather. Students spilled out of their classes and stopped to find out what was happening. A tightly packed cadre of fifteen students, many wearing army surplus ponchos with red armbands, gathered around the base of the statue.

In a few minutes, they were all soaking wet and cold and looking rather forlorn.

Eugene waved his arms and yelled with all the volume his lungs would produce. He carried a battery-operated megaphone that crackled in the wet conditions and screeched horridly every time he tried to shout.

"Listen to me!" he cried desperately, "You possess the power to shut this place down!"

The disciples at his feet bleated a few mournful-sounding slogans: "Power to the people!" "Students strike now!" "Get out of Vietnam!" "End racism and oppression!" "Students run the university!"

One longhaired girl with large dangling ring earrings and wire-rimmed glasses shouted: "The proletariat must seize the means of protection now!"

Fresh from psychology class, a snickering Randal Boots pushed his way to the base of the monument.

Vico spied him instantly and directed his discourse at Randal.

"Students unite! Strike now! The class war begins in class!

"Seize the university!"

"Seize the means of protection!" cried the girl whose name was Mary Anne and who majored in Painting. Generally, her subjects were semi-abstract grisely renderings of severed heads and dead birds. Mary Anne was quite proud of her Marxist vocabulary, which she'd newly acquired under the intellectual guidance of Chairman Vico. The Chairman had explained to her that this language was a sign of her new freedom from the slave-language of bourgeoisie capitalism, from false morality (he stressed to her that body and mind were interconnected and proceeded to free her body as well as her mind). He hastened to add that revolution would improve her art.

"Strike now!" Eugene shouted at Randal, "Boycott your classes. Empty classes make the university senseless. We are the destitute—the proletarian. Professors are the proletarian. Professors, join our movement!"

Vico paused and scanned the Kreis, looking for Professor Hallerman, who had promised to join the strike and speak from the monument. But there was no sign of him. Well, maybe the rain delayed him, or perhaps he was still busy gathering other sympathetic professors as he'd promised.

People began to drift away. Randal observed the spectacle with a look of profound contempt.

At precisely this moment, Sylvian wandered through the Kreis, head down, on his way home from Calculus class. He looked quite ill. Rain soaked his hand-me-down coat. Without looking up, Sylvian ran headlong into Randal.

"Hey asshole, watch where you're going! Oh shit, it's you. Hope you ain't decided to join Vico."

"Randal?" Sylvian peered up at him, trembling as he always did at Randal's eerie satanic appearance.

"Yeah."

"People's Will should join the strike."

"Ain't you learned nothin' yet? We're serious. Gonna do some serious shit when the Masters order it," Randal's voice, however, did not carry much conviction.

Vico suddenly hit a screeching note, "To the Union! Seize the Student Union now!"

An older, white-haired man, walking through the Kreis at that moment, dressed in overhauls and work jacket with the university logo on the sleeve (the logo just happened to be an abstract figure of the von Jahn oak), stopped directly below Vico and gave him a quizzical look.

"Workers and students unite!" Vico yelled down at him.

The maintenance man looked puzzled. "What'd the hell students got width a union anyhow?"

Vico looked puzzled in turn.

"Students ain't got no jobs. How come they got a union?"

"No, no, sir. I'm talking about the Student Union."

"Yup. And I'm askin' how come you got a union when you don't work or nothin'."

"No, it's a place—"

"Ain't you says you strikin'? How can you strike when you ain't got no job?" The man sounded peevish.

"We're proletarians like you." Eugene was getting frustrated. "Join us. Power to the working class. Strike!"

"For what?"

"For freedom from oppression. To end alienation. To end the fetish for commodities. To become self-realized—"

Mary Anne interrupted him: "Seize the means of protection! And usher the highest stage of. . . pure communism!"

The man shrank from her as if he had stepped upon a nest of poisonous snakes. "A commie!" He howled, "Gah-damn commie! Ought to be thrown in jail!"

The vanguard of the working class fled as if pursued by the entire Soviet army.

Randal laughed. "So much for revolutionary workers."

Screams suddenly split the wet air. The Kreis abruptly became a pandemonium of scurrying students. No one was listening to Vico, and no one was marching to seize the union, not to mention the means of protection.

"The pigs!"

Spilling from the administration buildings, the maroon and white clad troops of campus security entered the Kreis. This time there were no Students Helping Students among them. Within their ranks marched dark blue and gold figures of the Hinnom Valley sheriff's department.

Fifty officers had come with campus security, armed with shotguns, mace, teargas, and nightsticks. They wore helmets and bulletproof vests. They'd driven an armored car right into the middle of the Kreis. Its over-sized tires dug up the wet sod. The vehicle resembled a miniature tank, and was equipped with a water-canon that looked like a fantastic ray-gun out a fifties science fiction movie.

Vico shouted: "Down with the pigs! Down with the pig nation!"

His tight group of disciples abruptly dissolved like blocks of salt in the rain. Only Mary Anne remained rooted to her spot; her glasses fogged, she was dripping wet.

Raising her arm stiffly, Mary Anne, dead bird artist, clenched her fist, and shouted: "Power to the People!"

By now, the police and campus security had surrounded the monument. They were laughing and seemed to be having a good time.

"Time to go home, little girl."

Vico made a great effort to regain control. He thrust out his chin, straightened his back to reach his full height (a hair over five-six), and jabbed a finger at the nearest security man.

"Brothers!" he cried. "Join us and let us build a unified fraternal state. We shall all plough the land, work collectively as equals, and render the earth into a flowering garden so that our children and their children will believe themselves living in paradise. Yes, yes! Paradise. Once merely a legend, a dream to console people living in ignorance and misfortune, the longing of the oppressed, the sigh of the downtrodden. People yearn for paradise and justice. So they have said that paradise awaits them in the next life. But to believe in another world drains the energy from this one. People are dead even before they die. Join us, brothers! Let us improve mankind. Let us make men wiser, stronger, more profound, more harmonious—more musical. Rather say that we, the toilers, will build this paradise here in this world, for everyone, for our children—"

Vico was quoting something he'd read a while back, but he couldn't recall the author he'd heard or who'd given the speech. Therefore, Vico de-cided, he'd been the author.

"You're under arrest!" Someone from campus security said moving to-ward the student orator. "You're causing a disturbance!" The regular police howled with laughter.

Three campus cops mounted the platform and seized Eugene. They were cautious and made sure not to beat him or to hurt him in any way. They used a minimum of force, which because of Eugene's slight frame was fairly easy to accomplish. They cuffed him and dragged him down, ignoring General von Brunswick who did not raise a finger to help the young revolutionary.

"Police brutality!" screamed Eugene. "Fascist pigs—!" Suddenly he began to wail. "Oh please, don't hurt me—"

"Fascist pig oppression!" Mary Anne cried. But in that moment, nobody paid her the slightest bit of attention.

"Let's get the hell outta here," Randal yelled.

"Wanna fight!"

Sylvian held his calculus textbook with both hands as though to wield it like a club.

Randal grabbed him by the shoulders and shoved him against the wall of a red brick building.

Sylvian screamed and swung the book at his head. The massive tome, slick with rain, slipped out of his fingers and landed in a puddle.

"Oh, Holy Mother of God!"

Sylvian frantically dove for it, instead, he slipped on the wet pavement and went sprawling into Randal, smashing his head into Randal's groin. His first real revolutionary act, people would later say, was to strike a blow in the name of calculus.

Randal howled, lost his footing, and followed the calculus book into the puddle.

The police, observing what had now appeared to be a puddle-diving competition, dissolved into fits of hysterical laughter.

"No more playing in the puddle, children," a cop roared, tears rolling down his cheeks. "It's time to go home."

Randal scrambled out of the water and shook like a wet dog. Sylvian got to his feet, clutching the calculus-bludgeon to his chest.

"This way—"

Sylvian followed Randal as he lopped around the corner of the building and headed across campus towards the river.

Halfway to the river, Randal abruptly bent over, gagging and coughing.

"Fucking idiot!" he gasped between spasms.

Clutching his book like a life preserver, Sylvian gave him a disgusted look. "Coward. Should've stayed and fought pigs. Delusion is infinite. Must fight—destroy. Vow to uproot delusion as one digs rotten weeds!"

"Stupid little shit. You're a member of the People's Will not one of Vico's fuckin' stooges."

"Swore to destroy the Establishment. Fight's back there." Sylvian said, pointing behind him.

"Shit, man, protest ain't nothing. Merely a game. Didn't you hear Anita? A protest is political masturbation."

"Vico's doin' something. Anita's done nothing. The Nothing nothings."

"Anita's serious, asshole. Don't ever criticize our Leader." Randal's eyes darted about wildly. He had lost his glasses and couldn't focus. "You heard the *Catechism*. You'd better be with us when Anita finally acts," he said, shaking his fist.

Sylvian began to feel feverish. Was he possessed by this black-haired devil, just as Father Loeb had often warned?

"Can't be part-time revolutionary. It's a war to the bitter end. Us against the Establishment. We're going to wipe it clean."

Sylvian looked sick and doubtful. The fall had done something strange. He felt as if he no longer lived inside his dwarfish body; he felt transparent, invisible. Then, as if he'd stepped into a vivid dream, the old, singular Sylvian Matreya was no longer there in the rain, on the campus of BSU, in November, and it was not 1969. He was the oppressed, existing simultaneously in all times and in all places. He was one of the downtrodden, the sufferers who were slaves in the service of the soulless mechanical monster which was the System. He lived countless lives in multible times. Tears filled his eyes. All suffering became his suffering as if some disease he'd only known in the abstract attacked flesh and bone, causing him real pain.

All at once, he was Vico facing the heavily armed police. He was James Rutledge nearly beaten to death. He was the napalmed peasant in Vietnam, skin peeling like an eel. He was millions upon millions of suffering humanity. He was even the suffering animals.

"Shit, you gotta get real," Randal snarled.

Sylvian stared blankly.

"Fucking moron. Come on. Let's go."

Sylvian followed him like a shadow.

"Jeez, what an idiot—"

THIRTEEN

A Conspiracy Unmasked

THE POLICE HELD EUGENE and Mary Anne at the base of the monument. A gray-haired man stylishly dressed and wearing a perfectly cut beard approached them. His long face bore a look of sad beneficence. He gave the impression of someone who "has seen it all" and could not be caught off-guard, a man for whom contemporary events were trivial repetitions of deep history. He sported plastic golden buckles on his black leather shoes.

Vico knew the Reverend Richard Bentley, Dean of Students, President Craven's pet spaniel. The officers stood respectfully aside.

"A beautiful speech, Mr. Vico," said Dean Bentley, sounding sincere.

Mary Anne looked confused. "Pig oppression," she declared, giving Eugene a bewildered glance.

"Oh, please." Bentley exhaled a soft chuckle. "They're only doing their job. They're human beings like you, family men simply trying to make a decent living. Don't reduce them to animals." He made a slight motion with his little finger.

The police released Eugene and Mary Anne.

"There," said Bentley. "You're not oppressed. The police are here for your protection and to enforce the rules against unauthorized demonstrations. All institutions must be guided by certain rules, which must be respected if order and security are to be maintained—"

"This university is a big oppressive monster!" Eugene shouted in his face.

Bentley did not flinch, yet his smile went from calm sympathy to wounded frown. "How can that be?" he asked, spreading his arms wide as if bestowing a blessing. "BSU provides you with one of the best educations in the state."

"It's a goddamn factory turning out passive consumers. It doesn't give us anything. All we do is sit! Sit and listen and absorb and flush it out like toilet training. We're as empty as when we first came. University's lost all its moral authority because of money. Education's all about money—"

"Right on!" Mary Anne chimed in. "Money is evil."

"Your tuition is among the five lowest in the state," said Bentley, still looking hurt. "It's among the best buys in the country—"

"Ahrrr. . . You don't get it! It's everything! Grades, jobs, the draft, the war, racism. . . fitting in, discipline, success, hard work, artificial culture, empty ceremony, hypocrisy, sexual repression— everything."

Bentley shook his head. "Young man, you are becoming far too upset. After that fine speech, you are now verging on the inarticulate. You're far too emotional. Your statements are becoming illogical—"

"Fuck you!"

"Yeah, fuck you!" Mary Anne added with great sincerity.

"Profanity hardly counts as an argument."

"We don't want any more arguments. Arguments are bullshit designed for public relations."

"Yeah, bullshit."

"What do you want?"

Vico hesitated. "I said. . . what I said."

"Perhaps you would like a personal meeting with President Craven himself? To discuss your demands?"

The questions took Eugene by surprise. "Me?"

"Yes. The young lady too, if she wishes. I'm quite certain President Craven would like to meet with students of your obvious intellectual abilities. He's quite open to change. He's with it, you know."

"He'll listen to me?"

"Oh yes, he's very good at rapping with your generation."

"Wow!" Eugene sounded like a child who had just been told that he would get to spend an entire day at the circus, not as a spectator but as an actual participant, a clown.

"I'm certain that President Craven will want to establish some sort of official commission to examine your concerns. I'll suggest to him that you be appointed the chairman of such a commission, a special commission on student unrest at BSU."

Eugene glanced at Mary Anne, who was looking very confused. He drew a long breath and thrust out his chest.

"I've always said that moral authority is greater than physical force. I've always believed in the dialectical laws of history. Our negation has negated the negation. . . We've won. The administration is beginning to crumble."

Bentley smiled.

"Mary Anne, you don't need to come. You go to the Union and tell the Party that President Craven and I will be meeting to discuss our revolutionary demands. Sheer force yielded to the higher power of truth."

"You do have a beautiful speaking voice," said Dean Bentley.

"Oh Eugene," Mary Anne sighed, "You're just. . . historic!"

"Vico's turned traitor," Anita declared. She took a long drag on her cheroot and glared around the table, fixing each of them in turn with her mesmerizing eyes.

Tom shrugged. "Well, accidents have been known to happen. I seen a few in Nam. Officers nobody liked. West Point shits. Dopes that could get you killed. Stuff happens to 'em—"

Anita reached over and patted his hand. "No, no, not unless the Masters order it."

"And just when are these Masters gonna order something?" asked Randal sarcastically.

Anita frowned at him through the smoke. He scowled back, but only for a few seconds. Lowering his head, he mumbled: "I mean, wow, here it is December and we ain't done nothin'. Vico's an ass, but at least he did something—"

"Yeah, he done betrayed the revolution," Vesta snorted. "Sold out to the establishment is what he done. Gone and spilt to Craven."

"Then, revolutionary justice should prevail, just like the *Catechism* says."

"I'd have to agree," said Paul of the long ears. He looked away from Anita. "As long as the Masters are silent, I think we need to follow the principles of democratic centrism. The Central Committee should vote and act in the name of the entire People's Will."

Randal snickered. "Man, don't you jus' love that phrase, democratic centrism—"

Anita slammed her fist on the table. Except for Tom, everyone else cringed.

"THE MASTERS HAVE SPOKEN!"

Randal whispered: "They have? How? When—?"

"As they always have. Unexpectedly, unannounced, at night. In fact, the very night of that strike. I'm walking near Oakwood Park, and suddenly he's there. Only I can see him. They've chosen to appear only to me. I recognized him by his hooded cloak, his great height, and glowing eyes. They never show their faces. He spoke, and I went home and wrote it all down, exactly as he'd recited it, as though he dictated it as he stood over my shoulder."

She took a drag from her cheroot and exhaled like a dragon breathing fire. She was reading something in the swirling cloud above the table.

Randal blurted: "What the hell did he tell you?"

Anita's eyes swept the table. "Where's Cathy Butcher?"

"Wha. . . at?"

"The entire Central Committee ought to be here to receive the Masters' instructions. Where's Cathy Butcher?"

"Randal should know. He's got the hots for her," said Vesta.

"I ain't seen her for a month!" shouted Randal. "And she's nothing special to me, just another revolutionary comrade. She's a good cook, though—"

"She ain't been around here since early November," said Tom. "She's smart. Well-read. Got her own ideas. Maybe she got tired of all the games."

Anita glared at him but remained silent.

"Ain't nobody seen her," said Vesta. "I hear she ain't been to any of her classes."

There was a long interval of silence, rare for such vital meetings.

"It must be true, as the Masters said." Anita reached into the thick folds of her winter poncho and brought forth a folded piece of paper. With great care, as if she handled a brittle ancient relic, she unfolded the page and placed it on the table.

"I've pondered the meaning of this communication, its higher meaning. Revolutionary communication is always indefinite, of course, allegorical in a certain sense, to confuse the superficial System."

The others gave her nervous looks. She never sounded like this, almost as if—unbelievably—she were afraid.

"I wrote it after the encounter. No thoughts of my own guided my pen. *He* wrote through me."

She gazed at the crumpled page.

"My little poem begins with a chorus of women, as in Greek tragedy, but only women, women alone. They sing about longing and cherishing, all quite indefinite, but hinting at higher, sublime experiences. Some birds join them. The birds have red feathers, which are symbolic of revolution, naturally. They also sing indefinitely, though very profoundly. Then a wise lizard-like creature appears, dragging itself along on stubby legs. It gazes up into the heavens and pronounces the following sacramental words:

Be not deceived by Seekers
Hungry ghosts are they
That devour innocent flesh
As Clouds hasten to swallow the sun."

"The Clouds!" exclaimed Vesta. "I thought they're FBI."

"How can they be?" said Randal. "Pigs closed 'em down. They was nothing but another Manson family."

Vesta snickered: "Ain't you heard? Rumor has it they're hiding out in Oakwood and the pigs done searched the woods but they ain't found the loonies."

"Those verses were brilliant," Paul said to Anita. "Higher poetry than all poetry heretofore and forever. For the higher man—"

"Sounds crazy, like something that pot-head Jerry would write," said Randal.

"Where's Cathy?" Anita repeated her earlier question.

Vesta's half-closed eyes grew wide with shock. "You mean she's gone and joined those crazy Clouds?"

"Worse. Much worse." Anita thrust the poem at her. "Can't you read? Are you stupid? Hungry ghosts devour innocent flesh. Despite what Billy-goat Boots over here would have liked, Cathy was an innocent, a virgin."

"A higher virgin," Paul added.

"So. . . you're saying that the Clouds are really a bunch of Mansons? Not the FBI?"

"Seekers are deceivers. Capitalist pig Amerika is the land of deceivers. The bourgeois state knows no morality. All its talk about morality is double-speak. It is the most heartless and cold death-machine in history. The Establishment will use any means to maintain itself in power. It will take up any weapon. Amerika is not a government of the people or for the people. Amerika is nihilism incarnate, the emptiness of absolute moral negation behind the mask of ethics and decency. What sane country would napalm villages of poor people for whatever reason? The Establishment will adopt any evil to accomplish its ends."

"Far-out—" Randal breathed.

"Profound," said Paul.

"When the pig nation speaks, you know that the opposite is true."

"So they are FBI?" asked Vesta. "I'm confused."

"Are you deaf? I've said it."

"Said what?"

"THE CLOUDS ARE MANSON-CULT FREAKS MANIPULATED BY THE ESTABLISHMENT TO KILL REVOLUTIONARIES."

"Wow! Blow my mind!" Randal blurted.

"Don't you see the pig-plot? It's like those California freaks. FBI, maybe even CIA, recognized just how they could use them to discredit the revolution. They might have even cooked it up themselves, but I don't think the Establishment has the imagination. The cult grew by itself, and the pigs finally realized how they could use it—"

"You mean the FBI manipulates the Clouds? This sounds pretty far-fetched," said Tom.

"BELIEVE IT! You, Tom, of all people, should recognize government deception."

Tom sighed: "That's Nam. Wait till historians get their hands on it. They'll find the truth."

"I still don't see what all this has to do with Cathy?" said Vesta.

"Look at it this way: Assholes like Vico pose no problem to the Establishment. They're easy to manipulate. But dangerous revolutionaries like the People's Will are tougher to handle. The System can't dig purity, integrity, and, uh, uncompromising decency. What it can't corrupt it must destroy. The pigs get frustrated. They can't infiltrate us. We haven't done anything to give them an excuse to suppress us. So here comes some stupid mystical, flower power, drugged, psychedelic-Bolshevik pseudo-religion of loonies that ain't no threat to the Establishment 'cuz their senses have been stripped by supernatural wanderings."

"Now there are two ways of using these pseudo-Eastern psychedelic Bolsheviks. Let 'em alone till they do something crazy that discredits the revolution. The California pigs let Manson have his little nihilist bloodbath and then said: 'See what happens when somebody rejects good bourgeoisie order and Christian morality? Revolutionaries are nothing but wicked criminals.'"

"Control the leadership, set up their own guru-swami who's really FBI, leaving the rest of the membership nothing but ignorant stooges. Then, after the FBI guru-swami leads them into crime, make a big show of repressing the thing. But since the guru's their man, they let him 'escape' so that he's free to work his mischief."

"Which is?" Tom asked.

"TO HUNT DOWN AND KILL REAL REVOLUTIONARIES!"

"Ridiculous. Manson's in jail and Sharon Tate was no revolutionary."

Randal shook a fist at Tom: "Not ridiculous at all! Manson's double is in the slammer. And Cathy Butcher was a revolutionary saint. Pure and uncorrupted."

"The Clouds killed Cathy? That's hard to believe," said Vesta.

"Believe it. And believe this: They're coming after the rest of us. Amerika has no fucking morality. Ever read the Bible? I mean, not have someone read it to you. God sanctions every conceivable crime known to man, and then some. So we need theologians to explain away the tough parts—oh, that's a metaphor, oh, God's mysterious ways, but it all comes out for the best. When Amerika needs God to be a real shit and get people to act in ways not even a self-respecting rat would dream of, why, the worst crimes become suddenly moral, absolutely moral, 'because God said so.' Amerika is under God, right? The Establishment has got to pretend its crimes are moral. So we have Christian Amerika. We can obliterate whole countries. Slaughter entire peoples—napalm 'em like I said."

"How do these Masters know all this?"

"THEY KNOW!" Anita's tone indicated that no further argument on this point would be permitted. Tom shrugged but looked doubtful. The others looked as if each of them had suddenly seen a divine revelation in the dark nimbus of smoke around her head.

Paul said: "Well then, to quote Engels, what is to be done?"

"It's Lenin, asshole. Where's that little Hindu kid?" Anita sounded exasperated again.

"He was supposed to infiltrate the Clouds. Wasn't he?"

"You can't be serious," Tom said. "He's just a little kid. You didn't actually expect him to do something—"

"Kid's confused," Randal, added, "been hanging around Jerry Wolfe. Brain's fried. Probably thinks he lives in Middle Earth. He was at Vico's strike, and I had to yank the little shit outta there before the cops got 'em. He's really hopeless, man."

"Confused or not, the People's Will has need of such," Anita declared. "We will play the piggy game. Exactly as the Master ordered."

"Play what?"

"We will infiltrate the Great Truth Cloud ourselves and cut off its head."

"Cut off its head? You're saying assassinate that guru person. . . uh, what's his name?"

"Goodjohn Saccidanada. The Divine Woo-Woo."

"You want Sylvian Matreya to kill the guru-FBI man?" Tom asked.

"You will train him."

"Brilliant," Randal cried. "Who would suspect the little shit? It's genius—"

"The White Order is the genius of this age," said Anita.

"It's nuts," Tom whispered.

"Can you train him?" Anita fixed him with her most soul- draining stare.

Tom seemed to wilt. Puppet-like, he nodded his head. "I guess. . . but the kid's a real idiot."

"The revolution has need of such."

"I'll try—"

"And you will succeed. This will be the first great revolutionary act of the People's Will. We will strike a blow against the evil Establishment, the first of many. We will execute Goodjohn Saccidanada for his crimes against the People."

Sylvian came home to Chicago for Christmas. He acted sullen and moody. He had very little to say, and when he did speak, he sounded like the computer Hal when the astronaut Dave shut it down. His dear parents found nothing strange in such behavior. Naturally, they insisted he go to Confession.

Disturbed by what he heard—a great many of the stories seemed more garbled than usual—Father Loeb gave him a severe sermon about the twin evils of drugs and Marxism. For good measure, he tossed in the sins of pro- miscuity and homosexuality.

The general theme of his lesson that Sunday was that such evils are Satan's appeal to the weakness of self-indulgence. Many people forgo the difficulties of self-discipline and blame society for all their ills. Many suf- fer from envy; they demand from society what they do not deserve, what they have not earned. Free love, for example, turned babies into a cash crop since most of those who became pregnant were unemployed and in need of assistance.

Sylvian tried to recall some of Anita's sayings about false conscious- ness. Or was it Vico? He couldn't remember. For the first time in his life, he actually tried to argue with Father Loeb (a sure sign of drug use). But his words got twisted and distorted, and he devolved into Hal-like silence.

The priest called Anita a deceitful woman, indeed, she was certainly a witch. Oh yes, Father Loeb was quite familiar with witchcraft, which was not something to scoff at even in this age of science. He proceeded to quote extensively from the *Malleus Maleficarum*: Women are more carnal as well as intellectually feeble; Eve was taken from Adam's rib, not his head (the proof of their rational deficiencies); they are sexually insatiable and therefore susceptible to demonic lovers; they are liars, for when a woman weeps she deceives.

His mood declined into morose apathy, as bleak as the Chicago winter. It was only lightened by the news that he'd received the highest grade in the Relativity Seminar and thus would be allowed to study Quantum Mechanics with Professor Olaffsoon. Hallerman had given him a "c" even though he had not turned in a single page of "doing-philosophy."

But what did physics and philosophy have to do with the revolutionary abyss into which he gazed? The void, as Hallerman quoted (never revealing his source), gazed back. He made it sound as if he'd invented the phrase. Sylvian actually experienced it.

As his thoughts grew darker, the skies more ominous with the gathering of revolutionary clouds, a strange thing happened. One day Father Loeb commented to Lorraine how much lighter little Sylvian looked. Had he had taken a bath?

There seemed to be a bright glow around him. Neither Lorraine nor Leon noticed anything different about their youngest son. He remained an embarrassment, the family misfit. He was their special child.

BOOK II

Spring Semester, 1970

INTERLUDE

Memo

To: BSU Students, Faculty and Staff
From: H. Richard Craven, President

WELCOME BACK TO CAMPUS IN THE NEW DECADE

All indications indicate that the 1970s will be a decade of momentous change. We, the BSU Administration, fervently pray to God that it will be a decade of peace and progress for all people.

We must not ignore the difficulties of the past year: The War in Vietnam, and student protests against that War, the problem of racism that still lingers at the fringes of society, the upheavals in culture and values, and though it pains me to report, the demonstrations that occurred on our own beloved campus.

I would be remiss not to note that college students who oppose the War are pampered and ungrateful bums, thugs and hoodlums, and such as these have always plagued good people.

Happily, we must celebrate the triumphs of American-Christian values. Who among us did not feel the thrill of patriotic pride when on July 20, at 4:17 p.m., the Eagle landed on the moon? The plaque the astronauts placed on that desolate surface unarguably symbolized the most significant technological achievement in human history and the most profound hope of the human species: "We come in peace for all mankind."

Let us reflect upon this marvelous achievement—an American achievement—-the greatest in human history. Does it not clearly demonstrate that despite protest, our American way of life represents the pinnacle of human accomplishment? The lunar landing illustrates all that is right about America. It incarnates in one glorious moment, those timeless values of competition, and spirituality.

Let us always remember that we are an exceptional, beloved nation under God. We are a beacon of freedom, which is symbolized by the landing of the Eagle. What sane person would deny the fact of the greatness of America blazed in the heavens in July? History will surely say the year 1969 surpasses 1492.

As we return to campus in the new decade, let us not forget, amid the tumult of hysterical voices, that our education, interwoven with the righteous moral values of American culture, has provided and will always provide the skills and strength to solve any problem and meet any challenge. Young people fortunate enough to attend BSU do not wander aimlessly in an intellectual wasteland as they do in so-called elite institutions. Here they acquire direction and purpose, and, ultimately, changeless spiritual values.

WELCOME BACK

(Memo in rough draft, to be released and published in the first number of Hinnom Valley's newspaper, The Valley Voice, January 1970.)

A Muslim Commentary on Aristotle's *Physics*:

Thus, we at last, come to the conclusion of our Commentary on Aristotle's *Physics*. Before we pass to the *Metaphysics*, let us pause and reflect upon the difficult ground which we have recently traversed.

The Faithful are commanded by Allah (Blessed be HE) to study nature. The visible world is Allah's garden. All things exist by the Will of Allah.

Believers are rightfully thankful for the wisdom of the Greeks. Indeed, Aristotle is the Philosopher, and his *Organon* is the highest expression of human reason. It is the sharp tool of logic we require to weed the garden. We see the chain of causes and conditions on the earth and in the heavens. Aristotle tells us why heavy bodies fall downward to the earth, why wood floats on water, why fire rises in air, why the heavenly bodies, made from aether, the fifth element, maintain their eternal rotation. We grasp the four causes that operate beneath the lunar sphere. We recognize the essential nature of deduction, which proceeds by necessity from established premises. We possess the categories of logic, the iron laws of reckoning called syllogism.

We can wield these implements like a smith's hammer to smash superstition and conquer ignorance.

Let the Believer beware! Aristotle is intoxicating.

It could readily come to pass that a people made drunk by Aristotle would be tempted to set themselves against Allah. They might even strive to usurp the Divine Throne and in this act of Shatan destroy the earthly garden. For what sane man would risk his life to climb a high mountain merely to study its barren face, or to extract minerals for mere material wealth, or to visit a dead place solely to boast of the journey? Such a one would be pitiful, driven insane by The Philosopher. One must climb to God. One must gaze upon the universe as the product of God's holy creativity.

Believers, remember the story of the sage Abu Sa'id and the philosopher Ibn Sina when they met in a bathhouse.

Abu Sa'id asked if a weighted body seeks the center of the earth as Aristotle says. And when Ibn Sina said that this was true, the sage took a heavy metal vase and threw it into the air.

But instead of falling, the vase remained suspended. "Why is this?" asked Abu Sa'id.

Ibn Sina answered that natural motion would most certainly require the fall of the vase to the earth, and according to Aristotle, some violent *force* must be keeping the heavy thing suspended in the air.

"What is this violent *force*?" asked the sage.

Ibn Sina replied that it had to be the *force* of the sage's soul (*mail nafsani*—psychic force) that has acted upon the vase.

"Yet, the vase does not fall."

Ibn Sina had to admit that yes, this is very odd.

"Then purify your soul," commanded Abu Sa'id, "so that you can do the same!"

Abu al-Mashriqijah, "Commentaries on the Philosopher and His Followers," 1305, Bukhara; translated and edited by Ibrahim al-Rashd, Professor of Logic at Brunswick State University, in *The Islamic Doctrine of "al-tawhid,"* BSU Press, Hinnom Valley, 1968.

FOURTEEN

The Outer Limits

SYLVIAN NEVER FELT WARM at home, even in the summer. And this was winter.

A snowstorm resumed its assault on the city of Chicago. The storm had let up around noon; by four in the afternoon, a second arctic wave swept the city sending frigid air off Lake Michigan and into the faces of miserable Chicagoans. The second surge hit harder than the first, freezing train tracks with its biting wind.

Mother had gone to St. Stanislas. Father was busy at the bindery. Sylvian sat alone in the spaciously freezing mansion near the lake. Tomorrow, Saturday, he'd be leaving for Hinnom Valley. With spring semester looming, Sylvian, anxious, packed his things a week prior.

He sat in an over-stuffed green chair in front of a miserable black and white TV. Everything familiar now seemed strange. The dark wooden floors, the rusting frames of faded photographs portraying people he could not remember, the bleeding crucifix above the TV—his former life eroded bit-by-bit and his identity evaporated with it. Blank, uninhabited spaces opened, ragged holes tore apart his memory. Perhaps they'd always existed, and he'd been lying to himself to bridge them—to bridge the yawning gaps with stories he told about himself.

Sylvian was becoming a fable. Soon he'd be unbelievable.

Something, someone else was beginning to manifest. This something was something strange. Maybe someone. It was alien, uncanny, a being without a soul, a body without blood, flesh without spirit. The road to rebirth was splitting, however, slowly dividing, becoming two paths: Pearl and Anita.

Sylvian was fading. All that exists deserves to perish. Or was it as that French Jesuit, de Chardin would say, *everything that rises must converge.* Sylvian had found Pierre Teilhard de Chardin by accident one weekend. He'd become lost in the stacks, trying to find his way back to his coherent (and safe) physics books. The humanities books seemed to have been written in a different language than the hard sciences. Ironically, de Chardin's book, poorly translated, had caught Sylvian's eye and the phrase, he thought, could only derive from the language of science and logic. So what was it doing here? Another unlooked-for signpost along the way? But to where?

The TV was on. He hardly paid attention. Last year they'd yanked *Star Trek* off the air, claiming it a colossal failure. Naturally, they lied. All too often, the show questioned — merely questioned! —the legitimacy of the System. So they repressed the threat. Delusion was universal, like a law of nature, like universal gravity.

"Oppressed, repressed, suppressed. . ." Sylvian muttered.

Suddenly the television filled a blank space (a void) on his mental graph. He heard the voice of the announcer, it was warning, something about control, being out of control. . .control. . . we are in control, the voice was saying. Of course they were.

"We are controlling transmission. We control the horizontal (the screen instantly snapped into a horizontal line). We control the vertical. We can change the focus from a soft blur and sharpen it to crystal clarity. For the next half hour sit quietly and we will control all that you see and hear (yeah, for your entire life). You are about to participate in a great adventure (delusion). You are about to experience the awe and mystery that reaches from the inner mind to. . . *The Outer Limits!* " Bourgeois false consciousness, Sylvian noted, Amerikan culture was totally, *The Outer Limits*).

The local channel, channel eighteen, played nothing but old re-runs of defunct programs. No longer able to garner sponsors, the very existence of TV programs like *Star Trek* depended upon the will of capitalism. *The Outer Limits* would soon follow. Anything that challenged the complacent herd grazing on platitudes had to be forbidden. The network can't send shows that promote thinking out into the public—they couldn't let the people think about thinking. It would confuse their message of control! Television: yet another oppressed class.

Sylvian focused on the story. What ignorant writers. Fundamental knowledge of idiot-mathematics and baby-physics would have ended the career of many a famous author- most so-called literary profundity based itself upon scientific illiteracy. Writers lied from ignorance.

The episode: "The Man Who Was Never Born."

The opening scene: A beautiful girl (a blonde-forest-nymph) has captured a frog near a pond.

A hideously deformed monster is watching from the woods.

OH NO!

Oakwood Park, Pearl, Goodjohn Saccidanada. Sylvian's mind wandered.

Focusing back on the screen, Sylvian watched as they cut to a commercial. He recalled one of Hallerman's sermons—lectures:

Capitalist propaganda, meant to make us aware of how dissatisfied we are without said product. Then came the feedback loop—the products were intended to also create—like God—a new need you didn't know you had. Now, you see that you *do* need what they are selling, and more of it. It was psychological warfare on the senses.

Sylvian glanced back at the screen. *The Outer Limits* jingle—cut to the image of a rocket ship accompanied with a voice drooling about the "lovely loneliness" among the stars.

The spaceship passes through an unidentified time barrier and lands upon future Earth, reminding Sylvian of his desolate memories.

The monster reappears and confronts the astronaut. It is earth and the is year 2148! But, protests the space-traveler, I left earth a mere month ago, February 3, 1963.

"Son-of-a-bitch!" Sylvian said aloud, his face lit by the silver glow.

Ah, says Mr. Ugly-but-Wise Monster of the Future, time and space are inseparable. You passed through a space-time convulsion.

At last. Somebody who knows a tiny bit of physics. Sylvian's old friends "t" and "S" fused just as Olaffsoon taught. Except what the hell is a "convulsion?" It hadn't been on the exam.

But there's more. The monster says that mutating microbes, developed by a certain Bertram Cabot Jr., destroyed humanity. His mother, a woman ironically named *Noel*, contributes to the end of all Christmases and births, holy or not. The monster says that humanity, too busy with going to the moon, neglected to notice the threat.

At this point in the story, an opportunity presents itself: We can go back through the barrier and change the past. We can find a gate back and kill this Cabot, thus, restoring order to the universe.

They try it but only the monster makes it back successfully, and the first person he sees is Noel collecting a frog in "Oakwood." She runs from him. And then the reveal; he is no monster. No scientist either. He lets the frog go free.

Now a twist, a *deus ex machina*, contrived, of course, but necessary: Now, the monster that is not *really* a monster can change into a handsome man employing hypnotic suggestion. He comes upon a boarding house for students. He meets Noel. He's a professor of archaeology, he explains. She is Noel.

The terrible truth strikes him harder than a physical blow: She will be the mother of Bertram Cabot Jr., the agent of humankind's destruction!

The monster-man says: "I'm too early. . ."

"I'm too early," Sylvian repeated the words. "I'm too early." He began to sweat, and his heart beat faster. "I'm too early—" And then, by some odd, unconscious association of scattered ideas, he remembered Pearl's stupid question: "Why did the Matreyas come from Europe to America?" Why? "Did they come too early? Because I'm too early?"

Meanwhile, the show resumes with the predictable triangle. Noel falls for the future beast-hypnotist from the future, rejecting the father of the evil genius, Bertram Cabot.

The monster is torn. He can't kill her. He loves her.

They flee her wedding and hide out in the park (always the goddamn park!). He tells her everything. I'm hideous, he protests. But no, she responds, there is no ugliness in you. Take me with you, she begs. It is you I love, I want, I need.

We cannot change destiny, protests the monster.

Sylvian shivered. Cannot change destiny—the words kindled something inside him. All at once, he felt cold and feverish just as he'd felt in the park that day tripping on Jerry-beer.

He could barely stand to watch. There is no glorious future, protests the monster sadly, only a dark and empty road leading to misery and despair. We will make a better future, says Noel, we can change destiny.

She's right, of course. Taking her aboard the rocket ship, monster-man and his Noel pass through the barrier, changing destiny. They create a world into which he was never born. The monster that was never born. . . fades away as do all retired monsters, Hallerman might have said. The devil vanishes, and she sits alone in this newly created space in time, weeping. All that remains is this emptiness—and her memory of their love.

A disembodied voice fills the void: "If you move one pebble from the beach, you change everything." Love can change the future.

"Oh, Pearl!"

He cried alone like poor Noel. He could not say how long he wept only that the darkness of the snowy winter dusk had overwhelmed the weak light.

Then, he cursed Pearl and her Goodjohn. He cursed his parents, the Church, the schools, the Establishment, the Clouds, the idiotic television with its capitalist brainwashing.

And just as abruptly he began to laugh like a madman. What shit! The story assumed that the entire causal chain of existence could be reversed: The future, which was in some way already determined, could yet exert a causal influence upon the past. Was the past an indeterminate time dimension? The past could be altered. The past was an array of probabilities that determined the future and could be changed by some future event—the birth of the man who was never born. What a paradox. A man who was and was not born—whose unborn love changed the world. The causal string of events flowing backward, in retrograde—future to past—introverted could only mean that time is an illusion, a lie.

"Why did the Matreyas come to America?"

Sylvian turned off the TV and staggered down the dark corridor leading to the stairs.

He passed Karl's room. The door was closed. Lorraine forbade anyone entrance while Karl was at war, even Leo. It was due to something an old Polish grandmother had told her long ago: leaving things just as they are would bring him home alive. Disturb a single dust-mote and all things change, from existence to non-existence.

Sylvian felt a sudden urge to break the superstitious taboo and violate the sacred place. Karl had always been mean to him, occasionally cruel. Some memories hung on with stubborn determination.

The door was unlocked.

A faint light shone through the room's single window, the reflection of a street lamp off newly fallen snow. It drew a path to the large oak bed, which like the rest of the furniture was draped by dark blue cloth bearing a coat of arms.

Sylvian followed the path of light to the bed. He sat down and gazed out the window. Shifting his weight, he noticed that the bed rocked a bit. Glancing down, he saw that two bedposts sat upon two thick leather-bound books.

Now here was something odd: books in Karl's room. Karl never read books (except the Bible, and Sylvian doubted that).

He gently extracted the two volumes from their service as bed supports and examined them in the pale light. They appeared extremely old, fat leather-clad, loose-leaf folios, similar to old notebooks, or an artist's sketchpad.

Sylvian peered at the worn leather of the top volume. Something was engraved there, a faded golden form, yet still decipherable. It was the figure of a seated man, legs crossed, one hand raised in a kind of blessing while the other touched the ground. At his feet sat a tiny bird-like figure, resembling a dwarf or an elf.

He carefully opened the leather cover. Yellow pages, brittle and crumbling, fell to the floor. A few crackled into dust as he frantically tried to gather them up and rearrange them. The writing was small, a tiny, flowing script and not in English.

The title page carried the title, which he made to be something like: *Lebensphilosophie und das Lebenswelt. . . Bodenbeschuffheit und. . . Weidergeburt dem . . .Karl Janski-Metteyya (Sumedha)—*

Was this Karl's writing?

With great care, he closed the volume and took up its twin. The script was identical, hand-written, but this time in English. Parts of the title had faded away as with the German version (Sylvian remembered German from one of his physics books). The English title was, however, different from the German. In English, it read: *The Great Renunciation of the Bodhisattva.*

He turned the page and read from the text.

My father—so began the first page—of old Polish nobility was a Deist and revolutionary who resisted to his final breath the hated tyranny of the Russian Tsar—

The rest of the page faded into undecipherable scribbling. Of course, the light was terrible for reading, yet Sylvian realized he would never be able to decipher it with the best of lights. He turned the page and read:

. . .often warned me to guard my sanity against the intoxicating fumes of superstitious religion with its false promises, as well as various other forms of irrationality by which the mass of people is easily deluded by those things they understand least—to paraphrase—

Farther down the page, it read:

Alas, the valiant Count died in 1863, leading a cavalry charge against Russian cannon.

Voices came from the front of the house. His parents were home. Gathering the books under his arms, he slipped out of the room, closed the door, and as invisible as a thought glided up the stairs to his tiny closet of a bedroom.

He sat up all night reading, and even the next day during his long bus ride through the frozen northern countryside to Hinnom Valley.

New myths were born in those yellow folio sheets, and new memories filled the gaps in the old. Sylvian Matreya felt reborn, as if the memoir was about him. He recognized a version of himself within those antique pages.

On Sunday, the First of February, the fourth week of classes at BSU, they discovered the frozen and naked body of Cathy Butcher.

Children sledding in Oakwood Park found the corpse. They'd been using the hill on the bank of the lagoon, starting from the base of the von Jahn oak and sliding out onto the frozen surface. Their momentum carried them across the lagoon to the edge of the wood.

The kids swept the snow cover off the ice to increase their speed. Most people believed that the lagoon froze out along the banks except the one bordering the wood where it suddenly dropped off (nobody knew how deep). The kids spied the frozen body right under their feet.

She lay curled in a fetal position, completely naked, her skin a shade of bluish-brown but otherwise looking as if she were peacefully asleep. She was suspended in ice no more than two feet deep. They had to use saws to get her out. The children marveled at how alive she appeared.

An autopsy determined that Cathy Butcher had been dead since December. In the ice, the corpse, frozen had not started to decompose.

What was the cause of death? Her lungs were filled with water. Officially, then, the cause of death was drowning. The body evidenced no signs of violence. The autopsy, however, did discover evidence of drugs, including alcohol. The police refused to release any more details, although the papers said that she'd had sex just prior to death. All remaining evidence—if such existed— remained locked away.

A search of the lagoon found nothing (and no one) except for Cathy's clothes. They were discovered beneath an old pine, neatly folded—jeans, sweater, coat, boots with the socks rolled up inside—as if she'd deliberately disrobed and gone swimming. The tiny forest appeared deserted. Not one human footprint marred the virgin snow. The police found no sign of life, no animal tracks, not even a breeze.

The week after the funeral a Butcher family lawyer issued a lengthy statement—in fact, a diatribe—vehemently denying suicide, which the local newspaper had reported, noting that Miss Butcher seemed to suffer from some depression according to her classmates. The official statement, instead, blasted illicit drugs and immoral sexual license—free love, it lectured, meant freedom from responsibility, which was the beginning of insanity. Such evils had destroyed the young life of a beautiful, loving child whose future was most certainly bright and hopeful, coming as she did from such an outstandingly successful and talented family.

The statement concluded with an announcement that BSU had established a scholarship in the name of Cathy Butcher and Butcher Brewery. The Butcher family dedicated the scholarship to the promotion of a drug-free America.

The coroner's office finally ruled that Cathy's death was accidental, but due in no small part to the harmful effects of illegal drugs, as well as irresponsible behavior condoned and indeed stimulated by certain anarchist fringe-groups of today's youth culture (those "pampered and ungrateful bums")—which is how the reporter chose to paraphrase the report.

Naturally, rumors about Oakwood Park grew exponentially, as the old Sylvian might have phrased it.

"Anita's been askin' 'bout you, Sam," said Jerry Wolfe. Jerry had arrived back on campus two weeks into the semester. He had signed up for Professor Hallerman's seminar on epistemology. He was sure to get an "A," he said.

Sylvian got up from his bed, walked to his desk, and brushed his fingers over two full leather-clad volumes.

"That person's gone—"

"Hey, man, what're them books? Looks like Bilbo's memoirs—"

"Never mind! Don't touch 'em. Get your hands cut off if you do. They're. . . about making shit that'll blow you away if you goof up one tiny thing."

"Far-out."

"Don't care 'bout Anita anymore."

"Huh?" Jerry had to think for a few minutes. "She cares 'bout you, 'cuz, shit, man, you ain't gonna believe this, but the fucking FBI is killing revolutionary fighters."

"Murdering bastards. Who'd they get?"

"Cathy Butcher, man! Fucking pigs kilt Cathy."

"No."

"You ain't gonna believe this neither, but Anita says they's using the Great Truth Cloud. That Goodjohn son-of-a-bitch is like some kinda Timothy Leary, some sex-crazed, hypnotist swami, but it's a cover. Goodjerk's a government stooge using hippies and freaks to infiltrate radical parties, man. Some kinda twisted, evil Gandalf—"

"No—"

"Oh man, she was a beautiful revolutionary chick even though she came from the oppressor class."

"What 'bout drugs, Frodo?"

"Huh? Shit, man, Cathy was one of the cleanest people I knew—"

"No. You."

"Me?"

"This one of your trips to Middle Earth, Frodo?"

Jerry became indignant. "I toll you, Anita says it! The High Elves done told her."

"Are the High Elves stoned too?"

"Man, you gotta believe it. They ain't stoned. They're naturally high, all the time. It's 'cuz they eat elvish bread. The elves done told it to her. The Establishment is going to murder us all."

"So?"

"So? Ain't you heard nothin'! They'll come for you too, Sam. So we gotta go to Mordor and destroy the One Ring."

"What's that mean?"

"Me and you. Frodo and Sam. Infiltrate the Great Truth Cloud and kill Goodjohn Saccidanada."

"She wants us to kill the groovy guru?"

"Yup. Revolutionary justice."

"Revolutionary justice. Everything that exists deserves to perish."

"Right-on! Sam, you're back. You had me worried there—"

"Yup."

Later that night in Crawley Library Sylvian puzzled over the week's lectures on Quantum Mechanics. It was incomprehensible to him why Planck had first adopted that constant h, and thrown this bomb into the seamless energy equations. Sure, they didn't work in the high frequencies. But that could be due to experimental error. Olaffsoon had been awfully vague about the entire thing. Sylvian got lost in a physics class for the first time in his life.

The math was easy. Sylvian's old math-mind was as sharp as ever. He made his way with ease through the friendly wave equations, down to the familiar energy expressions. The physical meaning was crazy. Planck declared that continuous energy came in bundles, *quanta*, definite sized bundles, some bundles but not others, and interacted with matter as particles of energy, in bits, like static frames that comprise a movie film. Outside the particulate body of matter, however, energy remained continuous.

It seemed like magic, as when the priest elevated the bread and wine of the Eucharist and the elements became, in reality, the body and blood of Christ. He never understood the magic of the Mass. What on earth (and in the heavens) were sensate accidents such as bread and wine?

Did not any divine intervention into nature destroy the conservation of energy? In Sylvian's mind, the conservation law was an abstract mathematical object. Unlike God, Planck's magic worked mathematically. Experimentally, even with transubstantiation, the bread always remained bread, the wine remained wine. He couldn't grasp the magic of mere words. Father Loeb blamed his underdeveloped *sensus Divinitatis*. His family reacted differently: Karl called him an idiot; his father beat him.

Sylvian gazed out of the tall windows into a black campus night broken only by the dull glow of street lamps.

His mind began a journey, leaving childhood behind. As always, these strange night journeys took him to the leather tomes, to the incomprehensible memoir of his grandfather Karl. Surrendering to the dark spirit of temptation, he slipped the English version out from beneath his physics book and commenced to read, yet again, the words written therein.

FIFTEEN

The Memoir of Karl Matteyya

IT IS IMPOSSIBLE FOR me to reproduce the precise words of this ridiculous memoir. The translation cannot be precise. What follows was communicated to me orally, not at Confession, I might add. All I can say about what follows is thus have I heard:

The memoir begins with this pronouncement:

> I have two souls in one breast, and yet am I soulless. I am a citizen of the East and the West yet at home in neither. I am the son of Count Kalka Janski-Matteyya and yet I am a Tartar changeling. I have been ill for years, and yet I am the most robust of men. I am made of solid matter, and I am invisible.
>
> Herein stands my story. Judge for yourself.
>
> My father's ancestral fief was located near the tiny village of Mniszek on Poland's most eastern march. The Polish Tsar Dimitry (named false-Dimitry by the Russians; we Poles believe that he was the true son of Ivan the Awesome) awarded the fief to my family in the seventeenth century.
>
> My father's family was staunchly Roman Catholic even though our territory had passed into the hands of the Orthodox Russians, and many nobles were encouraged to surrender to the straight path. Our family produced several parish priests, two Bishops, and three regular clergy—two Dominicans and one Jesuit.

My father Kalka broke the chain of tradition. He rejected the Roman Church, pronouncing it feudalized superstition. However, he did not become Orthodox since, as he once said, straight-thinking superstition was infinitely worse. He became what people called in those days a freethinker, ultimately a foe of all gods. Some say that because of my father's apostasy, our family was cursed. The sins of the Fathers are passed down to their sons as Moses wrote, through the generations, much as the Jews inherited the Savior's blood-curse upon themselves and their children.

Count Kalka Janski-Matteyya was the first of his line to attend the famous university at Koeingsberg. It transpired that there, in the very womb of Kantian philosophy, a doctrine that priests in those days labeled the logical outcome of Protestant heretical foolishness, the young impressible Polish Count became addicted to German idealism and, ultimately, revolution.

He was drawn into the *Burschenschaften*, the German fraternity system, which was nothing more than a society of organized drunkenness and riot. He joined the Turnverein, a gymnastic club.

And he practiced another sort of student exercise: he met a young, robust German Fraulein who served his *Burschenschaft* and who herself dreamed of someday meeting a dashing Catholic Polish nobleman—she being a rare Catholic in the Protestant north—and one happy evening the inevitable came to pass. *Amoris vulnus idem sanat qui facit.*

Her name was Flora Sumedha, and she became the Count's mistress for the duration of his years at the university. She was my mother.

Inconveniently, the young Count's future bride, patiently waited in Poland, which in those days was named the Grand Duchy of Warsaw. The Matteyya family had many years previously negotiated a contract of marriage with the Ukrainian gentry clan of Zinsky-Jagwain. As soon as the Count returned to Mnisek, despite his vehement protests, he married Petrovna Zinsky-Jagwain. Marriage, he often remarked, was the moral death of the proud soul. A married woman becomes notoriously reactionary, prone to the highest (and lowest) sublime nonsense, as every religious charlatan seems to grasp intuitively. Perhaps it has something to do with the children and the mother's fear for their safety.

My mother Flora followed her Count back to Mnisek where she, employed as a cook and a maid, ultimately became a governess to his legitimate children.

Anya Petrovna Zinsky-Jagwain, the new Countess Matteyya, was quite the opposite of Flora Sumedha. Flora's fine-boned waif-like appearance reminded one of a delicate bird or a garden fairy— fragile and as light as a soft breeze. Her gossamer tresses shone like the morning sunlight upon a silvery forest spider web glistening with dew—and here I'm quoting the Count's own words. Although unnaturally dark of skin, plainly due to the Mongols, said the old Polish women), Flora glowed like the golden sun.

The Ukrainian woman, on the other hand, resembled a rampaging boar bursting like a storm out of its dark lair deep in the Polish wood.

She shared Flora's dark complexion (the Count would often comment upon her alleged Mongol blood, referring to her as his *"Tartar Termagant").* But here all resemblance ceased, for her large-boned, lumpy body sprouted unusually dense hairiness, almost to the point of resembling a beastly pelt. The tight black curls covering her head had already begun to recede, even in her middle twenties. By the time of her old age, she wore a wig.

The Countess, then, was a very manly Ukrainian woman, possessed of heavy—some said brutal—features that paradoxically served as a kind of foil for her deep Orthodox sentimentality and mysticism.

While she appeared monstrous at first glance, no one having studied her for more than a few seconds could fail to be mysteriously drawn to her as though she cast a binding spell. This eerie attraction was due to her mesmerizing eyes, which were the lightest blue, resembling those dazzling skies that hung over the golden meadows of her beloved Ukraine. Many people, including the Count, swore that she could grab hold of you with that stare, drink your will, swallow your soul, drain vampire-like your very life force. She had the eye.

And, despite her repulsive appearance, she possessed an erotic magnetism, an almost demonic sexual attraction, acquired, no doubt, during some nocturnal witches' *Saturnalia.* Combined with such unnatural magnetism, dense flesh, including a beast-like pelt, she stirred within every man the very deepest archaic cravings, unnatural and brutal lusts from the dawn of the race, before the advent of civilization. Poor Count Matteyya often pondered this dangerous sexual force that she seemed to exercise over him effortlessly. He thought it another version of Russian slavery.

The Count never truly loved her. To his lasting regret, in moments of weakness, his desire for her became overwhelming.

Her fierce insatiable passion smothered and excited him at once. His lust sickened him for he was powerless to resist it. He felt as if his marriage allowed him to legally indulge in the most disgusting, forbidden, and depraved acts. Afterward, he hated himself, which made him despise her even more.

The Count thought of himself as a fly entrapped in a sticky web, slowly consumed by the most loathsome spider in creation. The very sight of her nauseated him. And yet. . .and yet. . .

The Count's father had arranged this terrible marriage. Thus did the old count and his son come to hate one another, for as the son resented what his father had forced him into, so the old Count could never understand the ideas and beliefs of his German-educated offspring.

Their festering hatred became tragic as it simmered in the cauldron of Polish nationalism.

Sylvian thought of Noel and the monster. "I'm too soon. . ." Other thoughts arose. Disjointed thoughts. . .like Planck's quanta: Was the revolutionary inheritance a destiny? A fate he could not deny? The memoir was that barrier in time and space. It seized and dragged him into the past. He'd never been able to concentrate on non-scientific writings. Until now.

The western branch of the family, the Janskies, loyal followers of Tadeusz Kosciuszko, had bravely fought the hated Russians during the insurrection of 1794 at Krakow. Terrible reprisals followed the Polish disaster, and the western Janskies were all but extinguished.

Then, in 1812, the old Count's brother—Kalka's uncle, Casmir—marched into Russia with Napoleon and died in the horrific carnage of Borodino. Later, during the war that began with the November uprising of 1830 in Warsaw, one of the few remaining Janski cousins perished with General Sowinski in the cemetery at Wola, where the Polish army died amid the graves of their ancestors.

The old Count of Mnisek had seen enough. He engineered a marriage between his son and the gentry of the Ukraine. The children, a fervently Orthodox Anya demanded, were to be raised following the strict Orthodox doctrine. The old Count sent his son to Koenigsberg, since a good German education generally brought with it a position in the vast bureaucracy of the Russian Tsar. By such moves, he hoped to exercise the fatal germ of rebellion from the blood of the family.

He shielded his son from politics. He said the study of philosophy was useless, a generally passive exercise for young men of a mild nature. He protected Kalka from all unpleasantness, all things melancholy: premonitions of death, sentimentality, the kind of wistful music that wearies the soul, anything he felt that might cause the boy to ponder the constitution of things, meaning, teleology, fate. Better to recite the formulas of the Church than to ruminate over unsolvable mysteries and not sleep at night. The Spirit of Curiosity, he observed, was not a good Spirit.

The old Count had not foreseen, nor could he, the influence of the French Enlightenment filtered through Kantian philosophy, which was like a mighty steed, like an ancient chariot, carrying young Kalka beyond his naive existence and out into the world of *Vorstellungen, Darstellungen*, and *Ding-an-sichen*.

Bitterness poisoned the old Count's final years, the resentment, which inevitably accompanies the eternal struggle of fathers and sons. He and his son no longer spoke to one another, for indeed, they no longer spoke the same language. He died facing the wall, weeping over the doomed house of Matteyya.

Thus did the son become the new Count Matteyya.

It did not seem to take the Ukrainian Countess long to realize that the strange German girl was more than a simple servant. Yes, the Count was discrete. Yes, he honored the marriage contract. They had children, three daughters. The Count made sure they were raised Orthodox and designated his legal heirs.

Anya's suspicions bred resentment, which mutated into anger, finally smoldering fury, not the least out of fear for her daughters; for in 1850, an unmarried Flora Sumedha gave birth to a son. She named the boy Karl.

I can assure you Countess Anya hated the boy and passed many hours ruminating on his demise. The servants whispered that she tried to poison the child. Naturally, Anya considered herself to be a sincere and observant woman of faith. Her faith, nevertheless, did not stop her from dabbling in the black arts. To the Countess, her hatred of the boy was righteous and she did not shrink from dark paths. The old Polish women of Mnisek crossed themselves and said they could perceive the signs of witchcraft in the Countess: she had "The Eye," and everyone knew that Ukrainian witches could be recognized by their beast-like appearance, as they commonly metamorphosed into physical copies of their demonic lovers.

Fortunately, let us say it was nothing short of a miracle, Karl survived. His father brought a priest into the house—strange behavior for a freethinker—and asked the good Father to perform an exorcism of the boy, should the priest sense an evil presence hovering over him. But upon his first encounter with Karl, the priest wept copiously.

The good Father never explained the reason behind his emotional reaction. He became the boy's tutor, which was the Count's apparent reason for keeping him about the place, despite the Countess's petty acts of meanness—the servants often heard her declare that Christ's Sermon on the Mount did not apply to cursed heretics.

The boy grew strong and healthy, and in a few years, the priest disappeared, mysteriously, and for good. In all the time that the priest lived with the family, he had revealed next to nothing about himself, except his to say his name was Father Khristopher.

As Karl grew older, people marveled at his intelligence and beauty. The old women of Mnisek said that young Karl held the Count's favor. Someday, they agreed, the Count would force the Church—the Bishop of Krakow who was a distant cousin—to declare Karl, the legitimate heir.

The three legitimate daughters—Yelena, Eridya, and Olga—grew to resemble their Ukrainian mother: dark, hairy, short, given to fat; spiteful, suspicious, and gloomy. Count Kalka had the most difficult time finding husbands for them. In truth, he succeeded only with the youngest, Olga, who was slightly less repulsive than the others. He married her off to a German named Frederick Buscher, a wealthy merchant's son and university professor in East Prussia, Konigsberg, I believe, reputed to have converted to Orthodoxy.. He later became a Christian apologist, especially in response to the Higher Criticism of Scripture, which he detested. Somewhat like the Countess, he possessed (or was possessed by) a meanness in his character, and he took pleasure in small, hurtful acts—and he felt fully justified by his sincere defense of God's sacred Truth.

The two other sisters stayed in the Matteyya house located near Krakow, haunting the old mansion like malignant spirits, wearing perpetual frowns and heavy black gowns, forever complaining, gossiping, causing small and trivial injuries when they were able, like two spiders bloated with rot and disease. They were very religious, of course, fiercely devoted to the figure of Christ. They decorated the walls with numerous icons, of which the majority illustrated the horrors of crucifixion, usually of a semi-naked Christ, bloodied and beaten, wearing his crown of thorns.

In the spring of 1860, our German mother contracted what the doctors said was cholera. In a few short weeks, following the diagnosis she died. The old women of Mnisek spread rumors: an evil spell cursed her, possibly poisoned, a demon had laid claim to her soul. She was like a saint, they said (in tears), martyred for her deep Catholic piety. A ridiculous story spread that the doctors attending to her final days found that she, like our Holy Mother, had died a virgin, which surely counted as a miracle, thus one step closer to sainthood. The Catholic Church gives Poland its strength. It can also be its greatest weakness.

Flora had been the only ray of light in the house of Matteyya, the Count's true love, his song of joy and springtime. How the ancient crones feared for the son!

Karl was now at the mercy of the terrible Ukrainian witch. The Count had yet to make him his legitimate heir. Instead, he sent young Karl to the University of Berlin, where Karl demonstrated brilliance in mathematics, and even surpassed his professors. Also, he possessed an inborn talent for music, like an essential piece of his physiology, a blessing of nature. His free-thinking father refused to label it God-given. Perhaps it was for this reason (God will not be mocked) Karl developed a strange speech problem, in Polish and German, which worsened as he rose to the heights of the mathematical heavens.

Then came that winter night at the beginning of the fateful year of 1863.

Countess Anya happened upon her husband in his study. He was reading (in the original French) Jean-Jacques Rousseau's *The Social Contract*. The Russian rulers of Poland, the "butchers of Warsaw," as the Count called them, banned Rousseau, and many other authors of the French *siècle de luminaire*, the Scottish Enlightenment too, especially David Hume, strictly forbidding the reputed atheist's books throughout the Tsar's territories.

The Count, reading in his study one dreary afternoon, had just come to the words: "tranquility is best found in prisons. . ."

when Anya lumbered into his study and planted herself between him and the warm fire.

Her bloated shadow smothered the page. He glanced up and frowned, praying to the God in whom he did not believe that the fire would spit a spark and ignite her greasy black gown. He often uttered such wishes aloud.

Anya screeched: "Now Rousseau is forbidden! The Christ only knows that we've enough problems with the young Germanized liberals who dare speak of rights and constitutions in the presence of our Father Tsar's governor."

"Enough, woman!" The count closed the book so as to prevent her noxious shadow from defiling the noble words of Jean-Jacques.

"We Poles only desire to be free, as any free people, possessed of country and our sacred Catholic rites—"

"You and your conspirators are regicides!" she howled, waving her arms and her bulky black shawl as if she were some gigantic carrion bird descending to pick a corpse. "I know them as well as I know you, my honest husband—

"Revolutionaries and Jacobins! Infected by Germans. Corrupted by French. And you would bring this disease into Holy Mother Russia."

The Count sprang from his chair as if stung by a wasp: "Lest you forget, my dear Countess, we live in Poland. You Tartars have brought a plague into our lands, you Cossacks and you Orthodox—"

She laughed an evil laugh: "I'm Ukrainian, Kalka, you ignorant Pole."

The Count spat back: "Ha! Part Tartar, part Swede, part Russian, part Pole—bastard daughter of a bastard people. Tartar termagant!"

"Ah, and what of your bastard? Will you send him to that German pig farm you call a university to learn the devil's doctrine from those false Illuminati who would plunge the world into chaos? What blasphemous nonsense did the old heretic priest bawl over him?"

"Father Khristopher?"

"Yes, *Father* Khristopher," Anya mocked. "The Romans are all heretics, polytheists, with their *Filioque* and their Anti-Christ Pope."

He glared at her. She would never understand. Too typical a Slav: servile to authority, superstitious, lazy yet crafty, stuffed with guile and cunning—and thus did she judge all others.

"The priest was a good man," he sighed, slipping back into his large chair. Suddenly and inexplicably, he felt exhausted. "And I belong to a literary salon of loyal university men who admire and read the philosophes. We read Americans too, Henry David Thoreau, for instance—"

"No, no, your priest was a heretic, and you are a cell of foul revolutionaries incubated in the hothouse of German atheistic philosophy, infused like a virus into holy Russia by the Jews. Your German whore was a Jew. You insist on stirring stagnant waters when your foolish people are best left in awe and fear of the *Little* Father. You Poles should remain slumbering peacefully in this tiny corner of his vast domains."

"Crushed by his vicious iron hand."

"Ah, so you do conspire."

He considered for a moment if the old crones were right; a terrible Ukrainian witch haunted his house. Somehow she knew that he had lied to her. He belonged to more than a mere literary group. The group was a front. The movement was political, and he'd become a member soon after dear Flora's death. Becoming "political" seemed to assuage his grief, and the movement was happy to enlist Count Matteyya of Mnisek among those revolutionaries, dedicated to cleansing Poland of the hated Russian plague. He found it strange, however, that young Karl showed no interest in politics. And he'd indeed often wondered if Flora were part Jewish. How did Anya know?

"It will be terrible," she whispered in a dark voice, as if pronouncing a doom.

"That which produces freedom from tyranny is always terrible."

"No," she rumbled, her words barely audible, like a storm at the furthest limits of hearing, " It's terrible for you, for your Jewish bastard and all his descendants. I foresee a curse upon all your family's revolutionaries down through the coming centuries, here and in the New World."

"Rubbish! Be gone you sinister creature of the border country. *You* are the bastard. Neither Polish nor Russian, not even Tartar. Bastards all."

"A curse," she repeated, her voice rising like the howling wind, "I foresee it. Become revolutionaries, and the earth itself shall refuse to harbor you and your descendants. Yes, yes, I see it. . . Regicides and assassins. . . and consequentially. . . deicide! First regicide, then deicide. God-killers. Your descendants will deny the immortal soul, and when the soul has vanished, so will

God. But the Christ will come again in the East, and you shall perish in the flames of his wrath."

"Begone!" he screamed at her. He leaped from his chair as if to strike her.

She fled from him at that moment, as does the darkness from the sunlight.

It was then that Count Kalka decided to make young Karl his legitimate heir, which he did the very next day.

In the dreadful year of 1863, the Polish revolutionaries, including Count Kalka Janski-Matteyya, rose up against the Russian Tsar and his oppressive government.

And Russian arms crushed their revolution.

Many tried to flee into nearby Prussia only to be betrayed by the Chancellor Otto von Bismarck who handed them over to the Russians. Some managed to escape to America. Russian anger and its accompanying thirst for vengeance fell primarily upon the Polish nobility. Officially, it was recorded that Count Matteyya of Mnisek died bravely charging a Russian field piece. But here I will relate an entirely different version of his death.

Local stories say that the noble Count escaped the slaughter. His horse fell in a hail of Russian bullets, but he was only knocked unconscious and buried beneath the bodies of his brave cavalry unit. He awoke hours later, just in time to see the city burning and to hear the cries and screams of the population, those poor unfortunate souls who'd fallen into the hands of the brutal Tartars.

Groggy and bleeding from minor wounds, the Count stumbled through the shadows of the winter twilight and found his way around the Russian lines. He dared not return to the Manor. The victorious Russian army was sure to sweep the area searching out Polish nobility. He felt nothing for the fate of his wife and daughters. The only grief he felt was for his beloved Poland.

As for Karl, he hoped that the boy would be clever enough to remain in Germany and pass himself off as German. Perhaps it was destiny that he spoke his mother's language as well as Polish —at least he did before his curious speech problem, which the Count believed was due to an evil spell. He remained convinced even though belief in such foolishness as supernatural curses clashed drastically with his dedication to reason.

A gray winter evening descended like a shroud upon the Polish woodlands, bringing a biting, sleety rain. The cold and wet fed the Count's anxiety for his son. Once more, against reason, he prayed that the boy would eschew politics entirely and become a man of the Church, perhaps a Priest.

Lost, cold, wet and exhausted, he unconsciously wandered off the road and slipped through the trees like some forest spirit, taking the shortest track back to the Matteyya estate. He had changed his mind. He sought his death.

To his great surprise, no Russian soldiers occupied the Manor. The high stone turrets glittered cold and lifeless as sleet turned to snow. Their windows were dark, and the massive oaken doors sealed shut. Not a thread of smoke drifted up from any of the five chimneys.

How could the Russians have missed it? How could they have ignored the estate of a known Polish revolutionary?

Treachery! The Tartar termagant, spying on him, informing on his circle, her revenge. Why didn't he see it? The battle before Mnisek. . . the wicked Tartars seemed to know our battle plan before we could execute it.

He staggered up the circular staircase. He'd lost his sword and revolver. He still bore his two-barreled, Italian-made, derringer hidden in his sash within his great coat. An assassin's weapon, the gun many in his circle carried.

He drew the weapon from his stained red sash and cocked the hammers. The caps were in place. Dual barrels were loaded.

He found her sitting before the grand fireplace in the main hall, in his favorite reading chair, staring into the pit, her gaze fixed upon heaps of cold ash. She held an Orthodox icon, one of Christ being taken down from the cross, surrounded by mocking Roman soldiers, Romans painted to look like Jews. Candles burned down on the table next to her, drenching his precious French books in hot wax, sealing them.

Like thunder from the Mount that Moses heard, Anya's voice crackled. Without turning her head, she said: "So, my faithless count, returned from your chastisement, have you? Tell me, noble lord, what have you learned? Have you repented your godless revolution?"

He was glad she did not stare at him with those soul-drinking eyes. Freezing and half-mad, he couldn't be sure of his self-discipline.

The large, throne-like armchair hid her from view. Only the black silks that hung over the chair's arms were visible, like dripping night. The effect was uncanny.

"So, Kalka, have you brought me a gift? Ah, I see. The gift of the grave."

"Is Karl still in Germany?" he asked hoarsely. He was as shaken from her display of seemingly supernatural powers as he was from his brush with death in battle. More shaken.

"Ah, you need not concern yourself about your bastard. He's a clever boy, he is. German cleverness. He's fled this miserable country—despoiled by the Jesuits, a breeding ground for God-killers. Aye, to an even greater place of evil has your bastard fled. And I foresee further wanderings. . ." Her voice rang like a great iron bell with the tones of prophecy. "Yes, yes," she continued, "He'll journey further west into even greater darkness and evil, sinking into the west like the dying sun, away from the east, from the light, *ex Oriente lux*."

"You lie, evil witch."

"Ah."

And suddenly it became truly evident to him why he truly feared and hated her. He saw it without distortion.

He hated and feared her for her Orthodoxy, her mystical version of reality, somehow intertwined with her uncanny occult powers her very existence presented a challenge to his beloved rational philosophy, a threat to reason and sanity. Her very existence mocked him, mocked his Descartes and Newton, his Hume and Kant, his cherished Jean-Jacques—her cursed superstitious rejection of solid reality and, much worse, her apparent demonstrations of that rejection, which he'd never, *never*, believe, despite everything. Instead, he'd assume that he was deluded, that some rational explanation would be forthcoming. Inside her superstitious world, anything was possible. In her world religion exercised a monopoly on the supernatural and with such belief, the divine state—the Holy Tsar and all other God-chosen tyrants.

Then she said: "Ah, so the dying finally sees the Truth of their rebellious lives. Now, at the end of all things, are true causes revealed."

And he knew that she was reading his mind.

"No, no—" he muttered in denial.

"Ah, not all."

"Not. . . all?" The words seemed to catch in his throat. All the moisture in his mouth had disappeared and his tongue was swollen, making the smooth flow of speech virtually impossible.

"Yes, yes, there's more to it, Kalka. Not so? Now, here at the moment of your death, will you know yourself?"

"At my death?"

"Aye. Mine too."

She'd risen now from her chair: a black vulture rising, having fed from a corpse, she turned to face him. The dim candlelight glinted in her eyes, making them burn like live coals in her head.

"See it? Deadman."

"No." His Newtonian mind bruised and beaten was not yet defeated.

"Ah, but you do see," she said, reading his thoughts as if they were luminous figures of smoke swirling above his head, symbols that only Ukrainian witches could translate.

"Yes! Your bastard. Don't you know? You and your German whore have bred the Antichrist. He'll destroy all that is good and holy."

"No!" he cried.

He raised the small pistol and aimed it at those accusing eyes, those terrible eyes more dangerous than the Russian guns he'd so bravely charged with his cavalry. Cannon could only blast the body. A witch's stare destroys the soul.

"Lover, oh my love," she purred sweetly.

His hand was steady. Don't jerk the trigger. . .

He couldn't do it.

She laughed, mocking him. Then the tenor in her voice, became low and menacing: "The Antichrist—"

Suddenly, unable to finish her threat, she was interrupted by a stream of Russian soldiers flooding into the room, Cossacks from the look of them.

"He's here," Anya cried in the language of the Steppe.

The Count turned to face the intruders, assassin's pistol still raised—

And died in a hail of Russian bullets.

And his soul fled, pursued by her raucous laughter. Whither to Heaven or Hell, or Nowhere, is a matter of opinion.

What became of the witch no one knows. But in this, too, there are many opinions. The ancient Polish peasants, wise old men and women, say that she returned to the Ukraine, where she entered an Orthodox monastery. Others say she died in the same hail of bullets that took her Count. Still, others say she haunted the mansion till her dying days. And still some claim— and I count myself among them—that her evil spirit haunts our family down the generations, casting her spells, causing harm in small and petty ways, and sometimes great.

I became a science tutor in the German estates, teaching the biological sciences to the spoiled whelps of the wealthy high bourgeoisie. In truth, I prefer the exact and experimental sciences. But my true love will always be mathematics. In the pure heavens of abstraction I soar, as if on wings, freed from the chaotic waste and welter of human feelings, away from all superstition.

In those years there seemed less of a demand for Newton and Helmholtz as opposed to a near obsession with faddish *Darwinisimus*, as Darwinian natural selection was then called in Germany.

I attended the public lectures of the great Ernst Haeckel, which, by the way, would appear under the title: *Collected Popular Lectures on the Subject of Evolution*. I must also add, with some pride, that I'd written a small pamphlet summarizing these lectures for young people entitled: *Great-Grandfather Ape: An Antediluvian Family Saga*. On the strength of this piece, I was hired to tutor three daughters of the De Fry banking house: Louisa, Mina, and the lovely Maria.

It became my habit to sit on a park bench near the Rhine, usually in the late afternoon, and meditate upon those gray waters, which made Europe's central artery. I must confess I am a man given to sublime thoughts and artistic impulses; though my aesthetic is, at times melancholy, it is often profound. I especially enjoyed the summer storms. Bellowing, black clouds mount the treetops and come thundering down the Rhine valley, churning the waters like some invisible living force striking the river. At times, I would imagine the Walkure riding those waves or the ancient *Mannerbrunde*, the bearskin warriors described by old Tacitus with such civilized disgust, striding through the dark forests, shaking their fists and howling their curses at the higher civilizations of Greece and Rome. It often happened that my sense of identity, my sublime soul, dropped away like a worn-out cloak, leaving the raw experience, pure and uncontaminated by personality. My tortured memories eroded like rocks in the Rhine; I felt a serene,—*ja*—peaceful emptiness, and a strange sense of freedom. I felt the profound truth of Luther's words: "*Ich bin nicht.*"

Those storms penetrated me, every cell as if the Rhine flowed through my arteries and veins. I confess it, dear reader. The shock of my father's death had affected my mind. Materialist though I am, I can almost believe my Polish soul had died with the heroes of '63. Had it not been a mere compound? A composite of Polish and German and only God knows what else? Jewish perhaps? My body holds not a singular soul, not two—but a multitude, each as empty and nonexistent as the other. But there they are, as certain as the proofs of Euclid, my Euclidean souls, which I cannot rationally accept, only believe.

Nonetheless, people called me a freethinker, an agnostic as Huxley says. The Holy Father, Pope Pius IX, had, of course, condemned Darwinism. I remained a Catholic, perhaps out of habit, or respect for my dear papa, the martyred Count. This last memory seemed especially weak, even though it constituted the most profound shock of my life. It came to pass that I could barely recall what he even looked like, for my new life was like a rebirth, and the old worn out Karl Matteyya fell from the branch like a dead leaf.

Then one day, without any known cause, for no reason other than a dream in which a voice said: "Pick up thy dying corpse and go there," I took my leave of the De Fry family, packed my belongings, and journeyed to the holy city of Rome.

In the stony damp chill of St. Peters, I gazed upon the apostle's golden tomb. I strolled through the lush papal gardens in the still of the afternoon, and in those gardens, on one such afternoon, I chanced to meet a stranger, one who reminded me of an apostle's statue come to life. He acted as if he knew me, yet I did not know him.

The strange apparition explained that he had been a priest at one time, and a Dominican, but he'd awakened to a different path, one that led him east. He sought a physician of the soul, he said.

But you know, dear reader, that Holy Rome is a city of frauds and counterfeit holy men.

I scoffed: "What is thy soul-illness?"

He transfixed me with luminous eyes. At that moment, it began to rain huge drops that sizzled when they hit the sun-warmed stones.

"I search for him, one of mixed race, who knows the soul-illness, its cause, its cure. He will stand out like the red robe of a cardinal amid crowds of pilgrims."

"Again, I ask. This soul-illness?"

At that moment, the world was plunged into the darkness as in the hour of Christ's death. But the storm did not break.

He paused and stared at me. "Are you not an educated man? You still wear that hideous talisman of the false Church, the death-symbol."

"You know nothing of me," I snapped. "My crucifix is a sacred family heirloom. Be gone with your blasphemy."

"Ah, my dark-skinned friend, do you know? The true Church has never been." He raised his arm and gestured towards St. Peters. He resembled a black-robed magician casting a spell.

"You've heard, no doubt, that Satan too can quote Scripture."

"A cliché," I said.

"Ah, my friend, maybe. But once long ago the devils and small satans studied the most ancient text, the Holy Torah itself, and became adepts; for it is said that God Himself studies the Torah, His most precious gift to the world, the Divine Mind in Words. Now, the devils and small satans became scribes and scholars and thus gained something of the Divine Power—"

"This is. . ." I searched my mind for the term newly coined, ". . . antisemitism."

"Ah, no. Listen, thou. The devils and small satans memorized the holy verses whose recitation confers omnipotence that even God could not defeat them. They knew God's Holy Name. So He tricked them. He sent a sage who taught a false doctrine denying the existence of One God, who ignored the distinction between Jew and Gentile, who made light of the Torah, and condemned the sacred rites. And the devils and small satans became this one's disciples. They flocked to him, following his false doctrines. Thus did they corrupt themselves. Thus did God defeat them. For what is to be destroyed must first be corrupted. Thus were they are thrown back into Hell."

"Enough!" I cried. "Such foolishness. Occult nonsense."

"Ah, young man from the East. Surely you know. *Ex Oriente lux.* The Church, in whose bosom you rest, in whose doctrine you find comfort, in your heart of hearts, as you can see, is a trap for devils and small satans. What is destroyed must first be corrupted. Men, unfortunately, were also ensnared. Their Church is the byproduct."

"This sage," I asked despite myself, "was Christ?"

"The Christ, also known as the Ninth. Another is coming, the Anti-Christ, also known as the Tenth, and you must prepare the Way."

"Madness!"

He turned away, black robes flapping, and vanished into a wet fog that had suddenly arisen in the blessed garden.

Now, as I write this, I realize that he was a phantom, an illusion bred by despair and loss, the soul-illness of which he spoke. Diseases are real, even ones that produce delusions.

Ach! I confess it. You who come after—let this be a warning, to my descendants who inherit even a drop of Matteyya-Sumedha blood. At any moment, especially in times of elevated stress or passion, we are in danger of horrendously vile superstitions, of populating the world with phantoms and spirits, of imagining conspiracies and plots and believing nonsense. And—I can hardly bring myself to write this—having lost the moorings of strict reasoning, we drift down the river of madness in longboats crewed by ghosts of forlorn longings. We rebel against sanity. We are a race of rebels, like the fallen angels.

My confession: And yet, knowing this, I gave up my agnosticism and my science, my Newton and my Darwin. I came back to the Holy Mother Church, though I dared never set foot in Rome again. For it was within the bosom of the Church that I found my sanity and myself. I was a Catholic citizen of the Grand Duchy of Warsaw, I said. The Church restored my lost moorings. I no longer cared for "scientific reality," the uncertainties therein. First, I desired security. I craved certainty and authority.

And so I became a religious scholar in the service of the Church. I became an expert on the heathen religions that posed a challenge to the Truth.

Then in the spring of my thirty-fifth year, out walking one morning in the Black Forest near the small Bavarian village in which I'd taken residence, I came across an ancient pagan road, overgrown and practically invisible, and followed it—

Here the manuscript ended, or rather, the final leaves were missing. Sylvian counted the pages of the German volume, and although he could not, of course, be sure, he believed that the German version ended as well.

He discovered, however, scribbled on the bottom of the final page of the English version, most certainly in a different hand, a weird sentence:

Here ends the real and true account of the Bodhisattva.

Sylvian quietly closed the volume, opened his physics book, and studied the string of equations again. Radiant energy like heat waves arising from the hood of a car supposedly came in little tiny bundles (the quantum of action, "h"), grossly illogical it seemed to Sylvian.

Still worse, light, radiation in general, even matter, became particles when one measured for particles or waves when one measured for waves. The double-slit experiment worked for electrons too. Somehow particles going through the slits interfered with themselves, giving the wave-like interference pattern, as if they existed in two places simultaneously, as if. . . two universes existed, superimposed, until someone (but who?) decided to measure. Existence, so said quantum mechanics (according to Professor Olaffsoon who'd met Bohr), was neither this nor that but both at the same time when no one was looking. The electrons are probabilities (Olaffsoon rushed through the wave function and the Born rule), so when they come to the slits, they realize their probabilities and take *both slits*. Our concepts, our language, do not apply to the quantum level. Yet we come from it.

He stared out the darkened windows. Their old wooden frames were engraved with designs, now worn by age, designs that supposedly suggested oak leaves, branches, acorns, and distant hills. For the first time, in his life, he found physics difficult. For the first time he felt stupid in the presence of physical science. He could follow the math, but the physical meaning completely eluded him. His mind had become as dark as the world beyond the manufactured frames—the vacuity of space, smooth as water-worn stone.

Physics suddenly became as odd and twisting as Karl's memoir. Casual connections were beyond rational explanation. The time dimensions folded back upon themselves like the scrambled pages of a broken book. Time ceased to exist. Olaffsoon suggested that there might be hypothetical double-slit experiments in which future events determined the past—the causal chain flowed backward in time—dependent upon the *information*. He became oddly vague at this point, implying that this might be *his* contribution to physics, though he didn't relish talking about his work. At last, he resorted to incomprehensible mumbling, eschewing the vertical and the horizontal—like the *Outer Limits*.

And Sylvian knew that he'd inherited the soul-illness of his ancestors. Had not Karl returned to Catholicism? Should he return to the Mother Church? Did he ever truly leave?

It struck him then that somehow it all came to the path in the woods, to Oakwood Park.

Suddenly he knew why his ancestors had come to America from the Old Country. Sylvian couldn't put this knowledge into words. Only—silence.

SIXTEEN

"Threshold of a Dream"

ANITA GROANED: "I DON'T think so, Tom. Mindless terrorism only plays into the hands of the heartless state."

She rolled over, took another cheroot from the nightstand, struck a match, and vanished in a fog of tobacco smoke.

Tom got up and walked to the tiny attic window. Snow covered the streets below.

"Shit, we're talkin' murder, ain't we?"

"They're committing murder! That Goodjohn Woo-Woo bastard killed Cathy and made it look like a sex crime to discredit us. Anyone who dares challenge the fuckin' System is a criminal. Capitalism has no conscience, and Christianity makes murder a sacrament."

Tom stared at her. She lay on the bed, naked and smoking. God, how big and muscular she was, not a bit of fat. Still sweating, she glistened in the smoke. He felt exhausted. Even a powerful man like Tom had his limits.

"All these little plots," he sighed. "These meetings, discussions, secrets. . . Now murder?"

Anita exhaled more smoke. "We're being murdered by the goddamn Establishment."

"Vico's right 'bout one thing," Tom said. "The military, the FBI, CIA, even the university, are all stooges. We gotta go after the real power. Hit 'em where it hurts. Property. Blow up their factories, their estates, build bonfires with their money. Don't rob banks, burn 'em. Trash department stores, ridicule advertisement, mock ceremony, blaspheme everything sacred. Destroy property, not people."

"Tom, Tom, you just don't get it. That's a sandbox revolution. It plays right into capitalist hands. Do you know why?"

"Nope, don't have your education. Wasn't blessed with your opportunities. Never lived with a genius like Dr. Jonathan—"

"TOM!"

He'd pushed her too far. "I only meant—"

"Capitalists control the media." She sounded as if she were indulging a small child, "The masses are hypnotized; their real needs are twisted and perverted into capitalist needs. It's elementary observation, not theory. Everyone wants the same shit. Everyone is dissatisfied 'cuz they never get enough. The media pumps people full of false needs like drugs. Old Marx could have never foreseen such a development. TV alone has negated his proletarian class romance. Fifty years more of this opium and who knows what the result will be. Shit, Tom, they'll welcome terrorist acts. Entertainment. Fear sells like sex. Crime will become profitable. It'll give rise to whole new industries."

Her voice rang deeper than he'd ever heard, like a muffled roar.

"You gotta have faith in the Masters."

"I. . . have faith," he breathed.

"The Masters know."

"Yes, Anita—"

"Why don't you come back and get warm?"

He came back to the bed drawn by her heat as if she were a mass of glowing coals.

"I can still trust you, Tom?" she asked, gazing into his eyes.

"Yes, of course."

"It must not be a crime, not an act of terrorism, not even murder. Can't be entertainment. It must be an execution."

"I don't know if I see the difference—"

"Execution is murder transformed into a moral imperative. A law of nature. Capitalism hates true morality. We cannot *not* execute the people's oppressors."

"I still don't see. the Masters told you this?"

"Worked it out myself, Tom. The Masters are invisible. They indicate."

"So we kill—"

"Execution. Righteously. Without guilt. Without anger or hatred, following natural law in the name of the people. Murder with a smile."

Tom sighed again. "These thoughts are beyond me. I'm lost, like in Nam."

"You'll obey?"

"I. . . will."

"Trust the Masters."

"I do—"

"It's settled then. We'll use that little college kid. What's his name?"

"Sylvian."

"Yeah. Him. Hey, you know I saw him a few days ago. My eyes must be goin' bad, 'cuz I could have sworn that the kid looked lighter, kinda bleached. Thought he was Indian, but guess not."

"Yeah, he does look different. Must have taken a bath."

"You'll teach him then? With those weapons, we stole."

"I'll teach the punk how to kill," he said, sounding uncertain and exhausted.

President Craven had decreed that cavernous Boots Auditorium serve as the venue for the teach-in. Set on a gentle campus hill on tree-lined Hoffman Avenue just across from Oakwood Park, the old auditorium was a confused blending of architecture, a hybrid of a gothic cathedral and medieval castle, complete with turrets, wooden columns painted to look like marble, a monumental portico topped by a pediment and a dome. Gargoyles with pointy ears, large bellies, and smirking grins served as rain spouts. The main floor sat about five hundred people. An ornate balcony could accommodate another hundred, although the wood floors and supports were so rotted from years of inadequate drainage that the fire department permanently closed the gallery.

A large table with twenty chairs, everyone facing the audience, crammed the stage. Each participant was assigned a microphone, but at the last moment, Dean Bentley discovered that the antique electrical system would probably explode into flames if they attempted to install more than one mike, which, naturally, went to the President.

Less than two hundred participants turned out on this early Saturday morning of the first weekend in March. They were mostly SHS, students attending at the behest of Dean Bentley. A small number of students were members of ROTC, all in uniform and sitting together, along with an organization called the Crockett Rifles. Many of the remaining student participants were Young Republicans.

Eight members of the Student Revolutionary Vanguard (SRV) attended led by General Secretary Mary Anne Klein. Eugene Vico made the ninth member, but he took his assigned seat on the stage, without a microphone. His official title was now Chairman.

An official press release stated that President H. Richard Craven had organized the teach-in as a response to Chairman Vico's demands that the university deal with the credibility gap created by administration policies. Vico was primarily concerned with such "fascist" organizations as SHS, ROTC, the frats and sororities, but also the university's acceptance of government research grants, which led to such things as the napalming of poor peasants in Vietnam. Besides the war and campus repression of legitimate student protest, he also wanted the discussion to focus on the excessive weight of the local power structure in university affairs, specifically the Board of Regents. Undereducated businesspeople, fattened on profits squeezed from real human misery (his words), bored wealthy widows, and senile reactionaries forever on hold in the 1950's hardly served today's educational needs.

The SVR's list of demands included, but weren't limited to: abolishing the elitism of the grading system, universal distribution of the pill (to encourage free love and sexual expression), abolishing all required courses, legalizing pot and (eventually) acid, ending racism, the drafting of a general university resolution for the immediate end to the war, expropriation of university capital to pay for all student tuition, an interdisciplinary department for psychedelic studies (with a possible recruitment of Timothy Leary), and a weekly session open to the public, led by President Craven and Dean Bentley dedicated to self-criticism and open discourse.

Oh, yes, and the renaming of BSU to the People's University of Liberation Progress (PULP).

The teach-in was unofficially designated "Threshold of A Dream," from the latest Moody Blues album, On The Threshold of A Dream.

Chairman Vico occupied the center seat at the table. Next to him sat President Craven, on Craven's left Bentley. Craven invited chosen faculty. At Vico's request, Paul F. Hallerman was there, wearing jeans, a tee shirt, and love beads. Professor Valentine Zorsky occupied a chair, as did Professor Ibrahim al-Rashd (who went by the name of Benny Razor). Olaffsoon attended, representing the physical sciences; also Chairman of the Business School, Robert Matheson, who taught Personnel Management (what Anita like to call "Higher Sheep Herding"). A Priest, Father Watson Tempier, showed up; no one knew if he'd come by invitation. Bentley represented the Protestants.

President Craven opened the proceedings with a lengthy welcoming speech. He was wearing a brown polyester fish-bone jacket and black turtleneck. Horned-rimmed glasses perched on the end of his sharp nose clashed with the mod effect. His long, fleshy ears, burning red, unfortunately, ruined his artsy-hipster look.

He began by praising today's students for their social awareness and political maturity, their commitment, and honesty. Next, he spoke with deep sadness about the "criminal element," mostly non-students, who sought nothing more than mindless hedonism and destruction. They were enemies of civilization and education, and all thoughtful men.

". . .as, for example, what occurred only yesterday in Greenwich Village where a terrible explosion killed three misguided Weathermen. We at BSU must at all costs prevent such tragedies. I know that Chairman Vico shares these sentiments."

Craven spoke for about an hour. He devoted a great deal of time to defending the various measures he'd been "forced" to take in the name of campus security, and he concluded his talk with a brief prayer which drew resentful looks from the clergy in the hall.

He received a standing ovation led by SHS and the frats, which lasted for almost two full minutes. ROTC stood in unison and saluted. Crockett Rifles dozed.

Dean Bentley followed the President with another hour-long speech, of which many people heard only fragments. Seated in the rear of the auditorium, Vico's Student Revolutionary Vanguard became rude, shouting "speak up," forcing Security to escort them from the building.

Bentley reviewed accomplishments of the past year, discussing the various "official" university organizations, which included a lengthy introduction of the "platoon leaders" of SHS as well as the entire staff of the Dean of Students Office. Each lengthy introduction duly received a prolonged ovation.

With the opening remarks concluded, President Craven called for a half-hour break. The university food service graciously served coffee and donuts.

The President opened the next session. To set the proper tone for the conference, he said, it was necessary to take a few minutes and discuss what he termed "aggressive disrespect," "poor taste," and "destructive cynicism" practiced by a far-left fringe of the youth culture, "as we've just witnessed." Another example of this disturbing trend, he continued, casting his net wide, was the new Spiro Agnew watch picturing a cartoon Vice President dressed in flag shorts, giving the peace sign. Perhaps this was meant to suggest that Agnew was Mickey Mouse, President Craven wondered.

But then Professor Hallerman interrupted the President suggesting that perhaps Dr. Craven, whose degree was in education, did not understand the difference between aggression and *reductio ad absurdum*.

Before Craven could reply, Hallerman rushed on to discuss the various forms of argument as outlined by Aristotle in the *Prior Analytics*.

"Now, if vee take the premise that Agnew ist Micky, and Micky ist genial happy-go-lucky fellow, then Agnew ist genial und gut, vich is a contradiction unt untenable since Agnew ist evil moron, vile unt uptight."

Here Professor Benny Razor interrupted and much to Hallerman's annoyance pointed out various problems in old Latin translations of Aristotle. Razor thought al-Masur's translation far superior to any Latin or English version if of course Hallerman would care to learn Arabic. And of course Agnew is morose and mean, but the "is" may not indicate identity; and the name Agnew never appears in *Prior Analytics*.

"Vell!" Hallerman said indignantly, "I do know Attic Greek, and I vill tell you dis—"

He began quoting from his writings on the subject, to which Razor replied by quoting from his commentaries on various Islamic philosophers—and this went on until lunch, which the university donated out of the student general fund (so too the donuts).

The afternoon session commenced with an observation by Professor Matheson that the Spiro watch would probably have limited market appeal and would probably last no longer than other oddities like alternative typewriter keyboards or the Edsel.

But this observation brought forth a stinging rebuke from Professor Zorsky who accused Matheson of economic provincialism. Zorsky pointed out that the Spiro watch might do quite well on the Soviet black market. Zorsky was a professor of Slavic Languages and not very popular with the students because he mocked their intelligence and wondered how Amerika would be able to maintain its leading role in the world once their idiotic generation came to power.

Professor Matheson proved himself up to this challenge. He wondered just how much of the total Soviet economy, crude as it was in comparison to modern "free-market" systems, fell into the category "black market." The watch would hardly make a profit. He supplemented his argument by quoting pages upon pages of relevant statistics, apparently from memory.

Poor Professor Zorsky could only lean back, scratch his thick black beard, and mutter how the Western economy was hardly free-market at all, as government and the market were so intertwined that, vell, the entire thing was a "black market."

Abruptly, Zorsky's salvation from further embarrassment came from an unexpected source. Father Watson Tempier broke in with the condescending-toned remark that he found no "sin" in the harmless satire of a political leader as Agnew, for such was the nature of secular politics which lacked respect and good taste. But if some radical had chosen, say, the figure of the Holy Father, or, heaven forbid, a saint, or perhaps even a member of the Holy Family, then this would constitute the heinous sin of blasphemy—

At this, a huge man sitting in the front row, who identified himself as the Right Reverend List, rose to his feet and thundered: "Ha, ha, ha. . . just tell me about all those statues and talismanic figurines, and bones, and whole graveyards of junk you stash away in your cathedrals! Talk about idolatry. Talk about blasphemy. You Catholics!"

This learned observation brought on a furious exchange that included most of the faculty and not a few members of the audience (which had melted to half its size by the afternoon).

At last, President Craven rose from his chair and casting a glance at his secretary, Dorothy, sitting near the door, grasped the microphone and announced the conclusion of the teach-in. He thanked everyone for his or her efforts, especially Chairman Vico.

"We may all take pride in the progressive tradition of Brunswick State University. Here we discuss our differences in a most creative, imaginative, and orderly way, enjoying significant, meaningful, and relevant dialogue in an atmosphere of civility. We have accomplished a great deal in a short time. I, for one would very much welcome another teach-in soon. Say sometime in May."

With that, "Threshold of A Dream" concluded.

Chairman Vico found himself the center of attention, congratulated by all and sundry for his successful leadership and high-minded sense of duty, "telling it like it is."

Somewhat dazed, he staggered out the doors and down the auditorium stairs, nearly losing his footing on the slick pavement.

During the conference, a strong thunderstorm drenched Hinnom Valley. Now a steady rain fell. Vico was instantly soaked. It wasn't until he reached his apartment that he realized he'd been carrying his umbrella—unopened.

Sylvian stood at the end of the table in the basement of the secret house on Green Street and listened to the words: "By the decision of the Central Committee of the People's Will, we gathered here decree that the counter-revolutionary murderer, Goodjohn Saccidanada, also known as the Divine Woo-Woo, Groovy Guru, Avatar, Swami, be executed for crimes against the People."

Anita read the document. She fixed Sylvian with her famous stare and asked: "Do you, Comrade Matreya, agree to become the instrument of the people's vengeance?"

Sylvian looked as if he hadn't heard the question. His head hung down, his eyes were closed, and he seemed oblivious to everything going on around him.

"Do you, Comrade?"

Randal, Vesta, and Paul Big-Ears-Che snickered. Tom looked sad.

Sylvian took a deep breath and said: "He returned to the Church. It always comes to religion. But that's empty. He did not understand. . ." He raised his head and stared at each of them in turn. "I'm the Anti-Christ," he declared.

The snickers turned to open laughter. Anita gazed at him with a somewhat bewildered expression, rare for her.

"Well, the revolution needs that one too. You need to understand. The guru is not condemned for his, uh, religion, whatever it may be. He murdered Comrade Butcher. He uses Eastern shit to seduce potential converts away from reality, from radical action. As Marx said—opium—"

"Fuck 'em!" Sylvian suddenly interjected. "Hates all the gods, the whole crowd of 'em. All that exists deserves to perish."

No one ever interrupted Anita Anacharsis in the middle of a speech. They expected lightning to strike little Sylvian right there and burn him to a crisp. Miraculously he escaped this fate for Anita suddenly burst out laughing.

She laughed until the tears came. Then she lit a cheroot.

"I agree, kid. I'm for ending the son-of-a-bitch. Psychedelic revolutionaries ain't no good to nobody, ain't no threat to the Establishment. Shit, bourgeoisie love 'em! Pickin' cellophane flowers under marmalade skies is what bourgeois life is all about."

"Maybe we out to do Jerry Wolfe too," Paul suggested amicably. "Democratic Centrism, you know."

"Nope. He's useful."

Sylvian closed his eyes again. He barely seemed to be breathing.

"Tom, he's yours to train. Turn him into the People's agent of vengeance. The Central Committee has decided."

Eyes closed, Sylvian said: "I am Death, Destroyer of all the gods."

"Only need to take out one," said Anita.

❖❖❖

Sylvian passed into Tom's hands for weapons training. The technical aspects of the assassination, the time, place, and means of escape would be planned later after Anita had consulted the Masters.

Tom and Anita agreed that Sylvian would also need time to get back inside the Great Truth Cloud and close to Goodjohn. If things worked as planned, Sylvian would convince the fraudulent guru that he, Sylvian, could get to Anita herself—the old double, double-agent scenario—fool the pigs into believing Sylvian was an agent of the People's Will trying to infiltrate the Clouds. But he could be turned instead to infiltrate the People's Will and kill Anita herself, which he would pretend to do. All the while he'd be stalking Goodjohn, and she'd be above suspicion because, well, she'd be dead and Sylvian was an idiot. So when Goodjohn turned up murdered they'd look elsewhere, say in Vico's direction. She loved it.

She waited for the Masters to speak. They remained stubbornly silent. She even tried walking through Oakwood Park at night, all the way around the lagoon into the woods.

Nothing. No one approached her, not even a stray dog.

Anita tried sitting quietly in the dark late at night, her mind empty, listening intently for the voice of the Master to pop into her mind.

Silence. She fell asleep.

Tom still wanted to strike at the heart of capitalism by destroying property.

As March waned and the Masters refused to speak, Anita had to admit that Tom's idea seemed more appealing. Sabotage the mill, the brewery—burn the capitalist tools of oppression to ashes. The more she thought about it, the more sense it made. She could almost smell the burning paper and hear the explosions. True, she'd argued against mindless destruction. But her frustration with the silent Masters fed her craving for violence.

Anita called a special meeting of the Central Committee and announced a minor change of revolutionary strategy. Since the Masters had chosen silence—perhaps because of the danger posed by the Clouds—Anita would support the destruction of the capitalist means of production which was the very heart and soul of oppression and exploitation. Such acts would also serve to divert attention away from the assassination of Goodjohn, the government agent.

Anita stared at Tom. He looked grim, and seemed dejected, almost as miserable as the day he was drafted.

"Tom. What's wrong? Thought you'd be happy. What's buggin' you?"

Tom shook his head. "Won't be no guru assassination."

"The hell there won't!"

"Oh yeah? Maybe the kid'll stab 'em with his slide rule. He sure ain't gonna shoot 'em."

"Why? Ain't you supposed to be training him down in the basement?"

Tom's shoulders sagged. "You try training him. It's the weirdest thing. Every time the kid touches a weapon, he gets sick. Either he pukes his guts out and faints or pisses in his pants and gets delirious. Starts prattling on about paths in the woods. How he's the Anti-Christ and other nonsense. It's crazy! He gets the chills just at the sight of a weapon. I tried knives and swords I brought back from Japan. Kid puked—"

"Some Anti-Christ."

"I told you he's useless," said Randal.

Vesta nodded. "Yup, just like Czechago. Students ain't no more revolutionary than Howdy Dowdy. Stupid New Left bullshit—"

"Shut the fuck up and let me think!" Anita shouted. She pulled out a cheroot and began smoking. At last, she asked: "Is that all? What about poison? What about a pipe bomb, you know, like a Bangalore torpedo? We could mix up some potassium chloride and sugar in the sink, use sulfuric acid and burn 'em up. We got dynamite too—"

"Yeah, we could do it, but not the Indian kid. I'm telling you, just a whiff of chemicals and he's sick."

"I can't believe it!" Anita declared.

"Well, believe this. I've got Sylvian exercising, doing marine corps calisthenics, stuffing him with three squares a day. I even got him to practice the waterfall throw, the comet, solar flare, martial arts shit I learned in Japan. The *kikon waya*, too, soft eye. Taught 'em what I know about the philosophy. Know what? He loves the philosophy but goes as limp as hot wax during the exercise. Can't even manage a *kiai*, just a little high-pitched whine. He's impossible."

Anita looked flustered. "That Indian kid is the only one that's been inside the Clouds. No one knows where they went. Jerry says they were trying to recruit the kid. They'll find him. He's our only chance. What are we gonna do?"

They all sat with bowed heads, like a table of monks at prayer.

Suddenly Randal looked up and said: "Maybe Sylvian can get one of our own into the Clouds. Two infiltrators, one Sylvian and the other the assassin."

"Far out!" cried Vesta. "I can dig that. Let me do it."

"No. Has to be another student. Somebody freaky. A hippie. Maybe black. A dangerous one—"

"Blacks have all been expelled—"

"Me," said Randal.

"No," Tom said flatly.

"Why not?"

"They'd kill you just like Cathy Butcher. You're a Boots. Another dead rich kid blamed on the movement."

"Who then?"

"Jerry Wolfe."

"Perfect," Anita cried with glee. "I knew he'd come in handy. The perfect freak. It'd be like two roommates joining a fraternity. Sylvian will get them in, and Jerry will do the deed."

Vesta snickered. "Hell, if he's high enough he'd shoot his own grandmother."

Anita laughed. "Oh, this just gets better. We'll keep Jerry tripping on good acid and tell 'em that Goodjohn is that Evil Lord. . . What's his name?"

"Sauron," said Tom. "I read Tolkien in Vietnam. Sauron, the Dark Lord. Some guys said he was Johnson."

"Yeah, him. When Jerry trips on acid, it's always to Middle Earth."

SEVENTEEN

Failure

SYLVIAN FAILED HIS FIRST Quantum Mechanics test of the spring semester. Up to this point in his career, he'd never scored less than perfect on a physics test. To actually fail such an exam was far worse than Lucifer's fall from heaven. The preeminent archangel, Father Loeb taught the parish children, the Light Lord, Morning Star, second only to God Himself, was cast out and flashed down like a mighty comet, plunging into the outer darkness—the darkness furthest from the divine. Now, so had Sylvian.

The technical questions did not cause the disaster. Sylvian could do the calculations as easily as he breathed. But Olaffsoon, unlike other professors of physics, taught interpretation, which meant philosophy.

The exam required that the three students write essays on the Copenhagen Interpretation of Quantum Mechanics, the significance of Heisenberg's Indeterminacy for the Newtonian-Kantian concept of the Real, and Einstein's opposition to Indeterminacy. Sylvian could barely understand the questions.

He was feeling ill these days. He seemed to be running a constant low-grade fever. He suffered chills every morning, fatigue every night, a vague apprehension every second. He dreamed terrifying nightmares filled with fleeting visions of bloody murder. He saw himself as modern-day Jack the Ripper slashing away at a blonde woman he could not identify. It may have been Pearl. Usually, she resisted him easily. In one dream she tore the knife out of his hand and stabbed him. So much for Jack the Ripper Anti-Christ.

A cloudy and bitter March gave way to a miserably rainy April. Tom gave up "military training," and the People's Will gave up on Sylvian.

Then one morning, having suffered a particularly horrid dream in which he saw yet another version of himself, oversized and menacing, like his brother Karl. With a knife in hand, he was standing over Pearl's headless body, laughing ghoulishly. Suddenly, the headless torso is coming to life. . . He watched as it morphed into the wide-eyed wizard from Middle-Earth, Jerry Wolfe. . . And awoke to the real Jerry Wolfe

Jerry was shaking him. "Hey, man, gotta wake up. Now!"

"Go away, asshole."

"But Sam, man, we're goin' into battle with the Dark Tower itself, and—"

"Go away."

"Listen, Sam, it's finally going to happen. The Elves ordered me and you to sneak into Mordor and find the Evil Eye himself and kill the bastard!"

He fumbled in the sizeable square pocket of his army-surplus field jacket, which he constantly wore and even slept in, and brought forth a small snub-nosed pistol with a white pearl handle. It looked like a toy.

He held the weapon awkwardly. "Tom says I gotta put this a few inches from the Evil Lord's head and keep pulling the trigger till the clip runs out—"

"Evil Lord?"

"Goodjohn Woo-Woo, the Sauron of our age. Do it for the revolution, man. I'm Frodo. You're Sam. Vico's Gollum. We're goin' to Mordor. The time has come. . . today!"

"Put it away. I'm sick."

"Sam, you can't be sick now. You gotta get us in there. You know, with that chickadee."

"Don't know nothin'. Ain't seen Pearl or Goodjohn. Don't give a shit. Go away."

Jerry shrank back from the bed. He went to the window and stared out.

"Man, the One Ring is wastin' you. Dark Riders are abroad too. Did you see 'em? They passed overhead in the clouds. He's waitin' for us to make a mistake. He's poisoning your mind, Sam."

Sylvian moaned in real pain. "Fucking idiot. It's a fantasy. Like religion. Go away."

"Man, it's true," Jerry protested sounding hurt. "The Shadow takes many forms. A different form for each age. It's up to us to root it out in our age. That Goodjohn creep is the Sauron of our age."

Sylvian sat up, kicked off the blankets, and rolled out of bed onto the cold floor. Kneeling, he began beating his fists on the impervious tiles. Next, he tried banging his head. He crawled to his desk chair, pulled himself up, seized the ponderous physics book, and commenced to tear out pages.

He flung the pages at Jerry. Each projectile fluttered to the floor like a wounded butterfly.

Jerry ducked and hid behind his bed.

Sylvian was laughing, then crying, then back to mad laughter. "Lies. Fictions. Delusions. What about light, Frodo? It's a wave, asshole. Got an interference pattern. But Einstein says it's a photon and that's true too. Ha, ha. . . Squeeze off a photon. What've you got? Interference. But its particles doin' it. Do it at separate times, as long as no one knows, across the universe, and you get? Waves! Every fucking particle interferes with itself, no matter where no matter when. One particle takes two paths. . .is. . .fuckin' crazy."

He tore out more pages and threw them at Jerry, laughing and crying hysterically. He recited Olaffsoon's lectures.

". . .and every fucking atom in you, in everything. Do you see this page smoothly floating? That's a lie too. Path's not smooth. It's got gaps, stopping and starting, from this point to next point but not crossing any space between. It appears here, now it disappears and reappears here. An electron jumps in the atom, in every atom, in every molecule, in everybody, everywhere. Now it's in this shell, next another, without crossing the space between. Except, none of that's true either! Electron is a shimmering fog until it's measured. . . How about that, Frodo? There's your Dark Lord. He's crazier than shit."

Sylvian danced as if the floor had become a bed of glowing coals. Froth foamed at the corners of his mouth and spittle flew across the room.

"Yeah, yeah, yeah. . ." He began to sing, vainly trying to sound like the Beatles. "Loves it, yeah, yeah. . . yeah. . . Yesterday. . . This energy state. . . quantified orbit. . . but only this one and no other. . . like the girl with kaleidoscope eyes. And it can't pass through space in between. Otherwise, it'd radiate frequencies, which it don't. . . 'cuz it ain't none of that shit, it's a probability wave. . . probably this or that but only when you look. . . He says one and one and one is three. Got to be good lookin', 'cuz he's so hard to see. . ."

He threw the book onto the floor and stamped on it viciously. The book slid out from under him and sent him crashing down, banging his head on the desk leg and knocking himself out cold.

Jerry rushed to his side and lifted him onto the bed. Minutes passed. Sylvian opened his eyes.

"Oh man, you're really wasted."

Sylvian ran his fingers through his hair and found them smeared with blood.

"Man, you're wounded—"

He sat up. "Don't you see it?"

Jerry looked confused. "See what?"

"Reality. Nothing's anything without something else. Fucking Haller-man had a point. Nothing is. Everything depends." Sylvian suddenly looked pleased. "Shit, that's the answer."

He jumped off the bed and ran to the window.

"Hey, Frodo. Rain's lettin' up and it's Friday afternoon, and we ain't got any classes. Less take a walk, huh? Like to Lilac Street. No, no, to the park."

"Where?"

"Oh shit. . . I mean, Mordor. The Land of Shadows."

"What about it?"

"You gotta be real, Frodo. Can't hide out in the Shire your whole life."

He stumbled across the room to his closet, tore out his worn navy blue pea coat and put it on.

"Let's do the park," Sylvian said as he hurriedly buttoned the coat, getting the wrong buttons in the wrong holes. "Probability function has gotta apply to Mordor too."

Jerry shook his head. "Man, what's wrong with you? You're too wired—"

Sylvian grabbed him roughly by the arm and pulled him to the window. "Don't you see? Are you blind? You go there. The rain, skies, woods. . . reality is there. You gotta go there."

"Where?"

"The park, stupid freak! Mordor. Look for Mordor. The fucking park is Mordor. The Church is Mordor. Amerika is Mordor. It's all scientific, Frodo."

He went to his desk. Fumbling through a pile of papers and books, he filled the air with academic debris like a dog digging in the ground. At last, he held up an old engraved volume and began laughing.

"Ha, ha. . . What is to be destroyed must first be corrupted. But if the world is already sick, corrupting it will make it well."

"Man, you're really trippin'."

Sylvian tossed the book aside and went back to the window. "Come on Frodo we're goin' to Mordor."

"Sam, man, this is serious. We're gonna waste Goodjohn for the revolution."

"The end of Sauron for this age, huh?"

"Sam, how can he be in the park? The pigs combed every inch."

"Frodo! Don't you remember what Gandalf said? The Land of Shadows conceals many things from the eyes of mortals."

"I guess so—"

"Clouds live in the Land of Shadows."

"Yeah?"

"Come on, Frodo. You'll see."

"Okay, Sam," Frodo said, hand in his pocket, "but you're starting to freak me out. Sam was always mellow, even with the ring, man. "

"To Mordor!" Sam bolted out the door and down the hall. He took the stairs two at a time, burst out onto the street and sprinted down the sidewalk.

Frodo ran after him, and ruefully recalled that hobbits "are inclined to fat and do not hurry unnecessarily."

Anita lit one cheroot with another, smoking about half before going on to the next one. The basement atmosphere became a combination of smog and tear-gas. Eyes watered, stung by the pungent smoke. Throats burned raw with each breath.

A more significant assault fell upon the auditory canal. Anita's voice was a continual string of explosions.

"IT'S GENOCIDE! A HOLOCAUST! AMERIKA IS KILLIN' ITS OWN YOUTH!"

She screamed and pounded the table.

"Christ, Anita," Tom muttered, "I'm really starting to believe the whole crazy thing. Blacks, poor whites, working class. . . radical students. . . murdered—"

"OF COURSE IT'S TRUE!" she howled.

"Oh, I don't think so," Randal said, trying not to look at Anita, "they probably just split someplace. Jerry's brain is mush. Probably just freaked out—"

"Yeah," Vesta agreed. "That Hindu kid's an idiot too. Could never figure 'em. Could you?"

"Jerry turned him on last semester," Randal added, "made 'em into a head. Shit, you can tell by just looking at him. He's spaced out. As wasted as Jerry himself."

Vesta and Paul nodded in agreement. Tom, however, stared at Anita. He saw the signs: the twitching about her mouth, the blinking, rolling of her eyes, the furrowed brow and exaggerated breathing. She was like nitrogen tri-iodide, the most hazardous explosive of all. A breeze might detonate her.

"BULLSHIT!" She pounded the table. "You fools, just wait. They'll find the bodies just like poor Cathy. In the park, too, I'll bet, all cut up, mutilated like Sharon Tate. But pigs won't tell. Oh no, it'll be something like a drug overdose, and the fucking administration will wag their fingers and warn us poor children about the dangers of illegal drugs. It's the fuckin' FBI that's done killed them 'cuz they know that we're onto their fucking stooge."

"Tom, what's wrong?" Vesta asked suddenly.

Tom was staring at the table and quivering, his hands and head shaking. His cheeks were moist. He was sweating.

"TOM!" Anita cried.

He glanced up, gazing past her. . . "Goddamn highlands village," he mumbled, "deserted, we thought, but no—look out! Man, it was reflex. Didn't mean to do it, just had to let go—" He put his head in his hands and moaned. "Only a little girl. Let go before I knew—"

"TOM!"

He looked directly at her. His face was contorted, his eyes filled with agony.

"Look at me."

He gazed into her eyes, luminous and compelling, and gradually, his quivering ceased. Slowly, the turmoil drained out of him and soaked into the green felt of the table.

He exhaled and asked: "Who saw 'em last?"

Randal cleared his throat: "Uh, me, I guess. Three weeks ago, I thought. I ain't seen them since that Apollo Thirteen thing."

Something in his voice sounded off-key as if he'd rehearsed and rehearsed a speech and still could not get it to come out right.

Tom gave him a scornful look: "Hey Randal, you always know what's going on, don't you? Why's that?"

"I don't know what you mean," Randal answered warily.

"I mean, you're the youngest Boots kid, right? You ain't ever going to run your daddy's company, right? Just live your worthless life off a trust fund, right? What are you doing in the movement?"

"What'd you mean?" Randal tried to sound indignant. "Man, you're always such a downer, givin' off bad vibes."

"Just wondering if you're in for the thrills. Maybe you're a bored rich kid. Or are you in for the chicks? You know, like Cathy—"

"Hey, fuck you! I ain't no little-girl killer—"

Tom rose menacingly. "You're a slimy bastard, Boots. A rich, slimy bastard who knows everything 'cuz he rats on us. I think maybe we ought to execute you."

Randal's face twisted in rage. With shaking hands, he took off his glasses and got out of his chair to face his tormentor.

"Yeah, come on rich boy. Try it. Ain't gonna be like wrestling sweet little rich girls—"

Randal turned to Anita: "I must protest such abuse of a comrade, especially one on the Central Committee."

"TOM! Randal is a loyal revolutionary. Past social class is meaningless in the People's Will. We're not Stalinists here."

Tom slowly sank back into his chair. He began to quiver again. His voice sounded like someone scratching at the wood table. He uttered broken words.

"You never really know who's the enemy till it's over, and then it's too late. Only after smoke lifts and blood's soaking into the ground—"

"I protest these accusations!"

"Enough," Anita said. "Randal, SIT DOWN! You going to get yourself hurt."

Randal gave her a deadly look. Nonetheless, he sat down.

"Well, I don't know everything, but I do know that Jerry Wolfe ain't been to class for three weeks now. But that ain't unusual. The Hindu kid ain't been seen for a long time either. He hangs out in the park a lot."

"There's nobody in that park," said Randal. "The pigs searched it again and found nothing."

Tom glared at Randal. "Those hippies skipped town over the winter. They were never nothing more than freaked out hippies—"

"No!" Vesta interrupted angrily. "Pigs said they're gone but they ain't. And the pigs ain't never combed through the woods in Oakwood Park. They're scared like everyone else. Nobody goes in there. Tell it like it is."

"Oh really," Paul dared to sound scoffing. "Because of that stupid legend—"

"The von Jahn curse," said Randal.

"No, you idiots!" Anita shouted. "Because the pigs are protecting it. Because it really is the headquarters of the Clouds and they really are agents of the Establishment."

"And now they got Jerry and Sylvian?" Vesta said.

"That's right."

"Oh sure," said Randal.

"That's right!" Anita howled.

Randal glanced at her for a second and quickly lowered his eyes.

"It's true."

He tried to maintain a stubborn silence.

"It's true."

"It's true," he muttered.

"Far out," Vesta breathed. "So what are we gonna do now?"

Anita seemed to deflate as if the storm within her had finally passed, and the sun broke through the clouds.

"I wish the Masters would speak," she whispered. "I just hate to do something without their approval. They're the only hope of the revolution—"

"We've got to do something," Tom said. "If the Establishment is picking us off, we just can't wait. We gotta hit back. Hard. Where it hurts."

"Well, maybe we can't get at that Goodjohn bastard," said Vesta, "but property can't hide."

"BURN DOWN THE MILL!"

"The brewery too."

"Let's trash Craven's office," Randal added.

"When in doubt, burn."

Tom turned to Anita. "It is the will of the Central Committee that we burn the property of the murdering bourgeoisie exploiters. Democratic Centrism."

Paul grinned.

"If I only knew the will of the Masters," she sighed.

Suddenly she looked up, and her eyes seemed to flash like bolts of lightning.

"Shit, that's it. The Masters spoke. When in doubt, burn."

She extracted another cheroot from somewhere within the folds of her poncho, lit it, inhaled deeply, and blew a string of smoke rings that floated over the table.

"Yeah, burn, burn, burn. . . Let's start with this fucking table. Let's burn the fucking thing. I'm sick of tryin' to figure out what that carving means. I'm sick of being reminded of that son-of-a-bitch Jonathan Burke."

EIGHTEEN

Presidential Penance

PRESIDENT CRAVEN SLAMMED THE phone receiver into its cradle and recited oaths filled with profane imagery. His poetic, if somewhat ridiculous, graphic descriptions dealt with a variety of incestuous and carnal relationships within the important families of Hinnom Valley as well as certain members of the state legislature, and, not to be ignored, the Board of Regents.

Next, he directed his remarks at Dean Bentley who sat across from him. He mocked the Dean's "intelligence quotient," which the President compared to the minuscule measurement of a specific lower anatomical appendage on the Dean's person.

Bentley bowed his head in prayer. He tried to appear contrite and willing to accept the blame for what had happened. He'd warned Craven on many occasions, verbally and by a memo that the President should not dismiss this Goodjohn as a middle-aged con artist who concocted a crazy Eastern stew seasoned with a sprinkling of Sanskrit and magic to seduce naive nubile coeds. Craven had laughed him down with a snide remark that the Great Truth Cloud ought to be named the Great Drugged Fog. The President quoted Vice-President Agnew to the effect that today's college students were over-privileged, over-sexed, and over-educated, a "Spocked generation, packed off to school with Portnoy and pot." Of course, they were an easy mark for any pseudo-mystical religion that trashed humdrum reality.

All we needed to do was harass Goodfraud a bit. Nail his ass for illegal drugs. It wouldn't take him long to pack up and head for California grass. Frauds are notoriously mercurial.

Bentley said he believed otherwise. He took religion in any form more seriously than the President. It was an intuition, he said, some vague gut feeling that Goodjohn Saccidanada presented a threat more significant than the People's Will, which Bentley himself had worked so long and so hard to control. He did agree, of course, that Goodjohn was a fraud. But given an intoxicating dose of the supernatural—the Intergalactic Brain for God's sake!—the divine, the mystical, a blatant fraud had the potential to become dangerous.

On the other hand, he could truthfully say that he'd complied with Craven's wishes. The police had busted Goodjohn and the Clouds for drugs. The groovy-guru, or whatever he happened to call himself that week, had fled. And good riddance. Like expelling the militant blacks. Bentley couldn't be absolutely sure, however, that the groovy-guru had departed Hinnom Valley for good. So, he came up with something bizarre.

He planted the idea in Anita's brain that the Clouds were agents of the System out to assassinate revolutionaries. He knew all about her "Master's Trip," as the stupid Boots kid called it. Using the People's Will to discredit student radicals seemed to him a stroke of genius.

Anita bought it. The snotty Boots punk played his spy role perfectly.

But then, who killed Cathy? A Butcher girl, no less. None of them were capable of such a thing. Talk, yes, but murder? Bentley feared he knew the answer, but this he did not reveal to Craven.

Craven finally exhausted all possible combinations of obscene words in the English language.

"Drugs killed her."

The Dean asked carefully: "What did the Chief say about the park?"

"There's nobody there," growled Craven, shaking his head. "Place is deserted."

"Bet they didn't search the old wood across the lagoon."

"Oh come on, Dick, are you trying to tell me that even the Hinnom Valley Police believe that lunacy about old von Jahn?"

"Never underestimate the supreme power of ignorance coupled with superstitious nonsense, President Craven. You'll always find people willing to accept the most absurd things. Frauds like Goodjohn—and Hallerman for that matter—grasp this principle intuitively."

"So you still think that Shit-John's hiding out in Oakwood? You think maybe those two punks have joined him and his hippie freaks?"

Craven gave Bentley a funny look as if, for a second, he'd let fall a mask he never dared remove. Bentley had the fleeting impression that Craven was playing some sick, perverted game; that the President knew very well what happened in the park, which he did not.

But, Bentley told himself; the President is not that bright—

He looked again and saw that the mask of stupid outrage was back in place. No, not a cover, but Craven's genuine character, he fervently hoped.

"Well, you may be right, Dickey. I'm thinkin' that old schemer Dick Butcher is trying to fuck with me."

"You think the Chief of Police is lying about the park."

"Goddamn right he's lying. He knows what's in them woods all right. He's letting those stinking hippies take over the park in order to undermine my standing with the Board."

"Why?"

"He never wanted me in the family. Was against my marriage. Hates me, the bastard. Wants to see me disgraced, exposed— "

"You think he knows what happened to Cathy Butcher. She was his niece, right?"

Craven gave him another funny look. "Shit, everyone knows what happened to Cathy. Drugs, like I said, that's what you get for hanging out with hippies. That's why I say he's lying. He knows they're in the park. Trying to make a fool of me. Make parents think I've lost control of their spoiled brats, so I get fired."

"Well if that's true we'd better think of some counter-measures—and quickly. The Matreya family's parish priest is right outside this office waiting to talk to you."

Craven blinked, and his long ears glowed dull crimson. "Oh shit! Lemme see the kid's folder."

Bentley shoved a manila folder across the desk. Craven opened it, read a page, thumbed through two more, and read half of the fourth. He appeared more puzzled than angry.

"Kid's kind of a moron," he muttered, staring up at the ceiling. "Can't see him getting into activism or crazy Eastern religion. I mean, kid's pretty dull except for science. Who'd even notice him?"

"I agree. Must be Jerry Wolfe."

"But you said that Mr. Wolfe was deep into the People's Will garbage. And, by the way, I know all about your silly play-acting and your infiltrator. Really, Dick, you've been watching too many spy movies."

"You know?"

"Think I'm an idiot, Dickey? Never rely on a single source of information. I also know all about Mr. Wolfe."

Bentley struggled to appear shocked.

"Both punks are missing, probably hiding out in the park with the other freaks. Chief says nobody's there. Now I'm stuck with this Priest. By the way, why a goddamn Priest?"

"Family's old Polish Catholic. The Church is much more than religion. They'll only trust a priest."

"You called them as soon as this kid turned up missing?"

"I did. I explained to mom and dad that I believed their son had run away with Jerry Wolfe to Canada because he was due to be called up. In three years he's passed one course, Hallerman's I believe. An impressionable kid like Matreya could have been easily turned."

"What did the family say?"

"That Sylvian's brother is a decorated war hero and that his younger brother would never turn traitor to his country."

"So they didn't accept your explanation?"

"Guess not."

Craven gave a scornful laugh. "Hell, neither would I."

"What are we going to tell the priest then? Are we going to be honest and say that we think young Sylvian's hiding out in Oakwood Park doing drugs with some over-sexed guru and his band of limber female followers, and the police are protecting them to make us look foolish? And no one else goes in there because of some old legends about ritual murder?"

Bentley wanted to add that he was growing tired of having to scrape up university funding for the President's extra-curricular "perks." The last perk, a year ago, must have been someone significant. It had used up practically all the extra state funding. Bentley had made the final payment in early December, as usual to a particular university account number so that it looked as if he were merely diverting funds from one area to another. Without coming up for air, Craven had leaped right into the next potential mess.

It was getting worse too. Craven, at least, would make an attempt at being discrete: an empty office, a deserted classroom, a vacant dorm room, sometimes even the park. Now it seemed as if his sense of caution had snapped.

The President's behavior escalated over the years, becoming brazen and foolhardy beyond all reasonable limits. It seemed oddly parallel to the war in Vietnam. The more it ratcheted up, the more senseless and foolish it appeared.

"Well, let's not forget he's a Catholic priest. We could say that young Matreya's been brainwashed by a cult of drugged spiritual anarchists and they're adept at evading our understaffed police force. Peaceful Hinnom Valley is not equipped to deal with the sorts of criminals they have down in Chicago—"

"I like it," Craven said, glancing once more at the folder. "What about that Wolfe kid? Drugs and stuff?"

"Well. . ." Bentley produced another folder. "Wolfe's parents are divorced. Father's a hopeless alcoholic but a big-shot executive for a rival brewery out-of-town. Mother's turned into a middle-aged free-love hippie. She's living off alimony and taking classes right here at BSU. She's been taking Hallerman's courses. My sources say she's probably screwing him too. She's rediscovered her true femininity along with philosophy. Gets stoned a lot. Benny Razor thinks she may be psychotic; she claims an alien cosmic intelligence beams thoughts directly into her brain. She thinks higher thoughts. Hallerman encourages her."

"What'd they say when you called 'em and said their dear son had fled to Canada?"

"His father wondered if he was in debt and how much it would cost the old man. The mother hoped that young Jerry would be happy in Canada because he really doesn't like winters."

"Really? Maybe we can use some of this stuff later. You know, to get that son-of-a-bitch Hallerman just like we nailed old Jonathan Burke."

"Oh, I don't know. Hallerman's smarter than Burke. What are we going to tell the priest?"

"What's his name?"

"Father Tadeusz Loeb. He's with Dorothy at this very moment."

"Ah, Dorothy—" Craven suddenly seemed to lose focus.

Bentley frowned. How bad would it be this time around?

He waited a good minute and then said: "I think we ought to go with the line that young Sylvian has joined a hippie cult. That Jerry Wolfe brainwashed him and provided him with illegal drugs."

"Yes, yes. . ." Craven waved his hand distractedly. "They're all together right now in Oakwood Park. . . what'd they call it? Freaking freely?"

"It also helps us that Jerry Wolfe is Jewish on both sides."

Craven's nose began to twitch like a hungry rat. "Why yes, I see what you mean. That is helpful. We must keep bringing that up. The Jews, of course."

"Of course. Oh, one other thing. Father Loeb's a Dominican. He might know all about Eastern frauds, as well as the Jews."

Father Tadeusz Loeb settled comfortably into the large red leather chair at the end of the desk. He appeared very relaxed as if floating on a cushion of serenity, like a magic carpet. His gray eyes swept the office, briefly lingering on some framed document, a diploma, and framed newspaper clippings.

The priest smiled at the various photographs of President Craven with politicians, business leaders, but most often some celebrity, like the billboard sized glossy photo of Craven on stage with Anita Bryant.

His benevolent smile faded, however, at the sight of Craven's prized swords. Taking a breath, he smoothly adjusted his features and turned his attention to the task at hand.

Father Loeb dressed in the traditional black cassock, collar, and belt. A large, golden-chained crucifix with an excessively contorted and suffering Christ rested on his chest.

The priest's age was difficult to determine. He might have been forty or sixty, even seventy. His smooth skin joined with his silver-blonde beard and sparse hair, his deep-set, grey-blue eyes, all seemed to point in opposing directions.

Life had not carved its joys and tragedies very deeply into that face, but had lightly brushed the skin, gently passing over and leaving his features untouched.

Unfortunately for his priestly dignity, an enormous clown-like nose marred his composed features. Whenever he attempted to look grave and clerical, he resembled the classic picture of the sad circus clown. The more earnest, the more somber he tried to look, the more one wanted to giggle, laugh out loud, and inflate balloons.

Today he wore his most serious expression.

Craven studied a page on his desk. Bentley bit down on his tongue.

"Ah, hum, President Craven," said Father Loeb, repressing a slight lisp, "thanks so much for taking the time out of your hectic schedule to visit with me. You must understand, uh, I do not wish to sound overly critical of, um, your administration, but, well, I've known the Matreya family for over twenty-five years and I'm young Sylvian's confessor, his baptismal priest too, as I am to his dear brother—did you know that his brother has only recently received the Silver Star? Alas, I and the family, we, are very concerned with some of the things that have been happening here recently, at Brunswick State University I mean. Should I say have been allowed to occur? Yes, we are extremely concerned—"

Craven refused to look directly at the priest.

"Well, the Matreya family is very concerned," Father Loeb repeated, obviously expecting some response from the President.

Craven mumbled: "I can certainly understand that. Dick Bentley here is Dean of Students and bears full responsibility for the welfare of the student body. Uh, Dick?"

Bentley peeked at the priest. The man's expression made him think of Red Skelton, and he involuntarily chuckled.

"I see nothing remotely funny about this situation. It is dire to say the least. When loving and good Christian parents like the Matreyas entrust their precious children to a university, it goes without saying that they expect the school to assume the full burden of the child's safety and well-being. Why this is the minimum expectation. It is a moral responsibility. Indeed, it is a legal responsibility. I want to add that a school is nearly identical to a home, replete with values, duties, familial love and protection. Take note, gentlemen, only a few years ago, on a visit to Nazareth, the Holy Father proclaimed that family life is a communion of love, that the home itself is the school of the Gospel, sacred and of inviolable character—and, hum, I would say that this is also true of the school as the home of the child, of inviolable character, quoting the Holy Father himself—"

"Uh, Dick?" Craven croaked.

"Yes, yes, we couldn't agree more," Bentley, said as smoothly as he could manage. "We—the faculty and administration of BSU—all see ourselves as surrogate parents. We believe this makes us unique. We are not obsessed with prestige, which in truth cares nothing about the individual student but values everything in terms of funding and public relations. We do not sacrifice values on the altar of finance. However, like your Church, Father, we cannot lock out the modern world entirely, especially during this time with all of its turmoil, rebelliousness, permissiveness, and counter-culture. Your Church, Father, is in the midst of such a struggle. Not so?"

"Well, of course, this is very true. But as dear Paul once said—as you are, uh, undoubtedly aware—one must live in the world and yet need not be of the world. Allow me to add our Catechism teaches that moral permissiveness and outright rebellion against God rest upon an erroneous conception of human freedom, which of course arises from the fact that men inherit a sinful nature, and, uh, well, such a wounded nature is inclined to evil. If I recall the words exactly: 'Therefore, those in charge of education must provide children instruction respectful of this truth'—that their nature has been perverted by sin—which, alas, I must sadly note from personal experience has been lacking here at BSU, even among the faculty. I point out one, Professor Jonathan Burke from the Department of History, was dismissed some time ago for the sin of concupiscence, as we say. And, more recently, one, Paul Hallerman, is reported to suffer from the same, uh, weakness. In the classroom too he is quite irresponsible with his opinions—note I do not say facts— which he tends to pass off as knowledge but which, when viewed dispassionately, are outrageous blasphemies that pretend to be rather pathetic attempts at satire and irony. Alas, hum, also paganism and atheistic Eastern trash have contaminated this University. These things may sound lovely; on the surface, they are quite intoxicating to romantic youth and people of a weak nature. But such things conceal the Evil One's oldest and most successful temptation, to whit: *thou shalt be as God—*"

"I take it you're referring to the Great Truth Cloud, Father?" Craven inquired sourly.

"Why, of course, sir. I believe this person calls himself Goodjohn Saccidananda—which, as any educated person must know, cannot be authentic but is a rather silly and contrived compound of the Sanskrit words, *sat, chit, Ananda,* meaning being, consciousness, bliss. Only God knows what he's trying to say by the name Goodjohn except for the obvious."

What didn't the Dominican bastard know? Bentley wondered.

The good priest, as if reading his mind added: "Of course, there have been other troubles, grave problems in this town. It seems to me, gentlemen—and I say this in the spirit of Christian charity—that you do indeed bear legal responsibility for the welfare of the young people entrusted to your care and that you have been, let us say, less than diligent guarding your gates against the various forms of barbarism that afflict our society."

"Yes Father," Bentley said carefully, "we agree, and we have taken measures to fortify our gates as you put it. The police informed us that the Great Truth Cloud has fled Hinnom Valley due to our strict policies on drugs. It may be that young Mr. Matreya is with them and therefore beyond our protection, which naturally causes us great pain but is, as you say, a rather sad consequence of these troubled times we are living in—"

The priest smiled and closed his eyes for a second. He intended to seem understanding and sad at the same time. He ended up resembling the sad circus clown who'd just suffered a kick in the rump and suffered the indignity with a smile, (and clownishly which was unintended).

"Oh, come now, sir. I suppose; next you'll try to tell me that Sylvian has run off to Canada with that, you know, that. . ." dropping his voice to a almost a whisper, the Priest raised his eyebrows knowingly and feigned reluctance when he finally uttered, "Jewish boy, Mr. Wolfe."

"More likely with the Clouds—" Bentley stammered, "because of—"

"A young woman named Pearl. Ah hum, yes, I know all about her, and I think it quite unlikely. Sylvian is a chaste young man in his rather simple but humble way. No, he would not succumb to sexual temptations, or the doctrines of atheistic pantheism, and he is certainly not a friend to Jews. To be frank, I have counseled the Matreya family thoroughly in this matter and together we agree that our dear Sylvian has been kidnapped by this godless cult of hippies, and the administration, your administration, President Craven, bears the full legal and moral responsibility for this heinous crime, and I am here to impress upon you the family's concern that something be done."

"And allow me to assure you, Father, that the authorities are doing everything possible."

"Well, hum, this is precisely our concern. . . that everything is indeed being done, *by you*."

"Is there something specific. . . a specific family demand, Father?"

"Oh my, no. Of course not. No one is making demands."

He pensively stared at a place above Craven's head and said softly: "Alas, young Sylvian has been rather lax of late in his duties to Church and home. He's not fully communicated with his dear parents, as he should. I don't mean to be misleading—perhaps 'kidnap' is too strong a word—let us say brainwashed? Young Sylvian is a rather impressible lad. A less charitable person might call him dull. A cruel person might use the word idiot, although the lad is brilliant in a strange, albeit very specific, way, but not in the sad realities of our corrupted everyday world. Well, shall we call it 'emotional kidnapping?' Naturally, this says something about the state of education here. I mean to say; you must ask yourselves if you have provided young Sylvian with the moral values, and especially religious instruction, which might have shielded him from such temptations? You do bear that responsibility."

Craven struggled to suppress his rage. "We are doing everything possible. Given the rebelliousness of today's youth culture, I'd say we're doing splendidly. But there's TV, radio, records, movies, books—its cultural infection, bound to spread through weak, impressionable young minds. A great deal of responsibility falls upon the home and the Church, Father."

"Well, of course. Nevertheless, young Sylvian disappeared from this university, in this town, and the family is very, I repeat, very concerned."

"Yeah, well, there's still the chance that he went to Canada with Mr. Wolfe of his own free will."

"Respectfully, sir, I'm forced to disagree. I've never known Sylvian to associate with Jews."

Craven exploded: "WHAT THE HELL DO YOU WANT FROM US?"

Father Loeb frowned slightly and stared at his hands, which he held face-high fingertip-to-fingertip.

"Well, sir, as I've said several times now, the family is concerned that this university has done everything possible to educate impressionable young people, especially in the areas of morality and religion—"

"WHAT DOES THAT MEAN?"

Bentley bowed his head in embarrassment. The priest was able to play the president like a church organ.

"Traditionally, the Church provides numerous avenues of penance for the truly contrite. The Church recommends almsgiving, indulgences and such for those who grasp the true nature of penance. The Matreya family has been generous supporters of St. Stanislas, and moreover they would indeed welcome some demonstration from this university of a renewed emphasis upon the spiritual welfare of the young people entrusted to its care—"

"Would the family itself share in, let us say, the material nature of this renewed emphasis?"

"Most certainly. As you may know, the family business is bookbinding. And it so happens by a fortunate coincidence that the Cathedral school is preparing a rather substantial order for new Catechisms. *Vatican Two*, you know—"

"Allow me, then, to assure you, Father, that the Board of Regents upon my enthusiastic recommendation would most likely desire to make a handsome contribution to this educational project. Will such a contribution serve to alleviate the family's concerns?"

"Why yes. . .of course by *handsome* you infer the entire order. How generous. Perhaps the university would also care to sponsor a summer conference, or two, on morality and religion for the young people of St. Stanislas? Pay for transportation from Chicago?"

"Done."

"Of course you will pursue young Sylvian's whereabouts?"

"Of course."

"And notify me before informing the family. If the news is bad, it is best that their parish priest break it to them."

"Absolutely."

Father Loeb leaped out of his chair and shook Craven's hand. He turned and gave Bentley a vigorous handshake as well. The priest's flesh felt soft and spongy.

"Oh my, look at the time. I must be going. To meet a class actually. Did you know that I myself am a professor at our humble seminary in Chicago? Oh yes, my specialty is in the field of Christian Ethics. I'm also considered an expert in the theology of apophasis. I'm sure you're familiar with apophasis, Reverend Bentley. Perhaps not? Apophasis is the profound insight of Catholic theologians, in which the very concept of God exists beyond frail, limited human languages: To assign God any category of thought—say God is good, or great—confines God to human conceptualizations of goodness or greatness, which is preposterous for obvious reasons. Consequently, silence before the mystery of God is the only solid and true theology—and I've written many books about it."

Bentley yawned.

"I hope you have a good class," Craven said dryly.

"Oh, thank you, sir. I always do."

Father Loeb strode to the door and then paused. "By the way, I do admire your medieval swords, my dear President Craven. They seem quite genuine, although it is evident to the trained eye that they're replicas."

"Yeah, they're fakes."

But Father Loeb had already made it to the outer office and was talking amicably to the President's secretary.

SECOND INTERLUDE

Reverend Bentley

"...AND AS RECENT EVENTS here and throughout the country have shown, we are at a turning point in history, perhaps a rupture in the history of American civilization.

Ours is an age of crisis. Like it or not, we are the hinge upon which modern history now turns. We stand at the threshold of a new era.

Today we hear about relevance, liberation, activism, and a thousand other words which taken together prove beyond doubt that certain radicals are questioning the very essence of civilization. Some even ridicule our sacred traditions.

What is a young person to do?

We, the Administration of Brunswick State University, are deeply committed to the welfare of our students. We believe that contemporary problems will never be solved by secular means. We hold that such issues are at heart religious issues. The answers young people seek will not be found in the dangerous quicksand of cultural relativism, subjective romanticism, and exotic cults, which are actually fancy wrappings for sexual license and deviant nihilism.

Despite the present obsession with fads and "happenings," there is and will always be an objective, timeless, and sacred core of Truth, which can only be found in the Judeo-Christian tradition. It is the bedrock of American civilization, the essential foundation upon which young people must build their lives.

God is still the God who so loved the world that He sent His only Son, Christ Jesus, who died for our sins. It is God who inspired the founders of America. Without Jesus, there can be no salvation for men. God is not Krishna, Buddha, Shiva, Rama, Kali, Allah, Odudrea, Ra, Quetzalcoatl, the Tao, or the Great Spirit. God is One, found only within the Holy Scriptures.

Therefore, the BSU administration has decided to sponsor a Conference here in Hinnom Valley, and a Conference in Chicago, as well, at St. Stanislas Cathedral. The two Conferences will be entitled: *Religion, Youth Culture, and the Rebellion Against God*. Both will allow time for a much-needed discussion.

Schedules will be released shortly. Course credit will be granted.

The Administration would like to give special thanks to Butcher Brewery for their generous donation. Also, a note of thanks goes to the Hinnom Valley Chamber of Commerce for its help in the planning of the conferences.

We want to acknowledge Father Tadeusz Loeb, whose pastoral concern and exceptional talents are largely responsible for this renewal of Christian values. Such programs give lie to the silly things one often reads in recent irresponsible and parochial news magazines that gleefully proclaim: "God is dead." Rather, it is Man who dies without God.

The Reverend Richard Bentley, Dean of Students.
The Brunswick State University Administration.

OFFICIAL MEMO:

To be distributed across campus, published in local newspapers, and tacked to the Bulletin Board of the Student Union at BSU.

May 1, 1970.

Leonides of Corinth (a sophist): . . .and so you claim, Basailius, following your teacher Xenophanes, that this god of his resembles us neither in mind nor body? Remains in one place and yet is everywhere? Sees everything above and below? Hears, knows, and wills all that is? Without effort, Basailius, you say this one god moves everything? And finally, this god created all things?

Basailius: Aye, Leonides. This is Truth, single and immutable. God is One, infinitely powerful, all good. Today. Yesterday. Tomorrow.

Leonides: Such was your teacher's opinion then? Surely, he was writing comic verse. What of Zeus? Poseidon? The Lord of Delphi, Apollo? I myself have heard him speak.

Basailius: Xenophanes did not jest. Nor did he indulge in sophistry as your own master, Protagoras. For such gods as the Olympians love and hate as the case may be; are spiteful, cruel, jealous, vain, rude, perverse, drunken—as the case may be. If dogs could write Homeric verse, their gods would bark, pant with lolling tongues, sniff shit and urinate in their own temples.

Leonides: And this One God is unlike mortal men?

Basailius: The One is greater than can be thought. He is without lust or hate, anger, or pain. Neither does He endure sympathy, empathy, regrets, hopes, or vanity. Such qualities indicate a lack, a need, which cannot be *God*.

Leonides: HA! A contradiction. Two contradictions. The One is still human. His qualities are still mortal ones: total seeing, hearing, all-powerful. . . human qualities raised to monstrous heights. Is your god creator? Then your god must have desire. Before he created, the desire to create must have arisen within him as a yearning. So he changed: from a god without desire to one with desire: passionate and with longing.

Basailius: No. God cannot change.

Leonides: Is not the birth of desire change?

Basailius: God is sublime and perfect.

Leonides: Sublime? Perfect? Total power without feeling? With no possibility of compassion? Give me lecherous Zeus any day. Your One is a monster. How could anyone approach such a god? How could such an empty abstraction even guess the trials and weaknesses from which humans suffer, let alone comprehend the dark and twisting and contradictory drives that motivate us? Even if he created us, lacking such, our soul would always remain opaque to him. Indeed incomprehensible. And, say, someday he decided to be born among men, as an Egyptian perhaps. He would suffer all we suffer except for the very thing that makes us men. He would remain *Athanasia*, an Immortal, even if his flesh died. He would never experience, nor would he really know, the ultimate pain of men.

Basailius (growing angry):He knows the all!

Leonides: That is the contradiction. In knowing the all, he knows not the nothing.

Fragment 38, from *Fragments and Texts of the Lesser Presocratic Philosophers,* translated and edited by Paul F. Hallerman, Brunswick State University Press: Hinnom Valley, 1966.

NINETEEN

"Where the Shadows Lie"

SYLVIAN DIED. HE DIED every night and was reborn every morning. He died every morning and was reborn every night. Whether it be Oakwood, some rattling old house near campus, or on the street, the place and time were not necessary. Only death was significant, for there is no rebirth without it.

He possessed a vague memory of his past. He lived what came, as it happened. He told Jerry that they were searching for Goodjohn, but this was merely to keep Frodo off Sam's back. In truth, he wasn't looking for anything. Gradually, life became dazzling simple: eat, sleep, shit (and fuck?). A marvelous serenity grew from the inside, warming him on the coldest of nights. Was he living like an animal? Yes. . . and no.

Humans are animals and suffer what animals suffer. But humans add to suffering. Sylvian found an old discarded book without a cover or title page in the park. It told him the story of a wounded man, a man shot with a poisoned arrow, who instead of calling for the physician wanted to know who'd shot him, what village he'd come from, what family? "Only after I know these things will I call for the physician." That man would surely die.

"Had to be High Elves last night," said Jerry Wolfe.

Sylvian recalled little of the previous evening. He couldn't remember the people at the party. He couldn't remember a great many evenings, in fact; the dead have no memory.

The party house sat rotting away on a dark, sinister street not far from the brewery. Jerry knew a few people. Sylvian didn't know anybody.

208

People kept pouring in off the street. They were mostly brewery and mill workers, but there also appeared to be a trickling of hippies and students scattered about, and—surprise—a contingent of blacks, angry and loud. In this life, Sylvian admired blacks. They'd endured. They were still enduring.

He saw James Rutledge arguing politics with an old mill worker. We ain't an economic class, James declared. We's a nation. Oh yeah? How 'bout integration? The older man asked. Integration's for you whites, said James. America was born racist. Never will change. We're a nation. We demand five southern states. A black confederacy. Where we have the power, black power. Then we'll negotiate with whitey. The older fellow shook his head. Gotta work like everybody else. Get a job, earn some money.

James laughed. Identity first, he said. Self-respect. We've already worked. That's all we done in Amerika is work. Never got paid. Work got us nowhere. Only black power—

Someone gave Sylvian a joint, and the combination of bad wine and sticky pot made it impossible for him to follow the remainder of the argument, precisely, at least.

A mill worker brought out flutes and began to play like Jerry's High Elves. A crazy group dance formed in the middle of the room. It swept to the walls and sucked Sylvian into its vortex.

Everyone began singing a tune from the Byrds, *Mr. Tambourine Man:*

> Take me for a trip
>
> On your magic, swirling ship
>
> All my senses have been stripped
>
> And my hands can't feel to grip. . .

Sylvian's "stripped senses" caused him to spin out of orbit and crash into a wall. The cheap drywall crumbled upon impact and seemed to swallow Sylvian whole. People were screaming obscenities. Sylvian felt only contentment.

Sometime later, during this dark night of soulless wraiths, Frodo dragged Sam back to the Shire—in this age Oakwood Park—thereby rewriting Tolkien.

It had been like this for weeks. Nights a dizzying blur and days sleeping in the park, searching for Goodjohn, haunting the roads like restless ghosts, passing house after house until they came to a party—Jerry, like his hobbits, always knew of somebody having a party.

As the two hobbits passed silently through Mordor, they noted how windows glowed with the same counterfeit blue, casting the same spells, dispensing the same drugs, speaking in the same tongue, which was the foul language of the Orcs. Mordor's Evil Eye lives in the Amerikan home, Jerry pointed out, and Sylvian agreed.

Wherever they went, they heard rumors: the Clouds had been seen on campus, man, or in the park, or on some street downtown, but that was a few days ago, or last week, and nobody's seen 'em since. Don't fuck with them. And don't go into the park.

Jerry and Sylvian had taken up residence in the haunted park. Sylvian spent his days reading Hermann Hesse—he especially liked *Siddhartha*, *Magister Ludi*, and *Demian* but didn't care much for *Steppenwolf*. Most of all, he loved the book without a cover.

Sylvian often thought about how easy it was to die. He felt happily empty. He adopted a new identity every night. One night he was a revolutionary, the next he passed for a soul brother, and the next a pothead like Jerry and yet nights to be tested.

One night they found themselves at an SHS party, where a gathering was taking place in a fortress-like mansion north of town on a large private lake. A Board member hosted the party.

Sylvian had heard about the party at the student union. His first sight of the mansion seemed to bring forth an old memory, one from the old country, of castles and wars, of memoirs written in haste. The memory urged him to go.

He explained to Jerry that they were going to see the High Elves. "You know, Elves who are always high," said Sylvian, attempting, perhaps, for the first time in his life, a pun. "Elves don't need to get high," Jerry answered, not amused. In Jerry's world there was nothing funny about Tolkien.

By the time they arrived—it had taken all of the afternoon and most of the early evening to walk the distance from town—everyone was drunk including the Board member hostess, the widow Frieda Uberhuntin, who, at the moment of their arrival, was flirting with the young men. Later, she disappeared with one (or two).

Jerry proceeded to get drunk while Sylvian studied the crowd. He noticed, very imprecisely, the multifarious ways they suffered—some were in real physical pain; for others, the pain was a kind of gnawing anxiety, ill-defined yet tangible; real. He got the sense that no-thing, no happening, could relieve their mysterious dissatisfaction or brightened their subliminal darkness, though they acted as if they lived in a constant state of ecstasy. They knew not why. They drank and drank, smoked and laughed, fought and fucked until the mysterious illness went away— though only for a time.

Warmed by beer and other refreshments, the SHS women became oddly rancorous. The men seemed to enjoy their uncharacteristic behavior. The spectacle was captivating for a while, but as the women became decidedly more aggressive—the uncharitable might have said lewd—the males seemed to recoil, and quickly the mood shifted. The men became strangely, angry.

Booze-soaked anger turned into rage. Fights erupted, which the ladies appeared to enjoy and which seemed to induce further displays.

Sylvian watched, fascinated.

A beautiful SHS girl with long brown hair, pouting red lips, green eyes, loads of makeup, and a wicked smile, slithered in close to him. He studied her passively. She gulped down rivers of beer and spewed forth all sorts of details about herself and her home—she came from Chicago—and her hoards of boyfriends, of whom she'd dumped one after the other, for some inadequacy or another. As she rambled and guzzled, Sylvian noticed that she'd begun to drool and that her meticulously coiffed hair and finely engineered makeup had begun to show signs of decay, mimicking the peeling paint and drooping wallpaper lining of the house. Her once graceful, carefully assembled person dissolved into a lolling heap of wrinkled clothes sprawled out on Sylvian's couch like a rag doll.

Belching between sentences, she winked seductively and began pawing at him like a dog. He stared at her calmly and remained still, quietly relaxed.

At last, after losing interest and giving up, the woman flopped back into the cushions. Burying herself under pillows and blankets, she promptly began to snore. She rigorously scratched at her fuzzy sweater and in the process ripped it open, exposing her. . .ahem. . . endowments— which without the confines of a bra, rare for an SHS girl, were quite large and in full view.

Smiling, Sylvian calmly got up, bowed, turned, and quickly made his way out.

He explored the high towers of Gondor, searching for Frodo, room by room. In one darkened chamber he found the Mistress of Gondor in the act of torturing one of her young prisoners on a wide bed. He quit the towers and explored the dungeons only to find more interrogations in progress. He finally discovered Frodo in a dark alcove on the ground floor of the Steward's Tower.

Frodo was kissing and fondling a drunken elf maiden. Sylvian watched in silence while Frodo struggled to get her jeans off. He got them as far as her knees. She was attempting the same with Frodo, and with the same results. Frodo, cursing like a mill worker, attempted the act of copulation, which is somewhat tricky for hobbits and elves given the differences in their respective physiologies. The elf maiden grunted, and Frodo cursed again. He continued cursing as he discovered that his hobbit-sized member refused to acquire the prerequisite solidity. The power of the One Ring was no help in this enterprise, a detail Tolkien failed to mention.

"Fuckin' faggot!" screeched the elf maiden. She pushed him away, pulled up her jeans, and staggered off in search of another hobbit.

"Come on, Frodo," Sam said gently, helping him on with his trousers, "here the rings of power are powerless."

They found their way out, stepping lightly between bodies of passed-out revelers who were stoned, drunk, or tripping. Aspiring beauty queens lay scattered about like corpses after a battle. Their attractive features had gone slack and lifeless, and their beauty magically transformed. Limbs and bodies contorted, heads lolled—arms askew, legs spread, every secret place exposed. The transmutations were far from enticing; to Sam, they seemed hideous and disgusting. Some belched, others farted. One slept soundly guarding her vomit. Staring at them brought on a momentary bout of nausea—and sadness of an indefinite duration.

"High Elves, hey Frodo?"

Frodo frowned and fingered a sore spot on his forehead. "I think one of the bastards hit me. But they did give us magic waybread, Sam."

Sam gazed across the field to the lagoon. Bright and cheerful beneath the noon sun, the long grasses glistened brilliant green after the morning rains. Beyond this peaceful world, however, loomed the darkling wood of evergreens and ancient oaks, haunted by the ghost of von Jahn and, for this age, Cathy Butcher—and her killer, the wicked Divine Woo-Woo, FBI agent, fraud, criminal—Sauron the Dark Lord.

They were unable to muster the courage to enter there. Frodo always discovered some reason to postpone the attempt until the following day. Sam regularly found that Frodo's excuses made perfect sense.

"Waybread?"

"Yeah, look." Frodo opened the little rucksack he always carried and produced a dried and stale brown muffin. Crumbs broke off like old plaster. He took a bite and chewed.

"Take some, Sam. It'll keep us going for weeks. We eat this, and there'll be no more sneaking into the cafeteria and begging."

He extended the thing to Sylvian. It resembled a dollop of dried dog-dropping that had acquired a greenish fungus-like skin.

"Shit, Jer. . . Frodo. Stealing is a hindrance. Begging is better. It's humiliating. Humiliation is good."

"This is magic. We gotta go to Mordor. We gotta eat first."

"Why not do what we've been doing? Let Sauron bury Sauron."

"Shit, Sam. I'm supposed to kill Sauron. I ain't even got close."

"He's gone to California."

"No, he ain't! He's right here. In there—" Frodo pointed across the field, the lagoon, to the wood. "We just can't see 'em. Our senses ain't been stripped."

"Maybe Anita's wrong about him. Maybe he really is a god-like being, an Avatar."

"Fuck, Sam-man, you're losing touch with reality."

"He's beyond reality like Hesse says: a symbol which always stands outside the personal and the historical realms."

Frodo frowned with intense concentration. He scratched at his beard: "Sam, you're mocking me now—"

"Oh, no. Never." Sam pretended to be hurt. "Never would I do such a thing. I know what it is to be ridiculed."

"Think I'm so high that I can't tell Amerika from Middle Earth?"

"Certainly not. Middle Earth is real. Everything else is an illusion."

Frodo suddenly became angry. "This is serious, Sam! We're carrying out the orders of the great Masters of the Revolution. This ain't no fantasy. It's real."

"All right, all right. . ." Sam feigned sorrow. "Here, give me a bite of that waybread."

"It's just a spoiled hash muffin some chick gave me at the party. I'm gonna toss it—"

"No, no, wants some." Sam grabbed the muffin, broke off a large piece, and stuffed it into his mouth. It tasted bitter, like old mold. There was another flavor, pungent, vaguely sweet, one he'd never experienced before. He chewed and swallowed nonetheless as if he participated in a pie-eating contest.

"Are you crazy?" Frodo howled.

Instantly Sam felt dizzy. "Hey Frodo, have you heard of the Many-Universes Interpretation of Quantum Mechanics?"

Frodo stared dumbly. Hobbits hate science and know nothing about it.

"It's the simplest solution. You merely take the probability wave at face value. You merely accept that all the probabilities are realized simultaneously with each act of observation that assigns values to the quantum numbers and collapses the wave function. Simple huh? It means that the world is continually splitting into separate realities with each act of observation like branches of an infinite bush. This guy named Hugh Everett thought it up in 1955. Ain'it far-out?"

Frodo stuck his hand into the pocket of his field jacket.

"That's crazy." Sam shook his head.

"Man, you gotta come down! We gotta to do this—"

"Ho, ho, what's wrong, Frodo? Lost the Ring?"

"Man, you gotta get real and fight for the revolution." Frodo gritted his teeth. "You got enough acid in you to do Chezcago."

Suddenly, Sam began to stagger about in a kind of drunken parody of a dance. He spun and jumped, twisted about and nearly collapsed.

"He's over there. Follow me—"

Then he started to gallop in a zigzag run towards the wood.

Frodo screamed after him. "You'll get yourself killed! Come back here, you fucking idiot!"

Sam stopped at the edge of the wood. "He's in there, Frodo, waiting for us. Ain't gone to California grass 'cuz he's a wolf of the steppes and so hard to see, and we're all gonna come together right now over *he*. Let's go find Siddhartha!" Sam loved to recite ancient lore. Fear, anxiety disappeared whenever he recited the tales he'd heard from his gramps when he was a young hobbit. Delivery of the recitation was far more comfortable than thinking.

He plunged into the shadows trailing laughter behind him, which sounded like a siren speeding into the dead of night.

"Shit!" Frodo swore, fingering the automatic in his pocket. Stupid little shit's gonna give us away." He looked around expecting to see the blue uniforms of the Hinnom Valley police, or possibly the olive-green National Guard converging on the lagoon. But the park appeared deserted as usual, and the air seemed stagnant without the slightest breeze.

"Goddammit, this is serious," he said aloud. With this declaration, he too loped into the wood like a red wolf and disappeared into the darkness.

Somewhere in Middle Earth the sun still shone, although now in this place it rushed towards the rim of the world, searing the clouds that floundered in its wake like ocean foam. Somewhere the wind heralded an approaching spring storm.

But not in Oakwood.

Darkness became a palatable thing. It rose from the leaf-like litter of the forest floor, joining in mid-air with the deeper shadows of the evergreens. The sky, broken into shards and slivers by the forest roof, was dull gray. The forest was a borderland world between day and night, a place where both seemed to merge unable to decide on light or dark. Gloomy, laden with the sweet smell of pine, the wood appeared sunken in perpetual dusk.

Frodo heard Sam utter a cry.

"It's here—"

He sounded close. Abruptly Frodo crashed into him. He had stopped dead at a great oak tree. Eyes shut, he connected hard with its trunk.

"What's here?"

"A path."

"Don't see no path."

"Pearl's path. Like before."

His eyes were firmly shut.

"Ain't no fucking path. . . Hey, what'd you mean before?"

"The last time. . . Sam was here with the Clouds."

"What—?" No one lives in Mordor 'cept for Orcs and trolls. . . and the Nazgul. . . and the Dark Lord himself."

Frodo furrowed his brows, looking more like a red-bearded dwarf than a hobbit.

"They're waiting for us. . . She's here."

Sam stepped around the tree and began walking purposefully forward.

"Been here before. . . Been here before. . ." Frodo repeated the words, shaking his head. "He's lying! All this time. Been here before. . . Oh shit! *An infiltrator.* The infiltrator! Goddamn FBI."

He drew the weapon from his pocket. "It's you. You're the traitor."

"Come on, Frodo. Let's go find Sauron."

"Ain't no Sauron. Ain't no Goodjohn. You're the asshole who murdered Cathy."

"Frodo, you're in Mordor. Can't see clearly."

"That's fiction you little asshole-traitor."

He pointed the snub-nosed automatic at Sylvian's back. Sylvian turned to face him as if he felt the movement.

"I'm takin' you back to Anita. To the revolutionary tribunal. Revolutionary justice."

Sylvian laughed: "Now that's fiction."

Jerry's hand shook. "I'm. . . serious!"

"Fuck you," Sylvian said happily.

BANG!

That a toy pistol should make such a thunderous noise startled both of them, yet Sylvian didn't flinch even when a fragment of bark struck his arm. Jerry, on the other hand, shook violently.

BANG!

He fired again. A branch cracked and fell. Sylvian stared at him with vacant eyes as if every thought had been sucked out of his skull.

The look infuriated Jerry. "Son-of-a-bitch!" he frothed, as white foam ran down his chin and dripped into his wolfish beard. "I'll kill you myself."

Sylvian turned and bolted away, darting around trees like a rabbit, changing direction instantaneously.

BANG!

A third shot shattered the wooded silence. Jerry assassinated a tree.

Sylvian ran on. Gasping for air and chest burning, he ran as mindlessly as the wind blew.

The ground began to rise, growing steeper with each step. Last time there'd been a valley, now he climbed a mountain.

The pressure in his chest sent searing jabs of pain, one after the other, into his ribs and his right side. He wondered—his first rational thought—if Jerry had hit him. Although the echoes rang in his ears and seemed to shake the trees, he didn't believe Jerry had fired a fourth time.

He slowed to shuffling walk, and then in the next minute, he stopped altogether. He kneeled down in a bed of pine needles and cones. A nauseating dizziness overwhelmed him and a terrible pain shot through his temples as if a bullet had entered one of his ears and exited his forehead. His stomach ached, and his throat burned. He leaned forward and vomited.

Mercifully the darkness took him, and he swooned. He welcomed oblivion. It was good.

"I knew you'd come back."

Words fluttered somewhere above his head. Moist warmth settled upon his exposed skin as light broke through the needled canopy and stirred the dew of the forest floor. Warmth seeped into his aching muscles like a steam bath.

"What did you find?" asked the voice.

He sat up, back against an ancient oak. So serene, like a dream. The voice came from a dream solution into which memory had dissolved—

Warmth took form, stabbed into his head, too bright to be real. Colors danced and rotated like small wheels, sunlight reflected through scores of water droplets, passing through eyelid slits. . . like the double-slit experiment: particles give an interference pattern, yet light is a wave. He closed an eye. Rays of sunlight became particles. Light, too, was stoned.

"Dare you to challenge the great mystery?" The voice sounded irritated.

He wanted it to go away. The voice is ruining this happy numbness, he thought. Seeking to see the voice brought suffering. Better to remain in this dreamy state of limp detachment.

"Go away."

"Open your eyes."

"Go away."

"Open your eyes. Please?"

Arms and legs felt heavy, muscles ached and his skin itched. His eyes burned as if pierced by needles of pure flame. Nonetheless, he risked a glance—

"Pearl."

She was wearing a single piece, ankle-length white gown, low cut and sleeveless, constructed from a kind of silky, pure white material that reflected light like a mirror. Skin and hair seemed nearly as white and shining as the dress itself—incredible, he thought, photons, billions fused in the form of a girl. Form without density, weightless, indefinable, and insubstantial fused but not at rest, jiggling, position in space uncertain—the Heisenberg Uncertainty Principle. Brilliant emptiness in the form of Pearl.

"Don't want to see," he moaned. "Rest here. Stay high forever."

"You can't. It's a rule."

"Pearl, go away."

"You don't mean that. You love me. You crave me."

She smiled. Beneath the flimsy gown, she was naked. Her little breasts and sharp nipples pushed against the gossamer material.

He did crave her. He didn't want to. Behind her stood Father Loeb, frowning. She smelled as sweet as the fresh pines. She was temptation incarnate, discontent, desire, possessed of seven devils. Or was it three? Depended on the legend. He did love her.

"You do want me," she said, reading his thoughts as if they floated up like steam and formed words in the moist air.

"No—"

"Come to me. I'm all you ever wanted. I am Shakti. I am Parvati. I am Mary of Magdala. I am the play of the divine, the divine at play."

"Go away."

"You cannot deny your cravings. Would you deny yourself?"

"Sam will not move until he's found the way out of Mordor."

"This is a place of hungry ghosts. Why did you come here? Searching for me?"

"Go away."

"Why did your ancestors leave the old country?"

Silence.

"You want me—" She was breathing heavily. "Go ahead. Come to the divine."

She reached out and touched him on the cheek. It felt like being electrocuted. A current surged through his body.

He jumped on her then, knocked her backward. He tore at the soft material of her gown, ripping the dress completely off. Naked and glistening, she lay back and did not resist. She spread her arms, her legs, smiling.

He pawed at her. His hands slid down her thighs—

She was laughing, mocking and derisive laughter as if to ridicule his awkward fumbling.

Her mockery froze him. Then he realized that he had succumbed to another illusion. Another chemically-created, simulated reality. The girl with kaleidoscope eyes—

"No, no, come on—" she whined, grasping at him.

Her touch burned his skin like hot coals. The current flowed into every cell, and he knew he was going to die.

"You love me," she hissed as she opened his belt and pulled off his jeans.

Abruptly it all went wrong.

She clutched with greater urgency, clawing at him, bringing blood. She grasped his penis.

"Oh, Jesus!"

Oakland. . .putrid, rotten, and smelling like a Chicago slaughterhouse. . . rank and rotted vegetation after a flood. . .the living Park became a graveyard.

Temptation died.

. . .claws grasping, drawing living blood, pulling at him. . .

Frightful power energized the illusion. "Shakti," he heard her gurgle.

She laughed.

She growled, and coughed, and yowled.

Her hands held him tightly. Her powerful thighs, thick as the bowls of the trees, brown and as hard as bark, wrapped about his torso.

She burned terribly. She drew him in deeper, her laughter, echoing in Sylvian's ears . . .all the time mocking him with her laughter.

No! A lie, like the whole rotten world. Then from somewhere in his shattered memory he saw St. Barlaam. And he heard the saint chanting: "*Samyama, Samyama. . .*"

This is the day I die. . .

Mercifully, the darkness took him, and he fell away from the dream into a deeper dream, darker than any he'd ever experienced.

He dropped into a realm in which one hears only the voice of the saints: "*Samyama, Samyama—*"

"*Release, release.*"

TWENTY

The Battle of Oakwood

"GANDALF! I KNEW YOU'D come." Jerry Wolfe cried.

"Aye," the phantom in white said gravely. "The Shadow stretches forth its hand and covers the land. An age passes. I fear there are evil times ahead."

"Gandalf, man, you can count on me. One of the Ringwraiths attacked me, but I chased the thing off—" Jerry held up the automatic. Small and delicate, the pistol resembled one of those artificial cigarette lighters with its pearl handle and blue barrel.

"The Ring! Do not tempt me."

Jerry quickly put the pistol back into his jacket pocket.

"Do you understand the peril?" asked Gandalf.

Jerry thought very hard. At last, in a mechanical voice, reciting from deep memory, he chanted: "The One Ring is evil. It possesses you, not you, it. The more you use it, the greater its hold on you. Causes you to fade, decrease, become more and more attached, miserable, a repulsive creature like Gollum, malicious in small things, totally self-consumed, hating and loving at once, attached to both, for as the self grows weak obsession with self becomes stronger."

"Very good," said Gandalf. "Alas, you must also realize this is not the Third Age, nor do we live in Middle Earth. Hobbits are extinct as are Elves and Dwarves, and Orcs. And you are not Frodo."

Not-Frodo scratched his red beard dejectedly. He wished (and not for the last time) that he'd never left the Shire. "But. . . there is still a Dark Lord?"

"Many, as there exist many rings of power. It's harder to find them now than in the Third Age."

"I guess—" Jerry agreed reluctantly. The fact he was not Frodo would take some getting used to, but he had to believe it, this was Gandalf, after all.

"The land of Mordor doesn't exist where the shadows lie."

"No."

"All around us is a dark land."

Jerry rubbed his eyes. Gandalf's beard and eyebrows were as white as snow, his cloak white, just as the books said. His skin was fair, creased with age, and he smoked a pipe stuffed with the sweetest smelling pot. Curious though, when Jerry looked askance, glanced at the wizard from an angle, he could have sworn that Gandalf became invisible. Then he recalled that wizards kept their own counsel.

He remembered too that something terrible had happened to Sylvian. What that something was he could not recall.

Goodjohn? The bastard!

"Shit, acid really fucks with your mind."

"Like the Ring," Gandalf agreed. "Grass is better. Wizards know their acid, don't forget."

"What am I supposed to do?"

"What did Gandalf tell Frodo?"

Jerry thought hard, trying to recall the chapter and scene. "Let's see, Book One, Gandalf describes how to destroy the One Ring. Frodo himself had to make the journey to Mordor. But first, it was vital that Frodo's decision was his—he must make a choice freely and without coercion. Gandalf couldn't tell him to do it—"

"I don't know." Jerry was stumped.

"He merely pointed the way. He could only show him the path. Frodo had to choose to take the path and walk it himself."

"If you say so." Jerry didn't sound very convinced. It suddenly dawned on him that if he wasn't Frodo maybe this wasn't Gandalf.

"I do say. Over there. Over there."

Gandalf lifted his wizard's staff and gestured past the trees to the lagoon.

As wandering images cross the border of the dream world into being, here came a man and woman, making their way into existence.

They wandered up to the levy that circled the lagoon and spread a blanket on the grass.

The woman lay down. . . or the man forced her down. Jerry couldn't be sure. The man stood over her and began, what looked to be, undressing; shedding his suit coat, possibly a shirt, the whole time, talking, although the man's words were inaudible. Jerry felt as though he was watching a silent movie.

A sudden gust of wind swept the park and Jerry heard a shrill scream.

"Come down yet?" Pearl asked.

Sylvian opened his eyes, feeling dizzy and disoriented.

She sat a few feet from him. Her legs folded, heel to thigh. Back straight, head erect, eyes wide and focused on him, she was wearing a peasant dress of dark green material, glossy like the young oak leaves that hung over her shoulders. She folded her hands on her lap and barely seemed to breathe.

He stared at her blankly.

She exhaled slowly and said: "It's so far-out I found you here. You were heavy into that wild lady and her thing."

"What happened? What happened to us?"

She gave him a quizzical look. "Huh? I came to the park to meditate. Some people like the mountains. I am the daughter of the Mountain, except that I'm also partial to trees. I felt you come here and collapse. I waited for you to wake. Slept the whole day. I can still smell drugs."

"Drugs?"

"Drugs bring scorn. Affairs are ruined, and life is wasted. Delusion and the destruction of mental clarity. . ." She chanted the words and then grinned. "Must have been a bad trip, huh?"

"A nightmare."

"Knew it. I can tell, especially here. I'm, far-out, on the same wavelength. I knew you had a bad trip."

"Been having a lot of bad trips."

"Yeah. When you wake, it's you again."

"Like the whole fucking System," he muttered.

"Like wow, this is a dark time. Kali Yuga. People say whole Yugas pass without a world-honored one. Sometimes the old teachings get corrupted, which makes things worse. Everybody wants to feel happy. We need a Blessed One. It ain't the Divine Woo-Woo."

"You?"

"I'm Mountain Daughter, the goddess," she laughed. "Do you know me?"

"I know you—"

"That I'm the goddess?"

"Sure. Do you know me?"

"You are the One who recognized me. I knew it from the beginning. You're Matreya."

"I'm the Anti-Christ."

"You must be hungry, Anti-Christ."

She produced a ragged denim pack and extracted a fig-Newton tin, a canteen, and a spoon. She opened the tin, put the spoon into it, and passed it over to Sylvian.

He discovered a gruel consisting of milk and rice and started slurping it down. The water from the canteen was slightly metallic but clean and cold.

He glanced up and noticed that the sun rode high in the trees, partially hidden by spring-green foliage. The birds sang, crickets chirped, and somewhere in the woods, through groves of trees, he heard water splashing. Here, however, the forest air was heavy with the fragrance of pine. As he drank the cold water, he caught the smells of aspen and purple flower, the flora of the high mountains. The feeling was so sharp and real that he had to remind himself this was Hinnom Valley and real mountains were a thousand miles away.

He ate the rice milk and drank the water. She watched him with a bemused expression. She still sat in her contorted, pretzel form, back straight and head erect, yet somehow very relaxed, alert not tense, unmoving, not rigid.

He finished and gazed back at her as if he were seeing someone he'd forgotten, like a person he had known many years ago and after a long passage of time suddenly recognized anew.

"Pearl?" he spoke her name to the trees.

"Yes?"

"Dreamed about us. . . together. . . except it was terrible."

"Far-out. Was it real? Like when you're awake?"

"Don't think so."

"Sure? You have only the memory of the dream, you know, like any other event."

"Yeah. So?"

"Is dream memory much different from other memories, what they call real life?"

"Not much. Memory seems like a dream."

"Sometimes, less than a dream?"

St. Barlaam popped into his mind. "Yeah. But here. This is no dream."

"Won't it become a memory, something I can recall? Just like a dream?"

"Yeah. So?"

"The past is your dream, too huh? The future too? Only the now is real, yet it too is a dream—both fantasy and reality." She was reciting something, answering him with a formula.

"Don't know."

"I'm there and will be there. I'm all in all, everything in everything. I will reveal myself to whom I will reveal myself. I am love, compassion, hate, anger, soft, hard, light, dark, life, death—the female. Freaky, isn't it?"

Another chant began; it was formulaic, except for the conclusion.

"Pearl, this is weird." He shook his head. His old problem. The word-curse. The imprecision of words.

She laughed.

"Is this a dream?" He knew he shouldn't ask.

"A dream rounded with a sleep, as Shakespeare says, or the sleep between dreams. The web of *Maya*, the groovy-guru said. Can you truthfully say that this shining moment is not a vivid dream, or that your memory of dreams is not, in fact, reality?"

"You remember dreams?"

"I remember all my dreams. I'm the goddess. I dream the universe. Some are very short. Others long." She winked.

"Pearl. . . please. . ." He stuttered into silence like the old Sylvian. She was innocently mad, like the square root of a negative number. Only its complex formulation made it rational.

She rose and glided to him, bent down and kissed him on the forehead. Then she kissed his eyes and finally his lips. "It is good."

It wasn't his problem with language, he realized. The poor girl was mad. Nonetheless, he returned her kiss awkwardly. Then he pulled away and gazed at her. "What about Goodjohn?"

"What about him?"

"You and him?"

"I'm no gopi. I am Parvati. *Ayamatma Brahma. This Self is the Divine.*"

He blinked.

She watched him closely. She giggled. "Goodjohn is foolish. He did not recognize me. You did."

Sylvian smiled. "There seems to be several me's;. Sam, Anti-Christ, and now, this Blessed One. They all cancel each other out. It's math."

"He's far from me," she said, ignoring his words, reciting her own. "He's gone west."

Just beyond the trees, hazy in the distance, a suggestion of forms that may have been rolling clouds darkened the sky to a deep purple and blue. Sylvian imagined shinning mountain peaks and the dark green skirt of a forest. Contemplating the vision, he saw how the mountains seemed to move as clouds passed slowly overhead and cast their shadows in random and flowing shapes. Solid rock rippled like white-tipped waves on a dark green sea. Constant motion combined with rocky stillness. The mountains

rolled on amid the rain, snow, wind, and the glacial shifting of the conti-
nents. Mountains did indeed flow.

He shook his head, and the vision passed, for this was Hinnom Valley
and tiny Oakwood Park, plus, he was tripping.

"You must go another way."

"With you?"

"What do you think I've been waiting for?"

"Pearl. . . the other dream. There was a word, *Samyama*."

"Oh!" she clapped her hands happily.

"What's it mean?"

She looked surprised. "I don't know—"

"Release? Restraint?"

"Doesn't matter what it means. It is the mystery of the Divine."

"Just like the Church," he said sadly. "Everything ends in the mystery
of the divine."

"Does your Church teach impure and pure? Spiritual and material?
Self and other? Man and God? Man and Woman? All in opposition?"

"Yes."

"Far-out. People become what they worship; it is said that the world
becomes what people believe."

"More mysteries."

"Words make riddles. Don't take my word for it."

"*Samyama, Samyama*," he repeated the word. "Release."

"Far-out."

He began to laugh. His laughter grew louder and louder, like a child
who cannot stop himself from laughing—and does not want to stop.

She grinned and waited patiently. Our one-time idiot noticed for the
first time that her teeth were perfectly straight.

"Release words?" he asked.

"Groovy. Don't hang on, I guess."

He sat back and vainly tried to imitate her odd, pretzel-folded legs.
He closed his eyes and remained perfectly still. She, too, sat patiently, eyes
closed, listening.

At last, he opened his eyes and stretched his legs, grimacing.

"You and me together," she said matter-of-factly. "We are Divine—"

He took a deep breath. "I'm still high. Better to stay high all the time.
Tune in. Turn on. Drop out."

She frowned and looked sad, like one of those stone angels in a cemetery. Head bowed, she seemed to be weeping, if stone could cry.

"The world needs to be awakened—" she recited.

"Awakened?"

"A big jolt, but the groovy kind."

"All that exists deserves to perish," he said without thinking.

"No, No. Give up wanting. Desire not to desire," she chanted.

"Holy Virgin, Mother of God! Not wanting? Capitalism couldn't survive for a second."

"Yes. Extinguished."

It was apparent to him that her recitations, her dogmatic chants, were random strings of quotes she's heard or read, juxtaposed haphazardly in unexpected ways. They sounded deep, and profound and it sure as hell beat thinking. Stoned fairies must be like parrots.

Something in those meaningless words, perhaps their rhythm, maybe the sound-waves alone, abruptly caused him to recall his old dream of St. Barlaam; it was like seeing into a mathematical problem without conscious or logical thought, watching the symbols aligning themselves into the solution, revealing the answer by speaking to him in a wordless language of pure joy and clarity. He saw the terms canceling, the functions falling into place, operators revealing the gradient of the landscape, a whole marvelous world coming into being. Extinguish—to cancel. No craving, no opposites, no distinctions, thus the end of all obsession, and fear, to be replaced by serenity and peace.

Gracefully, without effort, she rose to her feet like a plant opening to the sunlight.

Jerry always had the best acid.

"Sylvian, you're coming with me, right?" she asked. Once again, she'd changed, her voice falling into its old habit of whining complaint.

He decided to follow her, although he had no idea as to why or how he made the choice. It just seemed. . . right.

She led him unerringly through the wood, following the path that seemed extremely old and overgrown. They walked for the entire afternoon and finally came to the edge of the park west of the lagoon.

He touched her arm. "Jerry's back there, and he's totally stoned—and he's got a gun."

She shrugged. "We go to the mountains—"

"Wait. Is Kris still here?"

"Kris? Who's that?"

He looked at her suspiciously. "You know, Kris. Of the Great Truth Cloud. Wears blue body-paint."

"All the Clouds went west with Goodjohn last November."

"You never met Kris, the blue hippie?"

"No?"

Sylvian shook his head. She was crazy, but she was the first girl at BSU to talk to him. He wondered what sex would be like when he wasn't high, surely not a nightmare.

They circled northwest. The winding path took them higher and higher, away from the valley towards the distant clouds. Sylvian turned back one last time and gazed over the park. He saw the von Jahn oak standing firm and proud, reflecting the orange glow of the setting sun.

He began to laugh softly, shaking his head.

Pearl reached for his hand and asked, "What is it?"

"Thought of a good joke."

"Tell me."

"I know the answer to a mystery."

"You've awakened," she said.

"The acid wore off, it seems."

"We are divine—"

He laughed at her solemnity, which he'd come to recognize as a sign of dogmatic recital. Catholics know these things. He laughed and said: "Why did the Matreyas come from the old country?"

She gazed at him, holding her breath.

"So I could sit beneath the von Jahn oak."

She nodded as though she understood completely.

She held up a tiny yellow flower, fresh with spring.

He smiled.

A stiff breeze blew into Jerry's face bearing the gritty sting of fine sand. It came from the east and churned the waters of the lagoon. He pushed on, head down, shielding his eyes, positive that he heard screams for help.

"I still got the ring!" he shouted into the wind. "I'll use it, Dark Lord or not."

The cries for help abruptly ceased. Jerry stopped and turned around, shielding his eyes, trying to catch a glimpse of Gandalf. The wizard had vanished, as wizards are prone to do. Now Oakwood seemed dark and impenetrable, immune to the blast of air, beyond the wind.

He shrugged and climbed the levy. Cresting it, he stopped and stared down in disbelief.

A woman—young, brown hair, slender, and naked—sprawled on a blanket, face contorted in frozen agony, her body broken like a wooden doll. Dead eyes stared directly into his.

He saw that her head was grotesquely twisted at an impossible angle. It was as if her last living perception had been Jerry cresting the rise. A mixture of blood and salvia seeped from the corners of her mouth.

The woman's corpse was the prelude to an even greater horror.

A twisted parody of a human being was at that moment pulling itself off the corpse. Grunting, it turned and faced him.

An orc! Jerry recognized the thing instantly. It was speaking the Black Speech of Mordor. A Great Orc. One of Sauron's evil henchmen, bred by the Dark Lord himself in a horrible parody of Elves. Odious thing.

Ripping his pocket, Jerry tore the automatic free. He screamed at the thing and waved the weapon.

"Bastard! Murderer! FBI Orc bastard! I'm the Ring-bearer of this age."

The thing glared back at him. If it genuinely was an Orc of Sauron, it was undoubtedly one of the most grotesque. Of course, this was the first Orc he'd ever seen in the flesh; yet nothing in the histories had prepared him for the real thing.

The real thing resembled a cartoon. It was like a sketch of a creature that somehow moved and lived against all the laws of biology (unfortunately, Jerry did not know anything about these laws because Jerry had dropped biology after the first week).

The cartoon Orc possessed an enormously fleshy head almost perfectly round with sparse hairs growing haphazardly from the crown. Hairs sprouted from giant red ears. The wicked eyes slanted across its face. The Orc's nose appeared thin and weasel-like, almost human. Jerry wasn't sure what to do with a humanized Orc?

The mouth was also surprising. He'd always thought that Orcs had oversized mouths filled with fangs and broken teeth. He couldn't locate the thing's mouth at all! No lips, no teeth, no jaw. . . but then he finally found it, it was a tiny aperture with a cheerio-sized round hole.

A monstrous head, pasty white and leprous, wobbled precariously on top a thin neck that resembled a dead tree branch about to crack in half. The orc's arms and legs were just as desiccated, hardly able to support its massive bulk.

And what bulk! The orc's entire mass was concentrated in its belly; its skin stretched like an over- inflated tire. The large belly pressed upwards to the chest and hung down to the knees.

The Orc lurched and swayed as if dragged about by the juices that sloshed inside that colossal gut. The stomach appeared to move beneath the taut skin, rippling and gurgling, possessed of independent life.

The Orc was naked. It sprouted a tiny, erect and dripping penis, enfolded by the fat of its abdomen, like a sewing needle someone forgets to take out of a fluffy pillow. The orc couldn't have possibly raped the poor girl lying dead on the bank. It must have tried and failed.

"How do you fill that belly, man?" Jerry cried, curious despite his disgust.

The Orc grunted something he did not understand.

"Shit, man. What kinda orc are you? You must always be hungry. I mean, always hungry. With a mouth that small."

Then Jerry remembered that this was no longer the Third Age, neither was it Middle Earth, and orcs must take on different forms just as the Shadow arises in each age in a different guise.

"You're FBI!" he shouted at the orc. "CIA! Shit, there's nothing but orcs in the Pentagon."

Then he realized that the Orc was struggling up the levy. It lurched forward like a drunken barrel. Its greedy eyes closed in on his. Whistling groans and grunts issued from the tiny mouth.

"Son-of-a-bitch! I got the Ring of this age and I ain't afraid to use it." Jerry's hand shook.

The thing came on like an avalanche, except one surging uphill.

He pointed the pistol at the thing's belly. His hand shook.

He waited a second too long. A rare gust of wind struck him in the face. He staggered back a step and lost his balance. The gun went off with a loud crack. The round went straight up into the sky. Jerry had assassinated a cloud.

"Shit! A breeze does penetrate Mordor."

The Orc was closing in slow motion. He aimed and fired again. The shot went wide and murdered the lagoon.

"Fuck!"

Jerry leveled the weapon, held it steady, and fired. He heard a sharp metallic click. Jerry had used up all five rounds. He stared at the weapon in disbelief.

The orc's claws were reaching for him—

Jerry let out a scream of terror smashing in the thing's monstrous head with the pistol. He struck the gruesome face, the crown of the head. His blows made a kind of sloshing sound, like the plop of wet cement. They didn't break a bone. There were no bones to break. No blood either. He was beating a spongy rubber doll.

Thick fingers grabbed for him. Black dirty nails dug into his flesh. The Orc had him in a death-grip.

Jerry fought with all his strength. The spindly arms, so unnaturally thin, were so unusually powerful.

One claw dug into his shoulder, pushing him down with cranking ratchet-like jerks. The other claw seized his throat. Long fingers of flexible cable squeezed out his life.

His feet slipped on the wet grass. The orc was pulling him towards the lagoon.

It dragged him to the edge, and with strength ebbing away, he watched helplessly as the darkness enveloped him. Forms began to waver and dissolve, flowing one into the other as if someone wiped over a freshly painted canvas smearing a landscape into chaos. The world became indistinct, fog mixed with steam; somewhere in his bruised mind the memory surfaced, of a class long ago, the Turner painting called "Rain, Steam, Speed."

Then, with the abruptness of awakening in the middle of a nightmare, Jerry experienced a sudden peacefulness and sharp clarity of perception. Steam and rain separated as does a drawn theatre curtain, and the world snapped into place. He suddenly came down from the acid—

The Orc became an old man, half-dressed, with sharp rat-like features, bleeding from numerous cuts about the face and torso. The man was choking him and trying to push him into the lagoon.

Desperate energy flowed into his muscle fibers. He tore the old man's fingers from his throat and grasped the wrist. A vicious wrench twisted it like rubber.

"You son-of-a-bitch! Murdering bastard!" Jerry screamed. Fucking FBI!"

Jerry grabbed the man by the throat and shook him like a wet rat.

The villain shrieked and tore at Jerry's hands.

They danced on the edge of the lagoon, slipping on wet grass. Suddenly, as if Jerry and the Orc old man rehearsed it many times, both of them lost their footing at the same instant.

For a moment they paused, suspended in the air, and then with a wild flop they rolled down, hit the stony bank in a series of bouncing crashes and splashed into the lagoon.

It was like diving from a springboard. The last bounce carried the two antagonists out from the shore. They sank like rocks.

Oakwood lagoon is relatively shallow except for the western shore near the wood. At this end is a frightfully deep shaft. So much is known.

Only the Jesuits knew that it was once a bottomless natural well surrounded by granite and flint, in these times vanished from memory, merged into the more enormous pool of the lagoon. The old Indians believed it sacred. The first Jesuits had named it Satan's Well—its depths reached Hell itself, they said.

Locked together, the antagonists sank into Satan's Well. An icy undertow sucked them down into the shaft and away from the light. Arms and legs flailing, their panicky frenzy gave way to cold numbness.

The next day police discovered the body of a young woman they identified as the secretary to the President of Brunswick State University. They recovered no other bodies.

She'd been raped and murdered.

TWENTY-ONE

The Spark

"I DON'T LIKE THIS," Anita whispered to no one.

She waited at the gate where they'd sawed the chain. Tom and Randal, carrying large cans of gasoline, walked boldly towards the mill as if they were coming in for the night shift.

"Nobody's here," Tom called back. "Toll ya the night guard's an old drunk. He's off downtown drinking boilermakers.

Anita knew it was true. Saturday night usually found old Fritz the night guard guarding his favorite barstool.

Nevertheless, she felt uneasy. The Masters had not ordered revolutionary action. But Tom had been so convincing: With this spark, they'd ignite the revolution of the oppressed against the oppressors, the exploited against the exploiters.

What a dilemma. Anita had given her pledge of obedience to the Ascended Masters of the New Order. Compliance was the measure of a revolutionary: obedience and sacrifice.

I'm not exactly disobedient, she told herself.

She gazed at the silent mill. In the dark, it resembled a enormous barn. Dammit, it was a barn. The owners treated their workers like animals— worse than animals, like so much grease and machine oil, human lubrication *Ex machina*. *What Is to Be Done?* Lenin asked. A spark, as Tom said, would ignite a revolutionary conflagration that would cleanse this wretched world. Even though Tom was quoting that goddamn Jonathan before the great man lost his mind and went down the path to strawberry fields, she knew that Tom was right. To destroy property was to kill God.

Might not silence be a nod of agreement? Withdrawal, a blessing? What good are oracles in the age of reason?

"Come on," Tom called urgently.

She cradled the pack beneath her poncho. The bag contained ten cardboard tubes stuffed with a mixture of potassium chlorate and sugar—incendiary bombs to fire the gasoline. Anita was concerned, however, with the corked glass vials of sulfuric acid which were the time delay detonators. Once inverted, the sulfuric acid eats away at the cork and comes into contact with the explosive mixture creating an intense fire. She had to be very careful that the vials remained upright until it was time to set the bombs and gasoline.

"You two, guard the gate," she growled, nodding to Vesta and Paul crouching behind her in the darkness. Vesta carried an old Springfield that Randal had stolen from his father's prized gun collection. Paul brought the military M-16, still without a magazine because no one in the People's Will had been able to find the correct ammunition.

Both dressed in black. Neither one responded. An impossible fright possessed them like some artic spirit of the eternal damned. Petrified beyond words, they could barely speak.

Anita felt it too. But the anticipation of fame dulled fear. She'd be another Lenin, grander than Lenin who was merely a man; she was a messiah. Cradling the pack like a baby, she hurried through the gate and began to cross the factory grounds towards the mill. "Careful," she whispered to herself, "careful—"

Floodlights suddenly blazed like a supernova. The yard became an island of light surrounded by the outer darkness. Tom, Randal, and Anita were caught in the center of an artificial exploding star.

A voice cried out from the darkness: "This is the Hinnom Valley police. You're under arrest. Put down your weapons!"

Several things happened at the same time, instantaneous events in different regions of space, Sylvian might have said.

The heroic revolutionary guards, Vesta and Paul, threw down their weapons—and themselves for good measure. They cried and cowered in sawdust like beaten puppies. Anita had forced them into a life of crime, they yowled. She was a witch. They were her spellbound victims.

(The two brave revolutionary fighters were taken into custody and later charged with sabotage, arson, conspiracy to incite a riot, resisting arrest, trespassing, receiving stolen goods, weapons charges, and a hundred other violations, and were found guilty on all counts. Given the circumstances and their relative youth, their susceptibility to charismatic personalities, they were each assigned a year of community service after which time they were encouraged to enlist in a branch of the United States military.)

Randal placed the two cans of gasoline gently on the ground and put his hands over his head. As he accomplished these feats, he glared at Tom, his severe features contorted into a mask of hate accompanied by a look of perverted satisfaction and mockery.

Tom reacted by reflex. He spun and crouched, dropping his cans and fumbling in the pocket of his field jacket. In the bright light, he saw the look on Randal's face.

He immediately knew what it meant.

"Treacherous bastard!"

Randal grinned back.

"Freeze now!" barked a disembodied voice.

Moving with a fluid quickness, Tom dropped to one knee, brought forth a military handgun, a .45, and took aim at Randal.

Randal's mocking expression abruptly vanished. He began to tremble. Tears suddenly spilled from his eyes.

Flashes in the darkness. Flames. Sharp cracks piercing eardrums—

For Anita, it was like watching a movie screen from the front row; everything was too clear and precise, too bright and large.

She saw the bullets tear into Tom shredding his field jacket like tissue paper. Bits of bloody cloth and flesh exploded into the air. Spinning around, he took a bullet in the left ribcage, then in the back, then square in the chest. He crashed to the ground without firing a shot.

Streams of blood flowed like small rivers into the sawdust and dirt.

Randal collapsed, screaming hysterically. He wept and screamed and wet his pants, and created his personal river of urine.

In the next second, he ceased his hysterical antics and shouted angrily into the darkness: "Shit! He could've killed me!"

"NO, TOM!" Anita was bellowing like a wounded cow. She dropped her pack and rushed forward. The pack exploded into flames.

The concussion from the blast threw her to the ground. Flames burned the edges of her black poncho. The fire singed her hair but she was otherwise unharmed.

Powerful hands grabbed her. It all happened too quickly. They tore the poncho off her body. Arms encircled her thick torso. Fingers dug into her hair and yanked her head back, nearly breaking her neck. Other fingers sought her throat.

Everything became a mad blur. With almost superhuman strength, Anita wrenched her arms free and fiercely struck at her invisible tormentors. Her fists smashed into flesh and connected with bone, until she heard a snap. Cries of pain split the air. In between cries and enraged curses, Anita screeched, "Tom, Tom, Tom. . ." pounding the name into them as she continued with a barrage of fists.

There were too many. They tackled her. Vicious blows rained upon her unprotected head.

"Don't kill her, idiots!" a gruff voice yelled.

A rifle butt smashed into her temple. Her skull exploded, and her arms and legs went numb.

"Assholes! I told you not to kill her."

Anita sank into a deep black hole. She drifted down, gently it seemed, her thoughts going out one by one like a row of candles.

"Tom, Tom. . ." she still cried his name as she sank into a bottomless well.

Pain brought her back. Her wounded head throbbed with each beat of her heart. The very pulse of life caused her agony.

She would have willingly remained in the void. Cruelly, the drumming pain refused to allow it. She sincerely wished that her heart might stop beating. It beat on nonetheless, oblivious to her will.

Gradually, like snow melting, she felt herself growing warm. The blood seemed to find its way back into her limbs, with a new pain all its own. She felt an immense agony spread throughout her body: bruises, cuts, maybe broken bones, and perhaps torn tendons. Searing pain, as if from burned flesh, raw and weeping.

The terrible throbbing inside her head. She wanted to die.

She moaned: "Please, let me die. My Masters, how could I betray you?"

A gentle voice, deep and beautiful in her ears, a voice made for soothing consolation, like a verbal balm: "Ah no, dear lady. You shall live. You've been through a terrible ordeal. But you will live."

"Tom?"

"Alas," said the soothing voice, "What pain you must feel. He is gone. It is regrettable. So unnecessary. Tragic. Poor misguided young man. A vet too."

Treachery! She desperately wanted to shout. The terrible pain prevented it. She could only manage a moaning whimper.

"Sleep now." The voice soothed her frayed nerves. Gently it pushed her back into the delicious void.

She passed once more into unconsciousness.

This time there was no void, rather a confusing stream of images and voices. She saw Tom dying a second death, as gruesome as the first. She saw Jonathan and heard him lecturing. She experienced her breakdown. She saw herself walking in the park and hallucinating a man dressed all in white, who she first took to be the ghost of von Jahn but later came to realize was the Master of the White Order.

The image of the Ascended Master lingered. He knew every secret. He saw into the future. He told her of the coming revolution, the great change that would transform the world into a glorious new and happy golden age of humanity in which all wars, every sort of oppression, all unfairness and suffering, all sadness, ultimately all diseases and death itself, the final and most terrible oppressor of mankind, would be abolished.

She heard the actual words, so joyful and yet carefully measured, pronounced with a self-conscious precision. Perfect grammar. Lovely sentences. Exquisite paragraphs.

Yes, dear lady, the great transformation is just over the horizon. Does not the decade seethe with restlessness and violence and yet with vast hope? Do not people sense something new? Does it not call to them from beyond the horizon, telling them that this moment in history is unique? Is not our time an axis?

Oh yes! Anita cried, ecstatically in her dream.

Does not history begin here? With us? With our generation?

Yes.

And yet—

The head shook sadly, although Anita never truly saw the head, nor the face within the dark folds of the cowl. Nevertheless, she pictured a white-bearded man of dark skin and wide eyes, full lips, and long silver hair.

And yet they do not know the source of their restlessness and anger. They cannot see it. They cannot see across the vast ocean of time, as we can see -we who *know*.

For we, the White Order of the Himalayas, direct history. History unfolds according to our will.

We are the Sustainers.

The voice was confident. All at once, it was hypnotic and compelling, speaking unquestionable truth.

She heard herself begging: Tell me.

This first encounter with the Ascended Master was her deliverance from madness.

She had come to the park that evening to sever the thread of her life. Beyond the lagoon, among the trees, she'd end the pain forever. That very morning Jonathan had bidden her farewell, packed up, and dropped out.

She knew he'd been under constant harassment by the administration, mostly trivial things like class schedules and committee assignments. He'd complained of severe headaches, pains in his limbs, loss of appetite. He said he felt disgusted with himself. At times—they were becoming more frequent—he'd forget his own identity.

Jonathan had been a lonely child growing up in a cold old mansion near Lake Michigan. He populated his friendless world with imaginary playmates—now, an adult, he began to say that they were real and often spoke to him. He rambled about something called the Intergalactic Brain.

She'd laughed it all off at first. Then she'd tried to get Jonathan to seek help. He'd refused, and his "episodes of distraction" became more frequent. During his decreasing intervals of lucidity, he'd lash out at her, as if he held her responsible for his misery.

"Exaggerated and silly," were the words he used to condemn his teachings. Everything sickened him, ideology was poison, the revolution was infantile, and life had become banal. It was her fault. He was quitting the struggle. He was leaving. . . her, academia, the revolution, his followers, the Movement.

All that exists deserves to perish.

Then Jonathan experienced enlightenment in the library, he said. By accident, like a serpent beneath a rock, he discovered a collection of old manuscripts in the Crowley archives. A nineteenth-century Dominican Father was the author, or so the label said.

The collection contained a bizarre tale of an old German family descended from nobility with perhaps a healthy dose of Mongol blood from the thirteenth-century invasions. The family's heirs had helped establish BSU of the North. Why else would a family memoir turn up in the archives of a third-rate library? Garbled, riddled with lacunae, the document contained a prophecy. At first, he believed it a typical occult version of the popular savior-myth: a saint, an adept, would arise from the family, come west, and teach a path of liberation. Thence followed a twisting, contradictory memoir about revolution and betrayal, and lost hopes.

Ex Oriente Lux.

He threw himself into an in-depth and probing study of the East. He learned the languages, he said, and the perennial philosophy of Eastern Wisdom. Gradually, the clouds parted, *he said*. He went to India and encountered an adept, *he said*.

The adept spoke to him from across the ages, from over the seas. The ascended one took up residence in the mind of Jonathan Burke. And the radical professor, who'd frequently quoted Marx (quite out of context) that religion was "the opium of the people," metamorphosed into the Divine Woo-Woo, the incarnation of the Intergalactic Brain.

Jonathan had experienced an epiphany. He was a Divine Being. *Aya-matma Brahma—*

She heard him distinctly. Dreaming now, she listened to what he had told her. He was the divine guru, an Avatar. He was a god. He'd shake the foundations of the bourgeois order. He was the greatest idea of all possible ideas.

She'd interrupted him. She didn't want to hear any more of this nonsense. She knew what had happened. It was shallow and trivial and all-too-typically *bourgeoisie*. The great and marvelous professor Jonathan Burke had become besotted with one of his followers, some empty-headed little twit who drooled all over him.

Oh, Anita had known for a long time that something like this was coming. She felt the fury mounting, reliving the scene with greater awareness and sharper clarity.

The dream-memory on the precipice of death became thousand times more distinct and vital than it had in life. She heard her disgusted and angry response: Young women were attracted to Jonathan because of his reckless-ness (which he was really not), his intelligence (which was merely his big mouth), and his passionate iconoclasm (which was a carefully crafted act).

He was the least spiritual of men. He was addicted to sensual pleasure. He drank heavily. He took pills for every little thing. He was the most cyni-cal of men. Did he think her such a fool as to believe that stupid Dominican story? Secret manuscripts indeed! Adepts from the East. . .

She saw him smiling serenely, unaffected by the storm of her anger. He possessed an eerie, even sinister detachment.

He'd answered her—now, for the first time in truth she heard the an-swer—yes, he had indeed experienced true enlightenment. As a god, he saw quite clearly that no amount of radicalism would replace a single bolt in the capitalist machine, much less the gears and belts of the infernal thing. Capitalism had become reality itself. Russia, China, Vietnam, Cuba or the United States, it didn't matter. There was no opposition, no true negations, no alternatives except in empty words and phrases. Everything was an il-lusion. Reality was a dream, opined the Divine Woo-Woo, speaking in her dream.

He kept talking nonsense, speaking without his affected mannerisms and exaggerated emotion, *in her dream.*

Bullshit!

Not so, he'd replied, still very serene. Anita knew that he'd stopped responding to her. For him, she utterly ceased to matter. She had become nothing more than a small, murmuring voice, perhaps the last shreds of his self-doubt, which he felt compelled to answer one last time.

"I saw the truth. Politics is nothing. It is an act that arises from the Spirit, *Purusha*. I am a new *Purusha*. I am the greatest event in the history of the universe."

Double bullshit.

Who is she? Anita heard herself shout at him. It was like trying to shout over the ocean; the words become lost amid the cries of gulls and the crash of waves.

Who is she? Who is she?

He turned and left her.

She was Anita Anarcharsis, dedicated revolutionary, and she didn't care. After all, wasn't marriage just another bourgeois contract? Wasn't it a typically alienating contract? Didn't marriage like all other contracts ultimately reduce people, especially women, to the status of things, valueless in themselves, mere ciphers, property, all the way back to biblical times—thou shalt not covet thy neighbor's *wife*?

It didn't matter if she'd never really loved Jonathan. He represented what she wished to be. Wedlock didn't matter. It was a sham, after all, based upon false romantic notions of love, served up in the form of poetry, literature, movies, magazines, therapists—Christ almighty, even the greeting-card industry.

Yes. All contracts are models of the first contract between the first tyrant and His slaves, God Himself and His so-called covenant. Bakunin said it. As long as God exists, we're all slaves. As long as marriage exists, women are all slaves: Father-god, sister-slave.

Go fuck yourself to death, Jonathan Burke. And he had.

Yet she'd still gone into the haunted park seeking the darkness. Vile bourgeoisie vanity, brainwashing, she thought. Even she'd been duped, even her, even Anita Anarcharsis.

What a horror to know, to see the brainwashing and yet not be able to do anything about it. The corrupt and inauthentic establishment morality flowed through her as profoundly as one's lifeblood. Knowing the truth drove her mad. Somewhere in the gloom of Oakwood, she would end her miserable life.

Then she met the Master and was saved.

She saw the emerging community. She experienced the moral imperative of the revolution. She knew with certainty that all the so-called wisdom of the past was so much propaganda in the service of the power-hungry elites.

She left the park and went on to form the People's Will. She dedicated her life to the revolution and the Ascended Masters. She would be loved once more—this time by the masses, not a miserably broken-down old fool with a god-complex. Loved and feared. Messiah, Anointed One. The Master granted further revelations. . . until now, until this time.

Why had he (they) fallen silent? She wept, in the dream too.

Why had they refused to respond? Why had they allowed her betrayal? "Oh, Tom."

The pigs had won. Boots double-crossed them. She saw it clearly. Why had the Masters allowed it to happen? She'd somehow failed. She'd proved unworthy of them.

Nothing remains but to die.

TWENTY-TWO

"Where the Hell is Dick Craven?"

"The doctors say your blindness may not be permanent," said a voice. "Only time will tell."

The male voice sounded identical to one in her memory, but then all male voices merged into the One Voice.

She awoke slowly, pulled upwards by the thread of the voice. She floated on a sea of pain and anguish. The Establishment proved far too strong, even for the Ascended Masters.

All resistance is in vain. "We control the vertical. We control the horizontal." Nothing remains but to die.

She opened her eyes. . . to darkness. The pigs had blinded her. She was, now truly, one of the blind ones.

She bit her lips, her tongue. She would not weep. They would not have that pleasure. She was a revolutionary and prepared to suffer. Remember the *Catechism*. A revolutionist must always be ready to inflict damage upon the evil Establishment and suffer the consequences of blind retaliation. Revolutionaries are marked persons already dead. The revolutionist must expect no mercy from the cold monster state. There is no bewailing the fate of the revolutionist.

She heard hums and beeps, the rustle of people moving about, indistinct voices speaking incomprehensible words. She smelled chemicals, the pungent odors of sterilizing solutions, and the faint taste of drugs, of alcohol.

A hospital. She felt the straps. She was strapped in, a prisoner. Those who reject the false reality of the System are sick, not criminals but patients.

A revolutionist expects death. The revolutionist is already dead. Prison is another form of death. The Establishment is fiendishly clever. Its hospitals are prisons too. Revolution is a disease, the revolutionists are sick, in the country of the blind, truth is disease.

She would not weep.

The air moved, someone was breathing.

She felt a presence. It was the same presence as earlier before her dream-memories had revealed their terrible truths.

It was almost as if she could see. Memory took the burden where sight stumbled and collapsed. *Flowing white hair, beard, and brilliant gown.* In her sightless mind, the cowl had been removed revealing dark skin and black eyes, deep-set and ancient—

An Ascended Master in the darkness of the oppressor's dungeon.

Surely the forces that ruled Amerika yearned to annihilate such a being. His very existence demonstrated the hypocrisy and self-delusion of Amerikan culture. Was not the Master a foil for Amerika's frantic obsession with religion? Amerika loudly professed its religious faith at every opportunity and with every opportunity violated its teachings. Amerika's religion was money-theism. The Master, as Amerika's counterpoint, was a contradiction. He should not be. Amerika had to kill him.

She couldn't see him. Her mind produced him. She heard him in her ears behind ears. To others, he was invisible.

The Masters walked invisibly among the blind, even into the dungeons of the damned.

"We failed," she whispered. "The People's Will failed you. I failed you. I hoped that I might gain your respect. . . your love."

She perceived a deep sigh.

"Patience," said the ageless voice. "Patience. Everything moves. The great wheel turns inexorably. You only need patience and trust."

"Forgive me. I'm blind."

She felt a beneficent smile.

"We understand your urgency, your restlessness. We know your hopes and dreams, Anita Anarcharsis."

He paused for what could have been several minutes. Anita felt him gazing into infinity.

She suppressed a sob. "How? When?"

"The great turning of the wheel. The earth will be transformed. Evolution slowly mounts the ladder to spirit. Each step is painful and many suffer. Evolution cannot be accelerated, only directed. We, the Ascended Masters, have been directing it, Anita Anarcharsis. Remain assured. Believe."

The voice in her head possessed a strange, unearthly quality, not really a voice at all, rather more like a choir singing hymns.

"What of the People's Will?"

"Ah, dear child, do not forget that the goal of human evolution is pure spirit. The new world will become an abode of pure love, love sincere, and faithful. Many false paths simulate the truth. There are many false prophets who impersonate the Masters. They are terribly mischievous and dangerous. They make false revolutions that lead many astray. They thwart, perhaps unwittingly, or perhaps with guile, true evolution."

"Goodjohn Saccidanada."

"The Great Truth Cloud. In truth, the great poisonous smog of lies and deceit. A debased cult of murderers."

"But it was Boots who murdered poor Cathy and betrayed us. All this time, Boots."

"Alas," the Master said flatly. "Boots is the prodigal son returned to his father."

"The Clouds," she whispered, afraid she might be overheard. "Are they FBI? CIA?"

"Neither."

"What are they?"

"Downward evolution. Devolution. Our adversaries throughout history. They seek to make men animals. They deny everything. According to them, all is emptiness. How may emptiness evolve? How may nothing become something?"

"They are. . . nihilists? Like Manson?"

"Far worse, I'm afraid. These people of the Spirit are neither rational nor irrational. They exist beyond all categories. They begin where thinking ends."

"Oooo. . ." she moaned in agony. The thoughts of the Ascended Master seemed to pierce her poor mauled skull like hot needles stabbing into sightless eyes.

"They are hopeless. They merely smile with their insane serenity—like imbeciles, idiots. They walk an incomprehensible path. Many, I fear, follow them blindly. Many find profound wisdom in their madness, the answer to life's most intractable puzzles, which is no answer. . .." And now the heavenly choir became a raging storm, and terrible anger pierced her heart like a spear of ice. ". . .for they would destroy the very will to live. They are nihilism's ultimate form."

"I see," she groaned.

"You know all this. I am not telling you anything you do not already know. Goodjohn and the Great Cloud of Lies."

"You know. . . Do you see everything?"

The Master paused, but not to look into infinity. When he spoke again, there was nothing ethereal about his voice. His words were not patient, and they came from the outside.

"I ask: what do *you* know of Sylvian Matreya and Jerry Wolfe?"

"She's been babbling like this all morning," said a raspy, frustrated voice. "I'll ask again: What of the two you sent into the park?"

"Gone," she whispered hoarsely, "all gone—"

The voice became demanding.

"The police have searched the park. Numerous times and found nothing. Not even a broken branch, a footprint, a cigarette butt. No one lives there. What's become of Sylvian Matreya and Jerry Wolfe?"

She couldn't answer. She had no answer, nor the strength to give one if she did. She began to slide back into the world of fairies, spirits and Ascended Masters from the Himalayas. Her thoughts began to shatter and fly away, like shrapnel from an exploding bomb, flesh torn from the body by bullets.

"Where are Matreya and Wolfe?"

Her sense of hearing must have shattered too, for as she sank away from all awareness, she thought she heard raspy voice mutter:

"And now Craven. What the hell has been going on in that park?"

He could not have said such things. The Ascended Masters knew everything. They never used profanity. They were evolved. She was confused.

Down a long tunnel, cold and black, rushing away into the most bottomless well. . . She dropped.

At last, her fall became a gentle floating, like a leaf spiraling down in a gentle breeze. Away from all sensation, from the terrible pain, drifting away—

"Well, Anything?" asked Bob Boots, owner and chief operating officer of Boots Lumber and Paper—prominent member of the Brunswick State University Board of Regents, Elder of Trinity Lutheran Church—who also sat on the Board of Governors of the Beaver Lodge, held seats on three bank boards, was the historical columnist for the local newspaper, and bore so many more official titles even he could not have listed them from memory.

The Hinnom Valley Chief of Police stood next to him. Detectives and uniformed officers mulled about the hospital floor, mostly getting in the way of the doctors and nurses.

No matter how stylishly dressed in the latest fashion, Bob Boots always appeared slovenly and rumpled, as if he'd just awakened from a long nap on the couch in his office. Perhaps this impression was due to his generous body-mass, maybe his beet-red face, flushed and sweaty, eyes bulging and mouth hanging open like a fish out of water. He struggled valiantly to fit the model of the modern executive found in magazines such as *Playboy*. He ended up looking like a grade school janitor on a Sunday morning.

"Nothing. She's in pretty bad shape. The docs don't know if she'll ever walk again. For sure she's blind. The psyche evaluation says she's borderline psychotic, depressive, suicidal, hostile, obsessive, narcissistic, and with a martyr complex. She keeps blubbering abstruse nonsense. Reminds me of maudlin practice sermonizing in seminary."

"Sounds like all you 'versity nuts."

The Reverend Bentley bowed his head. "Please don't generalize, Mr. Boots. Many fine academics don't suffer such mental disorders."

"Oh yeah—" Bob Boots glared at the Chief. "What do you have to say?"

"Serves her right," the Chief shrugged. "Should've stayed home and baked cookies. Baked a little more with that old Burke bastard too. Kept him from chasin' tail and herself from goin' nuts."

"Well, we nailed Burke. He split once he knew we were on to him," Bob Boots said. He glanced at Bentley.

"Oh shit. Hey, Dick, you really think that Goodjohn bastard was Burke himself in drag?"

"You bet," the Chief said. "Burke was fired, all of a sudden this rascal shows up, and all hell breaks loose. Lying bastard. . .claimed he went to India, but we checked. Never left town. Sweet little girls are hot for him just like 'ole Burke. A new gimmick but the same result."

Boots snorted: "Son-of-a-bitch! Preying on the gullible. Educated parasite. Always oozing sympathy for some cause, preachin' adolescent rebellion to adolescents. Educated fools, need to grow up, work for real—"

"We're talking about Burke."

The Chief grunted: "I don't know, Dick. We closed down their drug house. Arrested a bunch of 'em and discovered they's mostly from California, Colorado, Utah, just as we thought. We ain't found the old man yet. Ain't found nothing in the park neither. Pretty sure he's gone west."

"Goddammit Dick!" Boots howled suddenly, shaking his fist in the Dean's face. "Who the hell murdered the Butcher girl then? Where are those two Pollack kids? And where the hell is Dick Craven?"

"One of the boys is Jewish—"

"Fuck! Drugs! Always drugs," spat the Chief. "Even in the best families. In my family. My own niece. I warned Craven. I talked to Cathy. Did everything. Whole generation's freaked out. Anybody could've done it. Whole fuckin' student body is suspect."

"Except the decent kids," said Bentley quickly, "like the frats or Campus Crusade for Christ—"

Boots shook his massively bulbous head. "Don't know. The ole lady keeps finding pot in Randy's room. We're on him like flies on shit, but it doesn't do no good."

"We infiltrated the People's Will. It was the Clouds that always worried me—and the blacks, of course."

"I warned Craven," the Chief repeated. "I told him blacks aren't the only violent ones. No, nooo. . . he says, we got it covered. We got a plan. They got Cathy. Craven's responsible."

"We had a good plan."

"To use the People's Will against the Clouds?"

"That was the idea. Infiltrate the People's Will, plant silly ideas in Anita's head. She was already hallucinatory. I couldn't do anything with Burke. He was into this crazy Woo-Woo stuff that even I couldn't crack. Can't do anything with such people except get rid of them."

"Well? Doesn't look like it."

"Don't know. . . the Chief here says the park's empty."

"If it was Burke, he's been long gone," said the Chief. "Since Christmas at least. Them two kids probably up and went with him. Got 'em hooked on drugs and religion like poor Cathy."

"It was Burke with a new angle. Goodjohn. The kids might have joined him. He probably murdered Cathy. . . this ought to be our official determination. Either, way they're gone. Somebody else's problem now."

The Chief shook his head. "Goddammit, I ain't never lettin' my kids go to college."

"Where in the hell is Dick Craven?" Bob Boots asked.

Dean Bentley looked troubled. He gazed out of the hospital window in the direction of the park and said in a very soft voice: "I wish I knew."

The Chief grinned. "And now his secretary."

Bentley blanched.

"Gotta search that fuckin' park. A real search. Drag the lagoon." He grinned at the Dean. "Think you know what we'll find."

TWENTY-THREE

Bloody Monday

On Thursday, April 30, the day before Sylvian and Jerry entered Mordor searching for Sauron and the Great Truth Cloud, President Richard M. Nixon announced a major "incursion" into Cambodia's eastern provinces by some twenty thousand American and South Vietnamese troops. Lon Nol, who'd seized power while Prince Sihanouk was in Moscow, "invited" the incursion to prevent a communist takeover. The ultimate purpose, Nixon explained, was to drive the communists out of Cambodia in about six to eight weeks, strengthening "Vietnamization" of the war.

Minutes after this announcement, at Oberlin College in Ohio and Princeton University in New Jersey, student protesters spilled into the streets. From Thursday to Sunday, student protests and strikes erupted at some twenty other colleges and universities. Many campuses passed into a state of siege as if the incursion had reached across the seas into the heart of America itself.

While the campus of Brunswick State University remained peaceful over the weekend, violence at the mill that Saturday night troubled the citizens of Hinnom Valley far more than the invasion of distant Cambodia.

Sunday morning, local newspapers blamed the tragedy upon anarchists, nihilists, and other outside agitators who were bent on pure destruction, murder (they'd killed Cathy Butcher for sure and, quite likely, President Craven's secretary), and sabotage. Police officials stated that they were confident such random acts of savagery had nothing at all to do with recent events in Southeast Asia.

That same Sunday morning, in almost every church service in Hinnom Valley, the various ministers, pastors, priests and reverends universally condemned atheistic communism, secularism, the counter-culture, and drugs—for good measure they added Satan worship, occult paganism and heathen religions to the noxious brew. Mindless violence, they declared, resulted from the collapse of decency and morals.

The clergy admonished young people to devote themselves to the likes of the Reverend Billy Graham, to Christian NASA scientist Rodney W. Johnson, gospel singer Tennessee Ernie Ford, rather than Abbe Hoffman, Jerry Rubin, Timothy Leary, or Dick Gregory (for Catholics, the devotion should be to Jacques Maritain, the Pope of course, and in a few isolated cases, St. Thomas Aquinas). Students needed to balance their intellectual education with spiritual nourishment by attending services regularly, praying together (with designated prayer leaders), attending appropriate Bible study groups (but stay away from those idiotic Jesus freaks), and volunteer work spreading the gospel.

Some clergy talked about athletics. Attending a football game, for example, cheering for the home team, providing a far more wholesome outlet than, say, political protest, teach-ins, and, what hardly need mentioning, the destruction of property. Socials sponsored by church youth groups were far healthier than rock concerts or political rallies (oppositional rallies, that is), and radical study groups. Studying non-Christian religions should be avoided at all costs.

The spirit of curiosity is not a good spirit; one priest warned the young, especially when the result is the distancing of the believer from God. Without a firm foundation in Christian faith, education leads to confusion. He then quoted the Church Father Tertullian: "What indeed has Athens to do with Jerusalem?"

Not a few men of the cloth sincerely warned young people that although their school years appeared carefree, exciting, life changing, much of this was an illusion; college would end all too soon. Students will awaken someday to find themselves in need of a profession, responsible adults with families of their own, mortgages, debts, bills, taxes, incomes; in short, economic responsibilities which depended upon their training here and now. Believe it, the clergy warned, potential employers will scrutinize these "carefree years," looking not merely at grades and credits (who cares if you got an "A" in Shakespeare) but at behavior, out-of-class activities, and most importantly, character. So, young people, you'd better think carefully about what you are doing today outside the classroom. Consider those persons with whom you now associate.

This being Hinnom Valley, the services were well attended by said young people, and these sermons taken very seriously indeed.

Thus did BSU remain relatively quiet over the tempestuous weekend despite the militant violence that took place at the mill and the expansion of the War into Cambodia.

On many other campuses, there were strikes and protests against ROTC, Dow Chemical, and other symbols of the warmongering Establishment. These students, unfortunately, did not have levelheaded and superbly trained clergy, as did students at BSU to warn them against acting foolishly and naively. . . ". . .as dim-witted pawns in the hands of perverted power-hungry communists and assorted criminal subversives. . ." so said an editorial in the Valley Democrat. The editor also quoted some of the more fundamentally minded clergy who labeled the protesters "minions of the Prince of Darkness himself." The devil, they were quoted as a warning, inspired the radicals (wasn't the peace sign in fact a broken cross?) as he had inspired their intellectual mentors from Darwin to Marx, to Freud.

Less fortunate universities were shaken by violence, as young Americans, the same age as the protestors, died in Vietnam—and now Cambodia.

Dean of Students, the Reverend Richard Bentley poured himself a glass of bourbon and sat in his office that same afternoon staring out of the window overlooking the Kreis. The green grass shone bright and peaceful in the gentle May sunshine. Alas, the happy scene did little to lighten his mood. Richard Bentley could hardly recall enduring such a lethal combination of depression, anxiety, and frustration. It seemed to seep out of him like foul-smelling perspiration.

Dean Bentley had given one of those sermons this very morning. From the pulpit, at least, he had managed to sound upbeat and overflowing with wisdom, projecting his usual calm authority and certainty. In his mind, however, uncertainty, and its side-effect anxiety, grew like cancer.

Where was Craven?

What had happened to Dorothy? A blind man could identify the culprit. Did the Chief know?

A thought came upon him like some terrible nightmare from which he abruptly awoke only to discover that it had occurred in real life while he'd been sleeping. He had heard something in Chief Butcher's voice, something intangible, a momentary inflection, the wisp of a tone.

The Chief knew everything. He knew quite well that neither the Clouds nor the People's Will had murdered Dorothy or Cathy. My God, his niece!

Bentley felt as if he'd taken a blow to the stomach. The Chief knew and had done nothing.

"No, no, NO. . ." Bentley moaned. "I'm going mad."

"NO!" And this final "NO" sank the nightmare. It slid back down into the dark and hazy world of paranoid dreams from which it had arisen and where it belonged. He felt better.

Where was Craven?

Dammit. He'd solved the People's Will just as he had solved the Jonathan Burke problem. He'd done it alone, with minimal help from Craven and the Board. All he'd needed was Randal.

Why did it all have to rest on him? Wasn't this what immense bureaucracies are for, to evade responsibility and the subsequent guilt by fragmenting the decision-making process? Does the bureaucratic administration even have to know the truth behind their collective decisions? Bentley gulped down the bourbon, got up, and staggered to his desk. He slumped down and put his head in his hands, trying to soothe his pounding head. He wondered if his headache was as bad as Anita's—if she could even feel anything anymore. The hospital reports were not encouraging.

Suddenly he laughed and said aloud: "Hell, I'm a Man of the Clergy. People automatically believe me."

He turned to his typewriter, inserted official letterhead, and pounded out the following press release:

> President H. Richard Craven will not be in his office due to an extended fund-raising trip on behalf of BSU. It is not certain exactly when the President will return to campus.
>
> In the interim, Dean Richard Bentley will assume all duties of the chief operating officer at BSU until further notice.

He made quite a few typos, which he seldom did.

When he finished, he went back to the window and poured himself another drink.

He passed the remainder of the glorious spring afternoon sipping bourbon and feeling much better.

On Monday, the fourth of May, at 12:15 p. m., after a weekend of protest which included property damage, the Ohio National Guard fired a total of sixty-one shots from the grassy rise to which they had retreated in the face of rock-throwing crowds of students on the campus of Kent State University.

In about thirteen seconds, the Guard fired fifty-five rifle shots, five .45 caliber pistol shots, and one shotgun blast.

Four students died. Nine were wounded.

Led by SDS, the students had demanded that Kent State abolish ROTC, reject all funding by the Department of Defense, and abolish the university's degree program in law enforcement. A few radicals demanded the abolishment of the grading system, required courses, transcripts, degrees, and tuition.

The radicals claimed that the university, as almost all universities in modern Amerika, had become mere finishing schools dedicated to producing cringing slaves who served the military-industrial complex. The university as a community of scholars had, therefore surrendered its moral authority. And, far from being a mistake in diplomacy, the Vietnam War was the logical outcome of the hypocritical Amerikan Establishment.

Thus spoke a handful of radicals.

Ten days later, at predominately black Jackson State College in Mississippi, city police and the highway patrol fired into a crowd outside a women's dormitory on campus, killing two and injuring twelve. One of the dead was a high school senior.

By the end of May, an average of one hundred strikes a day swept across the country, closing many universities and colleges for the summer. Unofficial statistics said that about two-thirds of the some two thousand, five hundred institutions of higher education in the United States suffered student strikes. Rumor had it that many more, perhaps as high as eighty percent, were disrupted by student protest. Many schools decided not to report such events. Officially, at least, many schools claimed that their campuses remained quiet and orderly amid the turmoil.

One of these was Brunswick State University.

At precisely two in the afternoon of what was now being called "Bloody Monday," as radio and TV blared the news from Kent State, Eugene Vico mounted the base of General Klaus von Brunswick's statue and began to harangue a tightly packed mob of students. People crowded the greens. No one had ever seen anything like it at BSU.

Vico called for a general strike followed by a mass demonstration in sympathy for the dead. He also demanded an immediate end to the war and trials of the National Guard Officers, the Governor of Ohio, the Joint Chiefs of Staff, and President Richard Nixon. They were to be charged with murder and accomplices to murder.

Local radio and television dispatched crews to campus. The news media arrived almost immediately after learning of the events at Kent State and well before Vico called for a strike. It was only logical that editors and news-directors anticipate trouble at BSU, despite the school's well-deserved reputation for well-disciplined and serious-minded students, as its public relations brochures advertised.

One of the wealthiest board members reacted with outrage to the media's presence on campus. In a phone interview with a young commentator, she criticized overeager reporters for trying to create news rather than honestly report it. The students of BSU, responsible and patriotic young men and women, would be in their classes, she claimed, hard at work, learning, thinking, absorbing knowledge from highly qualified educators.

She concluded the interview by stating emphatically that President H. Richard Craven had called her only this morning and had assured her that everything would remain peaceful at BSU and not to worry, students were attending classes as usual.

The responsible and patriotic students did not go to their classes. Instead, making the best of a lovely warm and bright spring day, they spilled out onto the college greens to perform before the cameras and microphones, drink, smoke dope, and generally have a good time.

Before long, the party got rather wild. It was a coming-out party. Students shouted obscenities and abuse into every available microphone. They made all sorts of obscene gestures and faces in front of every available camera. They threatened the "Establishment" with all sorts of violent actions. Some business students started a bonfire and burned dollar bills—just as the Church burned witches in medieval times, explained a history major. Several of Professor Hallerman's philosophy majors made blasphemous statements about certain holy persons, ridiculed every bourgeoisie's virtue they could think of, and attacked what they called hypocritical and decadent bourgeois morality. No one, however, was quite clear on the specific nature of "decadent bourgeois morality." But that didn't matter. Since, as one student explained, the concept covered "all possible cases in every possible world."

Professor Hallerman himself was absent from the proceedings.

The students demanded the most outrageous things. Law students, for example, demanded that President Craven and Dean Bentley come down to the Kreis and submit themselves to a public trial for high crimes against the people. They were accomplices to the murders at Kent State perpetrated by the Pig Nation of Amerika, as well as generational genocide both in Amerika and Vietnam. The penalty for such crimes would be a public confession followed by twenty lashes, thirteen for each of the dead and seven for the seven deadly sins.

Neither President Craven nor Dean Bentley dared to leave the sanctuary of their offices in the administration buildings, thereby proving their guilt.

And so it happened, Eugene Vico clambered up the von Brunswick statue and called for a general strike. With a dramatic if somewhat maniacal flailing of arms, Vico gestured defiantly (and obscenely) at the President's office and called for the immediate "occupation" of the office by "the morally virtuous oppressed people."

"Seize the villain and bring him to the People's Trial!"

The crowd surged toward the doors, followed by eager, voracious cameras.

At this moment, the police arrived. Several hundred showed up: university police, city police, county sheriffs, and state highway patrol.

From his vantage point in the administration building, a slightly hysterical, bleary-eyed Richard Bentley called the governor's office to request that National Guard be sent to quell the student rebellion at BSU. An obscure aid in the executive office at the state capital ridiculed this request, flatly telling Bentley that under no circumstances was our governor going to allow himself to become another Jim Rhodes of Ohio. Local authorities better not use lethal force on the students either. . .

". . .and goddammit, where the hell was Dick Craven anyhow?"

Why hadn't Craven called the governor rather than relying on one of his flunkies? We know all about the problems at BSU. The FBI has kept us informed all year. And, goddammit anyway, we haven't got time for your mouse-hole because there're real schools in this state that have exploded. So take care of it yourselves, goddammit!"

Bentley said that Craven was out of town fund-raising. The governor's aid snorted: "Well, he'd better get the hell back to town!" and broke the connection.

Bentley had to rely upon the local authorities. This time, unlike in the fall, almost all the student organizations, even SHS, had joined the riot. He stood at the window and watched the confrontation unfold. He'd just begun working on his second bottle of bourbon.

Dressed in their new riot gear of helmets and padded jackets, carrying shields and clubs, the law enforcement authorities resembled a ridiculous combination of a medieval knight, football player, and Star Trek alien. Forming a phalanx on the south end of the green, they slowly and in good order advanced upon the crowd. Tear gas filled the air, and weighted clubs cleared a path to the monument. Their goal appeared to be Eugene Vico, spellbinding orator and dangerous agitator.

Students tore up bricks from the antique walkways, picked up rocks and stones, fallen tree limbs, anything heavy enough to throw. They grabbed canisters of tear-gas and threw them back at the police. They tossed vegetables, eggs, and bags filled with dog feces. Volley after volley struck the advancing phalanx.

The police line wavered. A few fell. But then with a maddened bellow, they charged into the students.

Now the students were driven back. They beat against the shields and helmets with rocks, bricks, and bare hands. But police clubs proved more effective. Law enforcement seemed to take special joy in beating the students and did so with great vigor and enthusiasm. Many students collapsed without being touched and were dragged away to jail. Many more ran away. The police aimed for shoulders, chests, arms, and legs, not heads. They wanted no fatalities and especially no blood.

They were very good at their job. Hitting the students in the right spots to maximize pain without making a mess, and operating away from the cameras, required a great deal of skill. The Hinnom Valley police were justifiably proud of themselves. They'd elevated this skill to an art form, having learned the lessons of Chicago.

It took less than thirty minutes to clear the greens. This "mouse-hole" was still BSU after all, and most of the student protesters had joined the strike to enjoy the sunshine, to party, socialize, and have some fun with the press. Many had come out of curiosity, others as an excuse to skip classes, yet others to pick up girls. Once they saw that the police were serious, they quickly realized that militant protest was no day at the beach—as one student later told a reporter—and, after all, what could students do to change the political system?.

A few professors, Hallerman being one, canceled their classes in a demonstration of unity with the strikers. Hallerman encouraged his philosophy students to join the protest. He gave a fiery and impassioned, if somewhat reckless, speech about civil rights, freedom, oppression, and what he called "the sexual repression exhibited by those in powerful positions," noting among other things, the phallic significance of nightsticks, not to mention the inauthentic nature of polyester worn by so many members of the Establishment and even some of the faculty. This oration occurred in his classroom, and it was too bad, he said later, that there were no cameras there to record it.

Eugene Vico shouted defiance at the police. Above the dim of yelling, cursing, screaming, animal-like cries and howls, he steadfastly faced the cameras and continued his revolutionary oratory. When he noticed that the cameras had turned to focus on the violence, he jumped down from the statue and with great dignity presented himself to the police for arrest.

Police Chief Butcher recognized Vico. Grabbing him by the collar, the Chief yanked him away from the melee and snarled: "Go home, punk, before you get hurt."

Eugene demanded that they arrest him immediately. But the Chief held him until the police cleared the green and the last students had scattered. Vico continued arguing with the police, interspersing his demands for arrest with extended essays on Marxism: How the police were actually slaves of the capitalist oppressors, standing guard over their enslavement which was private property, protecting things and not people. . . how they should join the people, under his—Vico's—leadership, and so on. . .

The police soon wearied of this. The news-people packed up their gear and retired from the battlefield in good order. The police broke into their separate units, and one by one disappeared. The student protestors were released that very evening. The City of Hinnom Valley profited from the riot; affluent parents of the detained students paid handsome sums to expunge the records of their offspring. In the end, there were no serious injuries.

Chief Butcher released Vico, admonishing him once more to go home. The party was over. This was still BSU and not Kent State. He did compliment Eugene on his exceptional speech-making abilities, which certainly could provide the foundations for a successful future career, say in politics or law if only Vico would get serious. With that, he drove away.

Eugene now stood alone in the late afternoon sun and resumed calling for a trial of the criminals in the administration. After a time—it was getting dark—his tone became rather forlorn and helpless despite the stern efforts he made to sound determined and defiant. No one heard the speech that went on past dusk except a drunken Richard Bentley sitting at the President's office window.

Weeks after the riot, university authorities made inquiries, and students testified before university discipline boards. Many claimed it was Professor Hallerman's philosophy class that had started the violence and attacked the police.

The university was unable to fire Hallerman, although it seemed evident that he was guilty on all charges. After he'd dismissed his class, inciting them to riot, Hallerman had gone home complaining of a migraine. He truly yearned, he said, to join the justifiable protest, given his dedication to justice. But, vell, you know migraines. . .

When questioned by the authorities, Hallerman patiently explained that he never meant his so-called fiery lectures to be taken literally. He adopted metaphors from present events to illustrate in contemporary language certain perennial philosophical truths. The authorities could hardly hold him responsible if somewhat illiterate students failed to grasp the distinction between concrete symbols taken from lived experience and deep abstractions, or if they wished, Platonic ideas.

He was certainly clear about his methods; the students were confused.

Naturally, there were also issues of academic freedom to consider. And Hallerman was a tenured professor.

The Board of the Regents had the final authority and would have dearly loved to fire him. However, they quickly realized that such an act would result in frightful legal entanglements. As one banker noted, the crazy jungle of academic regulations would require the expertise of a whole army of lawyers, which would be far more expensive than a hundred stupid riots and one infantile professor. In the end, they dismissed the case for not enough evidence.

Hallerman loudly proclaimed that his victory was, in fact, a blow against the oppressive and degenerate administration in the name of the iconoclastic morality of free inquiry and justice, in the tradition of Socrates before the court in ancient Athens.

Several board members took note of Hallerman's deft and exceedingly witty methods of operation. When sometime later the Chief of Police let it be known that Craven had simply run off with his young secretary, and it became apparent that poor Richard Bentley had become a hopeless drunk (ultimately he suffered a nervous breakdown and had to be institutionalized), the Board quickly came around to the view of those who suggested that Paul F. Hallerman would make a fine university president.

When they finally offered him the position, Doctor Hallerman was duly humbled and honored by the gesture. Of course, he was not worthy of such a tremendous responsibility, he protested, for he was merely a dedicated educator. But if they truly needed him, it was his moral duty to serve.

Despite his lack of administrative experience, Hallerman promised that he would make every effort to shoulder the burden of the presidency. And though he was not worthy of such an honor (he protested his unworthiness numerous times), he would rule in the tradition of Plato's philosopher king.

TWENTY-FOUR

Updating

THE CONFERENCE WAS PROCEEDING splendidly. Each day for the entire week, young people filled Boots auditorium. Mostly they were parish children, bused up from Chicago and assigned to the residence halls, provided with free meal tickets as well as personal stipends designated for "educational materials," sold exclusively by the University Bookstore.

Father Loeb was pleased.

He was less pleased with the tone of the conference and the content of the discussions—the Second Vatican Ecumenical Council with its sixteen high councilor documents absorbed much of the conference's attention. While Father Loeb agreed in principle that the Church needed to open its windows, he did not care for the increasing worldliness of the breezes that came sweeping in, especially the so-called Social Gospel.

Father Loeb, you see, was of an Augustinian frame of mind when it came to the world outside the Church. The modern world, he often said, with its secularism and openness to pagan religions (and Jews) teetered at the edge of a moral abyss. Without the grace that flowed through the Church and its sacraments, the very nature of man was incurably corrupted—man was born ill. The fresh winds bore a moral plague, in his well-informed view, and there was nothing apoptotic about it.

Speaker after speaker strode to the podium and heaped praise upon the so-called *aggiornamento*, the "updating" of Mother Church. Many were professors from top Catholic universities such as nearby Marquette, Loyola, St. Louis and others. Many were Dominican scholars like Father Loeb. A few were Jesuits. Father Loeb was less pleased with Jesuit enthusiasm for the

Social Gospel. He especially distrusted the new "people's theology" and its romantic image of the "worker priest."

Too often, priests who entered the factory became ensnared by the secular world, ceasing to exercise their religious vocation, though they still wore the badge of ecclesiastical authority. Such revolutionaries lent spiritual validity to the false doctrine of Marxism (some even joined the communist party!). It made him furious. And the fact that not a few secretly married women of the working class—as if worker solidarity went that far!—convinced him that their motives were hardly religious.

It especially irritated him when some of the learned professors, good Catholics all, dared quote the Holy Scriptures in support of secularly motivated (sexually motivated) Marxism.

A certain Father Christopher (Father Loeb never caught his last name) proved most obnoxious. Father Christopher spoke so softly that one could barely hear him even with a microphone. His calm serenity seemed almost supernatural. He acted as if he were alone in the great hall, as if the audience didn't even exist in the presence of his unearthly detachment. His dark skin, oddly bluish at a certain angle, coupled with white hair, gave him the appearance of an Indian guru; one of those heathen cheats prepared to take advantage of youthful gullibility. All of them majored in trendy pseudo-religious trash. Father Loeb recognized a consummate actor spouting an absurd doctrine.

Father Loeb had difficulty telling Father Christopher's age. With his white hair and beard, he appeared to be very old, yet he also seemed strangely child-like. The smallest things took him by surprise. He would unexpectedly squeal with delight at the most mundane phenomena, like the way the sun suddenly glittered through a window, or the shrill cry of a bird, or even a passing cloud. He especially loved children. He wore the traditional black cassock and strode across the stage with purpose and grace; enveloped, it seemed, by a golden aura of age and wisdom.

Father Christopher gazed over the heads of the audience and appeared scarcely aware that there were people in the hall. An objection, a frown, a fidget or a yawn made not the slightest impression on him. Even if the audience had turned ugly and rushed the stage to stab him with their pens—as legend told of the medieval students in England who stabbed the philosopher John Scotus to death with their quills—Father Christopher would hardly have noticed.

Today's audience harbored no such intention. On the contrary, the old priest hypnotized them. They were carried away into a state of breathless wonder. His words held them spellbound, and his very presence caused many of them to quiver with delight.

Father Loeb despised him. Surely Father Christopher knew as Father Loeb himself knew, that this audience did not possess the disciplined understanding to grasp even the bare essentials of his talk.

Enticing, captivating, smelling of heretical ideas, such higher wisdom seemed profoundly meaningful as long as listeners thought with their intestines, Father Loeb like to say. The more confident the more intoxicating, he added. In religion, mysticism meant "mist" and "schism."

Perhaps he could silence the old priest with the "evil eye." He glared with a smoldering hatred. Father Christopher, in return, smiled back. He appeared immune to the air itself.

Father Christopher said: "Now when Jesus declares blessed are the poor in the gospel of Luke, he has the choice of two Greek words to use for our word the "poor." He can say *penes*, which in the Galilee of his time would mean the working poor, artisans, peasants—the vast majority of the population—poor in comparison to the wealthy one or two percent of the Greco-Roman hierarchy, yes, but still owners of private property, or as we might say nowadays, *petit bourgeoisie*.

"Such are the poor, the *penes*. Does Jesus use this Greek word in Luke? Does he bless the *penes*? Is theirs the *Basileian Tou Theon*, the Kingdom of Heaven?"

Father Christopher paused for the proper dramatic effect.

"No, he does not."

"What Greek word does the Lord use for the poor?"

(Another significant pause). Father Christopher gazed upwards as if receiving his inspiration from the Kingdom of Heaven itself.

"Jesus uses the word *ptochos*, not *penes*. And what does *ptochos* mean? It means the destitute. The homeless. The beggars. The outcasts of society. Untouchables. Those poor that ordinary people see but wish not to see and so turn their heads away.

"Jesus blesses the outcasts, the destitute; theirs is the Kingdom of Heaven."

Had it not been for the fact that he was due to speak next, Father Loeb might have leaped from his seat and rushed the stage to snatch the microphone and protest this nonsense. After all, this was his conference.

"What, then, does Jesus mean?" Father Christopher's voice rose in volume although it seemed that merely a ripple of emotion marred the mirror-like surface of his serenity.

"My dear people of God, Jesus means that society is unjust, unequal, oppressive, power-hungry, addicted to self-indulgence, built upon the foundations of a lie. This lie says that possessions determine the worth of a person, that you are what you own. In such a society, only the truly destitute are innocent. Only those who own nothing, possess not a pebble of the common earth, *ptochos*, only these poor are not implicated by the wicked, sinful Rulers of the Age. Only such are guiltless of the terrible sins committed by the tyrannical state."

Father Christopher appeared to float in the air as if the words he spoke canceled gravity. The audience flew with him. He caught his listeners in a finely meshed net, for he was indeed a fisher of men. Was he not a true disciple of the Lord?

Father Loeb loathed him, although he had to admire the performance.

"Is this you?" Father Christopher asked the crowd. "Can you honestly say that you yourselves stand outside the wicked society of your elders? Are you Jesus people? Are you children of the Kingdom of God? Or are you corrupted egotists of Satan's system of exploitation, greed, and racism? Are you the oppressors?

"Give away all that you have. Sell your possessions and give the proceeds to the destitute. Let the death-merchants who run this country bury the dead they have created. My children, what indeed is the product of the all-mighty military-industrial complex? What is the one product the elite rulers produce? Corpses. Let the dead bury the dead.

"Blessed are the poor. How can you serve God and your bank account at the same time? Take your money now, in your hands, and bring it here. Make a pile of it. Then burn it. Thus will you purge your guilt and your sin. Better yet, take your money to a bank, a store, a place of business, and burn it there. Make a great bonfire.

"In a corrupt society, only the powerless are innocent. And this is also true of our Mother Church. Embedded in an unjust social system as it presently is, it cannot offer the true road to salvation. It can never become spiritual while remaining a captive of the powerful. You—" he pointed at the audience— "cannot become spiritual on a diet of manna. I do not say this. Jesus says it. In Luke, for all to read. It is the Word of God.

"To follow Jesus, you must reject the existing economic-political order. You must renounce injustice. You must wash away the stain of money. As Jesus has said, only within a fully egalitarian society in which the necessities of life belong to all the people, completely and fully, only in such a community may the Church preach the gospel free from hypocrisy—a genuinely spiritual good news.

"Marx does not say it. Engels does not say it. Lenin does not say it. Che does not say it. Mao does not say it—

"Jesus says it. Amen."

Frowning, Father Loeb rose unsteadily to his feet. Stumbling on the first step, he mounted the stage. He greeted Father Christopher warmly, clasping both of the old priest's hands in his.

He began by praising Father Christopher's talk. He remarked on the timeliness of the priest's ideas, how "with it," how "mellow."

Father Loeb had planned to speak on the evils of drugs and how Christ was the only true drug, "the medicine of immortality," and the only cure for corrupted human nature. He was going to take his text from St. Augustine. He would impress upon them how they all carried an incurable disease, which no magic mushroom or sacred peyote could eradicate. Only the wine and bread of the Eucharist. For outside the Church is no salvation.

Father Loeb now realized that this would not do. Somehow he had to turn the conference away from "wild updating." Father Christopher and his ilk were no better than pagans. They were atheistic Marxists hiding behind wild exegesis.

Father Loeb gazed over the audience and considered the problem. The Augustine talk with its emphasis on the corrupted nature of human beings, corrupted reason, the inability of humans to realize the City of God, would surely sound a discordant note. It would make a noise like sand scrapping against glass, especially as *A Finis* to Father Christopher's lovely aria.

What should he say?

He began slowly. Once again, he thanked Father Christopher. It was his profound hope and deep desire, he said, that the students take to heart Father Christopher's excellent and relevant—with it—observations—

Then he had a sudden inspiration.

"—and so you've heard the truth of Christ's message, how relevant it is to our times. It would be inappropriate for me to comment any further on Father Christopher's elegant lecture. There is nothing I could add to his brilliance, such powerful and beautiful ideas so perfectly expressed."

He graced the old priest with a smile.

"So, allow me, please, a brief footnote to his little treatise. My note reads: and obedient to the Father, Jesus was obedient unto death, the death of the cross.

"It is most important to remember this fact: Christ sealed His life and teachings with the ultimate act of obedience. Every single word that Christ uttered, every thought He thought, every act and every fiber of His Being culminated in death on the cross. Obedience unto DEATH.

"Look to yourselves. Look to your loved ones, those around you, rich and poor alike. Look and think: How many will be sitting here in a hundred years? Will I be here to ask the question?

"Alas for your beloved family. Their journey ends in the grave, your dear mother and father. When you marry and beget children, look at them and consider. They may be living in capitalism or socialism, wealth or poverty, destitution or abundance, all are of perishable flesh, fated to sickness, old age, and death. Your dear wife. Dear husband. Loving children.

"And now picture yourselves. Your young bodies are so strong and healthy at this moment. Your young minds, so fresh and glowing with the burning eloquence of Father Christopher. See it all decay as the years' pass.

"Slowly, painfully, sadly—oh, so sad! Do you experience the gradual decline? The fire begins to die. The coals grow cold. At first, it is imperceptible. This experience is not a part of your busy life. But it goes forward despite everything.

"Now picture yourself a corpse, putrefying, bloated, the sickening stench of death hanging about you like a toxic cloud. All shun you, even those who loved you most. You have become loathsome to them.

"Think of your accomplishments, your life's goals met or unmet. Think of your life's hopes and dreams, your struggles, pains, your happiest moments. Yes, your joys. The body you so carefully clothed and fed. The home you made, your children, your career. All of it comes to this ultimate conclusion.

"Do you despair? Absolutely. How can you live one second more with such despair? You cannot. You must flee from it.

"So you laugh and make jokes—graveyard humor. Life's a bitch, and then you die. Ah, so clever. So witty."

These last words brought nervous laughter from the audience. Father Loeb chuckled too.

"Yes, yes, you put your despair away, smile and laugh, and go on living. But you are living towards the grave. You laugh, you joke; you may even dare to ridicule those who remind you of this despair. You bravely tell yourself that such *morbid*—a good word—thoughts are useless. Childish, not for serious adults.

"So you ignore your despair. You laugh."

The audience sat in utter silence.

Father Loeb took a deep breath, paused, and counted silently to himself.

"You laugh at it. BUT YOU CANNOT LAUGH IT DOWN."

The words rolled like thunder. The auditorium itself seemed to shake.

"You cannot laugh it down. Your death comes for you without fail. It is the cold wind no coat can withstand. The chill penetrates through the layers that you have built up about your soul. It penetrates the threads of your life's raiment woven together by the needles of your possessions, loved ones, your net worth, small or great. Death-cold seeps through all."

A collective shudder passed through the audience. Not a few young people found themselves on the verge of tears.

Father Christopher sat in the front row, smiling even now in his detached, child-like manner. He preserved his serenity as if none of this had anything to do with him.

"No perfect society, even if it builds walls like the tower of Babel, will halt this death from invading your life.

"Only in Christ crucified, obedient, raised, does your salvation rest. Christ and no other. The virtues of obedience and no other. The only Son of the One True God. If Christ is not unique, if He was not raised, if you do not participate in the resurrection of Christ within the elect of His Universal Church, then you are indeed doomed to ultimate despair. Your only future is darkness, meaninglessness, and death. You suffer the full consequences of sin."

Father Loeb rested again, measuring the effect. And now, not a few members of the audience, including some professors, found themselves quietly weeping. Many were unaware that they were sobbing until they felt the moisture of their tears.

At last, even Father Christopher appeared affected. He folded his hands and closed his eyes, breathing very slowly.

Father Loeb smiled to himself. Outwardly, however, he held his face rigid and severe. He looked sad and hopeless. Sad clown, yet not very funny, not humorous at all.

He raised his arms and closed his eyes.

"And so must you *obey* the Holy Mother Church, as Christ obeyed the Father. Only Christ. Only his Church. Not Socrates. Not Mohammed. Not Marx and not Lenin. Not the Maharishi. Not the Buddha. Not a thousand Buddhas. Only Christ. God's Son. He is your only hope. Amen."

A great roar of approval swept the auditorium. Father Loeb lowered his eyes, searching for Father Christopher. But he couldn't find him. The old priest had vanished. Father Loeb was pleased.

Thus did the conference come to a triumphal *Finis*.

TWENTY-FIVE

Mount Meru

A TRINITY OF FORMER BSU students visited me the other day at my parish residence in Chicago. Two were young gentlemen, the third a young lady who resembled that ridiculous Cher. They claimed to know the whereabouts of Sylvian Matreya and thought I might wish to relay the information to his family. I thanked them and promised to do as they asked, although his family no longer seemed overly concerned where Sylvian lived or what he was doing; he'd betrayed his faith and no doubt suffered the consequences of apostasy—which, in the end, comes to madness. They'd made donations to the parish to have masses said for his soul.

One of the young gentlemen reminded me of a clownish caricature of Satan, the sort you see in grade-b movies; but the young man was obviously from means, well dressed, clean-cut, and appropriately deferential. He did most of the speaking.

Sylvian had gone to India, he explained, to Nepal precisely, for eight months, and had returned to Colorado to live with a Tibetan guru, or Lama, or something—I've never been able to make sense of all these absurd self-absorbed titles.

It seems that his BSU girlfriend had gone home to Denver suffering from a drug-addiction that caused her recurring episodic psychotic bouts. Her parents had reluctantly institutionalized her, yet the program allowed for infrequent passes to serve therapeutic purposes. On such days she'd visit Sylvian and his Tibetan parasite (the holy bum did no work but lived off the credulity of wealthy patrons). She usually returned to the institution in worse shape than before her excursion.

Why her parents allowed such behavior, or why a licensed institution encouraged such a thing eludes me. But there it is. Thank God we have the Church. Modern secular psychology, like evolution, is surely demonically inspired. I fear for the mental health of future generations.

Allow me to add in retrospect that except for a handful of radicals—aging tyrants all—the crazy sixties culture no longer significantly impacts modern society. Oh, I'll concede that the spirituality craze continues, which in these times has become empty chatter and double-talk, profit-inspired one might add. But no one of any intelligence takes it seriously.

The cartoon-devil deposited some hastily scribbled, nearly incomprehensible pages of notes he'd supposedly received from Sylvian. He asked that I pass them along to the family. They are in Sylvian's hand, he claimed. I agreed, although I've no intention of disturbing these fine people and causing them further pain. The boy, I'm afraid, is as mad as his girlfriend. Unless he returns to the Church, modern treatment is a waste of money. The Cher, by the way, apologized for any pain they may have caused the family. As they say these days, she observed, "one must move on."

I don't believe much of what the notes relate anyhow. If it is Sylvian, then he's finally "lost his mind," as they say. I'll have to reconsider my statements at the beginning of this sad chronicle. Here are the notes. Judge for yourself.

Thus did I read:

> Early morning in the mountains: thin, freezing air, patches of dingy snow like brittle sugar sprinkled on the ground—nonetheless, this is a summer morning. He knows the physics of it: at higher altitudes, the atmosphere is less dense and thus does air pressure decrease, along with the temperature. The sun, though, is intense.
>
> He makes his way along the narrow path from his hut to his favorite tree. He is careful not to catch the old priestly robe on the thorns that grew along the trail. He should cut the one particular bush— Ah, no. He might die in the next second and why waste the precious time that he ought to spending in practice.
>
> The mountains are immeasurable; vast distances divided peak from peak. Here nature is ancient and elemental: rock, air, and water.
>
> He is happy. Borrowing from Tibet's greatest poet, Milarepa, he chants:

Ah, Pearl,

In sadness, you called to me.

Sleeping, you woke me.

In darkness, you found me.

Weeping, you consoled me.

He chants the verses as he walks, visualizing Pearl trotting beside him, laughing and teasing. Reciting formulas is so much easier than thinking.

He comes to his tree. It is a small, emaciated spruce eking out its existence amid barren mossy rocks and eternal frost.

Seating himself carefully at the base, he continues his chant:

Honor to you, Pearl.

Save me from all creeds.

Contemplating compassion and love,

Dissolve all distinctions.

Contemplating earth,

Those that rule forgotten.

Their rules forgotten.

Form forgotten.

Nor emptiness.

Forgotten is the faith once believed.

Contemplating the death that comes,

Forgotten is hope and fear.

Contemplating the path,

Forgotten is the dread of hope and fear. . .

Then, he switches languages as the ancient texts taught. He chants:

Tayata om muni muni maha manaya soha,

Om mani padme hum.

Om mani padme hum.

Rupam sunyata sunyataiva rupam.

He chants the verses again and again until he lost count of the repetitions. He tries to focus on the syllables, primarily concentrating upon the word OM—A-U-M. . . A-U-M. . . consciousness, dream, sleep, silence; awareness, non-awareness, neither awareness nor non-awareness, silence.

Silence.

As many theories do, it worked best in books. Distracting thoughts come. He lets them go, allows them to slide by without friction. Let them go; let it all go. Beginning with the body, then feeling, followed by mental habits, finally objects. All are names; all are flowing, dancing away, like the mountains.

Words are imprecise, as he knows, even recited ones. It is so difficult. A lifetime of habit, millions of years of evolution, the world of form and desire, all allied to defend a soaring, impenetrable tower of lies and delusion.

Nothing is born. Nothing dies. Everything passes into something else. Everything is cause and condition; everything arises by causes and conditions. But this too was a delusion. Nonetheless, he chants: "No birth, no death, no want, no fear, no pain."

He mustn't attempt actually to do anything.

He mustn't follow any religion, any philosophy, any ideology. You don't get anything. You get rid of everything.

But the thoughts arise, demanding attention.

Mara, Lord Illusion. Mara is coming.

Yesterday the battle with Mara had been particularly vicious. Mara had come in the person of dear Father Tadeusz Loeb.

He was in the confessional with Father Loeb. He told Father Loeb everything that had happened. The priest's voice was chilling. It blew through the grating, muffled and cold. It admonished him, criticized him severely. It broke at every pause for breath. It threatened and blamed, mounted in anger only to fall in dismay. This faceless voice was so vastly different from the Father Loeb he knew as a child.

He knew Mara, Lord Illusion.

Mara wove a web of Cathedral illusion about him. The Cathedral became a city, cold and austere, spiked towers with exposed steel trusses. Strange, insect-like creatures haunted the Cathedral-city. They were loathsome creatures; their very presence caused him to shiver. Mara appeared in the Cathedral and took the incredibly lifelike form of Father Loeb.

He chanted from the *Maha-Prajna-Paramita-Hridaya*. Like creeds, chants were easier than thinking. Reciting formulas solved his old language problem. They were precise, like equations, even if he didn't know what they meant. Again and again.

Mara did not dissolve.

He confessed (another recital) to Father Loeb, traveling back day-by-day, through the events that had led him to the path, to the *dharma*. Mostly he spoke of Pearl, but also of the People's Will, of the Great Truth Cloud, of the ancestors and the legends. Father Loeb wrote it all down, changing a

great deal, adding, subtracting. The sad priest called him an idiot; his tale
was the tale about an idiot, told by an idiot as the poet had said, a fool, told
by a fool and a rebel against God.

He patiently recited another formula: How painful and futile this
yearning for ancient rocks that do not flow, like yonder mountains. He
blessed his suffering, that strange childhood malady that was the necessary
condition for discovering the *dharma*. "Let us bless our suffering," he chanted. "Without it, there can be no awakening. Let us welcome our demons,
embrace them, and not exorcise them. They instruct us."

The priest's cold voice interrupted him, to scold and scoff. He endured
the assaults until at last Father Loeb fell silent.

Silence, however, did not signal Mara's defeat. The Magician had prepared his attack quite cleverly. Lord Illusion was not so easily silenced.

His long confession came to an end but it had no conclusion. He rested
in happiness. He felt no guilt for what he had done. He experienced great
peace, as if he'd finally opened his eyes after a frightfully long and restless
sleep. He felt the kind of exhaustion one endures after a long slumber filled
with nightmares when sleep does not refresh, and the dark is not gentle.

Mara was not easily defeated.

Father Loeb commenced to scold, ridicule, and complain. The priest's
voice seemed to explode in his ears like a sudden gust of mountain wind.

Mara proceeded to unfold the world's sufferings, the suffering of the
poor and the destitute, the inevitable suffering of old age, sickness, and
death. He spoke of human despair in the face of such things which were the
wages of sin. He quoted St. Augustine: Poor man, so helpless before these
truths, impossible to heal thyself, impossible to end thy suffering. Poor man,
poison arrow in the flesh. Who shot you? From what country? For what
reason? Who blinded you?

Mara took the form of a corpse. The awful death stench filled the crisp
mountain air. The form changed. . . into his father, his mother, his brother. . .
into Pearl, and then, as the tears rolled down his cheeks, the corpse became
his own.

But he knew all about corpses.

Mara's evil voice whispered into his ear: "Thou art that. *Tat Tvam Asi*
in the ancient tongue of the universe. Thou art that. Thou art that corpse.
Thou art death. Despair."

"Despair," Father Loeb kept repeating. "See and despair. Gaze upon it
and tremble."

"Only Christ!" he thundered. "Not your Divine Woo-Woo, not Krishna, not Parvati, not Buddha. Not a thousand Buddhas. Only Christ and His
Holy Church. Amen."

The horrible noise grew louder. Mara's words. Father Loeb's thundering "Amens." The sound drowned out the chants that he'd learned. The storm broke his concentration. His breathing became ragged: the slow, rhythmical inhale-exhale turned choppy as when the wind whips the mirror surface of the lagoon in Oakwood. He no longer breathed. He gasped.

Amen. Amen. Thunder and storm.

And just when Mara's assault appeared to reach its most violent peak, beating him down victoriously, he cried out into the whirlwind:

"I will not rise from this earth,

until I have obtained my utmost aim.

And find a way beyond life and death."

No one had taught him these words. They came from the dream of St. Barlaam, the strange old symbols that magically aligned themselves and spoke in music. He knew to say them aloud when all else failed, and Mara mounted strong.

An intense gale spiked with ice pellets rained down upon him. Darkness came, but the stars did not shine. The moon gave no light. The mountains shook, the seas churned, and the night became deeper than any void.

Then the tremendous rolling clouds emitted lightning, Mara's angry thunderbolts. The shower became huge stones of ice.

He repeated the words. He made the vow. He did not try to shout over the din, nor did he make the vow in his mind, nor his heart. He made the vow in the pit of his stomach. He made the vow calmly, defiantly but without anger, free from desire, reciting the formula like writing a string of symbols.

"Here will I sit, ten, or twenty, or thirty years. Here will I sit and I will not move. Until the mystery of the world is solved, inside the world, not outside the world. I will do this for all who suffer, even the poor beasts."

The ice-rain fell upon his head. Abruptly, it turned into a soft shower of flowers. The wind dropped, became a gentle breeze, finally, a whisper, at last a vast stillness, as in the haunted park.

There is no mystery to solve, only a great peace to be realized.

He said to Father Loeb: "Dear Father, your fears are the illusion. Don't you see that all is coming to be and passing away? Don't you know? When appearing and disappearing have disappeared, when you think without thinking when rivers are rivers, lakes are lakes, when mountains are mountains, then there is great laughter.

"Dear Father, have you not eyes to see? You, dear Father, are the source of your suffering, and the cure. No Father, no me, no Mara, only dependence upon earth and sun, and stars, and galaxies. What then of death? What dies?"

I inhale, I exhale. . . His breathing became regular, stabilized. He smiled.

Father Loeb turned away. The priest's shoulders sagged. The confession was over. No penance had been given, no salvation received, no grace imparted. His Christ had failed.

That was yesterday.

Today the sun shines brightly, and the chill air tastes sweet. Again, Mara comes.

Mara, insidious, perverse, powerful—today Mara comes to him in the form of his beloved Pearl.

She sits facing him. She sits in full lotus, mocking his inability to achieve the great *asana*, the perfect form, base, and foundation.

He whispers: "Mara, I know thee."

She smiles her most seductive smile. Her teeth are perfect. She wears the scent of spring. She shakes her blonde hair, which is like rippling sunlight.

Desire overwhelms him. It rises like a serpent in the grass. Desire. Craving.

Lord Illusion's daughter.

She smiles and waits.

"Here I will sit—" he begins. But he cannot even finish the first chant. His concentration is shattered. The words will not come.

Desire is greater than fear—a thousand times greater, more powerful than despair.

His breathing accelerates. His legs begin to ache. Then, like a sudden chill, he feels the absolute futility of the practice. He sees her, the fairy-dust madness in her. *She is his teacher.*

A depressing pall settles upon his shoulders, causing him to feel stupid and idiotic. He thinks of all the things he ought to be doing. He remembers all the things he's left undone. Should he not be concerned about food, shelter, and clothes? About physics and career? About marriage and family? Shouldn't he be doing something even if it was merely getting himself down to that ski-town to beg from the summer tourists? He is sane again. He is turned-off and tuned-in.

A gust of wind penetrates his patched robe, and he truly does feel a chill. He is cold, although at this altitude the sun burns fiercely and bakes his skin. He's become darker, further removed from Polish nobility, closer to the Mongol ancestry. *Ex Oriente Lux.*

He stares at Pearl. He tries to remember that this is Mara's daughter come to tempt him and destroy his concentration.

Avoid all evil, cherish goodness, keep the mind pure. He read it somewhere, maybe in his *Catechism.*

He feels her lips, tastes her breath, the texture of her skin and hair. Discontent, Desire, Delight—Mara's daughters. They scatter his thoughts like leaves in a strong autumn wind.

Mara's weapon is memory. Memory also speaks of the future, of desire fulfilled in the not-yet. Desire breeds desire, for every fulfillment comes to an end. And so with every attainment of pleasure comes discontent. From discontent craving. From craving binding. From binding confusion, loss of mind.

An hour passes. Somehow, he remains seated in terrible agitation.

He refuses to move. The pain in his legs becomes an agony. The muscles in his back at the base of his spine cry out in protest against the torture. His shoulders and neck, rib cage, and sternum feel as if someone had stuck hot needles into the bone.

He sits, refusing to wiggle and squirm.

He forgets why he sat. He knows only pain and desire.

Just sit. When all else fails, sit. Father Loeb admonished him to sit still in the pew. Mother Mary admonished him to sit still. Christ too.

Maybe it happened when a stray cloud passed over the sun and caused the mountain peaks and crags to dance in shadow. It might have been a simple change in pressure or a variation in the angle of the light.

He thinks: If I move my leg? So what, the other still hurts. If I get up, the pleasurable sensation of movement will shortly pass. I'll get tired walking to the town. Soon I'll want to sit again, and my legs will ache once more. So it will go: pain gives way to pleasure gives way to pain gives way. . . gives way.

Who cares what Father Loeb says? Mother Mary? Christ? Their words are imprecise. They seem severe, but perhaps they are joking.

I am not this leg. I am not this pain. Nor am I this pleasure. Nor this sensation. Nor this name. Nor this body. Nor this place—

Nothing changed at that moment. The cramping pain persisted. The aching muscles cried out in complaint.

He gazes at Pearl, feeling the same fierce desire, an even greater craving, a deeper love. It was like the pain in his legs. The memory of her was like the aching muscles in his back and neck.

I am not. *Non sum, Non sum. Ich bin nicht.* The words of another heretic.

He perceives the truth of it. He sees the evolutionary necessity that propelled his cravings and made them so insistent. He understands how illusion served millions of years of survival. He understands that all these desires, loves and hates are but habitual patterns of energy reinforced over and over again in spacetime. The sequence of their coming to be and passing away is falsely labeled "Sylvian," the idiot. There are only waves in the sea of spacetime. The waves roll on: no birth, no death— He would have loved to explain it all to Olaffsoon.

He laughs.

Knowing is a tragedy. Not-knowing is a tragedy. Yet in the dark thunder of the unknown is greater laughter.

He laughs at higher laughter. It is comedy.

He smiles at Pearl and says aloud: "I am not these things."

Pearl looks forlorn. She no longer smiles.

"The world is as it should be," he said, laughing. *Nature just is.*

She stands up. She looks sad and hurt.

Laughing, he knows indeed that this is Mara's daughter.

She turns, sighs, and walks back down the path, her head hanging dejectedly.

He does truly love Pearl.

The sun touches the peak of the western range. He has not moved from his spot on the earth. The pain has moved on, pain like pleasure also passes. Another joke. He must remember.

Patience. He knows Mara would attack again, for the past is very powerful. Habit navigates the oceans. Patience. The path is long.

A century perhaps? Maybe longer. How strange and complex the world will be by then. He can almost see it forming beyond the western peaks: a bloated world, polluted, jaded, cynical, sophisticated, stuffed with knowledge, overflowing, dazzled, hypnotized, everything a product, everything for sale, even the *dharma.* How strange in that world his denials, his simplicity, his tranquility, the peace of the transient. He laughed. How revolutionary. What an anarchist.

"I am a revolutionist," he says aloud. "I am the Anti-Christ."

When the time comes, he will arise and go to them, to the overflowing ones who suffer despite their wealth. He will teach the teaching that even the World Honored One cannot teach. He'll frown at their humor and laugh at their truths. In such a complex, busy, and overflowing world, his simplicity will be a total revolution. All that exists deserves to perish.

For he is named *Maitreya. Tathagata.* The One Thus Come.

He will go to them and chant: "*Gate, Gate, Paragate, Parasamgate, Bodhi, Svaha!*"

"Gone, gone, gone to the Other Shore, passed away to the Other Shore."

There are times when formulas are the best thinking can do.

He remembers how it had been predicted, how he had discovered the prediction that day in philosophy when, lost to *Dasien* and paging aimlessly through the textbook, he came to a selection by crusty old Schopenhauer. He read and re-read and later devoured the book during the time he passed in the land of shadows with Jerry Wolfe. Schopenhauer had written:

> "...the ancient wisdom of the human race will not be supplanted by the events in the Galilee. On the contrary, Indian wisdom flows back to Europe and will produce a fundamental change in our knowledge and thought."

Then he thinks: this is not true. *There is no ancient wisdom.* Schopenhauer, like every other philosopher, was joking.

He looks up and sees the mountains walking on.

In the fading light, he spies a tiny yellow flower pushing up through the dead leaves and dry brush of the forest floor. Gazing upon its simple beauty, he experiences a sudden urge to pluck the flower from the soil and place the fragile thing in Pearl's hair, if the real Pearl comes tomorrow as he hopes. How she'd love the gift.

He reaches for the flower.

Then as his fingers come close to the petals, he remembers and withdraws his hand.

He leaves the flower to remain as it is, untouched.

THE END

www.ingramcontent.com/pod-product-compliance
Lightning Source LLC
Chambersburg PA
CBHW051145030726
47504CB00004B/1049